THE BRIGHT DAWNING

C

THE
BRIGHT DAWNING

Being the Fourth Volume in the classic Heron Saga

Pamela Oldfield

This title first published in Great Britain 1999 by
SEVERN HOUSE PUBLISHERS LTD of
9–15 High Street, Sutton, Surrey SM1 1DF,
complete with new text by the author.
Originally published in 1982 in Great Britain by
Macdonald Futura Publishers Ltd
under the title of *White Water*.
This title first published in the U.S.A. 1999 by
SEVERN HOUSE PUBLISHERS INC of
595 Madison Avenue, New York, N.Y. 10022.

British Library Cataloguing in Publication Data

Oldfield, Pamela, 1934-
          The bright dawning
          1.   Kendal family (Fictitious characters) - Fiction
          2.   Domestic fiction
          1.   Title
          823.9'14 [F]

          ISBN 0-7278-2294-2

All situations in this publication are fictitious and
any resemblance to living persons is purely coincidental.

Printed and bound in Great Britain by
MPG Books Ltd, Bodmin, Cornwall.

For Dennis Barker

While researching this novel, I read many fine books. My thanks to the staffs of the County Library, Maidstone, and Westcountry Studies Library, Exeter, for helping me to find them.

CHAPTER ONE

Devon, May 1574

The small brindled terrier trotted eagerly at the unwashed heels, keeping a wary eye on the stout stick which his young master carried. He glanced from time to time at the old leather bag slung across the boy's shoulder. A slight movement within the bag brought a whine to the dog's throat and without turning his head the boy said, 'Bide your time, Brin. You'll have some rare sport later.' The boy was thin, with narrow shoulders and bright ginger hair which hung about his peaky freckled face and fell into his pale brown eyes. He gave his unkempt hair a practised flick and could see once more. The day was nearly done and there was a mist which clung damply to his skin, but he was oblivious to the discomfort, his mind busy with ways of spending the money he would earn.

He slashed with the stick at a particularly high nettle in the hedgerow and his lips moved slightly in the beginnings of a smile as the green head of the plant flew upwards. Brin sprang forward, catching it as it came down, delighted with the chance of action however insignificant. 'Daft besom!'

He whipped off a few more plant heads and then squinted up through the mist at the warm bright glow that was the sun and nodded, satisfied. Tomorrow would be a fine day. He would walk into Exeter – a matter of two hours – and sample the heady delights of market day. A cart passed him, loaded high with logs and the driver raised his whip.

The boy replied with a slight wave of his hand and turned to watch the cart's erratic progress. The old man slouched in the seat, his lolling head betraying the amount of ale he had drunk. One of the cart's wheels skidded into a rut and the logs shifted alarmingly. The old man also swayed but managed, with an oath, to steady himself. Shaking his head, the boy grimaced and turning off the highway, shouldered his way through the dense hedgerow. Beyond it the grass sloped down to the river and Nat turned left and began to follow it. After half a mile he stopped, whistled to the dog, which had disappeared temporarily, and sprang lightly across the boulders which served as stepping stones. Landing on the far side, he found himself face to face with a young girl who regarded him critically.

'Who are you?' she demanded.

'Nathaniel Gully, ma'am,' he said with an exaggerated bow and a graceful sweep of an imaginary hat.

She looked at him from large blue eyes and then glanced nervously at the terrier who was following him across the water, barking shrilly.

'You must go away,' she told him. 'This is our garden and you . . .'

'Nathaniel Gully, rat catcher extraordinary,' he went on. 'Not a better in the whole of Devon, though I say so meself, and who's to deny me?'

'You can't come here,' she insisted with a toss of her long fair curls.

The terrier ran towards her, wagging his stumpy tail, but she withdrew a few yards to the bottom of grey stone steps which led away from the riverside garden and offered a retreat if it should prove necessary.

'Shoo! Go home!' she told the dog. 'You must both—'

'Nathaniel Gully at your service,' he continued, unperturbed. 'Here at the request of one Mistress Kendal.'

'Mama asked you to come here?'

The dog still leaped about, barking excitedly and she retired to the third step, clutching her skirts. He raised his stick menacingly and the dog crouched low, silenced but still watching.

'Not exactly,' he said. ' 'Twas Beth who sent for me and

said as how the mistress would pay me well for my labours.'

But the girl was no longer listening.

'Your bag!' she said, astonished. ' 'Tis wriggling. Your bag is wriggling!'

'A ferret,' said Nat and he plunged his hand into the bag and withdrew a slim furry creature with sandy fur, bright eyes and short spiky whiskers.

With a scream the girl turned and scrambled to the top of the steps crying, ' 'Tis a rat!'

'No, no,' he reassured her. 'Just a jill ferret as'll kill all the bad rats in your barn. See, she doesn't bite me. You want to stroke her?' The girl shook her head violently. 'Then will you tell your mama I'm here? Will you be a big girl and take a message? Say Nathaniel Gully is here as promised.'

The girl hesitated. 'Mama has ridden into town,' she said.

'To Ashburton? Then will you tell Beth?'

'Aye.' She decided that he was to be trusted and said suddenly, 'My name's Lorna, I'm six years old and I've a new gown of lavender silk.'

'Lavender silk, eh?'

'Aye.'

She studied him carefully to see that he was properly impressed by this information. He returned the ferret to the bag and smiled cheerfully.

'Lead on then,' he prompted and at last she turned and led the way. They went through the orchard and across the herb garden to the back door yard. Leaving the dog and boy on the doorstep, Lorna hurried inside. Beth was mincing mutton and heard Lorna's news without much enthusiasm.

'He should have been here a week since,' she said, 'but send him in.'

Her eyes widened when the boy entered.

'You're not Nat Gully!' she exclaimed.

'I'm his son, ma'am. Nathaniel Gully the younger at your service.'

He made her the same elaborate bow. Lorna, perched safely on a stool, watched with interest. 'And every bit as good as my father, and he'd be the first to say so, and I'm sent in his stead 'cos he's laid low with his guts and he's griping that bad 'tis a wonder he don't turn himself inside out.'

'Hmm.' Beth regarded him dubiously. 'You don't look much like him with that red hair,' she said.

'I take after my mother, God rest her soul.'

'Hmm.'

Lorna said, 'He's got a ferret in that bag.'

'I should hope he has!' said Beth. 'Can't catch rats without a ferret, that I *do* know.' She addressed herself to him again. 'So you reckon you're as good as your father, do you?'

'I do, ma'am – and is the mistress not at home?' It was his way of reminding the old woman that she was not employing him.

'No, she's not,' said Beth irritably, recognizing the lightly veiled barb for what it was. 'And what time d'you call this, to come rat-catching?' Twill soon be dark.'

'That's the best time.'

'Hmm.' She stuffed the last handful of meat into the mincer and swung the handle with a final burst of energy. 'Be off then, and get on with it. You'll not earn much standing here.'

Lorna slid from the stool. 'I want to watch him,' she said.

'You'd best not,' said Beth.

'Oh!' Lorna's face puckered up and her lips quivered. 'Mama would let me,' she protested.

'She would *not*,' said Beth.

'I'll keep out of the way,' said Lorna.

Beth hesitated. She was sorry for the child because her brother Piers had been allowed to go hawking with their father and the tutor.

12

'Will she get bit?' she asked the boy.

Nat shook his head. 'No, ma'am. Brin here will see to that. None'll get past him. Real fierce he is, with rats. Fast as lightning, as they say. A bolt from the blue. One shake and they're dead.'

'Then go, Lorna, and mind you do as you're bid and keep out of the way – but you'd best not tell your mama, just in case. You take Nat to the old barn – and not before time. I've never seen so many of the dratted creatures. There's not a sack without a hole in it and they've even had a go at the tallow.' As he turned to go she said, 'And what's the mistress paying you?'

'A shilling for the first three dozen and another shilling for each dozen after.'

'Hmm. You'll be making your fortune then.'

'I wouldn't mind,' said Nat. He held out a hand for Lorna and together they made their way across the yard.

The old barn was long and low and raftered. Sacks of provisions were stored in it, as well as straw and hay. Rope and nets were kept there also and in one corner logs were stacked against the wall. The dog ran ahead of them sniffing hopefully in every corner. Lorna looked around her in dismay.

'They've all gone,' she said.

'They've gone under the floor,' he told her. 'That's where they live but we'll soon have them out. But first we must block off all the runs and all their escapes. You can help me, if you've a mind to.'

She nodded.

'Watch me then,' he said. He took a handful of straw, twisted and folded it into a compact ball, then stuffed it into a hole in the wall. 'If I don't fill that hole they'll run away through it. We've got to fill all the holes except two. Then we'll put the little jill down one hole and watch the rats run out of the other. See, there's a hole, down there by the door. Take some straw and block it up. You can be my assistant – would you like that, eh? A rat catcher's assistant.' He grinned.

13

'I'd like it well enough,' she said and set to determinedly.

It took them nearly half an hour to find and seal off all the routes by which the rats could escape. At last Nat closed the door and decided they were ready.

'Now where are you to go?' he mused. 'You can't stay there for there'll be rats everywhere and we don't want them nipping your toes, do we . . . Ah, I see the very spot. Wait and I'll lift you up.'

A large chest stood to one side and this he pulled forward with much grunting, for it contained old farm implements and was very heavy. As he struggled with it, the little girl considered him thoughtfully from the shabby leather shoes and bare legs to the patched breeches and faded blue shirt. His arms were flea-bitten and his hair was greasy with dirt.

'If you were cleaner, I would wed you,' she said at last, but Nat burst into loud guffaws as he picked her up and stood her on the chest.

'You'd best not let your mama hear you say so!' he laughed. 'T'would turn the poor woman grey in an instant! Now then, stand still and no screaming.'

Gently, he took the ferret from the bag and at once the dog stood motionless, one paw raised in the air, his small dark nose quivering expectantly.

'Why are his legs so short?' asked Lorna.

'So he can squeeze down rabbit holes, now hush.'

He went over to a hole in the far corner and set the ferret down before it. The animal gave a slight flick of her tail and disappeared. For a moment nothing happened. Boy, girl and dog waited. Then all at once there was a scuffling and a large rat darted across the floor. In a flash the dog was on it. He gripped it by the neck, shook it and tossed it aside. Before Lorna had recovered from the suddenness of the deed, two small rats streaked past her on their way to a familiar bolt hole, only to find it blocked with straw. Their frightened squeals were silenced – one by a blow from Nat's stick, the other by the dog. More rats appeared, scattering and squeaking in fear as, pursued by the ferret, they fled to the safety that no longer existed. Mercilessly

Brin pounced, shook and dropped them, and Nat dealt with the others. Still the rats came tumbling out from the hole, their dark bodies moving at an incredible speed across the earth floor, difficult targets in the failing light.

Suddenly there was a lull. Nat waited, stick raised. Brin watched, panting and trembling, his dark eyes glinting with the thrill of the hunt. Dark, still bodies littered the floor. As Lorna opened her mouth to speak, two more rats ran out and the dog took them both. There was another pause and then the ferret appeared. Nat lowered his stick and gently coaxed the tiny animal into his hand and back into the bag.

'I'll give her a fine supper of rat,' he told Lorna. 'She likes rat.'

Lorna shuddered. 'Can I step down now?' she asked and her voice shook slightly.

'Aye, and well done,' he said, helping her. 'I'll count them up and see what I've earned.'

She watched, fascinated, as he picked the rats up by their tails and threw them into a pile.

'. . . forty-one, forty-two . . . and two more, that's forty-four . . . and another here that's – how many?'

'Forty-five,' said Lorna promptly.

'Aye. Forty-five, 'tis indeed. That's a shilling for three dozen and nigh on a fourth dozen. Not bad at all.'

They returned to the kitchen to find Maria home from Ladyford and she paid Nat willingly for his services.

'And you'd best come again,' she told him, 'and clear out the stables. They're alive with rats and Jon says they bother the horses and make them restless.'

It was agreed and then Nat was away, the dog at his heels, the coins clinking cheerfully in the old purse at his wrist. Heron would see him again.

In 1574 the people of England were enjoying a period of comparative calm after the alarms and excitements of the previous years. The Kendals at Heron shared this peaceful existence with their neighbours in the West Country and prayed that they might continue undisturbed to mine their tin and raise their children. The nation was still adjusting to the Pope's excommunication of Queen Elizabeth and the fact that it no longer owed allegiance to Rome. The dreadful events of St Bartholomew's day were no longer news, for two years had passed since the Catholics had heard of the massacre of thousands of Protestants in France. Catherine de Medici contrived at intervals to propose her sons as suitors to Elizabeth though with little success. In 1572 Mary Queen of Scots' plan to take the English throne with the Duke of Norfolk as her husband had ended in failure for Mary and death for the Duke. But in Devon the events of the outside world went mainly unremarked in the face of a too-familiar threat from within.

Maria Kendal set down her goblet and raised anxious eyes.

'Plague?' she echoed. 'In Ashburton?'

The years had been kind to her and at thirty-three her oval face still kept its firm lines. The grey eyes no longer blazed but held a softer expression which suited them equally well, and the dark hair beneath the beaded head-dress was barely touched with grey. Her strong teeth were almost as white as when she married and her smile was sweet. Now, however, the finely arched brows were knit. She was unsmiling for the subject was grim. Her daughter-in-law, Harriet, who sat opposite, waited for Hugo's reply.

Her husband, Hugo, nodded. ' 'Twas only in one street, I grant you, but the three doors bore painted crosses and in one a woman leaned from the upstairs window talking to another who waited in the street below.'

'Was there a watchman at the doors?' Harriet persisted.

'No, but the door was barred. And at the far end of the street a man unloaded brushwood from a cart.'

'For the bonfire,' said Harriet soberly. She was a small slim girl, with soft brown eyes and a gentle face. Her hair was held back by a neat velvet head-dress and her fingers played nervously with the new wedding ring which gleamed

16

on her left hand. She had been married to Allan Kendal for only three months, but had lived at Heron for the past two years. Allan was the eldest Kendal son - the only child of Simon and Hannah. Now a man of twenty, he was finishing his law studies in London and Harriet longed for his return to Heron at the end of June. They were ideally suited and the little time they had spent together augured well for their future happiness. At some time Allan would inherit and she would be mistress of Heron but she was still young and not eager for such responsibility.

At present she was content to share the pleasures of the Kendals' family home. Maria was like a mother to her and Hugo treated her affectionately - almost brotherly. She was fond, too, of Beatrice, Allan's sister, now eighteen and living in Exeter with her husband, Mark Quarterman. Life was very agreeable and she considered herself most fortunate. She wanted nothing to disturb their peaceful existence and Maria's talk of plague dismayed her. Barely sixteen, she had only the vaguest memories of the last serious outbreak to affect the West Country and now all her fears were for her beloved Allan. She adored her tall blond husband and longed to give him a family of tall blond sons to carry on his name. Her one fear was of losing him.

'Is it elsewhere, do you think?' she asked as casually as she could.

Hugo shook his head. 'I've not heard of it,' he said. 'Pray God 'tis a local outbreak and soon ended.'

'Then pray God 'tis not in London,' said Harriet, putting a name to her fear.

Hugo, understanding the direction of the girl's questions, smiled at her. 'There's no mention of it in London,' he said. 'And no mention of it in Exeter.' He put a hand over hers. 'We must put it out of our thoughts,' he told her. 'Three shut houses and a bonfire! 'Tis very little to be alarmed about. That may well be all there ever is to it.'

Harriet looked at Maria with new hope. 'Mayhap the crosses were old ones,' she suggested, 'from an earlier outbreak. And the women just gossiping and the bonfire was to celebrate—' Her voice trailed off as she failed to think of an alternative reason for the untimely appearance of the bonfire.

'Mayhap,' said Maria kindly. 'As Hugo says, we must not fret. We shall take precautions and all will be well. We'll have a few bonfires of our own to burn up any pestilence in the air – if there be any – and will stay away from Ashburton for a week or so.'

'Have we plenty of medicaments?' Hugo asked lightly and she nodded. 'Then we can speak no more on such a mournful topic,' he said. 'We'll finish our wine and then Harriet shall sing for us.'

Maria nodded and her smile to Harriet was warm and reassuring. However, as she sat later listening to the girl's thin sweet voice, her thoughts returned to the threat of infection and she determined to be safe rather than sorry. She would send out for more herb of grace and dragon water and sprinkle fresh herbs and flower petals among the rushes on the floor to sweeten the air. Tomorrow, too, she would warn Melissa. Content that she could do no more, she went to bed a little easier in her mind and, with Hugo's body comfortingly familiar beside her, the spectre of plague faded until at last she slept.

A week later, however, the number of reported plague cases in the town had trebled and there were isolated cases in the neighbouring hamlets. In Exeter there were a few more and Maria's concern grew daily for Beatrice. The baby, due in October, would be the first grandchild.

At Ladyford, a short distance from Heron, a bonfire burned day and night. There Melissa Benet, the children's aunt, kept a watchful eye on her own small household. Her husband Thomas was an old man and vulnerable. Neither Minnie, the cook, nor Jacob, the hired man, were ever ill and her son Oliver was away at sea. Nevertheless Melissa heeded Maria's timely warning and had visited the apothecary before the general alarm put the medicaments in short supply and sent the prices creeping up. There was nothing left then but to wait and pray and this last they all did with great fervour.

Kent, July 1574

Appledore, in Kent, shimmered under a fierce July sun which, late in the afternoon, struck the wooded slopes at an angle and sent long shadows across Romney House, nestled below them. They gave the white walls a cold look and the black beams stood out harshly, but were in their turn offset by the warm thatch grown brown with age and pitted with birds' nests. The house now belonged to Maria, but had formerly been the home of Harold Cummins, to whom she had once been betrothed. Now it had a neglected air and the gardens were little better. The once neat hedges sprouted rebelliously and the shrubs grew into trees, obscuring the red brick wall which bordered the garden. Harold Cummins would have grieved to see it in such a state but his sister Ruth, who had survived him, was unaware of the gradual deterioration for her sight had begun to fail two years after his death and now, four years later, she was blind. Maria had engaged a young companion for her, and Felicity Carr moved into Romney House. Maria also kept on the shepherd, Mark Wynne, for the dwindling flock of sheep and a part-time gardener who could do little more than tend the fruit trees and keep an eye on the bee hives.

Felicity tiptoed into the bed chamber and gently opened the shutters and pulled back the bed drapes. Then she sat beside the bed, closed her own eyes briefly and waited for Ruth to waken from her afternoon's sleep. At last the old lady stirred and her eyelids fluttered. She opened her eyes but saw nothing. She drew a shaking hand from the bed clothes and felt for the bed drapes. They had been pulled back and a cool breeze reached her, telling her that the shutters had been opened. She listened but there was no

19

movement in the room and she called feebly. 'Felicity? Are you there, child?'

'I'm here, ma'am.'

The voice was soft and caring and came from the left side of the bed. The old woman stretched out her left hand and felt young firm fingers close round it.

'I was waiting for you to waken,' said the girl. 'I made your draught but when I brought it up you were already sleeping. I thought it best not to disturb you.'

'Quite right, child. Quite right.' Ruth sighed heavily. 'What time of day is it?'

'Evening, ma'am. I opened the shutters when the sun passed. And—' she could not hide the excitement in her voice '—there's a letter come, ma'am – from Mistress Kendal.'

'A letter from Maria? Why didn't you wake me? Oh, help me up, child and then read it. A letter from Maria! Why, 'twas only yesterday I spoke of her, saying I was certain she would write.'

Smiling, Felicity helped the old woman into a sitting position, as eager as Ruth to hear the news from Devon. Although she had never visited Heron, and had met Maria only once, the news from the Kendal family was almost her sole link with the outside world and eagerly anticipated.

She plumped up the pillows and straightened the woollen bonnet which the old woman wore at all times to hide her scanty grey hair.

'There!' she said. 'All tidy. D'you want to take your draught now, then the news will take your mind from the bitter taste!'

Ruth was impatient to hear the letter but she allowed the girl to spoon three measures of the syrup into her mouth and wipe the drips that ran down her chin. Sometimes she wondered about the girl, trying to piece together an image from the modest descriptions Felicity gave her. A homely face, small mouth, speckled brown eyes set wide apart and long mid-brown hair. Hardly a beauty but kindly and dutiful – altogether a good choice.

20

And patient in the face of Ruth's occasional nagging, for her sudden blindness had in no way sweetened her temper and increasing age had not mellowed her sharp tongue. 'The letter!' she demanded. 'My chin's of no importance with none to see me but you. Read the letter and read it slow, the way I told you, else I can scarce take it in.'

Felicity handed her the rolled paper. Ruth liked to feel the seal to reassure herself that it was unbroken and that her young companion had not taken a preliminary look at its contents. Felicity watched her, a faint smile of amusement on her face, then received it back, opened it, and began to read.

'From your affectionate Maria this first day of June. In hopes that your health be much improved and pleased that the shaking in your limbs is less troublesome. Felicity writes a fair script and we value her reports on your progress. Lorna is stitching a sampler for you with thick wools that she says you may feel the design with your fingers and see the colours in your mind. Piers makes progress with his Latin though Master Parry declares him an obstinate scholar—' Ruth's face puckered suddenly into a smile and she laughed silently until the laughter became a rattling cough and Felicity leaned forward anxiously to put an arm round the bony shoulders.

'That young Piers!' said Ruth. 'So like my brother when he was a boy. Such a bad boy, he was, and never out of mischief. You did not know my brother, did you?'

'No, ma'am.' Felicity answered the familiar question patiently while her eyes skimmed the letter eagerly.

'He died,' said Ruth. 'He was a good man. Such a bad boy but such a good man. Maria would have wed him but his health failed him. Poor Harold. He loved Maria. They were betrothed. Did you know that, child?'

'Aye, ma'am.'

'And you did not meet him?'

'Indeed not.'

'He was a good man - a dutiful brother . . . But go on with the letter. Piers and the Latin—'

21

Felicity continued. '. . . an obstinate scholar and would beat him if I would approve such measures but I can not. My beloved Hugo is well enough, but the mine is a source of great unrest and he finds little pleasure in it and loses sleep and is grown tired and out of humour. I trust you do not suffer the plague in Kent, which is lately broken out again in these parts and with some speed leaps from one village to the next, and the heat of summer will nurture it so that we are grown fearful and stay at home. Beatrice is in Exeter and it is there also so we must all to our prayers and take all good care that we can do. I am thankful Martin is away at school and Allan in London away from the infection. Matt would be remembered to you and speaks often of you and Harold, God rest his soul. Now my letter closes and I wish God's grace and peace to all at Romney House.'

She let the letter fall into her lap and looked at Ruth for her reaction. The old woman plucked absentmindedly at the coverlet and stared unseeingly towards the window.

'Martin,' she said at last. 'She speaks of Martin. How old is he, this Martin?'

'Eleven, ma'am – or it may be twelve. He is at school in Winchester.'

'Ah, yes. And have we seen the boy?'

'No. Nor any of them.'

'Yet I see them, you know, Felicity. I see them as you read. How is such a thing possible?'

'Maria has told us. She describes them and you remember.'

'I do indeed, child. I remember all of them. My adopted family! Maria calls them my adopted family.' She sighed. 'I could have wed you know,' she said wistfully. 'Did you know that, Felicity?'

'Indeed, ma'am. You have often spoke of it.'

'But I chose to care for my brother.' The girl was silent, reading the letter again and the old woman's voice rose querulously. 'You don't answer me, child. I said—'

'You chose to care for your brother,' said Felicity hastily. 'That was well done.'

'Aye . . . but she speaks of the plague in Exeter. We are more fortunate here.'

'We are indeed.'

'Lorna . . . Have we seen Lorna?'

'No, ma'am. 'Tis a long way for such a child. Maria says she will visit when she is older.'

'Ah, yes. I recall . . . That Matt she speaks of. Simple in the head, poor lad. Matthew, his name was, but he would not have it other than Matt. Harold taught him his letters, did you know that?'

'No.' Felicity lied kindly for the story was one of Ruth's favourites.

'Harold was so patient,' the old woman began, 'and he persevered so. But this Matt, he had so few wits and his fingers were big and clumsy—'

Felicity settled herself for the account, smoothing her skirt and Ruth broke off suddenly and turned towards her. 'What are you wearing, child?' she asked sharply. 'Answer me truthfully.'

The girl coloured instantly and put her hands up protectively to hide the blue silk gown which was her best.

'Felicity! Speak truthfully now.'

'Oh, ma'am—'

The old woman's face hardened. ' 'Tis the silk!' she challenged. 'The blue silk. Answer me, I say.'

'Aye, ma'am. The blue silk.'

Ruth sucked her breath in sharply. 'How many times have I told you that gown is for special occasions? For visiting and such like. I have told you repeatedly *not* to wear it about the house when there's none to see it. The kersey is quite good enough for the likes of you—'

'I'm sorry, ma'am. I—' She hesitated, reluctant to point out that Romney House saw so few visitors that the dress might well never be worn at all. It was the girl's only luxury – to wear the blue gown and feel the silk, smooth and cool to her hands, and to hear it rustle as she walked.

23

'Make me no excuses you ungrateful child!' cried Ruth. 'You take a cruel advantage of my sightlessness and laugh at me.'

'Indeed no, ma'am!' the girl protested, her sensitive feelings hurt by such an accusation. 'I never laugh—'

'You mock me!' Ruth insisted. 'You—' She was seized by a fit of coughing. The girl hesitated but, as though sensing her concern, Ruth waved her away. 'Go change the gown!' she told her angrily, 'and then stay in your room. I can't abide such deceptions. You are a wicked girl!'

Felicity's mouth trembled as she stood head-bowed and made no answer.

'And come back at seven with my hot posset – and leave the letter in my hands. You shall read it again later.'

Felicity handed her the letter, crossed to the door and closed it quietly behind her. Ruth sank back against the pillows and closed her eyes. Her anger had exhausted her and she breathed deeply while her fingers fumbled with the folded paper.

'Martin . . .' she whispered, 'and Lorna and Piers . . .' She stopped, struggling for breath, '. . . and Matthew, such clumsy hands—' She stopped again and her head seemed strangely heavy for her neck and fell sideways. Her vacant eyes rolled slowly upwards and her jaw dropped, but she was still aware of the paper between her fingers and knew only that she was still alive.

Beatrice Quarterman lay on the truckle bed immediately below the window and watched Amy's fingers thrust the needle in and out of the white linen. Perspiration glistened on the maid's broad forehead and her frequent glances towards her mistress were fearful.

'Put that away,' Beatrice told her, 'and look out again for Mama – Ah, that will be her now.' There was a banging on the door below. 'Run down at once and let her in. I feared she would be too late.'

Amy obeyed and Beatrice was left alone in the small

24

upper room. Her own body was bathed in perspiration and she lay naked under a single sheet. Her limbs ached and movement was agony for her. The infection had advanced rapidly from the initial fever and now affected all her glands and she felt as though a fire consumed her body from within. She kept her eyes open with an effort. If she closed them she isolated herself from the world entirely and knew only the loneliness of darkness and pain. No one had put a name to her sickness and she acknowledged it only to herself. Footsteps sounded on the stairs and she turned her head painfully, hopefully, towards the door. Her mother had come. She would know what to do. She would save her from the dread . . .

' 'Tis the doctor, ma'am!' cried Amy, her panic clear in every word. 'He would come in, ma'am. I swear 'twas not I that fetched him. Oh, ma'am, I swear I—'

She thrust an anxious fist into her mouth and waited for her mistress's wrath. The plague doctor followed her into the room – a gruesome figure in the familiar protective clothing, floor-length leather coat and a matching hood. This completely covered his head and face, apart from the two round eye holes and beak-like protuberance for the nose which was filled with scented herbs and garlic. A slight groan escaped Beatrice at the dread sight, but as she struggled to sit up the doctor spoke reassuringly.

'Don't stir yourself, mistress, and calm your fears. 'Tis only I, Master Phillips—'

'Master Phillips?' gasped the maid. 'Faith, sir. I didn't recognize you.'

He laughed. 'Hardly surprising in this guise,' he said, 'but I assure you 'tis no stranger who attends you.'

Beatrice breathed a sigh of relief and her most immediate fears lessened. She had known Daniel Phillips since she was a child herself and he had confirmed her pregnancy earlier that year.

'Fearfully hot, these robes,' he told her as he knelt beside the bed. 'In this heat I am slowly roasting and will be nicely cooked by supper time.'

'A cool drink—' Beatrice suggested and he nodded as he turned back the sheet.

'Fetch ale for the doctor,' said Beatrice, then winced as his gloved fingers probed gently for the telltale swelling.

'Nothing in the neck,' he said. 'Now gently – I want to lift your arms and feel the arm pit . . . Nothing there—' He lowered the left arm and moved round to the other side of the bed. 'Slowly does it. I won't hurt you – Ah! That's what I was looking for. The bubo. 'Tis forming under this arm. A good sign, child, for the infection will gather there and be expelled. A very good sign.'

He nodded and through the holes in his hood she saw that the kindly faded eyes crinkled in a smile.

'Then the house . . .' she began.

He sighed as he stood up moving clumsily in the unfamiliar garments. 'We'll have to shut you up,' he said, 'and promptly. Is no one here to nurse you but young Amy?'

'My mother is coming,' said Beatrice. 'At least, she is sent for. I thought you were her.'

Amy returned with a tankard of ale but the doctor shook his head.

'I'll drink it in the back yard,' and his voice held the hint of an apology. 'Then I'll write you a prescription and Amy shall run to the apothecary for anything lacking in your own cupboard.'

A sudden rapping on the street door sent Amy rushing to the window. ' 'Tis your mother!' she cried thankfully, and hurried down to admit Maria.

'A timely arrival!' said the doctor. 'I shall speak with her before I go and the watch will be along shortly to make fast the door. But don't fret. Thirty days will soon pass and all will be well again. You have a mild attack and with your mother's devoted care will soon be whole again. Pray for others less fortunate.'

And with a nod he left her and went downstairs to give the rest of his instructions to Maria.

'When the swelling in the arm grows purple, lay a

poultice to it,' he told her, '—as hot as can be borne but not so hot as to blister the skin, like some I've seen. Eighteen pennyweight of garlic cloves, fresh butter, lemon and a handful of scallions. Wrap it in calico and when 'tis cooled replace it with another until the bubo is drawn and the poison expelled. She is fortunate – no sneezing and no sign of the tokens on her skin. Aye, 'tis a mild case and she'll recover, God willing. Not like some poor wretches – six gone in one family in Castle Street. Six in less than a week but that's how it goes and who are we to question? Once the house is shut up you know the rules – you must admit no one and no one must leave for thirty days. If you need anything send the watchmen. They're idle wretches mostly but will stir themselves for a coin or two and 'tis mournful work they do, in all conscience.'

Maria followed him outside into the small courtyard at the back of the house and Amy handed him the ale. He took off his hood and took several deep breaths of the bright sunlit air to clear his lungs, then he applied himself gratefully to his cool drink.

'And the child?' Maria forced herself to ask the question. 'The unborn child she carries?'

'All should be well,' he said. ' 'Twas, as I told you, a mild case.'

'And will you call again?'

'If time permits, but I leave her in good hands. The plague, like poverty, is always with us and if the stars be propitious we shall cheat death a little longer. Are all well at Heron?'

'Aye, so far thank the Lord.'

'Then I'll bid you adieu and be on my way.'

'God be with you,' she said and he replaced his hood and followed her back through the cool house and out once more into the unrelenting noonday sun.

As he had predicted, Amy only just got back to the house in time. Within an hour of the doctor's visit a burly watchman arrived and nailed a bar of wood across the front door. The hammering reached Beatrice as Maria fed her with spoonfuls of warm honey water and she 'tutted' at the noise.

'Thirty days!' whispered Beatrice. 'How will they fare at Heron without you for so long?'

Maria laughed. 'Oh, they'll survive no doubt. Beth is most capable and Harriet will enjoy playing "mistress of the house". Hugo will keep a watchful eye on things and Matt will scurry to and fro to bring us news.'

Beatrice smiled faintly. ' 'Tis a wonder he is let you come here alone. He has been your shadow for so many years.'

'Aye, he's a faithful soul. Poor Matt. He'll never wed, being so child-like, yet I think he is happy enough. There now. You sleep and I'll see that Amy has fetched all that we need. If not then the watchman must go. Let's hope he's an amiable man and willing.'

As she turned to go Beatrice cried, 'Mama! The baby. Did you speak to Master Phillips of the child?'

'I did and there is nought to worry us. Your babe is safe. Go to sleep now.'

In the kitchen she found Amy unloading her basket, a satisfied smile on her face.

' 'Tis all here, ma'am,' she told Maria and ticked the items on her fingers. 'Vinegar, scallions, treacle, butter and cloves – and from the apothecary cedar wood, rose water and rue!'

'Well done, Amy. Now, we shall prepare the poultice and set a pan of embers – Ah! that banging goes on and on!'

She went through to the front of the house and put her head out of the window.

'How many nails does it take to bar one door?' she asked. 'My daughter is trying to sleep.'

A rough-looking man of indeterminate age looked up from his work, a hammer poised in his hand. His hair was tousled and his smile revealed several missing teeth, but he took the rebuke cheerfully.

' 'Tis the very last nail, ma'am, begging your pardon,' he told her. 'I'll be painting on the cross next but that'll make no noise at all. Then the blessing and I'm a fair hand with words. I make a real neat job and never had a complaint. Why, my last family was so pleased the husband gave me a gold ring off his own finger for my trouble and . . .'

'Well, there's no husband here,' said Maria sharply. 'The husband is away in Ireland so there'll be no gold ring but you'll likely earn an honest penny if you can run an errand without taking all day.'

'I can, ma'am. Indeed I can.'

'We shall see. But now knock that last nail in and be done with your banging. And catch the next water carrier that comes by – we're getting low.'

He touched his forehead, gave the final nail three blows and raised his hand triumphantly.

'All done!' he announced, but Maria had already withdrawn her head and closed the window tight to keep out the smoke from the bonfires.

'Thirty days!' she muttered. 'A whole month! But 'twill pass . . . Aye, there's much to be done and the time will fly.'

But she was not entirely convinced. Thirty days' quarantine was a heavy sentence for the sin of ill health, but the regulations were very strict and if it prevented the spread of the disease then she would willingly comply.

Sighing, she thought for a moment of the rest of her family, thankful for Heron's isolation. Little chance of infection there, she reassured herself and, comforted, made her way back to the kitchen to supervise the making of the poultice.

CHAPTER TWO

Piers, perched on top of the stable door, watched while Nat made a final count of the dead rats as he gathered them into a large sack.

'Sixty-three, sixty-four – Ah! This devil is still alive! See that, Master Piers!' He held a large black rat by the tail and they watched it wriggle. 'Too heavy to climb up its tail like the young 'uns. But see here he starts to twirl. Round and round he goes to try and shrug off his tail skin. That way he'd leave me with the skin and he'd be away – free as air. Oh no, you don't!'

He dropped the rat into the waiting jaws of the little terrier who eagerly shook the last vestiges of life from it.

'Sixty-five,' said Piers. The rest of the bodies went into the sack. 'Seventy-one in all! 'Tis more than you took in the barn!'

'Aye.' Nat grinned, pleased with his evening's work. He whistled the dog and they stepped out into the yard. At the far end young Ben waited with the horses. 'You can put 'em in again now,' Nat shouted and Piers darted off to lead his own pony back to its stall.

Ben paused. 'Sorry to hear about your father,' he said and Nat's face clouded over.

He shrugged. ' 'Tis God's will, I daresay, but he was a good old man.'

Ben nodded. 'I hear you buried him in the woods.'

' 'Twas his last wish,' said Nat. 'I got some strange looks but—' He shrugged again. 'He never could bear the church yard. Real mournful, he called it.'

'I'm eight years old,' Piers interrupted them, 'but I'll soon be old . . . and then I'll be buried in the family grave.'

'Eight years old,' laughed Nat. 'You've a long way to go. No need worrying your head about it yet awhile. And where's that sister of yours? I thought she'd have been out here with you to see the fun.'

'Kept in at her lessons and Master Parry hit the table with his fist – like this!' He brought his clenched hand down through the air, '. . . and called her a young ninny.'

Ben, emerging from the stable, winked at Nat, 'Young Master Piers is the perfect pupil, of course!'

Piers was not at all disconcerted. 'My sister Beatrice is well again,' he told them. 'She had the plague but is quite recovered and now Mama is home again Harriet has a fever.'

The other two exchanged startled glances.

'What fever would that be?' asked Ben, for his sister Ellie was part of the Heron household.

'An ephemer fever,' said Piers. ' 'Tis not the plague. Ah, here comes Lorna now.' He raised his voice as the slight figure of his sister appeared round the corner of the barn. 'You're too late!' he assured her. ' 'Tis all over and Nat has caught seventy-one rats.'

Lorna reached them, her face flushed, skirts held high, her hair dishevelled. She looked from one to the other in dismay.

'Too late?' she wailed. 'But I have run all the way.' She put a hand out to fondle Brin. 'Oh, how I hate that Master Parry!'

Ben grinned. 'Who's a young ninny, then?' he asked.

Before she could reply, Beth came into the yard, a scowl on her round face. She had eaten too well of her cooking over the years and had put on too much weight, so that she moved with an effort and was quickly out of breath.

'I called you, young Lorna,' she grumbled. '*And* you heard me so there's no use pretending otherwise. There's nought wrong with your ears so you'd no call to rush past me like a wild thing and me having to traipse down here after you . . .'

She paused for breath, a hand to her chest, and Lorna said, 'I wanted to see Nat catch the rats – the way he did before. I told Piers to ask Nat to wait for me but he didn't.'

31

She looked reproachfully at Nat who in turn looked at Piers. He looked guilty. In the excitement he had forgotten the message and Nat, to avoid a confrontation, said hastily, ' 'Twas the fault of my little jill ferret. She's in a strange mood today and so restless. I dared not wait any longer or she'd have bit a hole clean through the bag and—'

'Never mind you and your ferret,' said Beth. ' 'Tis Piers and Lorna I'm after. Poor Harriet has took a turn for the worse and you're both to ride to Ladyford with Ben and stay a few days.'

'How worse is a turn for the worse?' asked Ben.

Beth avoided meeting his eye. 'They don't tell me much,' she hedged.

'But is she sneezing?' said Ben. 'Your own ears will tell you that!'

Beth hesitated and there was no need for the brief nod that followed.

The men crossed themselves and the children's expressions changed.

' 'Tis the plague?' cried Lorna. 'Harriet has the plague!'

'I'm afeared so,' said Beth, 'but you two will be well out of it—'

'Will she die?' asked Piers, wide-eyed at the unwelcome news.

'Not if the mistress has her way!' said Beth. 'Beatrice didn't die, did she? Maria has sent for the doctor and will nurse Harriet herself, though how she'll find the strength, I don't know, for she's only just come back from Exeter, poor soul, and has gone so thin with the worry of Beatrice.'

'And now she's another patient on her hands!' said Nat. He swung his sack over his shoulder and waited hopefully for someone to remember his fee. But Beth was hustling the two children to saddle up their ponies, refusing to allow them back into the house, promising to send clothes and toys after them.

'Your mother wants you out of Heron at once,' she told them. 'So no "ifs" or "buts". And she says to do as your Aunt Melissa bids you and be no trouble to her.'

Brin barked suddenly and darted off after a large ginger cat which sprang down from the stable roof. Nat coughed loudly and Ben said, 'Ah, your money. Seventy-one rats, you say? How much is that then? I'm no scholar. You'd best see the mistress.'

Beth said, 'There's none to be allowed into the house. He must see Hugo when he comes back from the mine, which will be within the hour. Wait here, Nat, and the master'll pay you.'

Nat lowered his sack to the ground, settled himself on the cobbles beside it and took a hunk of cheese from his pocket and began to eat hungrily.

Protesting half-heartedly, the children were finally mounted on their respective ponies and Ben threw a saddle over the old mare's back. 'No message then?' he asked Beth as he swung himself up.

Beth put a hand to her perspiring forehead and tried to think. 'Say as the doctor's sent for and please to keep them until she gets word. And there'll be a letter in the morning. And say Harriet's sneezing and—' Her lips quivered suddenly and Ben looked at her sharply.

'And what?' he demanded his voice rough with fear, but Beth shook her head helplessly, unable to utter the dread words. 'Not . . . ?' Ben's face paled.

Beth, with a glance towards the children, nodded. Beneath Harriet's fair skin a scattering of faint blotches were already visible. The dark tokens indicated the later stages of the most virulent form of the disease.

Ben drew in a deep breath then slowly let it out. Then with a forced smile he turned to the children.

'Let's be on our way then!' he said, and Nat and Beth watched in silence as the small cavalcade passed through the yard and out of sight.

Nat whistled. 'I've seen folk fit as a fiddle at sunrise and dead by nightfall!' he said with more truth than tact, and then cursed himself for a fool as Beth burst into loud, ugly sobs and made her way back to the house, her large body shaking with fear and grief. ★

33

Harriet's skin burned as her temperature soared. She could bear no covering over her and was only soothed when Maria bathed her with tepid water, but as soon as the water had dried off she would once more pucker her face in discomfort and moan for water. Her lips had cracked and her dry tongue licked them ineffectually. Maria applied butter and goose grease but they, too, gave only temporary relief. The all important bubo did not appear and the scattering of dark spots increased almost hourly. The physician called later in the afternoon and could offer no hope to the despairing Maria.

'But there must be something else we can try,' she pleaded fearfully. 'I beg you tell me some other hint, no matter how foolish it may sound. I must try everything. Everything. Poor Allan – they have been wed so short a time. Only three months—'

'I know it,' he said, 'but death takes no account of such reckonings. If 'tis God's will you must resign yourself. We have tried everything—' he shrugged hopelessly, 'and we have failed. I sympathize with you but now only your prayers could save her. Turn away God's wrath and mayhap he will be—'

Maria's tired eyes blazed suddenly. 'Wrath? What cause has God to feel wrath for this poor child? I'll warrant she has never harboured an unkind thought in that sweet head of hers! Oh sweet heaven, Allan will be beside himself if she dies. They are so much in love.'

The physician shrugged again and began to close his bag. 'I'm sorry,' he said. 'To lose a loved one is never easy. We are surrounded by death yet never learn how best to deal with it. I must go—'

'No! I beg you,' cried Maria, putting a hand to his arm. 'One moment more, Master Phillips. Help me, I beg you. There must be some way, some trick. You saved Beatrice. You cannot let Harriet die.'

'Forgive me,' he said gently. 'Beatrice was fortunate. It was a mild case, as I told you. This is a most virulent form and—'

At that moment Harriet cried out in sudden pain and flung up both hands to clutch at her head. Maria looked at her aghast as the girl began to mutter feverishly, tearing at her head, pulling out her hair.

'Oh my dearest child,' cried Maria, kneeling beside her and trying in vain to stay the girl's hands. Master Phillips shook his head and turned to go.

'You cannot leave us!' cried Maria. 'Help me, I say.'

'I'm sorry,' he said. 'I have told you there is no hope. I am needed elsewhere. God willing, I may be able to save a life. You must be strong, mistress, for she is going to die and her husband will need your support. Now I must go. There is no need to shut up the house. You are isolated here.' He paused at the door and looked back. The leather hood hid his expression but his tone was gentle. 'Someone else must share the burden with you,' he said. 'You will exhaust your energies.'

Maria shook her head. 'No, no,' she protested wearily. 'The infection—'

'You have sent for her husband?'

'Aye.'

The physician nodded and withdrew. A scream from Harriet made him hesitate but then, shaking his head, he made his way downstairs and let himself out of the house. The outbreak had lasted nearly two months and he had seen a great deal of sickness, misery and death. His emotions were mercifully blunted but so young a woman, and so pretty! He sighed as he walked towards his horse, which Ben held for him.

'Will she get better?' asked Ben.

Master Phillips put one foot in the stirrups and half turned. 'She will soon be at peace,' he said, but the euphemism did nothing to soften the news.

In the garden beside the river eleven-year-old Ellie crouched in the grass, her two hands cupped and waiting. In the long grass a toad blinked in alarm as she bent

35

forward and her head cast a shadow over him. Before he could move, her hands were round him as, with a squeal of disgust, the little girl held her wriggling captive at arm's length.

'Keep still!' she hissed. 'Ugh! Stop wriggling, you stupid creature.' She dared not close her hands for fear of harming him. A dead toad would be useless. The charm would never work. Slowly, awkwardly, she stood up and set off towards the house. She hated the feel of the toad's cold body, but at least he had stopped trying to escape and sat passively in his small prison, and she tried not to visualize the ugly body with its thin angular legs and alien head. She shuddered, nevertheless, and quickened her steps. Ellie was Minnie's daughter, a faithful copy of her mother but taller and less moody. She lived at Heron and attended Harriet and Maria as personal maid. Minnie, maid to Melissa, tried hard not to show her envy. Her own long-cherished dream was to return to Heron, but she was happy enough at Ladyford and willing to bide her time until the Lord saw fit to answer her prayers. A smile played around Ellie's lips as she reached the kitchen door, kicked it sharply and shouted out to Beth.

'Let me in at once, Beth. 'Tis most urgent, I swear it.'

Taken aback by such impudence, Beth sent Ben to admit her and they both looked at her in astonishment as she held out her cupped hands.

' 'Tis for Harriet,' she told them, her small dark eyes glittering with ill-suppressed excitement. ' 'Tis a toad to cure Harriet. I've—'

Another piercing scream reached them and Beth crossed herself hurriedly.

Ellie glanced upward. 'Is that Harriet?'

'Aye,' said Beth. 'Screaming her agony and her wits quite gone, Maria says. The master is with her, too, trying to hold her down, for she's that wild – Oh, I can't bear to think on it!'

Ellie's face had paled a little but she made to pass Beth, who spread her arms wide.

36

'And where d'you think you're going?' she demanded.

'To take this toad to the mistress. 'Twill save Harriet from the plague. My ma told me.'

Beth snorted. 'Toad indeed. Well, you're not taking it a step further. If a toad would cure her then Master Phillips would have prescribed it.'

'But mayhap he doesn't know of it,' protested Ellie. ' 'Tis a secret, you see, passed on to my ma by her ma and passed on to her by—'

'That's enough Ellie,' said Beth. 'I know you mean well, but I'm that weary I've no time for such tricks.'

Ellie turned to her brother. Ben was three years older than she was and at most times a loyal champion.

'You tell her, Ben,' she pleaded. 'How you hang the toad by his leg until he dies and the life stuff drips out of him on to the patient. You heard ma tell it, Ben. You tell her.'

Ben shook his head. ' 'Tis no use, Ellie,' he said as kindly as he could. 'And Beth's had bad news of her own a few moments since. Her own sister is sick of the plague and like to die.'

Ellie looked at Beth in dismay. 'So many folk dying!' she said. 'I'm afeared. If Harriet dies will we all die?'

'Don't say such things,' said Beth. 'Heron's a big place and you're well away from the infection. But now I must get on with some baking for if my sister dies I'll be bound to see to her poor old husband, for he's been crippled these past five years and can't care for himself.'

'You mean you'd leave us?' asked Ben. 'Leave Heron?'

'Happen I'll have to,' said Beth resignedly. ' 'Tis all I can do for my poor sister and that's little enough. I could scarce leave her old fellow to starve to death. Still, we'll wait and see. Pass me the rolling pin, Ben, and Ellie – that toad goes out! This very moment and no ifs or buts! And don't pull that face. You look just like your mother when she was a girl. Now where are the currants? Oh dear, I'm all at sixes and sevens.'

An hour passed and Harriet's screams grew thankfully less frequent as the pain in her head subsided. Her temperature remained high, however, and her delirium increased. She spoke in a rambling voice, quite unlike her own, and for Maria, sitting beside her, the high-pitched murmuring increased her distress. She wondered if Allan would reach Heron in time and secretly hoped he would not. It was a poor sight to see the once beautiful girl in such a condition, her body marred by the dusky blotches which sprinkled the fair skin of her breasts and shoulders and began to appear on her face and neck. Her bloodshot eyes were wide and staring and from time to time she shivered so violently that her limbs jerked uncontrollably and her teeth chattered. She had bitten her tongue and blood oozed from the corner of her mouth and ran along the cracked skin of her lips. Maria wetted the small towel and wiped it away. Was it her imagination or had Harriet's breathing changed? It seemed more rapid and the shivering increased. Harriet tried to speak but her voice was no more than a painful croak and Maria leaned over her to try and hear what she said.

'What is it, child?' she asked gently. 'Are you cold? Or thirsty? Is it Allan you speak of? He will be home directly, never fear. We have sent for him. Take a sip of wine to ease your throat.'

Harriet struggled to speak and Maria helped her to sit up a little and raised the flagon to her parched lips. Harriet managed a mouthful before she caught sight of her arm, and gave a moan of fear. Her pale wrist was speckled with three dark spots. Harriet understood their significance and stared at them, transfixed with horror.

Maria held her hand, patting it reassuringly. ' 'Tis nothing,' she told her. 'Three little spots!'

But now Harriet rubbed at the marks, uttering shrill cries of alarm. The sound, like an animal in distress, chilled Maria's heart. The girl turned her head slowly and became aware of the tokens on her right shoulder and then she looked down at her body and saw her speckled breasts.

She began to claw frantically at her skin, trying to rid herself of the offending spots, and she summoned deep reserves of energy so that her movements were forceful and her nails tore into the skin, streaking it with blood. Dimly, Maria was aware of hoofbeats outside and her heart sank. God forbid 'tis Allan, she whispered, but she knew it was very probable.

She pleaded frantically with her daughter-in-law, aware of Allan's imminent arrival. 'Stop that, Harriet! No, you must not. D'you hear me, child. Oh, stop. I beg you.'

But the demented girl fought off her restraining hands and then there were footsteps on the stairs and Allan ran into the room.

'Help me, Allan. For pity's sake, help me,' cried Maria.

He flinched at the sight that met his eyes – Harriet was half out of bed, screaming hysterically, her body running with blood from countless self-inflicted weals.

'Help me hold her. Oh, what is to be done with her? Should we tie her down? Allan – Ah!' She winced in sudden pain as Harriet lashed out at them, and a powerful blow caught her across the side of the head and sent her staggering off-balance. As she fell, she struck her head against the corner of the four-poster.

'Mama!'

Allan turned his attention momentarily from Harriet to Maria and in a flash the girl pulled free of his grasp and ran out of the room.

'Are you hurt, Mama?'

She shook her head dazedly. 'Harriet – go after her,' she gasped, and he left her and ran out on to the landing. Already, the girl was at the bottom of the stairs. She ran straight into Ellie, who was turning the corner carrying an armful of freshly ironed linen. The little maid took one look at the dreadful sight, dropped the linen and fled back to the kitchen, white-faced and speechless with shock.

Beth could get no sense from her so she hurried out into the hall in time to see Allan run out of the front door.

'Now what's amiss?' she demanded and, looking after

39

him, drew her breath sharply and crossed herself. ' 'Tis the end, poor child! 'Tis the way they go, some of them. Some die slow and others burn themselves out in a flash.'

Ellie, who had crept out after her, burst into tears and clung to Beth, who put a comforting arm round her.

'Harriet! No!' shouted Allan, for the girl was running in the direction of the river. She reached the top of the steps which led down to the lower garden. She turned abruptly and her expression was strangely calm. Allan hesitated as she held up a hand to warn him.

'Harriet,' he stammered. 'Come back to bed. Come with me. Oh, my dearest, take my hand. Let me hold you. Let me care for you. You shan't die.'

For a moment it looked as if she would comply. Her lips parted in a travesty of a smile and then she glanced down at her ravaged body.

'Come to me, Harriet,' he repeated gently. 'All will be well, I swear it. Don't run away from me.'

She looked up and he saw that tears glinted in her eyes. 'I'm ugly,' she said simply. 'The tokens are ugly – I must wash them away.'

Allan took a step towards her and held out a hand. 'I shall wash them away for you,' he said. 'Come back to the house and we shall make you clean. You will be pretty again, I promise.'

With her hands, she brushed at the blood on her breasts then raised her fingers to look at them curiously. Allan took another step towards her and she glanced up at him with a strange smile on her face. 'I'll wash them away,' she repeated. 'Aye, that's it. I'll wash them away.'

Only ten yards separated them, but before Allan could shorten the distances she turned suddenly and stumbled down the steps. As he ran after her, he heard the splash as she went into the river and when he reached the bottom of the steps he saw her standing waist-deep in the water. She was splashing water up over her body and she glanced up at him with a crazed expression. She flung wide her arms and laughed. Then the laughter died in her throat, her arms fell slowly to her side and she looked at him with sad eyes.

'Oh dear God!' cried Allan, plunging into the water, struggling to reach her before she collapsed. As he reached her she closed her eyes and fell lifeless into his arms.

It was past midnight when Harriet's body was finally laid in the straight wooden coffin which rested on two trestles in the bedchamber she had shared with Allan for so short a time. Maria and Melissa had laid her out and now stood beside her, looking down into the sweet face, perfectly composed in death. The long white robe hid the lacerated body and white chalk successfully concealed the dark spots on her face. A white bonnet covered her soft brown hair and her eyes were closed and long lashes fringed her smooth cheeks. The candlelight was kind to her.

'She was a bonny girl,' said Melissa. 'She looks so serene now. Allan will feel better when he sees her this way.'

Maria sighed heavily. 'Poor Allan. He took it very hard. When I found them he was sitting on the steps, cradling her on his lap. He was talking to her - trying to reassure her that she was still beautiful. Her head was against his shoulder and her hair was wet. I thought she was still alive.'

'Poor little girl.'

Maria put out her hand and gently stroked Harriet's cheek. 'Still downy, this poor little face. Allan used to call her his little swan.' Her lips trembled and she turned to Melissa. 'If only I knew where he had gone. He was so strange. At first he would not part with her body but carried it into the house and sat in the bedchamber with her. I thought she would - I thought her limbs—' She broke off and Melissa nodded without speaking. 'I thought we *must* take her from him but I couldn't find the words. My head ached from the fall and I felt sickly. Then Hugo came back - 'twas a mercy he did. He argued with Allan and then he - Allan - laid her on the bed and ran out of the room. He rode off, no one knows where. Oh Melissa, he looked so strange.'

''Tis natural enough,' said Melissa. 'Such a terrible shock, poor lad.'

'But Allan is—' she hesitated, biting her lips, afraid to put her fears into words.

'He'll be back, you'll see. He'll ride out his grief and return to us.'

'I hope so. Jon said he rode like one possessed.'

'He'll be back,' Melissa's tone held conviction.

'I hope I was kind to her,' Maria said suddenly. 'I think I was. Such a pitifully short life. I hope she was happy.'

'Indeed she was,' said Melissa. 'A husband who adored her, an affectionate family, a comfortable home. Of course she was happy. How could she be otherwise?'

'But to die before she had a child. Such a grievous loss, never to know a child's love.'

Melissa was silent, thinking fleetingly of her own son, Oliver, now a young man of twenty-four. He had left home ten years ago to go to sea and she had not seen him since. They had an occasional letter and these she treasured, reading them again and again, trying to picture her quiet son, wondering how he survived the rigours of a sailor's life. Nightly she prayed for his deliverance from danger and for his eventual safe return.

Maria fussed with the dead girl's gown, twitching the folds into place and tucking the hem more securely under the small feet. 'She looks very beautiful,' she said. 'Tomorrow I shall search for white flowers, some to tuck into her hands, others to circle her head. What d'you think Melissa?'

'I like it. Flowers lend a certain delicacy.'

'Aye. I think so.' She sighed again. 'And Beth is to leave us tomorrow. Did you know?'

'Beth? Why, no.'

'Her sister is also stricken and leaves a crippled husband.'

'Sweet heaven! And this is a mild outbreak! Where will it end? But how will you manage without her?'

Maria turned to her hopefully. 'I meant to speak with you on the subject. I wondered if I might have Minnie here if Maggie would come to you.'

'Maggie Ball at the bakery?'

'Aye. She has often said that she might one day give it up. She is greatly aged this past two years and might welcome the idea. Will you think on it?'

Melissa considered the idea and found it agreeable. There was a bond between herself and Maggie which no one else could share. They had both loved Simon Kendal and both had lost him. In a way Melissa admired the forthright Maggie for her independent spirit and ready humour. Melissa smiled wryly. 'I dare say Maggie would rather come to Heron and be near her beloved Allan. To her he is almost a son.'

Maria shrugged. 'Minnie would never recover if she did. *She* has been trying to find a way back here since the day she moved to Ladyford.'

They both laughed. Maria moved the candles nearer to the head of the coffin and Melissa looked at her curiously.

'I know,' said Maria. 'I fidget. 'Tis foolish but I want to satisfy myself I have done all that I can for her. I cannot quite believe that she is dead and beyond the small comforts of life.'

'Her soul is on its way to God,' said Melissa. 'The passing bell rang long and loud. She is at peace now. Let her be.'

Maria took a deep breath and smoothed her own skirts. 'You are right. 'Tis no use fretting over the dead. 'Tis the living need our help. Tomorrow, if Allan is not returned, I must send Matt in search of him.'

'And I will speak to Thomas about Maggie and most likely ride into Ashburton to see her. You will need help with the funeral feast with Beth gone. How strange to lose Beth after all these years.'

With a final glance at Harriet, they moved quietly to the door and out onto the landing. The rest of the household were already asleep and the only noise was the wind in the chestnut tree. It was too late for Melissa to return to Ladyford so she would sleep at Heron. She took the proffered candle from Maria and kissed her lightly.

43

'Sleep easy,' she told her. 'You have done all that you could.'

Maria's eyes were large in the flickering light. 'I hope so,' she said earnestly. 'I truly hope so.'

Allan had ridden fast and furious, across Dartmoor. Oblivious of his destination, he had ridden due east over the sprawling moorland unaware of the darkening sky that heralded nightfall. He rode without stopping, spurring his horse unmercifully so that it raced desperately, heart labouring under the unexpected effort, nostrils flared, specks of froth whipped from its mouth by the wind. Allan rode with his eyes closed against the pain, careless of his own safety, unconsciously challenging death to take him also, so that he could be once more with his beloved Harriet. At last the rumble of passing cartwheels opened his eyes and he found himself on the far side of the moor, on the furthermost outskirts of Tavistock. With an oath, he turned his exhausted horse and headed north-east so that he moved across moorland once more. He longed to ride forever until he fell, but it was in fact the horse that stumbled, throwing him head first to the ground.

He was lucky enough to land in soft marshy ground which broke his fall. For a moment he lay where he was, his anguish welling up afresh but then with a deep, trembling sigh he scrambled to a kneeling position and stared into the darkness. His horse was grazing nearby. He could hear the teeth closing and the small sound of grass parting from its roots. The half moon was rising and there were no clouds.

'Harriet!' he whispered. 'Harriet . . . Harriet.'

He longed to see her as she had been, when he lay with her, sweet and loving under his caresses, an excited smile lighting her face, her breath coming in soft gasps. Instead he saw her wild eyed and bloodied. He groaned aloud and threw himself face downward on the cool turf and there he lay all night, unmoving, sleepless, while the moon rose

44

over him and the night creatures watched him cautiously, skirting the long still form, startled by the blond hair which shone silver in the moonlight.

His stillness belied the turmoil within him, as grief and shock gave way to a deep misery that was physical – a misery that weighed on him like earth upon a coffin, pressing him down into the soil beneath him, while the darkness hid him from the world. He was abandoned, solitary, cut off from his fellow men, unable to see or hear, a forgotten object. He was buried alive in the dark recesses of his mind. He was at one with his sweet wife. He prayed for oblivion and wanted the all embracing darkness to go on forever.

But at last the sun rose, touching the cold sky with its rosy light and warming the earth with the promise of a new day. The sounds of night vanished with the dawn and reluctantly Allan Kendal opened his eyes and forced himself to face the rest of his life.

His body was cramped and his clothes clung damply to him. His mind was numb, all rage, fear and pain had merged into unreality. His horse was gone but he stood up and stamped his feet and swung his arms, and felt the stiffness leaving him. Breathing deeply of the cold air, he turned to face the sunshine, imagining that it warmed his face. Then he turned eastward and set off for home. After an hour's walk he came upon his horse, which came willingly when he whistled. So he rode slowly back and the hours passed at a walking pace until the spire of Ashburton church gave him his exact whereabouts. On a sudden impulse he turned away from Heron and headed into the town, and just before five had tied his horse to a hitching post and was knocking at the door of Maggie's bakery.

She came grumbling to the door, a shawl thrown round her shoulders, her figure hidden in a shapeless nightgown. Her protest died on her lips as she recognized him.

'Sweet heaven, 'tis Master Allan – and in such a state! Come in at once and let me take a proper look.'

She pulled him inside and closed the door and for a few

seconds her eyes took in his haunted expression and the crumpled state of his clothes. Hands on hips, she surveyed him, tutting softly to herself, then she flung her arms round him and hugged him fiercely.

'Whatever ails you 'tis not the time to speak of it yet,' she said shrewdly. 'When a young man turns up on my doorstep at this ungodly hour, there's only one thing to do and that's feed him. So you sit yourself down, young Allan, and nurse the fire along for I've only just lit it, and I'll get a bite of breakfast and a drop of hot spiced wine. That'll warm the cockles of your heart – mine, too – and we'll eat and drink and life'll be worth living again. That's right, love, throw on a few more sticks. They're in the basket behind you. Make a nice blaze. Now let me see, there's a couple of veal pasties in the larder and a bit of cold capon. Tasty that was, though I say it myself. Cooked it slow with a few sprigs of rosemary and the flesh fell off the bones. We'll finish that – and there's a bit of curd cheese, or did I finish that off? My memory these days! I'm getting old, no point in pretending.'

Allan said, 'You'll never be old, Maggie,' and she smiled to herself to see that he was 'coming round'. Chattering on, she gave him no time to think his own thoughts and suddenly she laughed. He turned from the fire to see her regarding him cheerfully.

'You look just like your father, kneeling there,' she told him. 'The image of Simon. He was a grand lad, your father. A grand lad – and you're like him. No two ways about it. Oh dear, it's smoking a bit. Wood's damp I expect. The bellows are behind you, love. Give it a bit of a blow. Show it who's master.'

And she bustled about the small homely kitchen, resisting the urge to find out what had brought him to her door.

'We'll have a picnic,' she told him, and capon, cheese and pasties were set down beside the fire which suddenly flared into life and gave out a comforting warmth. Glancing at Allan, she was pleased to see the colour creep back into his face and a little of the pain fade from his eyes. 'There now—' she said, setting down two bowls of hot wine. 'A breakfast fit for a king so help yourself and don't wait to be asked. Manners are not my strong point, as you well know, so let's fill our bellies and talk after.'

Allan was surprised to find that he could eat the simple food which tasted better than any he could remember. The hot wine warmed him, sending a pleasant glow through his cold body, and gradually he began to relax and the horror of the previous night receded, routed from his mind by Maggie's determined cheerfulness and the warmth of her affection for him.

Slowly he began to talk and the telling of Harriet's death, though anguished, was bearable and the pain less than he had anticipated. Maggie nodded from time to time and the sympathy was plain in her eyes, but she continued to press food and drink upon him and her occasional comments were made in a matter-of-fact way. She let him talk on until the horror and anger died in him and only the grief remained.

'You had a sweet, loving wife,' she told him. 'Most men are never so fortunate. You've known true happiness. Many men would envy you for that. Be thankful for such mercies and when you lose them, why, treasure the memories. You know what they say – better to have loved and lost—' He nodded. 'Put a few more sticks on, love, and that bit of a log. I must chop some more later. Ah, that's better. I love to see the sparks rise, don't you? Sad how often we lose the ones we love, but that's the way of the world and 'tis no use railing against God's will. We must take our joys when they're offered and pay for them when the reckoning's due. Life goes on. Do they know where you are – at Heron, I mean?'

He shook his head and a flash of panic showed in his face.

'Not that there's any hurry,' she said quickly. 'They'll no doubt send Matt after you and that'll keep him out of harm's way for an hour or two. You bide here a while. I don't often have the pleasure of your company and if mistress Harriet could look down and see us here, all cosy,

47

she'd be well pleased. Traipsing over the moor all night! I don't know.' And she shook her head and a smile lit up her plump, homely face.

Allan looked at her curiously. 'You loved my father, they say. Is that true?'

'Oh, it's true enough. Great times we had and a lot of fun. We often sat here, just like this. That was before he knew he was a Kendal. Simon Betts, he was, when I first knew him. Simon Betts, the baker's lad.'

She laughed and Allan smiled with her. 'Head over heels in love I was and he fancied me. Oh, you needn't grin like that. I was pretty then with brown curls and—' She stopped and sighed, fingering her greying hair.

'You're still bonny,' he told her. 'Go on with the story. I've never heard it all told.'

Maggie laughed. 'Not much more to tell, really,' she said. 'I was crazy for him, but one day he met your aunt Melissa and that was the end of my romance.'

'Aunt Melissa? But—'

'Ah, we know they're related but you see they didn't. Not then. No one knew. Being a bastard, he'd been given to a family called Betts. Oh, he was a fine lad, your pa. I was so jealous. I knew there was someone else, you see. I spied on him to find out who it was. Followed him one evening and saw them together. Then I went to his father and told him.'

'Maggie!'

'I know, I know. 'Twas a spiteful trick, but I was so in love with him and it broke my heart. Still, it was as well I did for they was brother and sister and only the father knew it. Dear oh Lord, that stirred up a hornet's nest, I can tell you. He was sent packing and I never saw him again. Not until he was acknowledged, that is. Once his brothers were both dead, he was the only heir and Luke Kendal brought him into Heron.'

'And Aunt Melissa later married Thomas?'

'Aye – and very happy they've been, bless them. She's forgiven me. We're friends. Your father wed Hannah and they were very happy.'

48

'And poor old Maggie—'

She laughed ruefully. 'Life's funny,' she said simply. 'Simon loved Melissa and he grew to love Hannah, but 'twas me that was with him the night he died. I'll always be thankful for that.'

Allan nodded. He had heard the story from the servants. 'You met up on the battlefield outside London,' he said.

'Aye. That Wyatt and his ill-fated rebellion! Next day I found Simon dead of his wounds and sat with him until they came for his body.'

'And then—' he prompted, to turn her thoughts away from sad memories.

'Then? Oh, you know it. Hugo was widowed and in time he wed Hannah. They had young Beatrice, bless her.' She smiled. 'And all the time Maria was pining for Hugo but she had a long wait. She despaired, I reckon. Took herself off to that nunnery, poor soul. But then the Lord saw fit to take Hannah when she gave birth to Master Martin. Oh, a real scamp, he was . . . So then there were three motherless Kendal children.'

'Until Hugo and Maria wed.'

'Aye and a real love match that was. Then they had Master Piers and little Lorna.' She shrugged suddenly 'And what do *I* do during all these excitements? Why, I make pies and puddings and apple dumplings—'

'The *best* pies and puddings,' he corrected her cheerfully, but she shook her head and sighed.

Allan was silent, then he put an arm round her shoulders. 'Poor Maggie,' he said softly.

'Aye. Poor Maggie. Poor Allan. We all have our griefs and we all live through them to happier times.' She sighed deeply, then with an effort, shook off the melancholy. 'Now then, young Allan. That's enough talking for one day. "Poor Maggie" has got work to do. Pastry to roll and pies to bake and here I am sitting over the fire gossiping.'

'I'll help you, Maggie,' he offered but she shook her head.

'I'd love to take you up on it, but your place is at Heron. Maria will need you. She must be at her wits' end.'

'Just for an hour, then, Maggie,' he pleaded. 'Let me help you for an hour and then I'll go home.'

She hesitated. 'A Kendal rolling pastry and chopping meat?'

He smiled. ''Twas good enough for my father.'

'It was indeed,' she said. 'Right then, you shall help me for an hour. Stir your stumps, young Allan, and'we'll make a start.'

And so it was that when Melissa arrived with her message she found Simon's son up to his elbows in flour and a wink from Maggie told her that the worst was over.

They laid Harriet to rest two days later in the family grave and the sun shone thinly through the autumn mist lending a mystical quality to the proceedings. Allan watched impassively as the coffin was lowered into the ground and he was first to toss in the rosemary twig. His lips moved, then, in a whispered farewell. His sorrow was in his eyes for all to see but his control was greater than anyone expected. The Minister's voice rose and fell with the familiar words and brought home to the mourners the frailty of life and promised them riches in heaven. He spoke movingly of Harriet's short life and sympathized with the bereaved. Then he commended her soul to God and the bell began to toll. As the mournful sound echoed in the still air, Allan's eyes lifted for a moment from his wife's grave and sought out Maggie's. Wordlessly, he expressed his gratitude and she acknowledged it with a brief nod of her head. Then, as tradition demanded, he took up the spade, drove it into the loose earth piled beside the grave and scattered it over his wife's coffin.

CHAPTER THREE

The river which flowed past Heron continued its way
through field and moorland and then wound round the
bottom of a small wooded hill. Here, half overgrown by
bushes, was Nathaniel Gully's home – a small building,
little more than a hovel. It had a hole in one wall which
served as a window and a doorway covered by a well-worn
hide. The smoke from his fire in winter found its way out
through chinks in the turf roof. In summer he cooked
outside. Three chickens and a goat shared this humble
dwelling and the smell was considerable.

Lorna wrinkled her nose in disgust and said, 'Pooh!'

Piers nudged her with his elbow but it was too late.

'Your house smells,' she told Nat.

Looking up from his netting, he laughed in mock
dismay. 'Don't you like it, ma'am?'

'She does,' said Piers.

'I don't,' said Lorna. 'It smells horrid.'

Piers, embarrassed by his sister's honesty, averted his
eyes, and wished he had come alone on the long promised
visit. He snapped his fingers at Brin and the little terrier
heaved himself out of his corner and trotted over eagerly
to be patted. Nat's nimble fingers twisted the hook in and
out of the mesh and tugged a new length of string free of
the ball.

'Oh,' he said. 'So you don't like my house? Not as grand
as Heron, is it, but it suits me. I've a roof over me head to
keep out the rain and four walls to keep out the wind.'

'But there's only one room,' said Lorna.

She and her brother sat side by side on the log that
served as a seat. Nat sat on the only stool, making a new
rabbit net.

'One's all I need.'

'But where's your mama and papa?' she insisted.

'Dead and gone,' he replied cheerfully. 'And my sisters are wed and gone. That just leaves me.'

'And Brin,' said Piers, 'and the goat and the chickens.'

'Do they lay eggs?' asked Lorna.

'Well,' said Nat, 'they don't make honey, that's for sure!'

She looked at him suspiciously but he was intent on his work once more.

'To tell you the truth we're a funny lot,' he told her, ' 'tis the goat that lays the eggs and the chickens give milk.'

She stared at him wide-eyed while Piers tried hard to keep his face straight. After a moment she said cautiously, 'What does the dog do?' and Nat and Piers burst out laughing.

'He's teasing you,' cried Piers. 'Oh, you should see your face! Serves you right for being impertinent.'

She sprang to her feet, squealing indignantly and the log tilted, throwing Piers off-balance. He cried out and the dog, sensing a game, rushed between them barking excitedly. Nat watched with amusement as the two children wrestled and then Lorna tripped backwards over the log and fell sprawling on the earth floor.

'That's the way,' said Nat. 'Get yourself all muddy and your ma will want to know where you've been.'

They were immediately sobered. Piers helped his sister to her feet and made a half-hearted attempt to brush down her gown. Without another word they sat themselves down once more on the log. Lorna put her hands in her lap and her feet neatly together.

'I only said it smells because it does,' she muttered and Piers, groaning, put his hands over his ears. Seeing that Nat appeared quite unconcerned, he took them down again.

'Everyone is dead,' said Piers. 'Harriet is dead and Beth's sister is dead and old Ruth is nearly dead.'

'Old Ruth?'

He nodded. 'Old Ruth at Romney House. She's had a fit and can't walk. Mama is gone with Matt to visit her.'

'Your poor mama,' said Nat. 'Always nursing sick folk. She'll be worn to a frazzle. Isn't there any good news? A little bird told me—'

Lorna dropped her hands. 'Oh yes, the baby! Beatrice's baby! 'Tis a little girl born on the first day of November. Emily Mary Quarterman. And now I'm an aunt and Piers is an uncle.' She giggled, putting her two hands to her face.

'An aunt and an uncle,' said Nat. 'Well, I never did. I shall have to mind my manners with such important folks around.'

At that moment the goat, ambling around the room, decided to investigate the back of Lorna's neck and gave her a little nudge. She leapt off the log with a scream.

'Your goat!' she cried. 'He tried to bite me.'

' 'Tis a nanny,' said Nat, 'and she's friendly enough. But shoo her outside . . . There now, I've finished the net. That'll do me very well tonight when I go rabbiting – but 'tis time you were off home. Your folks will be looking for you before long.'

'Can't we watch you rabbiting?' asked Piers. 'You did promise.'

'Ah, so I did. And so you shall, but not today. We'll have to ask your folks, all right and proper. Next week, mayhap.'

Reluctantly the two children left the little hut. Nat walked back with them along the river until they came to the stepping stones that led into the garden at Heron. Nat watched them safely to the other side, waved a farewell and whistled for Brin who had followed them over. Then he set off for home, still chuckling. Nat Gully was very fond of the two youngest Kendals.

Maria sat upstairs with Ruth in her bed chamber. Matt sat in the large kitchen with Jem and reminisced about 'the old days' when Maria had been betrothed to Ruth's brother and Romney House had been their home. Outside, a November mist hung over the river and encroached over the marshes. There was much hilarity, and upstairs Maria smiled to herself. Beside her the old woman dozed fitfully and Felicity sat by the window sewing. Maria was trying to decide what should be done for the best. The old woman was very frail and her right side was paralysed, but the physician thought she might linger on indefinitely. Alternatively, she might shortly have another 'fit' and die. He could not predict what would happen. Maria studied the old woman compassionately. The face was wizened and the mottled skin stretched tautly over the bones. Her sparse hair was tucked under her bonnet and the right eye oozed moisture.

And she cannot see either, thought Maria, pitying her the meagre existence. And yet still the old woman clung to life, talking interminably. But then speech was all she had left and no one could begrudge her that. Maria sighed heavily. What was to be done with her? It was a burden for Felicity to care for her alone. Maria had offered to take her back to Heron, but Ruth had refused outright. She had grown quite vehement on the subject and Maria, fearful for her health, had withdrawn the offer. Felicity had suggested hopefully that Maria might return to Romney House until Ruth's death, but that was out of the question. She had a husband and family and her first duty was to them. No, Ruth must remain at Romney House and somehow provision must be made for her proper well-being. She would talk to Felicity again. Not an easy task, for the girl was so shy. She glanced at her, head bent over the white linen, and saw her pause and stroke the blue silk of the gown. She was almost fourteen but so immature. Beatrice had been more confident at twelve years old!

With another glance at Ruth, Maria stood up and, taking the stool with her, crossed the room and sat beside Felicity who glanced up, a look of trepidation on her young face.

'Tell me,' she began gently, 'when did the cook leave?'

'Nigh on five weeks ago.'

'But why did you not write to me of it?'

'I did, ma'am, but later I learned that the bearer of the letter had met with an accident along the way.'

'I see. But who has cooked since then?'

'I have, ma'am. We have eaten sparingly, I swear it.'

'I don't doubt it for a moment but—' Maria was momentarily lost for words. ' 'Tis such a burden for you, to care for Ruth and cook, also. I had no idea.'

'I'm happy to do it, ma'am.'

'Where did she go - and why? She had no right to leave you.'

Felicity twisted her fingers nervously in her lap, the sewing neglected. 'She said she had a better offer but—' She hesitated.

'Well? What is it, child? Tell me.'

'I don't - you won't tell him, ma'am? Oh, promise you won't tell him?'

'Tell who? Felicity, what are you talking about?'

Maria looked at her, bewildered. Felicity lowered her head. 'I told you in the letter, ma'am,' she mumbled.

'Told me what?'

' 'Twas the looker, ma'am. She was afeared of him.'

Maria looked at her, baffled. 'The looker?'

'Aye, ma'am - him as looks after the sheep.'

Maria's bewilderment grew. 'Do you mean Mark Wynne, the shepherd?'

'We call them lookers on the marsh, ma'am. Aye, 'tis him. He's a bad man. We were all afeared of him - except Jem. Oh ma'am . . .'

She stopped abruptly as though she had said too much already. Slowly, with infinite patience, Maria persuaded her to tell the whole story. It seemed that Mark Wynne had taken to spending more and more time at Romney House and less and less time with the sheep. His quarters were now above the old stable, since his cottage had fallen into disrepair, and he would frequently retire to bed with a flagon or two of wine and later get up again and force his

55

way into the kitchen. His drunkenness disgusted the
women, but as long as Jem was present there would be no
further problems. Jem, however, was courting the daughter of a neighbouring farmer and was frequently out in the
evening. On these occasions, Wynne's behaviour was
bullying and his language obscene.

'Bullying?' said Maria, horrified. 'In what way?'

Felicity was obviously struggling with her emotions and
found it difficult to speak of the incidents without distress.

Maria took her hand in her own. 'You must tell me,' she
said. 'I must know it all or how can I help you?'

' 'Twas all in the letter,' said Felicity.

'But the letter didn't reach me! Tell me, how did he
bully you?'

'And you won't tell him 'twas I that told you?'

'If what you say is true I shall get rid of him, Felicity.
You have nothing to fear.'

'He said he was without – without a woman of his own.'

'But he has a wife and family. I have spoken with them.'

'His wife died, ma'am, a year since – maybe more – and
Judy, his daughter, left him. She ran away in the summer.
They quarrelled and some say he beat her because she –
she would not – be his woman.' She hid her face in her
hands as her voice dropped to a whisper.

Maria sighed heavily. 'Go on.'

'He said at first that neither of us would serve him.' She
swallowed at the memory and her face paled. 'He said cook
was too old and I was too young but he'd—'

'Sweet heaven! I shall have him flogged!' Maria's face
flushed with anger. 'If he has laid a finger on either of
you . . .'

'Indeed no, he hasn't, ma'am, though lately he said he
would have me, whether I would or no. Oh, ma'am, he
says he means to wed me. I cannot bear it!'

She burst into tears and flung herself on to her knees.
Maria held her close, comforting the trembling girl, her
thoughts chaotic. Remorse filled her at the thought of them
in such sad circumstances and she blamed herself bitterly

for not taking a more positive interest in the little household Harold had left her. Forgive me, she prayed silently. I swear I will mend matters.

'Mark Wynne will never wed you,' she told the girl. 'You have my word on it. So dry your tears, wash your face and be of good heart. I shall deal with Wynne in the morning. But for tonight I must think carefully on what must be done.'

Maria ate her supper that evening in a preoccupied silence and after the meal walked in the grounds with only the dogs for company. She wished fervently that Hugo was with her. He would advise her. Now she had to face the problem alone. It all stemmed from lack of money. Harold's small fortune had ebbed away and the only income was from the sheep. Of late even this had dwindled, but she had trusted Wynne, who had been with the family for as long as she had known them. Each year he had produced a plausible reason for the poor return – a drought, disease, a fall in the demand for wool. Had he been keeping back some of the profits? Had it been spent on loose living? Or were the poor returns genuine – a result of his negligence? There was probably no way of knowing. She had only herself to blame if he had cheated her. Heron had absorbed all her energies and Romney House had come a poor second. But reproaches were useless, she told herself firmly. The problems must be solved and it seemed drastic measures would be required.

A new cook was the smallest of her worries. She would make enquiries. Ruth and Harold had several friends who would, she felt sure, be pleased to recommend a likely replacement. She would start with James Moore, whose farmland adjoined Romney House on the west side. Wynne she would give a month's money and dismiss him instantly. No – on reflection that would not be practicable. There would be no one responsible for the flock until she found a new shepherd. But would he work a month's notice? More likely he would revenge himself by poisoning the sheep! No – he must not know until it was too late for him to do any harm. But how was that to be achieved? Frowning, she paced the narrow paths between the hedges and suddenly became aware of their overgrown state. At the fish pond she stopped, peering into the water, but it was too dark to see whether the fish were alive or dead. What had happened to the gardener? Did he collect his wages and do nothing to earn them? Who would notice? Ruth was blind and Felicity was little more than a child and she had more than enough to do within the house.

One of the dogs had startled a rat and the two dogs now streaked across the lawn, whining in their eagerness for a kill, but it eluded them and they returned to Maria's side, disappointed.

'You must be quicker,' she told them. 'You eat too well and grow fat and lazy!'

It grew late and the moon shone. By its light she saw apples and pears rotting on the ground below the trees where they had fallen. She ground her teeth in vexation. They should have been picked, wrapped and stored for the winter. Such terrible waste appalled her. But could she get rid of the gardener also? There would be no one left! Briefly she smiled at the prospect, but it was no laughing matter. The gardener must stay but she would speak to him severely and he must mend his ways. Maybe a period of trial – six weeks would be fair. Yes, she would see to it. He must understand that if the garden was not greatly improved within six weeks he could look elsewhere for employment, and without a reference that would prove impossible. But Wynne remained her biggest problem. Wynne and the lack of money. She sat down on a small stone seat, pulled her cloak more closely round her and stared unseeing across the moonlit garden. The air was chill but she would not allow herself to go back into the house until she had found a solution to the problems. She shivered and was glad when the dogs settled themselves beside her, one leaning against her legs, one sprawled across her feet. She sat there for nearly an hour and then suddenly she had an idea. It was so simple, so perfect! She considered it from every angle and then nodded in a satisfied way and stood up. The dogs sprang up, eager to go back to the warmth of the hearth. Maria patted them fondly and set off towards the house. Next day was Wednesday and she would set her new-made plan in motion.

James Moore was the local magistrate and he listened keenly to what Maria had to tell him about Wynne.

'Hmm,' he said when she was finished. 'A fine looker gone to the bad, I fear. I did hear rumours about his daughter, poor little lass. We had the constable out looking for her but she was never found. 'Tis a wicked world, my dear Maria. A wicked old world.' He smiled and the faded brown eyes glinted at her over the rim of his goblet. 'As to helping you, why, there's no question but I'll do all I can. Don't be too hard on yourself. I, too, meant to call more often than I did. I promised Harold and then there was always some more urgent task to attend to. The weeks slip by. We're all guilty of the sin of procrastination. A cook – now let me think . . . I dare say my wife will be more help on that subject. We'll talk to her later.'

Maria looked at the weather-beaten face under its thick white hair and saw the firm way his gnarled hands closed round the stem of his goblet. '*You* have changed very little,' she told him truthfully and he looked pleased at the compliment.

'Ah, I've plenty of life in me yet,' he assured her. 'I can still sit a horse and enjoy the thrill of the hunt. I can outride any of the young men – and my sight's as good as ever. Hawkeyes, my wife calls me. But I digress. Some more wine – that's the way – and back to business.'

'The looker,' Maria prompted.

'Ah, yes. You've made a wise decision. The wretch will have to go but you're letting him off lightly. He should lose a hand. Stealing's a serious offence and we must make an example—'

'But I've no proof,' said Maria hurriedly. 'I've only my own suspicions. The loss of a hand is too severe.'

He shrugged. 'He's *your* man.'

'Aye. And the rest of the plan?'

He laughed grimly. 'I'd give a sovereign to see his face! Aye, 'tis the best you can do in the circumstances. I'll take a hundred myself at the current price and the rest'll go. I'll send my man, Merritt, over to round them up. Your two lads'll never do it without a dog. You say Tutherington will take some?' She nodded. 'Then we'll fetch mine. The rest will go by cart. You'll need four or five. Leave it with me and I'll see what I can do. Ah—'

He looked round, hearing his wife approach. She kissed Maria warmly and they exchanged pleasantries. It was ten years since they had last met and Alice Moore had aged considerably. But her mind was as alert as ever and she promised to find a new cook for Romney House as quickly as possible. Then she spoke at length about her grandchildren and Maria told them about her own family and life at Heron. Finally, it grew so late, they persuaded Maria to stay to dinner and it was three o'clock before she finally left to ride home. She was pleased with her efforts so far, but she had not quite finished.

When Mark Wynne first woke it was barely light. Something had disturbed his sleep but he was too befuddled to consider what it might be. Too thick headed, in fact, to realize the need to consider what had interrupted his sleep. He realized only that his head ached as usual and his belly rumbled protestingly over last night's intake of cheap ale, followed by the remainder of a flagon of wine stolen from the cellar up at the house. They never did mix, ale and wine. He knew it – everyone knew it – but still he tried the impossible. At the time it had seemed a reasonable experiment. Now the griping pains told him the attempt had failed. He felt ill and sorry for himself. Below him he thought he heard voices, whispering, and the champing of horses. There was a clatter, quickly muffled, and then silence. He told himself he'd imagined it. No one would be rousing before daylight. Clumsily he turned over, groaning and cursed roundly as the change of position increased the pains in his belly. But it was too much effort to change back again. He lay on the straw on his right side, still fully clothed, his face turned to the roof which sloped past him. He scratched at a flea bite but even that was too much effort and he closed his eyes and drifted back into an uneasy sleep.

When he awoke for the second time, his head felt clearer but his body was sluggish as he struggled into a sitting position. Blearily he regarded the motes of dust which danced in the slivers of sunlight that found their way through chinks in the thatched roof. Hell's blood! The sun was well up. The day well advanced. He might be seen sneaking back to the fields where he should have spent the night 'looking'. He was a short, stocky man with broad shoulders. His small head looked bigger because of the burly dark beard and wild mane of curly hair, but his bushy eyebrows made his small eyes look meaner than they were. He had a scar across his cheek where a savage dog had once bitten him. He had fought it bare-handed after it killed his own dog. Then, he had been one of the most respected lookers on the marsh and Harold Cummins had been proud of his man. But that was all in the past. All that had gone. Everything had gone. Wife, family, a reason for living. He had become a cheat, a drunkard, a bully. And he had developed a dangerous temper. He did not know how it had all come about and he no longer cared.

Breathing heavily, he pulled himself to the edge of the ladder, turned and began the slow, precarious descent.

At the bottom, he steadied himself and saw with some surprise that both horses were missing and there was no sign of Jem. Outside in the yard he shaded his eyes from the bright November sun and stared round him. No sign of Matt, either. It was strangely quiet but he was too hungry to give it much thought. Unsteadily, he made his way to the kitchen door and found it locked. He stared at it in disbelief and banged on it with his fist. That Felicity would give him a bite to eat – too scared to refuse him. He banged again and waited, leaning against the door jamb. She was a scrawny little thing but she was only half grown, he reflected. Not quite as old as his Judy. His lip curled spitefully as he thought of his daughter. Wayward little bitch! He'd find her one day. He was a patient man and could wait for his revenge. He banged again, surprised that no one hurried to open it. He moved along to the window and looked in. The kitchen was empty but a sound above him made him look up and he saw Felicity looking down on him from the upstairs window.

'Go away,' she said somewhat shakily. 'You'll get no breakfast today.'

Before he could answer, she withdrew leaving him staring upwards, open-mouthed at her insolence. God's teeth! She'd grown bold all of a sudden. He felt the first stirrings of disquiet. On an impulse, he ran round the house to the front door. That, too, was locked and he cursed angrily and stood for a moment trying to understand what was happening. Something was very wrong. He felt vulnerable. He was in the wrong place at the wrong time. He would go out to the flock and think it over. Slowly, he made his way back to the stables and crossed to the gate at the far end. He lurched along the lane, his head down, his brow furrowed in thought. An empty cart passed him and he flung himself into the hedge to avoid it, and saw as it passed him that Matt Cartright was driving. He heard Matt break into loud boisterous laughter and wondered sourly what the idiot had found so amusing. At last he reached the field where the flock had been left to their own devices – and found it empty. He stared slowly round, stupefied. For a moment he doubted his own senses, then he doubted his memory. Was this the field? But the neighbouring fields were also empty. Leaning heavily on the gate, he covered his face with his hands and tried to puzzle it out.

Minutes passed and he was no wiser. Three hundred sheep could not be spirited into thin air. But where were they?

The sound of hoofbeats brought his head up once more, like an animal scenting danger. He was suddenly afraid. Three riders came into sight, round the bend in the lane. One was Jem, one was Mistress Kendal – and one was the magistrate! He began to run but Jem rode after him and, flinging himself from his horse, brought him heavily to the ground. There was a short, sharp scuffle but Jem was fortunate. Mark Wynne was far from his peak physical condition or he might have proved a dangerous adversary. As it was, he was quickly taken and, hands bound behind his back, was led to where Maria and the magistrate waited for him. The former looked down at him coldly.

'You are discharged from my employ, Mark Wynne, without notice and without a reference,' she said. 'You have scandalously neglected your duties and I believe you cheated me. You have behaved in an improper manner to members of my household and you can count yourself fortunate I have neither time nor energies to investigate further into your activities over the past year. I'm committing you into custody and you will be punished accordingly. Have you anything to say to me?'

He looked stunned by the speed of his downfall. 'The sheep,' he muttered. 'Where are they?'

'Sold,' said Maria. 'The entire flock. The lands will be rented out until my own son is of an age to take over the management.'

'You whore!' he shouted, but a blow from Jem knocked him down. 'You bitch! You think you can do this to me!'

'I've done it,' Maria told him and her voice was steady. With a brief nod to the magistrate, she rode back to Romney House.

Wynne was lodged in the gaol and later flogged half naked from one end of the village to the other at the cart's tail. He was followed by a small jeering crowd who watched the whip descend thirty times until the broad shoulders ran with blood. No one at Romney House was there to witness the spectacle or hear his threats of revenge. At the end of his ordeal a bucketful of water was dashed over him and he was deposited outside the town limits and forbidden to return on pain of death. As far as the inhabitants of Romney House were concerned, the matter was at an end.

By the time Maria rode back to Heron, two weeks later, the household had been reorganized. The money from the sale of the flock would supplement what little remained of Harold's fortune. Meg Forbes, a small cheerful woman of indeterminate age, had been engaged as cook. The gardener had been given a chance to redeem himself and he would move into Mark Wynne's cottage as soon as the repairs were completed. Matt was to stay on for another month and would then report back to Maria. It had also been arranged that the physician should call regularly once a week to attend Ruth – and Felicity was the proud owner of two new gowns – a pale blue brocade and a grey wool trimmed with yellow braid.

Maria rode back to Devon feeling well content with the result of her efforts. She had made amends and was at last free from the uncomfortable prickings of her conscience.

CHAPTER FOUR

In early December Minnie left Ladyford and rejoined the Heron household as cook. Maggie left the bakery and moved into Ladyford where Melissa greatly enjoyed her company as well as her cooking. Oliver was still at sea and Thomas divided his time between Heron and the mine. Maggie, prudently, had decided not to sell the shop but to put in a man to run it for her. She chose a certain Samuel Tegg, who had once worked for her as 'a lad' and with whom she had enjoyed a relationship that was more than platonic. He had wanted to marry her but she had refused him as kindly as she could and he left her employ to nurse his rejection elsewhere. He later married a young widow and they had seven surviving children. Maggie reasoned that fact alone would make him a hard worker and she trusted him to deal honestly with her. She was not disappointed in either respect.

At Heron preparations for Christmas went ahead almost immediately, but in the event it was not quite as cheerful a celebration as in previous years. Everyone made an effort for the children's sake, but an unspoken concern for Allan affected the adults and robbed their merrymaking of some of its usual enthusiasm. He had borne up well after the funeral and for several weeks following, but he then sank into a depression from which no one could rouse him. He rarely spoke and then only when spoken to and his face wore a haunted look. He lost all interest in food and often went for days without a proper meal. Maria scolded him cheerfully and tried to coax him to eat and to please her he would take a few mouthfuls, but as her 'nagging' continued he grew irritable and was often absent from the table altogether. The physician recommended bleeding but Allan refused that, also, denying that he was sick. He sat through the Christmas festivities and smiled dutifully, but his manner was both sad and distracted. Instead of lifting him out of his despair, the excitement around him seemed only to increase his solitary brooding and their concern for him grew daily.

The new year announced itself with a heavy fall of snow and Heron and Ladyford were separated by deep and treacherous drifts. Piers and Lorna made the most of the opportunity and spent as much time outside as they were allowed. For nearly three weeks the kitchen was draped with damp clothes and boots stood steaming in the hearth. Beth would have found it a great nuisance but Minnie, recently installed in her place, was so delighted to be back at Heron (where she firmly believed 'everything happens') that she made no protest and the children's joy continued. It was halted in the last week of January by an abrupt change in the temperature. Heavy rain, which washed away the snow, continued for nearly a week with disastrous effect. The ground was still frozen and unable to absorb the combination of rain and melting snow, and the surplus water found its way into the rivers, which rose alarmingly. Piers woke one morning to find that the rain had stopped and the sun was shining. He scrambled out of bed and ran to the window whooping with delight. Then he gasped in amazement.

'Lorna! Come quick. Come and see,' he urged. 'Do wake up, you ninny, and look. I won't tell you again, you must see for yourself.'

He jumped up and down impatiently until she struggled to her senses and, somewhat crossly, ran to join him. She, too, stared in amazement at the sight which met her eyes. Large areas of the surrounding moorland had disappeared under a vast sheet of water which sparkled in the sunlight. From it the tips of shrubs emerged and startled birds swooped above it uttering shrill cries of alarm. The higher ground was unaffected and a few stray animals had found their way to it – a small group of ponies who grazed unconcernedly and several sheep.

Lorna looked at her brother, her young face suddenly

grave. 'All the animals!' she said. 'The rabbits and foxes
– will they all be drowned?'

'I doubt it,' replied Piers, who was none too sure. 'But
make haste and dress and we'll ask Papa if we can ride
out.'

She needed no second bidding and before long they were
hurrying down to the kitchen where Minnie was already at
work. The fire blazed and the porage was bubbling.

'We can ride out to see the flood,' Piers told her
breathlessly, 'Papa said so.'

'But first we must eat a good, warm breakfast – Mama
said that.' Lorna grinned and they sat down at the table
while Minnie ladled out two helpings of porage and
added a spoonful of honey to each dish.

'You go careful,' she warned them. 'We don't want you
falling in.'

'We won't,' said Lorna. 'Papa has told us not to leave
the horses. We are to stay mounted. And we must not go
too far. We promised.'

'Well, see that you do as your pa says. There's neither of
you can swim yet and water's very wet stuff!'

The two children giggled, scooping the thick, sweet
porage into their mouths in their haste to be off.

Once outside, they raced to the stable and were soon
mounted. Jack watched them go, hands on hips. 'And you
mind what your pa told you and keep on the horses,' he
yelled, but they merely waved in reply, too intent on their
adventure to waste words on an answer.

They rode out of the stable yard, skirted the house and
went down the hill on the far side until they stood at the
water's edge. The river banks were hidden under the
swirling brown water and the original course of the river
was no longer visible. A solitary dabchick paddled furiously
against the current, making no headway.

'I wonder what the fish think of it,' said Lorna, gazing
down and trying to pierce the murky depths. 'The eels and
the roach and the mullet . . . they'll all get lost.'

'Fish don't get lost,' said Piers. 'I'll wager our lower

garden is flooded. The steps, too, most likely. We'll have a look later. Ah, there's a kingfisher! Did you see it?'

Lorna shook her head. She was watching something further out. 'It's a tree,' she cried, pointing excitedly. 'See, Piers, a whole tree floating along with its roots and branches.'

'Aye, I see it. The current must be very strong. And look to the right – the stone bridge is half hidden. The arches are out of sight.'

They looked at each other soberly.

'Will it come higher?' asked Lorna anxiously. 'Will it reach Heron?'

He tried to picture it happening, screwing up his face in concentration. 'It might,' he said at last, 'but we would climb upstairs if it did.'

'And if it came up the stairs?'

'We'd climb out onto the roof.'

'Oh.'

A sudden thought struck her. 'Nat Gully!' she cried. 'I wonder if he is flooded. Should we go and see? Is Nat Gully's too far?'

'I think not,' said Piers, so they turned their horses and rode alongside the water. When they drew opposite to his hut they saw that it was above the water line – but only just. There were three or four yards between the doorstep and the encroaching water. Of Nat there was no sign. They shouted but there was no reply.

'Brin's not there either,' said Piers. 'He would have barked.'

'He would have been pleased to see us.'

'Aye.'

'I wonder how far is *too* far?' said Piers. 'I wonder if the old wooden bridge is too far. 'Tis built higher than the stone one. We might be able to cross it and then we could look for Nat on the other side.'

They looked back the way they had come. Heron was still in sight, its thatch just visible through the hawthorn trees. While they were deliberating, the sound of barking came faintly to their ears.

''Tis Brin!' cried Piers. 'They must be up ahead. We'll surprise them.'

They urged the ponies to a trot and rode on a few hundred yards then stopped and listened again. The barking continued, but now it was quite obvious it came from the far side of the swollen river. They reached the wooden bridge and were dismayed to see that it, too, was almost submerged. The wooden supports were out of sight and the water flowed over each end of the bridge to a depth of a few inches. Only the centre was free of the water where the curve of the bridge reached its highest point. The barking was nearer now and Lorna opened her mouth to call to Nat but Piers put a finger to his lips to silence her.

'We'll go and find them,' he told her. 'We can cross the bridge.'

Lorna glanced down at the dark water which swirled around the wooden beams.

'We daresn't,' she protested. 'We must stay on the horses.'

'We will! We'll ride over the bridge. 'Tis strong enough. Cattle cross it.'

It was true. An excited gleam shone in her eyes.

'Then let's make haste,' she said eagerly, and headed her pony towards the water's edge.

'Can horses swim?' she asked as they splashed through the shallow water.

'Aye,' said Piers, who did not know whether they could or not. 'But I should lead the way. 'Twas my idea.'

His protest went unheeded for already his sister's horse was splashing on to the wooden bridge, his eyes rolling nervously.

'Go *on!*' cried Lorna crossly, digging him with her heels. 'You stupid old thing, go on!'

The sound of Brin's barking drew nearer and they heard Nat laugh.

The old pony was jerking his head from side to side, unaccustomed to the gleaming expanse of water which surrounded them. 'Hold him steady!' cried Piers, trying to persuade his own mount to follow Lorna's on to the bridge.

Suddenly, Brin dashed from the cover of the trees and ran towards them and Lorna's pony took fright and reared up. Somehow Lorna clung on but by now Piers' pony had moved onto the bridge.

'Take him forward!' cried Piers, but Lorna had lost control and the pony, backing away from the excited terrier, collided with Pier's mount and sprang forward with a shrill whinny of fear. As Lorna tugged at the reins, the horse swung sideways and the bridge rail creaked ominously. Brin had reached the bridge and dashed on to it, straight under the hoofs of the terrified animal which made a frantic leap. Lorna lost her hold and was flung sideways. With a despairing cry, she clutched at the rail as she fell, but her hands could find no purchase on the smooth wood.

Piers screamed, 'Lorna!' and then Nat appeared running towards them.

Piers was struggling with his own pony and trying to avoid Lorna's. 'Lorna!' gasped Piers. 'She's in the water!'

Nat took in the situation at a glance. Lorna's head surfaced for a moment and she screamed, too far now to try and take hold of the bridge supports for already the current was carrying her downstream.

'I'm coming! Stay with the horses!' cried Nat, as he dived into the water and swam after the little girl.

Sometimes he saw her head or an arm as she struggled in the fast-moving water. Sometimes she sank from sight and Nat's heart sank with her. It seemed impossible that he could catch up with her before she sank for the last time, but suddenly she was carried up against the torn bough of a tree which slowed her progress momentarily and gave Nat the vital time he needed to reach her.

They were both chilled from the icy water and Lorna was scarcely breathing. Nat prayed that he could drag her to the bank in time. Piers had managed to get both ponies back on to the bank and now he galloped after Nat and Lorna, his face white and shocked. He raced ahead of them and then forced his pony into the water in an attempt to head them off. The horse obeyed him reluctantly and with only seconds to spare they were in position as Nat and Lorna were driven towards them. As they swept past, Nat reached out and caught at the horse's leg and Piers swung himself down to clasp his wrist. Slowly, he backed the horse into shallower water and at last they were all on dry land.

'Make haste!' cried Nat, through chattering teeth. 'Help me turn her.'

Together they lifted Lorna's unprotesting body and held her upside down until a rush of water emptied her lungs and she swung choking and spluttering – but mercifully still alive. Piers gulped back tears of relief as she burst into loud, uncontrolled sobbing and Nat, shivering and exhausted, tried to comfort her. When she was calmer they rode back to Heron. Nat rode Lorna's horse, with Lorna on the saddle in front of him. He sat with one arm round her, trying to warm the frail, trembling body as she leaned against him, half fainting with cold and shock. Their arrival at Heron sent the household into a near-panic. Lorna was carried into the house and straight up to bed. Clean dry clothes and three hot bricks brought the colour back to her pale face. Minnie heated milk and added a spoonful of brandy to warm and soothe her stomach. Later there would be plenty of explaining to do, but in the meantime Nat Gully was the hero of the hour.

After the snows and heavy rains of the first two months of the year the high winds of March were welcomed by one and all. They dried out the low-lying pastures and the sheep returned to their grazing grounds. Once more men moved freely about their business and journeys that had been delayed were embarked upon. Ploughing was started and the ground prepared for early corn. Hunting was resumed and the population waited eagerly for the first signs of approaching spring, when tight buds would open and the children would scurry forth to search the trees and hedges for birds' eggs. The sun shone but there was little warmth in its rays.

Hugo sat by the fire in the Hall, a letter in his hand. Beside him Piers worked at the table, busy with a piece of writing which wholly absorbed his attention. Lorna, at his side, practised plaiting with three leather thongs and waited patiently for him to finish. He leaned over his work and the tip of his tongue protruded.

At the far end of the room Maria worked at the loom, deftly sliding the shuttle backwards and forwards, soothed by the monotony of the movements. She glanced up at the windows. It was already growing dark and she saw that Hugo had turned the letter towards the firelight to read it more comfortably.

'Fetch a taper,' she told Lorna. 'You shall light the candles for us . . . and ask Minnie for an extra candle for me. I shall work on for a while longer.'

The little girl hurried out and Maria looked across at her son.

'What are you writing so diligently?' she asked him. 'I wish Master Parry could see you. He'd be most impressed with your perseverance.'

Piers looked up. 'I must write one full page in my best hand to present to him in the morning.'

Hugo glanced at him curiously. 'And what is your subject?' he asked. 'Won't you read it aloud?'

Piers hesitated, then dutifully began to read:

'The fox. A treatise . . .' he began.

'A treatise on the fox?' Hugo repeated, astonished. 'Who teaches you such matters?'

'Nat teaches me. He knows about all animals. He knows about foxes, badgers and martens. He hunts squirrel and rabbit and . . .'

Hugo laughed. 'Go on with your treatise. I am convinced.'

Piers began again: 'The fox. A treatise. The young fox is called a cub but after one year, 'tis called a fox and later an old fox. Two foxes make a brace and the tail is called a brush or drag. When the fox mates 'tis rightly called clicketting and the she-fox is with cub when she carries her young. The fox is hunted with hounds and in cold weather leaves the strongest scent—'

Hugo said, 'Nathanial has taught you well. I trust he will not teach you to poach also.' Piers kept his eyes on his writing and made no answer.

'And is there more?'

Piers nodded.

'Then let us hear it and then away to the kitchen for your supper. Ah, here is Lorna with the taper.'

The boy continued. 'The fox is hunted with the horn also and will oft go to earth. Then must he be dug out with a broad spade. Or else he will be caught above ground and the hounds will kill him and his body be raised up on a pike staff.'

He reached the end and looked up at Hugo for his appraisal.

'Well done,' said his father. 'You will make a fine huntsman – one day. Next year you shall go with me after an otter or a stag.' He took the taper and lit the candle which Lorna then carried and set beside Maria. Hugo lit the two candles that stood at each end of the table and also the torches ensconced on the wall. 'And now, away with you,' he told the two children. 'Your mother and I have much to discuss. Remember your prayers and sleep well.'

When they had gone, he re-read the letter which was from Melissa's sister. For a while he was silent, considering its contents. Then he glanced at Maria.

'Leave your weaving,' he urged. 'Let it wait until the morning. You will tire your eyes.'

Maria obeyed willingly and, blowing out the candle, crossed the room and settled herself beside him. He put an arm round her shoulders and she nestled closer, enjoying his closeness. 'This girl that Abigail so warmly recommends for Allan,' began Hugo. 'What do you think on the matter? This Eloise Ballantyne. She comes from a good family and Abigail says she is well versed in music and dancing as well as household management.' He glanced again at the letter. 'She says she is in sound health and of comely appearance with a pleasant voice and manners. Do you think Allan will consider her?'

Maria hesitated. 'I cannot say. I confess it would please me but mayhap 'tis too soon. He has scarcely recovered from Harriet's death and his mood is so sombre.'

Hugo nodded. 'The more reason for a new interest,' he suggested. 'He is young and he needs a woman in his life. He is he eldest son and needs an heir. This Eloise sounds very suitable – comely, a sweet voice, pleasant manner . . .'

Maria smiled. 'Quite a paragon in fact! I think you are half in love with her yourself.'

'I think not,' he laughed, tightening his arm around her. 'She is very young, not yet fifteen, and I am an old man.'

'Old? You will never be old! Forty-one is no age at all.'

'Nevertheless I shall not succumb to her young charms. I have all I want in my Maria. But shall we go to Rochester and see the girl? It can do no harm. Mayhap we could visit Abigail and meet her and speak of it to Allan on our return.'

'And if Allan won't consider it?'

Hugo shrugged. 'We cannot force him to wed but I am hopeful. Allan has known the joys of the marriage bed. He surely will not choose to stay celibate for ever. If he will not wed this year, then it must be next year. Why delay? 'Twill serve no purpose.'

'But will *he* think that way? Oh, poor Harriet! Why did she have to die? They were so happy. If only I could have saved her.'

'No one could save her. You did everything possible. You must not reproach yourself.'

'Poor Allan. Mayhap a new bride *will* restore his spirits. I confess I grow anxious. He has changed so these last few months.'

'He has lost his wife! *I* would change if I lost you. I would be melancholy.'

'But would you choose only your own company for days at a time? Would your temper grow short and would you shout where once you spoke calmly? I am fearful. Do you believe 'tis just the melancholy?'

He turned and looked at her troubled face and kissed her gently. 'I do,' he said lightly. 'We men are strange creatures. Allan is mourning Harriet, 'tis no more than that. We will send word to Abigail to thank her for her letter and to advise her of our visit. If we like what we see we can broach the matter with Allan. We shall ride to Rochester at the beginning of April, when hopefully the highways will at least be passable . . . Eloise – 'tis a charming name. Let us hope she is as charming as her name. By this time next year you may well have a new daughter-in-law.'

Abigail had done Eloise an injustice. She was not comely. She was beautiful. Her thick chestnut hair fell almost to her waist and, by contrast, made her fair skin appear paler than it was. There was no blemish on her face – not a scar, not a pockmark. Not even a freckle spoiled the translucent quality of her skin. Her blue eyes were large and flecked with dark green and her nose was small and straight. Even her teeth were white, and free of decay. Only Abigail, trying hard to be dispassionate, would have described her as merely comely. Eloise was the second daughter of James and Stella Ballantyne. They had six children. The first two, both girls, were James' children by his first wife. The four younger ones, all boys, were Stella's.

Although Abigail and Stella met rarely, the husbands were on friendly terms and their business interests overlapped. Adam Jarman, Abigail's husband, now owned the flourishing boatyard which had been in his family for seven generations. James Ballantyne owned a ship's chandlers from which he made a more than comfortable profit. He had settled his older daughter Bridget with a generous dowry and a middle-aged husband. He did not like his elder daughter and was thankful to be rid of her. Now he could devote himself to finding a suitable, and acceptable, husband for his beloved Eloise. Of all his children Eloise was the only one towards whom he felt the true affection a father should feel for his child. She was his pride and joy from the first moment she opened her eyes and nothing was too good for his beautiful Eloise. All her life she was petted and favoured and her transgressions, small or large, were either readily overlooked or else they were acknowledged and promptly forgiven. The other children grew jealous. Even her mother protested at such blatant favouritism – but to no avail. Eloise could do no wrong in her father's eyes and she grew up accepting male adoration as her due. Her body developed early and by the time she was fourteen her good looks were complemented by fashionably small but perfect breasts, a neat waist and long slim legs. She was precocious, wilful and indulged, but promised, within a very few years, to be a great beauty.

Steven Kennet, who worked for her father, knew it. Now he looked into the blue-green eyes and his own were narrowed with shock.

'Betrothed?' he cried, almost stuttering in his dismay as his emotions churned desperately. ' 'Tis news to me. You spoke nothing of a betrothal. What of me, and my love? Am I nothing to you? Tell me 'tis a lie Eloise.'

She stared at him coolly, enjoying his dismay. So he *did* love her. He had never said so before and she had tried often enough to wring the admission from him. Almost as often as he had tried to persuade her to submit to his passion. Neither had been successful. Eloise remained a virgin and Steven remained unsatisfied. And now it seemed time was running out for him. His face darkened and he leaned forward, his face close to hers as she leaned back against the open door. Through the doorway the slanting rays of the afternoon sun pierced the gloom of the lean-to store behind the shop, picking out coils of rope, barrels of tar, chests and trunks full of locks, hinges, handles and an assortment of buckets, baskets and brooms.

The shop itself fronted the road and, by rights, Steven should have been there, for trade was flourishing and Friday was always a busy day. But James Ballantyne had sent him out to the store to fetch a rope sample and there he had found Eloise waiting for him, with the news that had so shattered his composure.

' 'Tis no lie, Steven,' she told him calmly, 'nor jest, either. His parents are on their way at this very moment, come all the way from Devonshire.'

'But you've no need to take him!'

'Mayhap I'll want to. Think on that, Steven Kennet.'

'But – but you said you love *me*. You promised yourself to *me*. Spoke it with your hand on your heart! You can't deny it.'

'I don't deny it,' she said with a slight toss of her head, 'but I cannot disobey my parents and he is rich, this Allan Kendal. And a grown man of twenty-one.'

'And you fourteen and only half grown!'

She lowered her eyelids so that he should not see her expression. Half-grown, indeed. Who did he think he was to speak thus to her? He was no more than a hired man with no prospects – and he had never said he loved her. Now he would regret his reluctance. She turned her head away, and looked out towards the tangle of masts and rigging that was the river Medway. The waterfront hummed with activity and occasional shouts and snatches of song came to their ears above the interminable flap of sails.

From the shop James Ballantyne roared: 'Steven! What's keeping you, lad?' and panic showed in the boy's eyes. He was sixteen and lusty and no longer a virgin. He had taken two girls to date, one willing and one not so willing. This one was proving more difficult than he had expected, but he had felt fairly confident of the ultimate outcome. Now time was of the essence. She was about to be snatched away untried. He cursed his luck inwardly while his mind raced. How could he pluck this ripe peach before she was handed to another? He had waited patiently for her surrender but now it seemed he would have to change his tactics.

'I'm coming!' he shouted in answer to his master, then seized Eloise roughly by the shoulders, forcing her to turn and face him. 'And I'll be back again so you wait for me, d'you hear? I'll think of an excuse and I'll be back. Answer me, Eloise. I'm telling you to wait for me. D'you hear me?'

'I do, Steven Kennet, and I'll thank you to keep your hands to yourself. You don't know your own strength and you're hurting my shoulders.'

She tried to wriggle free but he leaned his full weight against her, pinning her to the door. Her body sprang into an unwilling awareness of his and she saw the desire smouldering in his eyes.

'You'd find how strong I am if you'd so much as nod your head,' he boasted. 'I'll wager I can show you more tricks than your so-called betrothed.'

'Then you'd lose your money,' said Eliose triumphantly, 'for he's been wed already and you haven't. His wife's dead.'

'Dead? What of?'

'I don't know.' She wriggled again as his lips moved against her own. 'Get off me, I say. You'll get nothing out of me, Steven Kennet, until you say the words – and maybe not then!'

Steven relinquished her mouth and let his right hand rest against her thigh. Slowly it travelled upwards until it cupped her breast and he saw her eyelids flicker with delight. If words were all that held her back she should have them.

'What words is that?' He stalled for time as his fingers slid under the lace and down over her cool, softly rounded flesh to feel for the small nipple that stood up eagerly against his fingertips. Her father roared again and Steven, cursing, withdrew his hand. He leaned forward suddenly and flicked her parted lips with his tongue.

'Be here when I get back!' he warned, but as he turned to go she snatched at his sleeve.

'You know the words,' she said. 'If I don't hear them I shan't wait.'

He looked at her beautiful face which glowed with a combination of mischief and desire. He felt his body stiffen and saw her eyes go down to it in triumph.

'Say it, Steven,' she begged him, her eyes imploring through the half-lowered lashes.

He took a deep breath. 'I love you, Eloise. I want you ·and by Christ I'll have you as soon as I get back. I swear you'll not go to your betrothed a virgin – nor will you regret it.'

She closed her eyes to hide the satisfaction which welled up inside her. So he had said it at last! Steven Kennet had said he loved her. He had persisted for nearly three months, but she had won. There was no need to endure his company further.

'Quick!' He was tugging her inside the doorway, into the gloom of the store, pointing to the ladder that led up the sail loft. 'Wait for me up there,' he said. 'I'll be back.'

He snatched up the required rope and ran round the side of the store back to the shop. Eloise waited, listening to his retreating footsteps. Then she smiled, rested her hands on her hips and said, 'So, Steven Kennet plans to deflower Eloise Ballantyne.' Throwing back her head she laughed aloud and ran back to the house and up into her bed-chamber. She watched from the window until she saw him hurry back towards the store, relishing the thought of his disappointment. She waited until she saw him come out again, his face furious. He glanced up at her window and she waved a dismissive hand, then turned away, humming lightly to herself. Allan's parents should arrive before nightfall and she was eager to meet them. She did not doubt for a moment that they would find her acceptable but she wanted to impress them. She would ask her mother if she could wear her best apricot silk. If she said 'No' she would ask her father.

Maria and Hugo arrived at the Jarman's boatyard earlier than expected. They were greeted lovingly and were soon refreshed and eager to meet the girl who might one day be mistress of Heron. Abigail sent out one of the servants to the Ballantynes with a message that the guests had arrived.

The lad returned with the message that James and Stella Ballantyne would call on them at nine o'clock with their daughter, Eloise. They had already eaten but would welcome a glass of madeira.

'There!' cried Abigail, clapping her hands with excitement. 'They will be here at nine o'clock! Oh, Maria, I do *hope* you like her. I am sure you will. You have come so far it would be a tragedy to be disappointed by her but I don't think you will. Indeed, I think you will find her in every way suitable. Won't they, Adam? Oh do say something, Adam. I am chattering like a magpie, I am *so* nervous.'

'Calm yourself, Abby,' he laughed. 'It will hardly be such a disaster if they do *not* like her. But I agree with you.' He turned to Maria and Hugo. 'We do not know Eloise very well but I know her father. He is a good neighbour and honest in business. We have spoken with the girl on several occasions and I don't doubt for a moment that all he said about her is true.'

'She has such a sweet face,' cried Abby, 'and a smile that would melt icicles. She was a bonny little girl but is suddenly, in the last year, grown into a young lady. Oh Adam, they *must* be charmed with her.'

It was Maria's turn to smile. She leaned forward and patted Abby's plump beringed hands.

'If you say she will make Allan a good wife, I see no reason to doubt it,' she said warmly. 'We are grateful to you for your interest. 'Tis never easy to find a wife for a son and more difficult to find a second wife. There must always be comparisons.' She shrugged. ' 'Tis natural enough and the boy still grieves for Harriet. He is so pensive and his eyes seem to stare without seeing.'

Abby looked anxiously at her husband and then back to Maria.

'He is . . .' she searched for an appropriate word that held no hint of criticism, '. . . recovered?'

'Yes, indeed,' said Hugo, almost too hastily. 'You must not heed Maria. He is quite recovered. He was always pensive and he has lost someone dear to him. We are convinced that a new wife will gladden his heart.'

They all fell silent at once and the pause became an awkward one. Adam stood up. 'Then we'll drink to that,' he said. 'I have a fine madeira. We will have a toast to a possible union between Allan and Eloise. And we will let matters take their course.'

While he busied himself with the new Italian glasses of which he was very proud, Abby's chatter filled another awkward silence.

' 'Tis such a joy to see someone from home,' she said. 'I love my home and I love the river but sometimes I long for Heron - to see you all and my dear Lissa. Is she well? Since my chicks have flown the nest I feel the need to talk, to be with someone of my own. Adam doesn't understand. Men don't, I think. Melissa must feel it, with Oliver so far away. I thank God none of my boys have gone to sea. Poor Lissa. At least mine are all safely wed and within reach. I am really most fortunate and shouldn't grumble.'

'Melissa is content,' said Maria. 'She has news of him from time to time. Sometimes a letter, sometimes a visit from a fellow seaman on his way home. He threatens to turn up at the door one day without warning.'

The glasses were filled and handed round. 'A toast—' she began, but at that moment there was a loud rapping on the door and she lowered her glass.

'That will be them,' said Adam and they heard the maid run to open the door.

Maria and Abby patted their hair and straightened their skirts and the two men rose to their feet as the Ballantynes were ushered in. Mother and father were introduced first and then they stepped aside to allow Eloise to come forward. Maria could not restrain a gasp of delight.

'My dear!' she murmured and glancing at Hugo saw that he, too, was pleasantly surprised. Eloise wore a gown of apricot taffeta which accentuated the colour of her eyes and hair. She dropped a brief curtsey and smiled shyly at them all in turn then cast her eyes down demurely.

'So you are Eloise,' said Hugo and he turned to James Ballantyne who stood proudly by, awaiting their reaction. 'Adam did not exaggerate your daughter's charm,' he said. 'She makes a pretty picture.'

Abby beamed her delight and a bench was drawn up to accommodate James and Stella and a stool was brought out for Eloise. She sat down gracefully with her knees drawn up, her skirts well down, hands clasped about her knees. She was slightly lower than the others and when she looked up the effect of her eyes was startling. Hugo was entranced and Maria thought delightedly of the effect the girl would have on Allan. Surely such a charming girl would make him happy and would bring him out of his self-imposed isolation. More glasses were filled and a toast was drunk, to Queen Elizabeth.

Then the talk turned naturally to news of the Queen and the perennial questions were raised. Would Elizabeth ever wed and if so who would she choose? Spain had wooed her unsuccessfully and the house of Valois in France had had no better success. Some thought she would never marry if it could not be the Earl of Dudley.

They toasted the future safety of the realm and the prosperity promised by expansion and trade abroad. As the wine flowed the company relaxed and the talk ranged easily from politics to personalities and from personalities to fashions.

Eloise joined in from time to time, but otherwise maintained a charming deference towards her elders. Whatever the topic under discussion *she* was the centre of attention and the reason for which they had come together. The thought gave her great satisfaction and she played her role with remarkable poise. When asked to sing she did so readily. Her voice was sweet and she sang in tune and with a natural sense of rhythm.

The evening wore on and all were reluctant to end it. The Ballantynes were impressed with the Kendals and they, in turn, found James and Stella good company and could not fault the family. Abby's round face glowed, partly with wine and partly with the success of her scheme. It was arranged that Eloise would visit Heron in the near future and meet Allan. If the young couple liked each other plans would be made for a betrothal.

Only one thing marred the evening. A thundering on the front door just before midnight frightened them and sent the three men out into the dark street, armed with their pistols. They found no one and the meaning of the incident remained a mystery – except to Eloise, who kept to herself the realization that it was Steven Kennet expressing his frustration in the only way he could.

'Allan! A word, I beg you.'

He turned to see Maria hastening towards him down the steps. Behind him the river ran cold and swift – the river in which Harriet had died. He often sat there, his thoughts heavy, his mind full of grief. Here he need make no pretence but could allow his fancies full rein. Could imagine that Harriet sat beside him, her small neat head against his shoulder, her slim fingers twined in his. Here by the water he could be alone with his thoughts where the sounds of the river soothed and refreshed his tired spirits. Reluctantly he stood up to greet her. He had expected Maria to approach him since her return from Rochester the previous day. Now he must listen to her account of the visit and a description of the young woman of whom his aunt had written with such enthusiasm. Maria had referred casually to the matter before they left for Kent and he had tried to convince her of his indifference. Harriet's sweet ghost was still with him, haunting him, and he had told Maria that she need not find him another wife.

'I've looked for you this past hour,' she told him breathlessly. 'No one has seen you since noon and Minnie thought you had gone to the mine but Jon said "No" you had not taken the mare.' She smiled at him as he made room for her on the fallen tree trunk which served as a seat. 'Where were you?' she persisted.

'Here.'

'All this time? 'Tis not good for you to be so inward looking, Allan.'

'Grief is ever a lonesome state,' he said quietly.

'Only if you will not share it,' said Maria. 'We want to help you, Allan. Let us share your grief.'

He made no reply and the conversation faltered and Maria fussed with her skirts in an effort to disguise her nervousness. Allan made no attempt to help her.

'You do not ask if we enjoyed our visit to Rochester,' she said.

'I am certain you did. You and Aunt Abby have always been close.'

'Indeed we have. We are more like sisters than sisters-in-laws. Dear Abby. She was in good spirits. A little older and a little plumper but such cheerful company. And Adam also. They made us most welcome.'

'I'm glad to hear it.'

Maria tossed a twig towards the river but it fell short and she gave a soft exclamation of annoyance. The silence lengthened and still Allan gave no sign that he knew the purpose behind her presence beside him.

At last she sighed deeply and made a small helpless movement with her hands. 'Will you not ask me, then, Allan? About the Ballantyne's girl? About Eloise?'

Allan's expression hardened. 'You know my feelings on that matter, Maria. I spoke clearly before you left for Rochester. Must I pretend an interest I do not feel? If so then – do tell me about the Ballantyne girl. 'Tis a pointless exercise but—'

'You would not speak that way if you had seen her,' Maria cried. 'She was beautiful, Allan! A real beauty! I swear I don't exaggerate her charms. Abby did not do her justice in her letter. I was stunned by her and so was Hugo. You'll see for yourself soon enough but in—'

'So you have invited them to Heron?'

It was less a question, more a reproach. Maria glanced at his face and her nervousness increased.

'But I told you we would do so, Allan,' she stammered.
'You asked me if I objected to them paying us a visit.
I said I was indifferent on the subject. I still am,' said
Allan.

He stared out across the water. His face was impassive
but his tone was grim. Maria recognized with despair the
stubborn streak that he had shown since childhood. Once
his mind was made up he was usually unshakable.

'But when you see her, Allan, you will feel differently,
I know it. She will melt your heart as she did ours. Oh
Allan, will you not consider her for my sake? For the sake
of Heron if not for yourself. You must remarry, Allan.
And Eloise will be a bride that all men will envy! She has
a radiance - such confidence and poise. She can talk
intelligently and sing and is a good cook—'

'Quite a paragon, it seems,' Allan said coldly. 'But is she
gentle or loving? You do not say so.'

'But indeed she is. At least, I'm sure on it! Aye, she is
all those things. Say you will be courteous to her Allan.
Promise that you will consider her in all fairness. That
you'll reserve judgement until you meet her.'

He shrugged without answering.

'Allan! Answer me!'

He turned slowly to look at her. 'If you must have an
answer then 'tis this. Harriet is still my wife. A poor dead
wife, mayhap, but I love her, still. If I *must* wed again at
some future time I'll consider your Eloise. But I make no
promises, Maria, and do not try to force a decision. I will
be courteous, aye, but no more. And have you considered
this - that she may not care for me when we meet? What
then of your fine plans? Have you thought on that?'

Maria shook her head. 'She *will* care for you. She *must*.'

'There's no *must* about it,' he said harshly.

'But if you *do* like her, Allan, and if she cares for you -
then will you agree to a betrothal? 'Twill be next year
before you can be wed. She will be fifteen then.'

'I've told you, I make no promises, Maria. If you are
determined—'

'Hugo thinks it wise, Allan.'

'And you?'

'Now that I've seen her, I agree with all my heart. She will make you happy, Allan.' She sighed deeply and stood up. 'So I can tell Hugo you will consider her?'

He nodded reluctantly, already regretting his acquiescence. He had allowed himself to be swayed by her eloquence. He cast around in his mind for a loophole. 'On one condition,' he said.

'And that is?'

'That she is told of the Gillis strain in me.'

Maria gave a shocked gasp, and her face paled. 'Oh no, Allan!' she begged. 'Not that, I thought it was decided long ago that—'

'I was younger then,' he reminded her. 'And prepared to take advice from you and Hugo. You advised me as you saw fit but now I am older and make my own decisions. I will only agree to a betrothal if she is told the true facts and still wants me.'

He felt a sense of freedom as he delivered the ultimatum. The Gillis blood was a convenient route by which he could escape. Strange that after so long he should find a use for the unpalatable facts of his birth. Another glance at Maria's face showed him that he had indeed found a weapon which he could use in his own defence. Eloise would feel the sharpness of its edge! There was a rich irony in the prospect. *He* would accept Eloise but she would reject him. Then the blame would lie with her. He would be the wronged party – the innocent victim of Fate. It was a trump card. No one could press him into a loveless marriage. Eloise would go back to Rochester and he would be left in peace with his beloved ghost.

Maria faced him wearily. 'And is that what I must tell Hugo?' she asked. ' 'Tis your last word on the subject?'

'Aye,' he said. 'The very last.'

86

CHAPTER FIVE

Martin Kendal was like his father, in colouring, at least. He had the same swarthy skin and gleaming dark hair and the same humorous brown eyes. However he was not stocky like Hugo. His limbs were longer and his neck was slim. He had inherited his father's confidence and was cheerful, trusting, assuming his fellows to be friends until they proved themselves otherwise. He was popular at school and enjoyed his life. Winchester had a lot to offer and Martin worked hard and was a successful student. He was thirteen years old but already tall for his age so that people believed him to be older. The school term ended on 20 July and he arrived home in high spirits, prepared to enjoy the delights of home. He was soon being regaled by Piers and Lorna with the latest news. That Minnie had moved into Heron he discovered for himself. Meeting her in the Hall, he swung her off her feet and kissed her cheek. She squealed and put up a token resistance and then confided that she had roasted a mallard especially for him.

'And beetroot in almond sauce?' he cried.

'I remembered that also.'

' 'Tis well done, Minnie, for I'm ravenous. Will there be boiled onions?'

Minnie rolled her eyes. 'Oh, 'tis boiled onions as well, is it? Then I'd best be off and prepare some. Boiled onions, he says. Tut! You haven't changed at all, young Martin.'

'*Young* Martin?' he teased. 'Why I'm twice your size.' He held out a hand and touched the top of her head. 'I do believe you are shrinking, Minnie. 'Tis old age, and your bones are crumbling.'

And he darted away before she could retaliate and headed for the garden with Piers and Lorna skipping beside him excitedly. Minnie watched them go with a smile

87

on her face but she thought, They'll be grown up soon, all of them and Heron'll be a quiet place. She knew that negotiations were in hand for a new bride for Allan. At thirty-four Minnie had not outgrown her habit of eaves-dropping and was always well informed.

'And dear old Maggie has moved into Ladyford,' Piers told Martin.

'And Allan is to be wed again. Her name is Eloise and she's to move into Heron the day after tomorrow and she's pretty and she sings and Nat says we can go and watch the lurcher races.' Lorna paused for breath and looked at Piers to see if she had omitted anything.

'And Ruth is ill again,' said Piers, 'and Mama must go down there at once. She's an old, old lady and must surely die.'

Martin sat on the grass with his back to the broad trunk of the chestnut tree and leaned back, his hands clasped behind his head. He always made for the same tree and did not consider himself truly home until he sat there. He considered the chestnut tree his own property, for he knew every branch and fork and had spent many years as a boy hidden within its dense leaves. There were two notches in the bark, toe holds from times past that Matt had made for him when he taught him to climb it. The initials M.K. were carved in it – his own handiwork – and Maria, diplomatically, had asked his permission before Lorna's swing had been hung from the lowest bough. Higher up there was a small rotting hole where the squirrels hid their nuts which was known only to Martin. He regarded Piers and Lorna fondly for a moment as they knelt beside him, then he took his hands from behind his head and with a sudden movement pushed them both over backwards. Then he sprang to his feet and galloped off, slapping his thigh and making a fair imitation of a hunting horn. The two younger children picked themselves up and raced after him as he careered wildly across the lawn. At last he threw himself face downward under an oak tree and feigned death.

'Get up, you ninny,' said Piers. 'We know you're not dead.'

'We know it,' piped Lorna. 'Get up, Martin.' He lay quite still, his face hidden in the grass. Lorna looked at him anxiously and then at Piers. 'We know it,' she repeated with less conviction.

'Martin!' cried Piers pushing him with the toe of his shoe. 'Martin, *do* get up.'

With a sudden terrifying roar, Martin leapt to his feet, snatched Lorna up and pretended to devour her. 'I'm a wolf!' he cried. 'A hungry wolf!'

When at last her squeals subsided and the excitement was over, he settled himself under the tree, hands behind his head and looked at their flushed faces. 'And now,' he asked. 'Tell me about the lurcher races?'

Maria was so busy with the preparations for Eloise's arrival that she was not aware until the middle of the afternoon that Martin, Piers and Lorna were all absent from the house. Puzzled and vaguely annoyed, she checked with Minnie to see if they had gone picnicking. Minnie shook her head.

'Not to my knowledge,' she said, 'and they've not come to me for food and drink so I doubt it. When did they go?'

'I scarcely know,' Maria admitted. 'I thought they must be in the garden or—'

'Most likely gone riding,' said Minnie. 'Jon would know.'

Jon was swilling down the stable floor ready for Eloise's mount. They were expected early evening. He shook his head in answer to Maria's query.

'Haven't clapped eyes on 'em,' he said cheerfully. 'Young Lorna's not even been out to feed the ponies. Off gallivanting, I expect, and I wish I could join 'em. Fine day and all. At least the visitors will have a pleasant journey.'

'I hope so.' She sighed crossly. 'I wanted all the family

to be here to greet them. Hugo is coming home early from the mine. Oh, how very vexing!'

Jon seized a broom and began to sweep the water out of the stable door and Maria backed away hastily and retreated to the house. Upstairs, she took a last look at the room she had prepared. She was pleased with her morning's endeavours. The small bed chamber smelt fresh and clean. There was clean linen on the narrow bed and a pomander hung in the window on a red ribbon. The sun's rays warmed it, giving an orange tang to the air which mingled with the lavender which was generously sprinkled on the rushes on the floor. A sheepskin rug lay beside the bed and a candle stood on the small wooden chest beside the bed. This would be Eloise's room until she was married. It had been Maria's room and Hannah's before that. Alison had slept there before her marriage to Luke and earlier still it had been Elizabeth's. Now she, Maria, slept with Hugo in the main bed chamber, but one day they would relinquish it to Allan and his Eloise. The thought held no regrets for Maria – she found it strangely comforting. Pray God it will always be so, she thought, a Kendal man to rule Heron and a Kendal woman to love and cherish him.

For a moment she let her thoughts wander. Eloise seemed a very suitable match for Allan. Hopefully he would accept her and they would marry when Eloise was fifteen. They had not met each other, but Allan was an attractive man and Eloise should find no fault with him – if he would put aside his morbid thoughts and shake off the memories of his recent tragedy. Eloise would make him happy if she allowed it. Maria was sure of it. Eloise would give him sons and daughters and his life would be full and happy. It could happen and it must, she told herself. So why did a nagging doubt persist? Was it a doubt or less tangible than that? A feeling of unease? She shrugged the thought aside. She was a foolish woman to allow such notions. The visitors might arrive at any time. With half the family missing it was even more important that at least the mistress of Heron should be properly attired and ready to greet them. She hurried along the passage to her own room, calling to Ellie to come up and help her dress.

The lurcher races were held once a month during the summer and were to be found at a variety of venues around the town. They were haphazard affairs at best, starting in the afternoon as soon as enough dogs had arrived at the arranged meeting place and ending when it grew dark or when no one had any money left to wager, whichever came sooner. On this particular day, Nat had told them that the meeting would be held further along the river bank, beyond the wooden bridge where the land was flat, before it reached the first granite outcrops. Martin, Piers, Lorna and Nat walked along with Brin trotting dutifully beside his master. Lorna thought secretly that with such short legs he would scarcely win a race but she hoped to be proved wrong.

'And remember,' Nat said for the third time in as many minutes, ' 'Tis not my fault if Allan's bride-to-be arrives and you're not there. I've no wish to face your father's wrath nor your mother's, neither. 'Tis you wanted to come.'

'Oh do stop chuntering,' said Martin. 'We *won't* be late back and they *won't* arrive early. But what if they did? 'Tis Allan she's going to wed not one of us. She'll see Allan and that's all that matters. Anyone would think 'twas the wedding we were missing. 'Tis only Eloise and her father arriving from Rochester. They'll manage well enough without us.'

Nat, still nervous, opened his mouth to argue but Lorna interrupted with a shrill cry.

'I can see them! I can see all the people. And all the dogs!'

They had rounded a bend in the river and the sight of the crowd of men and dogs put an end to all their doubts. The long awaited excitements loomed and at once Eloise and her imminent arrival faded from their minds. In some way the meeting was a clandestine one. The races were held in out of the way places so that those who attended could do so safe in the knowledge that loved ones, employers and other interested parties would not discover them. There were men of all classes there and a few women. Some of the men were flat-capped prentices who had feigned illness to escape for an afternoon's sport. Others were tradesmen who had 'gone off on business' and left their wives to watch the lad in the butcher's shop or make their excuses at the smithy. The saddler's son wandered through the crowd carrying an armful of leather dog collars and his mother was draped in a selection of leads. An old man offered canine remedies which would cure all known distempers, and charms that would guarantee fleetness of foot. A few, like Martin, were gentlefolk prepared to wager small sums on the outcome of the races. Others were like Nathaniel Gully – an owner, fussily competitive and eager to see his dog race for the sheer fun of it and the occasional heady taste of glory if the animal won. There were several tinners there, somewhat dismayed to see Martin Kendal, and Lorna recognized Colin Parry, the cousin to their tutor as well as Mistress Bellamy, the cobbler's wife.

They were just in time. Stakes were being driven into the ground to prop up the wattle hurdles which would separate the dogs at the start of each race.

'That way they each get a fair chance,' Nat explained, 'and the dogs can't bite each other. Their owners will hold them – you'll see in a moment – and then the whistle goes and off they go.'

'But where do they go to?' Lorna asked, mystified.

'They chase the hare, ninny,' said Piers, abashed by her ignorance.

Nat smiled at her. 'But 'tis only a make-believe hare, not a real one,' he said. 'A lump of wood wrapped in a hare's pelt and dabbled with blood to make it smell like one. 'Tis on a long rope and the rope is wound on to a drum. Come – I'll show you. 'Tis cunning, the way 'tis done.'

They followed him in and out of the tangle of owners and dogs and leashes until they came to a 'wall' made of straw bales. There was a hole through the straw large enough for one dog, and behind the straw there was a narrow wooden drum set on its side on a spindle with a handle at each side and a rope round the middle of it. Piers and Lorna looked at it, no wiser than before and Nat laughed at their expressions.

'I'll tell you how it works,' he said patiently. 'At the end of the rope there's the make-believe hare, you see? The hare lies in front of the dogs who are lined up at the start, separated by the hurdles so they can't see each other. All they can see is the "hare".'

Martin, he noticed, had wandered off and was deep in conversation with a man holding three leashed dogs.

'When the whistle blows two men up this end start to wind in the rope and that pulls the hare along so the dogs think the hare is running away. They rush out and chase it. When the quarry – that's the hare – reaches the straw it's pulled through the hole and the first dog to go through the hole after it is the winner.'

They were very impressed and after a few more questions were satisfied that they understood. Men, with their dogs, were still arriving, some walking, some mounted, a few even rowing downstream to the meeting place. As the crowd grew the noise increased as dogs whined and barked and their owners boasted about their own dog's invincibility. An enterprising ale wife arrived in a rickety cart carrying three large barrels of ale, and she was soon doing a steady trade. The talk grew wilder and was punctuated by bursts of loud laughter. The sun shone and the river ran by, gurgling round the boulders. On the far side of the river a dozen or more long haired cattle watched curiously through sleepy eyes, their heads raised occasionally as the scent of the dogs was carried across the river by the light breeze.

Lorna and Piers were left to their own devices as Nat hurried to the start of the course to enter Brin in the first terrier race. There were six pens and Brin went into number three. Two men crouched at each end of the traps to watch that no dog was released by its owner until the whistle blew. The fourth dog was put into the pen next to Brin and everyone waited impatiently for the last two. These were all black and white short-legged terriers. The lurchers belonged to the gypsies. They were long-legged with shaggy broken coats, cross-bred between collie and greyhound. Lurchers and terriers would run alternate races. In went another terrier and then the last. There was a roar from the spectators, who crowded to the edge of the hundred-yard track and began to shout for their dogs even before the whistle. Piers and Lorna had squeezed a way to the front and now joined in the general excitement, screaming loudly for Brin. The whistle blew and the hare jerked forward as the owners released their dogs and the six small animals surged in pursuit of the bloodied bundle of fur which tantalizingly leapt just ahead of them, no matter how hard they ran.

'Brin! Brin! Come on, Brin. You can run faster than that!' shouted Piers. 'You can win! You must. Go on, Brin. Go on!'

The excitement was almost too much for Lorna. She imagined that the blur of fur was a real hare and, fearful that the leading dog would reach it, she covered her face with her hands and prayed for its survival. Piers, beside her, continued to shout but as Brin fell behind his excitement gave way to disappointment and his cheers to groans. A dog by the name of 'Wrangler' was declared the winner and the next race announced and wagers invited. Martin reappeared briefly to smile at the children, then he was pushing his way through the crowd and was once more lost to view. Nat returned with Brin beside him and the two children made a great fuss of him as he stood panting, his sides heaving with the effort of his race.

'He'll do better next time,' Nat assured anyone who

94

would listen. 'He needs the first race to warm up, you see. Never does well until the second or third but he'll go! Aye, he'll win before the day's out. Now watch, the lurchers are almost ready. Watch number five. He'll win. Can you see, little Lorna? Stand in front of me, that's the way. Ah, they're ready – they're off!'

Before the whistle blast had faded the dogs were away and once again the spectators shouted themselves hoarse as the air rang with their cries of encouragement. Number five came in third but Nat was not at all put out.

'Off form,' he told them airily. 'That's a youngish dog and still moody. I still say he's the best of that lot. Just a bit off form. You'll see.'

Most of his money had been lost but he went off to wager what remained on Brin. If Brin won he would gamble again, if he lost he would enjoy watching other folks parting with their money. He had a cheerful disposition and was not easily cast down by failure. He glanced round for Martin and saw him some distance away, talking to a small unshaven man with darkly glittering eyes. Nat groaned inwardly as he recognized the man. It was Jonah Gillis, the old woodcutter from the other side of Ashburton. The man was a well known rogue and had narrowly escaped the clutches of the law on several occasions. He had a nervous tic and frequently jerked his head to the left side and blinked his eyes. Nat wondered what business Martin could have with a Gillis. They were a strange brood, the Gillises. Shiftless and not to be trusted. His wife, Aileen, was not right in the head, or so folks said. Word had it she sang strange songs and made no answer if folks spoke to her except to wring her hands and shake her head. He gave a shout and Martin turned to raise a hand then turned back to continue his conversation. Ah well, Nat Gully wasn't playing nurse to a boy of his age. No doubt he could fend for himself and he, Nat, must get along to the start or Brin would miss the next race and that would never do.

★

95

Martin and the two younger children had not returned when Eloise and her father rode into the courtyard outside Heron and Maria, Hugo and Allan went out alone to welcome them. Eloise wore a dark green travelling robe and her hair hung down her back in a mass of chestnut curls. They had stopped a half mile back to freshen up with the help of damp towels, combs and brushes and in her slim, well-fitting clothes Eloise looked a picture of youthful health and good spirits. Allan wore grey, the doublet slashed with red and his blond hair gleamed in the late afternoon sunshine. Hugo called Jon and Matt to hold the horses while they alighted and Allan went forward to assist Eloise. He smiled politely and reached up to help her. His hands went round her waist and then set her down.

'Welcome to Heron,' he said. He was nervous and the words sounded more formal than he intended. As he looked into the beautiful face he knew he should say more – pay her the compliment she deserved; express his joy at seeing her for the first time. She looked up into his face, waiting, and there was an unspoken arrogance in her smile. As clearly as though she had spoken Allan heard her thoughts – 'See how beautiful I am? Confess yourself more fortunate than you had dared to expect'. Yet the smile was friendly and she dropped him a low curtsey as he lifted her hand to his lips. The words died in his throat and he could not retrieve them. Instead he stared into her eyes searching for a hint of gentleness, warmth or understanding, but found only a confidence which he himself lacked. She gave him a slightly mocking smile with her head on one side and he found himself stammering. From the corner of his eye he saw Maria glance towards them and he cursed his stupidity. Here was a man of twenty-one outfaced and discomfited by a girl not yet fourteen. It was ridiculous.

'I – I trust you had a good journey,' he said.

' 'Twas fair.' She watched him with growing amusement, not helping him, not making it easier for him. He saw Harriet in his mind's eye, timid and loving, so different

96

from this bold Eloise. He wanted to close his eyes and see the ghost more clearly but the beautiful blue eyes were holding his in an unflinching stare, demanding his attention.

Aware of his reaction, Maria turned quickly, drew Eloise into her arms and kissed her warmly.

'How good it is to see you again,' she said, 'and looking so fresh. I thought you would be weary from your long journey. And you are hungry, no doubt. We will eat shortly. Minnie has excelled herself in your honour and has prepared a huge meal so I hope our appetites will do justice to it.'

Hugo was talking with James Ballantyne and now he introduced the two men, who smiled and bowed to each other and exchanged the usual pleasantries.

'Your sister-in-law did not exaggerate,' James told Hugo. 'Allan *is* a fine man. You must be very proud of him. They will make a handsome couple – and raise a handsome family! I think I could not give my daughter into safer hands. I'm well pleased.' He spoke as though the matter were already settled but Allan made no comment. Hastily Hugo sent away the grooms and horses and Maria led their visitors towards the house.

'We cannot stand gossiping on the steps forever,' she laughed. 'We will go in and show you to your rooms.' She turned to Eloise. 'And what do you think of Heron – what you have seen so far? We love it and I hope you will also. 'Tis rambling but comfortable.'

Eloise admitted that she was very impressed with its size and position.

Maria laughed. 'Tell her what happens in winter, Allan.'

Allan smiled. 'We are always snowbound,' he told her, 'but it has its compensations. We toboggan down the slopes and the little ones make snowballs and the kitchen is full of drying clothes. But we are well provisioned and never starve.'

James Ballantyne said, 'You won't lack fuel for the fire, either. We passed plenty of trees.'

'We put our woods to good use,' said Allan, 'for they also provide pit props and shuttering for the mine.'

Maria, relieved that their son was now talking more freely, relaxed slightly and sent for Ellie to show the guests to their rooms. She had not referred to the absence of the rest of the family and still hoped they might return before the meal. She was angry with them for their disappearance, but she was at pains to hide it until the visitors were upstairs and beyond earshot.

'Where can they be?' she demanded of Hugo, although she knew it was a pointless question. He knew no more than she did.

'I don't know but 'tis no use fretting,' he said. 'As long as they have come to no harm we must be satisfied to see them when they *do* return.'

'Come to no harm? Why, Hugo, you don't think—'

'No, no. I don't think it likely but it never does to make rash judgements. There may be a sound reason for their lateness.'

Maria glanced in through the hall doorway to reassure herself that the table looked as good as she remembered. It did and she nodded distractedly.

'I think they liked each other,' said Hugo and she hesitated before replying that she hoped so. 'Don't *you* think they did?' he persisted.

'I'm not certain of it – but maybe I expected too much. They need time alone, to talk, and get to know each other.' She smiled. 'I'm too eager, I dare say. I was always so sure of my feelings for you, I expect others to know their own minds just as surely. I thought Allan was . . .' She searched for the right word, '. . . reluctant, somehow. Do you think he is determined not to like her?'

'Who can tell. We must wait and hope.'

'Aye. But, Hugo, we only want his happiness. We cannot restore Harriet to life but we can give him another love. Is that wrong?'

He drew her into his arms and kissed her gently. 'No one says we do wrong, Maria. If we have acted too quickly 'twas no more than a mistake and from the best intentions. We have no cause to blame ourselves. Most likely the match will turn out well. You must not fret. We will all relax and help them as much as we can. Now stop frowning. It doesn't become you. They will be down again before long and we must greet them cheerfully.'

They finally began the meal to the accompaniment of black looks from Minnie who had cooked for eight and saw only five at the table. She knew where the other three had gone but had said nothing. She could not reveal her knowledge since she had gained it by eavesdropping, so she had to content herself with a few muttered comments and the occasional banging of lid upon pan, until a whispered reprimand from Hugo sent her scarlet-faced and furious into the kitchen in one of her sulks.

A creamy onion soup was followed by roast venison and vegetables. The wine was plentiful and the. talk became animated. Even Allan joined in the conversation and was attentive and charming to Eloise who radiated high spirits. Her eyes shone and there was an excited blush in her cheeks. Hugo made a passing reference to the absence of Martin, Piers and Lorna, saying that they had obviously been delayed and Maria turned the talk immediately to the topic of the mine. Minnie had made a peach tart and a syllabub and there were nuts and fresh fruits. Ellie, carrying in these delights, hoped most earnestly that the diners were already full and would leave most of the desserts so that the servants might finish them off later.

Suddenly there was a commotion outside. They heard Piers cry, 'Not yet, Lorna. Come back.' But she came flying into the room. She was hot and dusty and her long dark hair was dishevelled. Her face was flushed with excitement and she carried a black and white puppy under her arm. 'Mama, Papa, look here. Martin has bought a puppy.' She held him up, oblivious to the presence of strangers and too excited to register the disapproval on her parents' faces. 'See how bonny he is? 'Tis a dog and Jonah Gillis says he'll be a winner but Nat says Jonah Gillis is a rogue. He says the Gillises are all either bad or mad but . . .'

Piers had now appeared in the doorway, a stricken look on his face as he saw the effect of his sister's appearance. He hesitated, torn between the desire to silence her and the desire not to be involved himself.

She went on: 'There were five pups for sale and this one will be the fastest because he has the best lines. I am to care for him while Martin is away at school and in the holidays—'

She faltered suddenly and looked at Allan who had gone very white and half rose from the bench. Hugo cursed under his breath and Maria stared at Allan beseechingly. Eloise and her father exchanged glances, puzzled by their reactions to the girl's prattle. There was a moment's silence as though they all waited for the drama to be resolved.

'His little nose is - is cold and wet,' stammered Lorna. 'That means he is - in good health—' She turned to Piers who moved reluctantly towards her.

'Lorna!' cried Maria. 'How dare you burst in this way—'

She didn't finish but threw an agonized look at Hugo. He said sharply, 'That will do, Lorna! You know better than to come to the table in such a state. Take the pup away. I will talk to you later.'

Lorna stared at him and the tears started in her eyes.

'We'd best go,' whispered Piers but she remained apparently rooted to the spot and he snatched the pup from her and ran out of the room.

The little girl burst into loud sobs and Maria stammered, 'Please excuse her. 'Tis very amiss—' and made as though to leave the table, but Hugo shook his head discreetly and indicated to Allan that he should also sit down again.

At that moment Martin came into the room arms outstretched towards Lorna who flew to them. He picked her up and hugged her and whispered something that immediately silenced her tears. With a cheerful grin he addressed first Hugo and Maria.

'Please forgive the untimely interruption. We did not intend to disturb your meal. We are so late and the fault is entirely mine. I shall ask Minnie to feed us in the kitchen for our sins. 'Tis all we're fit for at present.' He turned to James Ballantyne and made a small bow. 'I trust you will forgive our rude manners,' he said. 'We meant no disrespect.'

'Why, none taken, young man.'

'And you must be Eloise—' Martin gave her a bow also. 'My brother is most fortunate. I envy him.'

'You are very kind,' said Eloise, slightly taken aback by the easy charm of this young man with the dark good looks.

'Then we'll leave you to enjoy the rest of your meal in peace.'

He carried Lorna out of the room and for a moment the diners looked at one another in silence. James was first to speak.

'A charming young man,' he said. 'He reminds me of my own youth. Oh aye – I was just as wilful at that age and careless of life's little courtesies. But he apologized most handsomely. I hope you will not rebuke them on our account.'

'You are very generous,' said Hugo. 'but—'

'No buts! I insist the matter is of no importance. Their absence in no way spoiled our meal, and they have obviously enjoyed themselves. Youth is fleeting. We must make allowances. That syllabub looks very good. I wonder, could I . . . ?'

'Most certainly.' Maria nodded to Ellie who served him a large helping and the meal was resumed and the conversation returned to other topics.

After dinner Allan announced abruptly that he would take a short ride out. Maria's heart sank.

'Then take Eloise with you,' she suggested. 'You can show her the moor in its summer colours.'

But Eloise shook her head. 'I must decline,' she said. 'Riding is not one of my accomplishments. I ride the streets of Rochester but only at a walking pace and then only when the street rubbish makes it necessary.'

Allan stood silent. Hugo said, 'Allan will have to teach you. Without a horse you would not get very far here. Not even to the nearest town.'

Eloise nodded. 'I shall learn most willingly but today I am weary and too full of good food to move from this stool. Do go alone, Allan.'

'I will.'

In the stable yard Maria caught up with him and plucked at his sleeve.

He kept his face averted.

'Allan! I know what grieves you,' she said, 'but pay no heed to it. 'Twas no more than a child's careless prattle. It means nothing, believe me.'

'They were Nat Gully's words, not Lorna's. Don't pretend with me, Maria, I am past such make believe.'

He threw the saddle over the horse's back and bent to adjust the strap.

'But Allan, you take everything to heart so. You must learn to put the matter out of your mind. 'Twas so long ago.'

'She was my grandmother! You can't imagine how that feels.'

'But she's long dead, Allan. 'Tis all forgotten.'

'Not by her grandson.' He straightened up and faced her and she saw anger in his eyes as he went on:

'If Isobel Gillis had lived a normal lifespan she would be alive now and then how would it be? Would I visit her and listen to her ramblings about my grandfather and their illicit love affair?'

'Allan! Don't speak that way—'

'Would she visit us? Would the Kendals be on speaking terms with the Gillises? All bad or mad, he said, and he's likely right. They are despised in these parts and we all give thanks that Isobel died young. That may be well enough for the rest of you, but 'tis I have her blood in me! Nothing can change that. Which attributes have I inherited, Maria? Will I go mad or to the bad? It's not a choice for the squeamish.'

He jerked himself free from her restraining hand and swung himself up into the saddle. 'I need space,' he said, 'and time to think.'

'Allan, for pity's sake. Think clearly, Allan. Your father was her son. He was neither bad nor mad.'

'Mayhap he didn't live long enough to become either,' said Allan. 'He managed to die nobly in battle. Let go of me, Maria. I must ride out, I tell you.'

Maria clung to him more fiercely. 'But you did like her, Allan. I saw it in your face. Tell me you did like her. She is as beautiful as I predicted, is she not? And she was taken with you, Allan. I saw that also.'

'I have to think,' he said. 'She should not be kept in ignorance. Yet I doubt she will have me when she knows.'

'Then do not tell her, Allan. In God's name promise you will keep silent on the matter. Allan, answer me!'

But he leaned down, his face a mask, and wrenched at her fingers until he was free, then spurred his horse to a canter and rode off towards the darkening moor.

He rode with Lorna's words ringing in his ears until Heron disappeared from view. Then he dismounted and flung himself down on to the springy turf, leaving his horse to graze. Clasping his knees, he stared at the sunset, but his eyes were blind to the trailing glory of pink and grey which streaked the yellow sky. He was deaf to the lark which rose nearby and oblivious to the scent of sun-baked heather.

For his eyes saw only Eloise and only her laughter rang in his ears. His heart beat for her and his body ached traitorously for hers. All his senses were alive in a way they never had been before. He felt a new awareness as though only now was he fully alive. Eloise Ballantyne! His mind raced and he fancied he heard his blood coursing through his veins. Dazedly he shook his head, astonished at the sweet confusion into which she had thrown him. Eloise! Dear God, he whispered. This cannot be! The girl he had been so reluctant to meet had swept away his defences with the first challenging look from those cool blue-green eyes. He was amazed, ashamed, delighted. Maria had warned him and he had paid no heed. 'You will care for her,' she had told him. Care for her? He almost laughed at the memory, shaking his head in disbelief at the wonderful, inexplicable joy that drowned his senses.

But had anyone else been aware of the strength of his feelings? He had tried so hard to hide them; tried so hard to keep the image of Harriet clear and strong in his mind. But he had finally lost her. Harriet had faded little by little, driven away by the power of Eloise's presence. And he had surrendered her with scarcely a fight! Now he felt remorse pricking him and his joy was involuntarily dimmed. His sweet Harriet! He had betrayed her. Pray God she need not know of it, he thought, yet even that awful thought could not spoil his newfound happiness. The plain truth was that Eloise Ballantyne had bewitched him. He confessed it unreservedly, trying to come to terms with all that the confession entailed. He would wed the girl – if she would have him.

But would she accept him when she knew of the Gillis blood? A coldness seized him at the mere possibility Eloise Ballantyne might refuse him and who could blame her? Such a beautiful woman surely deserved a better match. If he told her the truth she could make up her own mind. But if she chose not to wed him could he accept it? And if she chose to go ahead with the betrothal – she would bear him sons and daughters that were part Gillis!

He sighed deeply and flung himself face down on the grass, his head cradled in his arms. For so many years – ever since he had known about Isobel Gillis – he had struggled to believe what Hugo and Maria told him – that there was nothing for him to fear and no reason to feel shame. He had married Harriet and, against his better judgement, had told her nothing. They had lived together lovingly for a few months and then God had seen fit to take her from him. But was it retribution? Was it God's will that there should be no more Kendals marred with Gillis blood? Now a fresh thought struck him, sending a chill through him. Was he behaving abnormally by coming here to wrestle with his problem? 'Oh God,' he whispered, 'is this the beginning? Am I obsessed with my past or is it normal to have such fears? If it were Martin in my place, would he be prey to the same anxieties? Sweet heaven, am I going mad? Is this madness? Or if I let my thoughts run wild will I then go mad?' Desperately he tried to review his life so far to discover any strangeness in him that might forewarn him, but he could think of nothing untoward. Maria had spoken truly when she mentioned his father. Simon had no badness in him, and no madness. It had been churlish to answer her the way he did. Maria meant well but she did not understand him. He was the odd chick in the brood – the only child of Simon and Hannah. They were both dead and he had no one of his own to turn to. Beatrice and Martin shared Hannah and Hugo. The little ones shared Hugo and Maria. But he alone inherited Heron!

Slowly he sat up, clinging to that thought. Simon had made him heir to Heron. And what a heritage! He knew Martin envied him. Piers would one day envy him also. He, Allan Kendal, was heir to Heron. The Gillis blood could not alter that. Had Fate compensated him? The idea cheered him, a warm glow among the icy fears. He strove to nourish the idea and draw comfort from it. He was Simon's only child. Simon himself had been a bastard – the bastard son of Luke Kendal and poor mad Isobel Gillis. Yet Fate had restored him to his rightful place in Heron and had given him a son to continue the line. So perhaps he and Eloise were meant to wed to continue the *rightful* Kendal line. Hugo, Simon's cousin, had been an outsider, who had come to Heron through his marriage to Hannah.

If Allan left no heirs, the house and mine would pass to Martin and then to Piers.

Gradually his hands unclenched and the muscles in his face grew less taut. He breathed more easily and the darkness that had enveloped him lifted. He let his thoughts dwell on the luckless Isobel. Poor woman. She, too, had been a victim of Fate. Born a Gillis, what chance did she have, he wondered? And how she must have longed to be free of her family as Luke Kendal's bride. And Luke had betrayed her. Wasn't that enough to send a woman out of her mind? They said she was very beautiful. Poor mad, beautiful Isobel. He scrambled to his feet. He would no longer fear her poor little ghost. He would set aside all morbid fancies and at some time would speak openly to Eloise of his unfortunate grandmother. He would take his inheritance *and* his bride and they would fill Heron with Kendals! A smile touched his lips, he sighed deeply and for the first time the haunted look began to fade from his eyes.

The next day Maria set off for Romney House where Ruth lay ill. She had delayed the trip as long as she dared, determined to see Eloise settled in to her new home. Torn between her duty to Ruth and to her own family she had chosen the latter, rightly or wrongly, but she was now quite content to leave them and ride out. This time, to Matt's dismay, she took Martin with her as escort. Her intention was to give Allan and Eloise some time alone to get to know each other. The two youngest children would be occupied for most of each day with their lessons and would amuse themselves under Ellie's watchful eye for the rest of the time. Martin, however, was on holiday for several weeks. Maria had seen the interest in Eloise's eyes when she first saw Martin and wanted to ensure that Eloise was not able to make unfair comparisons.

Allan had returned from his ride in a calmer frame of mind. He had kissed her lightly, whispered, 'I will say nothing for the moment. Let her stay', and the subject of the Gillis blood had not been referred to again. James would remain at Heron until the end of the week to satisfy himself of his daughter's happiness and he would then return to Rochester. The immediate crisis seemed to be over, and presumably the betrothal would go ahead. Reasonably content, Maria turned her thoughts resolutely to whatever lay ahead for her at Romney House.

CHAPTER SIX

Felicity came out of the old lady's bedchamber with a tray in her hand and almost collided with Martin.

'Oops!' he mocked and put out a hand to steady the tray.

'I'm sorry,' said Felicity.

'Sorry? 'Tis I should apologize. 'Twas I bumped into you.'

'Oh no, sir.'

'Felicity! How many times must I tell you not to call me "sir". You make me feel old.'

'Forgive me. I—' she broke off, embarrassed as usual by Martin's manner. She was unused to teasing and although she knew Martin meant it in a friendly way she did not know how to deal with it. She was two years older than him and yet felt much younger. In her eyes Martin Kendal was a worldly young man and she had never met his like before.

'How is she?' he asked gently, seeing her confusion.

'She is failing rapidly. Poor soul—' Her lips trembled.

Hastily forestalling the tears he asked, 'Is Maria with her?'

Felicity nodded and swallowed hard.

'Then why not take back the tray and walk with me in the garden? I'm very bored and very lonely.'

She looked at him, startled. 'Walk with you? Oh no, I think not, sir - I mean Martin.'

'Well done! You said it!' He grinned at her. 'We are making progress. Now the next lesson is to teach you to accept when invited to walk in the garden. Why won't you come? I won't eat you.'

Felicity's spirit quailed at the very idea. She would have

nothing to say and he would find her a dull companion. 'I'm too busy,' she said. 'The cook will want me—'

'And *I* want you. I want your company. Here, give me the tray and I'll return it to the cook and tell her you are coming out with me for a while.'

'Oh no!' She clung to the tray like a drowning man to a straw, but he eased it from her.

'Wait here,' he commanded. 'I shall be back in two shakes of a lamb's tail, as Minnie used to say!'

He was gone before she could protest further, leaving her standing on the landing and then he was back again, taking the stairs two at a time. ' 'Tis all arranged,' he said. 'It won't be so bad, I promise you. I'll tell you the story of my life and you'll tell me yours.' As he spoke he took her hand and led her down the stairs and out into the garden.

When they reached the pond he turned and surveyed the house. ' 'Tis the first time I've seen Romney House,' he told her. 'One day I shall be master here. Mama has promised it to me because she has no use for it and Allan will inherit Heron.'

'And your other brother?'

'Piers? Oh, he will have nothing because he's the youngest. I dare say he will go to London. I shall come home and breed sheep or cows – or pigs or chickens!' She laughed as he intended her to do. 'Will you still be here?'

'I don't know. If the old lady dies—'

'She will die, Felicity. She is over eighty and she has no joy in life. Don't pray for her to live. Do you envy her that sad existence?'

'No, no, but if she dies . . .' She stopped again, unable to put her fears into words.

'What will become of you?' he prompted.

She nodded, turning her head away.

'Maria will not throw you out into the world. I am sure of that.'

'Don't speak of it, I beg you.' She turned to face him and her long lashes were spiked with tears. 'Let's talk of something else.'

'Felicity, don't look so forsaken. Believe me, you will be well treated. Mayhap they will find a husband for you.'

'Oh!' She blushed furiously. 'I think not. I'm not attractive and I have no dowry, nothing.'

He put an arm round her shoulder and gave her a comforting squeeze. 'I find you attractive,' he told her gallantly. 'So stop fretting and sit with me. We'll throw twigs at the ducks and you shall tell me your life story.'

'You tell me yours.'

Martin laughed. 'You know it already,' he said. 'Mama has told me that old Ruth talks of nothing else to you. Poor girl, you must know as much as I do, if not more, about Heron and the Kendals. Deny it if you can.'

'I can't deny it!' At last she laughed with him.

'Felicity! You look so bonny when you laugh and you have such grey eyes. Ah! I've embarrassed you again. Then I'll say no more. Tell me your life story – from the very beginning. I want to know all about you. Come, sit down.'

They settled themselves on the grass and he plucked a long grass and began to chew it, staring out over the pond. An old boat floated on it and dabchicks called to each other among the reeds that edged the water.

Felicity hesitated and then began. She spoke haltingly. She had no memories of her mother. She had died giving birth to her. Her name was Alice. Felicity paused.

Martin took the grass out of his mouth and ran it along her bare arm. 'Is that all?'

She jerked her arm away as though the grass had scorched her skin. Shocked, she looked at Martin to see if he knew what he was doing.

'I'm still listening,' he told her.

He did not know. She breathed out slowly. He was only a boy still, in spite of his size.

'There's so little to tell,' she protested.

He reached out again with the grass but she snatched it away. Ecstasy, however fragile, was a new experience. It had made her forget where and who she was and she was startled by the intensity of her reaction. Martin sprawled on the grass beside her, cupping his chin in his hands, watched her with amusement.

'I'm still waiting.'

Slowly, she added a few details, careful not to look into his dark eyes. He nodded and waited and with an effort she continued. Her father's name was William and he was a charcoal-burner from Bedgebury. He was a large man, honest, and sparing with his words. His summers were spent in a rough hand-made shelter, tending his fires. Having no wife with whom to leave his daughter he was forced to take her along.

'All summer long? But what did you do all day?'

She shrugged. 'Played among the trees, helped my father. He was always busy for while one stack burned he'd prepare the next.' She smiled shyly. 'I am quite well versed in the act of burning. I could lay a hearth, set the chimney round the stake, and layer the logs round it. Have you never seen a charcoal stack?'

He shook his head, amused by her earnest expression.

'Then you should. There is an art in it, a skill – and my father was one of the best. A well stacked fire must burn very slowly and I was set to watch that the flames never broke through the crust.'

'The crust?'

'The earth crust which seals in the heat. My father was a craftsman in his way.'

He detected a note of defiance in her voice which puzzled him.

'I don't doubt it,' he said gently.

'My mother came from a good family but she ran away with my father and was never forgiven. Even when she lay dying and my father sent word . . . they would not come to see her.' Her face darkened. 'My father was very bitter from that time on. He never saw them again.'

'And they never came to see *you*?'

'Never. I was never acknowledged. It mattered little to me for you don't miss what you've never had. I grew up with my father. In winter we shared a small cottage on the edge of the forest. In summer we lived in the heart of it.'

'A lonely life for a young girl.'

'Mayhap, but I had known no other way of life. I was content.'

Suddenly she stopped, afraid that she was boring him. While he waited for her to continue he picked a small posy of daisies from the grass and presented them to her.

'Oh, my thanks.' It was the first time anyone had given her such a gift and she was touched by the gesture.

'I shall take them back,' he warned, 'if you don't go on with your story. How did you come to Romney House? 'Tis a far cry from a charcoal burner's hut.'

'Aye.' She held the daisies to her nose and sniffed delicately, twirling the flowers, admiring them from every angle. 'How did I come to Romney House? 'Twas this way. My father died. I was eight or nine, I'm not certain. He had an accident. He was chopping wood and the axe slipped and injured his foot. It wouldn't heal and there was no money for doctors' fees. I nursed him as best I could but—' She sighed deeply, 'He took a fever and his mind wandered. I knew then that he was dying. I lay beside him to warm him but when I woke in the morning he was dead. They buried him in a pauper's grave.'

Martin was silent, no longer teasing. 'My poor little Felicity.'

She stared past him, hardly hearing what he said. 'I walked eleven miles to the big house where my grandparents lived and asked them what I should do. The gentleman was kindly and would have given me a place there but his wife would not hear of it. Their name was Lattimer.'

She saw herself again in the large room, the focus of all eyes. George Lattimer, small and round with his fussy manner. His wife Miriam, tall and austere, dressed in sombre brown and three other grandchildren, wide-eyed and curious, standing together by the window, occasionally whispering together. She heard Miriam's voice, 'Dead, you say?' and saw herself nod, numb with grief and weariness. And Miriam's answer: 'I knew no good would come of it!' Then they had argued about her future as though she were invisible, without speaking to her. They did not ask her to sit down, and she had waited, weak with hunger, until she fainted.

Martin waited. He said nothing but regarded her intently. In her nervousness she had twisted the daisy stems to a pulp and he took them from her and tossed them away. As she began to protest he put a finger to her lips.

'I'll pick you another posy. Finish your story.'

For a moment she watched his slim fingers darting among the grass blades, plucking the small white flowers. In search of more he rolled over so that he faced away from her and she considered the long, lithe body in the well fitting clothes. His dark hair curled slightly at the nape of his neck and his broad shoulders and back tapered to a slim waist. He would soon be a man, she thought, and recalled the touch of the grass against her skin and the warmth of his arm around her shoulder. He had taken her hand, too, when he led her down the stairs. She did not want to forget.

He rolled back and gave her the second posy. 'And don't spoil them!'

'I won't.' She would press them, she decided, between the pages of a book.

'And then . . . ? The Lattimers?' he prompted.

'Oh – then another man came in. James Lattimer, one of my uncles. He said he had friends who might find a use for me in their kitchen. I was taken there later that same day and they agreed to give me a trial. Their name was Cummins.'

'Aha! Now we're getting warmer!'

She smiled faintly. 'Aye, Victor Cummins was a second cousin of Harold. When Harold died they were unable to come to the funeral but they visited Ruth a few weeks later and recommended me, if ever Ruth should need a companion. They were well-meaning, you see, and saw a chance for my advancement. Later when the old lady's sight began to fail, she sent word to Maria to ask for me – and here I am.'

'And you are happy here?'

'Indeed I am.'

'Hmm.'

She wondered, suddenly anxious, if anything in her story had offended him.

He said, 'And who taught you to read and write?'

'Victor Cummins had a governess for the children. I attended their lessons twice a week.'

He stood up and pulled her to her feet. 'I challenge you to a race round the pond.'

'A race?' She was astonished and excited by the unexpected proposal.

'I shall give you a start of three.' He pointed. 'That way round – No, I shall accept no excuses. You have legs. Use them. Ready – Go!'

He gave her a push and she began to run, holding up her skirts, her head thrown back, her long hair tossing behind her. At the count of three he ran after her but she was fleeter than he expected and not such an easy conquest. But he reached the starting point a few yards ahead of her and turned to wait for her. As she ran towards him, flushed and dishevelled, he opened his arms wide to stop her and then held her at arm's length.

'Now,' he said lightly. 'We are friends – and you will never call me "sir" again!'

'I shall be along to see you next week,' said the physician, pausing in the doorway. 'I shall want to hear that your appetite is better. You eat all that they give you, a little white fish—'

'I don't care for white fish,' Ruth quavered and Maria, already outside the door, smiled at him. He pursed his lips humorously. He had dealt with plenty of cantankerous patients but none so old as Ruth Cummins. He was proud of her long survival and boasted of it to his friends and colleagues, taking an understandable pride in his care of her throughout the latter half of her life. He saw a great deal of death, many babies within a week of their births, more children before they reached the years of adolescence. Then he would lose boys to the rapacious consumption – eager young men who began to waste and grow pale and who would cough their way out of this life. And he, and other physicians, would stand helplessly by, unable to save them. Then the women would go in the young prime of their lives, taken by the dread childbed fever, living only a few days – a week or two at most – before losing sight of the beloved child and husband. And any that survived all this would live precariously, a prey to all manner of disease. Frequently, having steered them safely through these he would be finally robbed by an accident or design – a grandfather of forty-eight years run down by a wagon and horses, or a rich gentleman poisoned by his son for his money.

Ruth Cummins was proof that he could sustain life and he treated her as he would a rare plant, with devoted attention and not a little pride of achievement.

'Then ask the cook to make it with almond sauce,' he told her, 'and a coddled egg each morning and a glass of madeira with every dinner and supper—'

'I shall be pickled!' argued the old lady stubbornly. 'One glass a day is—'

'Who is physician here, you or I? A good wine is an excellent aid to the digestion. A short sleep at noon and another in the early evening—'

' 'Tis scarcely worth opening my eyes if I'm to sleep again!' said Ruth irritably. 'What nonsense it all is. I cannot tell night from day as 'tis, if I sleep as you prescribe I shall scarce know one day from another! And will it be of any consequence? I would be better dead—'

Quietly he withdrew and closed the door. Despite her gloomy protestations she clung on tenaciously to life.

Maria looked at him anxiously. 'So little left to live for,' she echoed. 'And yet 'tis a sin to wish a life away. She doesn't mean it.'

'Indeed not.' He patted her arm. 'She is an amazing woman, quite amazing. This last stroke – it was minor, I grant you – but at her age! 'Tis quite astonishing. And she will go on yet. Oh, make no doubt of it. Her heart is sound. She has her speech and hearing. Felicity talks with her and reads aloud. Your letters are a great source of pleasure.'

They went downstairs slowly, talking as they went until they reached the front porch.

Maria said, 'My problem is to know whether I dare leave her and return home. Felicity is very young and 'tis a heavy burden. If Ruth should die I cannot be here in less than two days, three if the highways are bad.'

'Go home, Maria. You are needed there. Your staying cannot save her if death reaches out for her. If God wills it, she'll go – and most likely peaceably in her bed. A fortunate end to a long and enjoyable life. Most people would envy her.'

'I feel I am deserting her.'

'Nonsense, woman. I tell you to go. Let me persuade you thus – your presence excites her and young Felicity's mind is distracted from her duties by the handsome prince who has suddenly ridden into her life!'

'Martin?'

'Aye. She is quite enchanted with him.'

Maria frowned. 'I had not noticed. I have been so concerned for Ruth.'

The old man shook his head. 'The old woman's quiet routine is upset. The whole household is upset! You have done your duty and you came when sent for. Now take my advice, go back to Heron with an easy mind and let Romney House settle once more into its dull routine. That is what Ruth needs, the even tenor of her life.'

Maria laughed. 'You make it very easy for me. I can see through your wiles and yet I thank you for it. Tomorrow we shall ride back. I will write often and you will keep a watchful eye on her.'

116

'I will, never fear,' he cried. He allowed Maria to help him on with his surcoat. 'Ruth Cummins is the golden seal at the end of my long career!'

A wind blew up in the early morning, bringing grey clouds which massed overhead with the threat of rain. By eight o'clock it was showery with heavy droplets which rattled against the shutters. By eleven the wind had dropped and the showers had given way to a steady downpour which hissed into the lawns and seeped in at the stable doors. An hour later the rains had stopped though the moon was still hidden for most of the time. Inside the house Ruth lay on her back, already asleep, snoring lightly with her mouth open, one mittened hand thrown up on the pillow beside her face, which looked skull-like in the candlelight. In the room next door Felicity lay awake, her eyes staring at the pale rectangle of light which was the window. She was thankful that the wind had dropped. Her shutters did not fit properly for one hinge was loose and on windy nights they creaked and shook and sometimes sprang the catch and parted. Then she would have to close them again and wedge them with cloth or anything that came to hand. Now she thought of Martin, secret, joyful thoughts which she had never dared to think before. She was no better than a servant but he had shown her great kindness. He had listened to her brief life story and had not mocked her. He was, she was certain, a good person. In Felicity's life people were either good or bad, there was no in-between. Her eyes closed sleepily but she jerked them open, fighting sleep. She had so much to think about she could not afford to sleep so soon.

In the next room Martin slept, tossing restlessly as he always did. The sheet and coverlet were already tangled round him like the wrappings of an Egyptian mummy and now restricted him so that he fought to free himself and dreamed that he was being sucked into a quicksand and powerless to free himself. In the dream Allan was there, only yards away, towering above him, watching him go under. Martin tried to ask his help but no sound came from his lips and his terrified thrashings brought his end that much nearer.

Maria had fallen into a deep sleep with the ghost of a contented smile still playing about her lips. Tomorrow she and Martin would start for home and, God willing, another two or three days would find them at Heron and she would be in Hugo's arms where she belonged. She had fallen asleep with his name on her lips and she lay curled up like a mouse in a nest.

Outside the house a man moved in the shadows. He moved surely as though on familiar ground, going quickly from tree to tree, his eyes on the house. Only one window was lit and that he knew was Ruth Cummins' bedchamber. She would not sleep in the dark after her brother died and, even though she was blind, she insisted on a candle beside the bed and would put out a hand to feel for its warmth to satisfy herself that no one tried to deceive her. That lighted window told him which room Felicity slept in. That bitch! He knew it was Felicity who had brought about his dismissal. They had denied it at the time and Maria had tried to take the responsibility upon her own shoulders, but only Felicity could have known why the cook left. He had misjudged the damned girl and the thought tormented him that, but for her, he would still be a looker with a job, a warm bed, and a full belly. Instead he was an outcast, forced to beg or steal every rotten crust that went into his mouth and he had a back full of weals that festered and would not heal. Felicity Carr had a lot to answer for and she was going to learn that no one messed with Mark Wynne and went scot-free. She thought he was gone out of her life but she was in for an unpleasant shock. So great was his hatred that he had made his way back into the area, although he knew the kind of punishment he could expect if he was discovered.

But he did not intend to be discovered for he knew the land like the back of his hand as well as all the places where a man could hide. His plan was simple. He meant to hound her until she was frightened out of her wits and cursed the day she had betrayed him to the justices. Felicity Carr would learn not to meddle with men like Mark Wynne. Tonight was the beginning of a hate campaign that would shatter her peace of mind – and restore his!

Skirting the pond he crouched low, each hand clenched round a small rock. He prayed 'let her window be unshuttered'. He was soaked to the skin and shivering with cold but his anger warmed him. He ran closer still and then the dog began to bark and he threw himself full length in the sodden grass and thanked God there was no moon. If anyone woke and looked out they would not see him. The dog barked again, but he knew it was in the kitchen out of harm's way. His eyes were accustomed to the dark now and as he squinted up at the house he saw by the outline of Felicity's window that in fact her shutters were closed. Hell fire! He could do with better luck! He waited but the dog continued to bark and then he heard it scratching at the back door. Stupid animal. And bloody stupid household to keep a dog in the kitchen where it could do no more than bark. Suddenly he heard the click of a shutter and then – his luck was changing! – Felicity was at the window, leaning out. He could dimly distinguish the pale oval of her face. After a moment he heard the faint sounds of the shutter hooks and knew she had left them open. He allowed himself one more minute to check his facts. Jem would be asleep over the stable and *he* was all that Mark Wynne needed to consider. The old lady was bedridden and Felicity would never dare show her face in the garden at midnight. He lay still until the dog was silent and then stood up and cautiously moved nearer still.

Then he took aim and threw the first rock at Felicity's open window. His aim was true and even as it left his hand he knew it was on target. There was a muffled thud and then a scream. Felicity had only just climbed back into bed when something flew over her head to strike the wall and crash heavily on to the large pottery jug that held her washing water. It smashed and a sharp fragment flew up into her face, narrowly missing her left eye. Martin in the next room woke instantly and ran out of his room and into hers. She was standing by the bed, terrified, one hand to her face. Downstairs the dog was barking frantically.

'Through the window!' she gasped. 'Something came through the—'

Before she could finish the sentence another missile whistled past, narrowly missing them, and Felicity screamed again and threw herself into Martin's arms, clinging to him desperately. Another thud followed as it hit the wall and fell on to the bed where, a moment earlier, Felicity had been sleeping. Martin's instinct was to rush to the window and look out but Felicity held him back.

'There may be more!' she cried. 'Don't go to the window, I beg you.'

She began to tremble as the shock surfaced and Martin pulled her into the corner out of the line of the window and held her close, trying to comfort her. At that moment Maria ran in, barefoot and holding a lighted candle.

'What's happening?' she cried. 'Felicity! Your face – it's bleeding.'

She looked at Martin, utterly bewildered, but he stepped forward and pulled her into the shelter of the corner.

'Those rocks,' Martin cried pointing, for now in the light they could see the cause of the damage. 'Someone is throwing rocks through the window. You stay with her, I'll go down.'

'Take care,' cried Maria, putting an arm round Felicity. 'Rouse Jem. You are not to go alone. D'you hear me? We don't know how many there are. Oh – Ruth! I'd better see – No, no, of course. I closed her shutters. Now don't shake so, dear. You're in good hands. Jem and Martin will deal with it. There now, weep if you want to. What a wicked, senseless thing to do. Now calm yourself, I say. The danger is over. We will go downstairs shortly and bathe your face. And look at that jug – in smithereens and water everywhere!

What are we coming to, when folk cannot sleep safely in their own beds?'

The sudden shrill barking told them that the dog had been let out but they both resisted the temptation to look out of the window.

'Put something warm on,' said Maria, 'and we'll go downstairs. Perhaps we can find out – Ah, that's Jem's voice. Good.'

They paused, listening, and heard Jem's deep voice. 'Find him, boy. Seek him out. Where is he, eh?'

And then Martin's voice, excited, higher pitched, and Maria said silent prayers for his safety. From Ruth's bedchamber they heard a quavering voice demanding to know what the noise was all about.

'I'll go to her,' said Maria. ' 'Twill alarm her to see you in that state. Put on slippers and a robe and I'll see you downstairs.'

The old lady was sitting up in bed, clutching the blanket to her withered chest and staring sightlessly towards the door.

' 'Tis a disturbance in the garden,' Maria told her. 'Most likely a poacher taking a short cut home! Jem has set the dog on him. There's nothing to fear. Go back to sleep, dear.'

'A poacher, you say?'

'Mayhap. We don't know. Or else a fox.'

'A fox? All this commotion for a fox? What time is it?'

'Time you went back to sleep!' said Maria soothingly. 'Will you take a little warmed milk?'

'Warmed milk? Indeed I will not, but a little quiet would not come amiss.' Her hands went out towards the candle.

' 'Tis alight,' said Maria. 'Will you try to sleep again.'

'Aye . . . warmed milk at this hour! A fox, you say . . . ?'

She allowed herself to be settled down and Maria kissed her and hurried thankfully out of the room.

Felicity stood at the open door and Maria joined her. Fleetingly the moon appeared from behind the clouds and dappled the garden with silver and dark shadows. For a moment all was still and they glanced at each other fearfully.

Mark Wynne had discovered his error too late. Expecting Jem to appear from the direction of the stables he was taken by surprise when the dog, an ancient border collie, raced from the kitchen followed by another man.

'God's blood! There's two of 'em!' he muttered and hesitated, trying to decide on a new means of escape now that his way out of the main drive was blocked. 'Get down, you mangy cur! I'm not scared of you!' He lashed out at the old dog who, recognizing his scent, was instantly puzzled and unsure whether or not to treat him as an intruder. He leaped up but without baring his teeth and the looker brought his foot up under the dog's chin and kicked him savagely. Howling with pain and shock, the dog fell backwards into a shrub as Martin arrived on the scene. The two had never met and Mark Wynne assumed by the boy's height that he was older and therefore a more dangerous adversary. Aware that Jem was on his way, he chose flight and turned to flee.

'You won't get away,' cried Martin and lunged at him wildly. In his excitement the blow went wide and he almost lost his balance, staggering to regain it while he shouted to Jem. As Wynne ducked to avoid the blow he stepped backwards and fell over the dog. At once Martin was on top of him, but he was no match for the older man, hardened by years of outdoor life. They wrestled but Martin was taking a severe pounding.

'I'm here!' he yelled as Jem came rushing through the bushes in search of them. With a tremendous effort Wynne threw off Martin and rolled free as Jem leapt for him. Then the bush was between them but Martin was back on his feet.

' 'Tis Wynne!' cried Jem. 'Corner him against the wall!'

Seeing the danger, Wynne charged between them before they could close in on him, then he turned to the right and made a dash for the orchard. The dog ran up again, leaping at him, hostile now. He caught at his sleeve and hung on.

With an oath Wynne swung him off the ground and into a broad tree trunk. As he yelped the dog released Wynne's sleeve, but now Jem had doubled round. There was only one way to go and that was towards the pond.

'Stop the wretch!' cried Jem. 'After him, boy!'

Wynne managed to keep just ahead of them and reached the water. He waded out and began to swim. Jem waded after him shouting back to Martin, 'I'll hold him. Go fetch a rope. We'll need to bind his hands. Behind the first stable door. Go!'

Martin hesitated then ran back the way they had come. Jem reached Wynne to find he had snatched the oar from the old boat and now faced him with it. He braced himself as the wooden blade curved murderously towards him then grasped it and jerked as hard as he could. Surprised, Wynne stumbled forward and released his hold of the oar, and seizing his chance Jem brought the oar round and down on the back of Wynne's head. Wynne gave a short cry and fell face downwards into the dark water. Jem dragged him to the water's edge.

'I reckon I've stunned him, sir!' he cried when at last Martin reappeared, 'and thank the Lord for that! A vicious bastard, this one.'

'Is there any need then, to tie his hands?'

'Aye, 'tis safer. He'll come round shortly and he's going to be desperate!'

They twisted the man's hands behind his back and knotted the rope securely. Then together they dragged him up to the house and on to the steps where Maria and Felicity waited anxiously. It was only when they examined him by the light of the candle that they discovered his neck was broken. Mark Wynne was dead.

It was four days before Maria and Martin were able to leave for Heron. Hugo was waiting for them and listened to the account of the episode with horror. When Martin described Wynne's death he said, 'And a good riddance!

'Tis quite intolerable that such scum should prey upon innocent folk. Felicity had a narrow escape. Dear God! When I think how it *might* have ended. But what then? How did you dispose of the wretch's body?'

Maria took up the tale again. 'I'm ashamed to say we left it in the hall for what was left of the night. The truth is no one knew what to do with it.'

'Jem wanted to toss him back into the pond!' said Martin with a grin, 'but Maria would not have it.'

'He can smile now,' said Maria, 'but 'twas no laughing matter, I can assure you. What did we do next? Next morning Jem rode into Ashford to the justices and they sent a man with a cart and took Wynne away. There were a few legalities. Martin and Jem told how it happened and the clerk wrote it down. They put their signatures to it—'

'Jem put his mark,' Martin corrected her.

'And 'twas all over,' she said, ignoring the interruption. She sighed heavily. 'A sad end, in some ways, for I believe he had given Harold good service for many years.'

Hugo put an arm round her. 'You are too soft hearted.'

'But what makes a man go to the bad?'

Hugo shrugged. 'Who can say? Drink, mayhap, or some base aspect of his personality. The stars, mayhap, ill placed at his birth.'

Martin said, 'Rumour has it that he had a woman once and beat her 'til she ran off. So Jem says.'

Seeing the depressing direction of their conversation Hugo said forcefully, 'Jem may be right. But let's talk no more on the subject of Mark Wynne. He brought about his own downfall and has no claim on our pity. Now, Maria, tell me how Ruth fares—'

'The physician was well pleased with her recovery.'

'And Felicity is none the worse for her ordeal?'

'She, too, is quite recovered.'

'Good. Then the incident must be forgotten and the sooner the better.'

At that moment the two younger children appeared with the puppy and flung themselves first on Maria and then on

Martin with cries of welcome. They then dragged the latter away to show him various tricks which they claimed to have taught the pup during his absence. As soon as they had gone, Maria turned to her husband.

'How goes the match?' she asked eagerly. 'Allan and Eloise – do you think they like each other? Has there been a sign or a hint? I thought of nothing else until Mark Wynne appeared on the scene. Hugo, do tell me what has been happening.'

'I will, I will!' he laughed. '*If* you have done with your questions, I may venture some answers! Do I think they like each other?' He paused reflectively and Maria bit back an impatient comment. 'I think Eloise is disappointed that he does not show her more affection, but knowing Allan as well as I do, I think he is giving her more attention than I expected.'

'Hugo! What does that mean? Have you answered my questions?'

He opened his hands with a helpless gesture. 'How can I say more? As far as I can tell they do not quarrel and they spend a fair amount of time together.'

'A fair amount! Is that all? Oh, what is the matter with the boy? There are times when I could shake him.'

Hugo shook his head gently. 'No Maria, he's no longer a child. No one can influence him. I think he finds her more attractive than he cares to admit. His manner is – guarded. He needs more time, that is all.'

'And Eloise? Is she all we hoped for? You have seen her this past week. What is your true opinion of her? I must know. Did we make a wise choice?'

Again his reply was slightly guarded. 'Eloise is – intelligent and has great charm but she is used to her own way, I feel. Her father has obviously indulged her in everything. That much was evident in the time he was here. She is also rather vain but who can blame her. She is already a beauty.'

Maria was chastened by his observations and Hugo regretted her disappointment.

'You did ask for a true opinion,' he reminded her, 'and 'tis hardly a calamity. On the other side of the coin she is interested in the management of the house and the mine—'

'The mine?'

'Aye. We talked at some length on the subject and she is eager to learn all she can and has a ready understanding. She asked Minnie for her recipe for mincemeat and has won *her* heart completely. She has won everyone's affection – Ellie, Ben, Matt. They all adore her.'

'Oh.' Maria felt a slight twinge of jealousy but quickly suppressed it, ashamed of her reaction. 'So there's hope for them?'

'If Allan can give her all the love and attention she craves – aye, there's hope for them. We must put our trust in God. I think all will be well. But why are we still standing on the steps. We'll go in and find you food and drink. Oh Maria, I have to let you go away, for 'tis so *good* when you come home!'

Eloise was delighted to discover that Maria and Martin had returned. She had been looking forward to a supper at which the whole family was present and she could take her place as Allan's bride-to-be and 'second' mistress of Heron. Since her arrival she had worked hard at winning hearts and influencing her future father-in-law. Her father had done his best to promote her, but she had finally grown tired of his constant efforts to convince Hugo that she was the perfect bride for Allan. Why did no one try to persuade her of Allan's suitability as her husband? Her original doubts about him had mostly been dispelled for she sensed the suppressed desire which he believed well hidden and knew he could not maintain his passive role indefinitely. Twice during the week he had ridden out alone and he had spent one whole day at the mine. When they walked together in the garden he was polite and spoke earnestly on a variety of subjects, but Eloise Ballantyne was never one of them. So far he had proved impervious to her feminine wiles and despite her thinly veiled encouragements, had done no more than kiss her hand. But he longed to do more. That much she read in his eyes and knew intuitively that an admission of his feelings for her was just a matter of time. How much time remained to be seen. She was not known for her patience. She was curious about his relationship with Harriet and asked discreet questions of the servants. Their replies confused her. They had seemed an ideal couple, Ellie confided, and very much in love. Had Harriet been beautiful? Sweet-faced, Minnie told her, with a soft smile and gentle ways. Eloise was unimpressed and decided she had little to worry about. Maria and Martin would soon be back and with a little help from the latter she would soon jerk Allan out of his indifference.

The meal was well under way and Eloise was enjoying herself immensely. Hugo, at the head of the table, was properly attentive and Allan, opposite her, was relaxed and unusually talkative. The talk flowed freely as Hugo told stories of his earlier exile in France and Maria spoke with affection of her protracted stay in the nunnery at Arnsville. Martin amused them with descriptions of some of the more eccentric boys and teachers at his school and the two younger ones endlessly extolled the virtues of the puppy who had finally been named Beazel.

'Poor old Leonie,' laughed Maria referring to the older dog. 'I expect she is worn out by his youthful antics. She has had the house to herself for so long.'

'Oh but she loves Beazel,' Lorna insisted earnestly. 'She plays with him and they chase in the garden. Tomorrow you must see, Mama, how they romp together.'

Martin looked up wickedly. 'Oh, there's nothing like a young pup to liven an old dog – wouldn't you agree, Allan?'

'Allan's not old!' cried Eloise, quick to take the point of the remark, 'he is mature.'

'You make him sound like a good wine,' said Martin.

'And you make *me* sound like a scatterbrained pup!' She pretended indignation but her eyes met his, challenging.

'Talking of good wine—' said Hugo hastily, 'my goblet is empty. Help yourselves and pass the flagon along.'

Martin picked it up and offered wine to Eloise.

'Have you had enough?' he asked.

She lowered her eyes fractionally and said, 'Of wine? Aye.'

'Only of wine?' he persisted, refilling his own goblet. 'What else do you lack?'

He passed the wine to Piers and Maria said, 'No more for you, Piers, you and Lorna have had enough.' And she took the flagon and refilled Hugo's goblet.

Lorna giggled. 'Allan's twenty-two!' she said. 'He's an old man!'

Hugo leaned over and tweaked her ear. 'Take care what you say, young lady. I'm more than twice Allan's age remember. Would you have me with a long grey beard, then, and no teeth?'

She clapped a hand to her mouth, shrieking with laughter.

'You know the old saying,' said Eloise. 'Many a good tune is played on an old fiddle!'

She glanced at Allan opposite her and then across at Martin.

'Do you like music?' he asked innocently.

Maria was fully aware of the undertones, but unsure how to put an end to them. Hugo had drunk rather too well and was taking the exchange at face value.

'I propose a toast,' he said, 'to old fiddles and mature wine.'

Eloise raised her glass. 'But some wines are best drunk young,' she said and held Martin's eyes steadily over the rim of her goblet. 'Are you a connoisseur?'

'What is a connoisseur?' asked Piers.

'A connoisseur—' Hugo began but Martin interrupted him.

'A connoisseur is someone who knows what he likes. *I* know what I like so I suppose I am a connoisseur.'

Martin knew by Maria's expression that she was about to challenge him so he hastily turned his attention to the pile of walnuts on his plate and began to crack them.

'So you can define the word connoisseur?' said Allan. 'It seems your teachers have taught you something. Let us be thankful for small mercies.'

He stood up abruptly and turned to Eloise. 'If you have finished you might care to walk down to the river with me before the light goes. There is often a kingfisher at this hour.'

'A kingfisher? How splendid. I've never seen one.' She stood up obediently and Maria breathed a sigh of relief which was short-lived for Eloise continued, 'Will you join us, Martin? I should be flattered to have *two* handsome brothers to escort me to the river.'

Martin hesitated. He dearly wanted to accept but dared not. The man in him longed to challenge his brother but the boy in him feared Maria's wrath.

'I think not,' he said. 'They say two's company and three's a crowd.' And he watched them leave the room with regret. Avoiding Maria's eye, he turned back to his plate, picked up the nutcrackers and gave the walnuts his undivided attention.

Allan and Eloise walked across the garden, past the orchard and down the steps to the stretch of garden that bordered the river. Neither spoke. Eloise was a trifle apprehensive but unrepetant. Allan was disturbed but anxious to conceal the fact. He was grateful that Martin had not accompanied them but knew well the reason. They stood side by side, looking down at the water which gleamed softly with the last of the light and lapped the stepping stones with a familiar sound that soothed Allan's ruffled feelings. At last he said as calmly as he could – 'So what d'you think of my young half-brother?'

'You are very different.'

'Neither of us took after our mother and we had different fathers. We do not look alike or think alike.'

'He is mature for his years,' said Eloise. She pulled the dead head from a yellow iris and threw it on the water and they both watched it being borne away.

'But you like him,' said Allan.

'I do. Don't you want me to like him?'

'Of course.'

'Then I'll make you happy and tell you that I find him most agreeable. If Hugo was like him at that age I can see why Maria found him so irresistible.'

A fish jumped and they watched the pattern of widening ripples as though their lives depended upon it. The silence lengthened and Eloise wondered nervously if she had overstepped the mark.

'Mayhap,' he said at last, 'you should be betrothed to Martin.'

His forthright words stung her. She had not expected such a direct challenge.

'He has a boyish charm and pleasant manners,' she retorted. 'Most people find such qualities agreeable. He is cheerful company and makes me laugh. I do not wish myself betrothed to him, however, but I'm offended you appear so indifferent on the matter. Mayhap *you* wish me betrothed to him - and don't, I beg you, speak to me of Harriet. I am aware of her virtues. If 'tis another Harriet you seek, then I am *not* for you!'

'You are jealous of her ghost.'

'And you are jealous of your brother!'

They still did not face each other but addressed their remarks to the air above the river where a cloud of midges danced crazily in the cooling air.

'If you find him such a paragon,' said Allan quietly, 'why do you choose me?'

She shrugged. 'You are my betrothed,' she said.

'That's a poor answer.'

'Then you answer this - *why* don't I please you for 'tis

plain I don't. Is it Harriet's ghost that comes between us? Was your love *so* perfect that no one else can take her place? Did you show her love and affection that you will not show to me? Oh you pretend to be cold, Allan, but I read the truth in your eyes.' She was almost shouting now. 'But what am I to do? Am I to throw myself at your feet, begging for a kindly word or gesture? If that is what you are waiting for you will be disappointed. I do not grovel, Allan Kendal. I don't need you to tell me what I am. I *know* I am beautiful. I *know* I am desirable. I see it in men's eyes – aye and boys', too. I see it in Martin's eyes. He is not ashamed to find me attractive. You are, it seems. Or else I do not please you and I have imagined the passion in your eyes.'

Allan's face was white and his eyes blazed as he looked at her. Suddenly he caught her fiercely by the shoulders, but with an effort controlled his voice and kept it low. 'You don't please me if you flirt with my brother!' he said. 'You don't please me if you want me to fall in love with your beauty and wit. That's not what I see in a woman. My woman must be tender, with a loyal and loving heart. If 'tis a declaration of love you seek then I cannot make it. I scarcely know you. As to passion – I will declare it in my own time or not at all. Now I have had my say. 'Tis your turn. Say what you will and we'll be done with this folly.' She struggled to free herself but he would not release her. 'Say it, Eloise. Say if 'tis Martin you want, not me.'

With a last effort, she wrenched herself free from his grasp and stepped back. The colour burned in her cheeks. The words trembled on her lips but with an effort she refrained. She closed her eyes to conceal her anger and fought to breathe more steadily and still the pounding of her heart.

' 'Tis not Martin I want,' she said at last, her voice low. She opened her eyes, saw the hope spring into his, and hastily lowered them as with a muffled cry Allan pulled her towards him.

She raised her head and looked into his eyes, and was

shocked to feel a fierce longing sweep over her. So this man who was to be her husband *could* reach her emotions!

Allan's lips were close to hers. He is going to kiss me, she thought, and knew that if he did her body would respond. She would not let that happen. Not yet. He must wait for her.

'Don't,' she whispered drawing back slightly. 'Not yet. This is a bad beginning but you are right. We have plenty of time.'

His arms fell back to his side and his eyes darkened with disappointment.

'Then say it again,' he murmured. 'Say that 'tis me you want. I need to hear the words again.'

'I want *you*, Allan Kendal,' she whispered.

CHAPTER SEVEN

The two women sat in the kitchen on opposite sides of the table, each busy with her own thoughts. Melissa was chopping onions with fierce concentration. Thomas had developed another heavy cold and it had suddenly settled on his chest. She had insisted that he spend a whole day in bed, for the raw November weather aggravated the condition and the bouts of frantic coughing exhausted him. He was over sixty and had never been robust, although he had always denied this fact. Every winter a battle developed between husband and wife, with Melissa urging him to don his sheepskin vest and Thomas delaying as long as he dared. He no longer worked a full week and rarely went to the mine, but attended to the various accounts either at Heron or in the comfort of his own home.

From upstairs came the sound of coughing and Melissa 'tutted' anxiously. 'Listen to that!' she said to Maggie. 'And he'd have ridden over to Heron today if I'd allowed it. In this weather!'

She waved a hand towards the window. Outside the fog swirled lazily, hiding all but the nearest trees. 'A fog like pea-soup and Thomas would be out in it. 'Tis quite beyond me. Men are so stubborn.'

'Aye, they are,' Maggie agreed. 'They're most likely born stubborn.' She was knitting a blanket for Beatrice's baby and her fingers moved jerkily as she worked, occasionally tugging a new length of woollen thread from the bag beside her. The wool had been bleached a soft creamy white and Maggie had spun it herself – a labour of love for, as she was first to admit, she had no talent for anything but pies and puddings. Melissa laid the knife aside and scooped the onion into a small iron pot. She added a cupful of cider-vinegar and a large spoonful of honey and hung the pot over the fire to heat.

'Finest thing there is for a racking cough,' she said. ' 'Twas Minnie taught me that. I must remember to tell that to Eloise. She'll no doubt be collecting recipes and remedies for her household roll.' She seized a cloth and wiped the chopping board.

'I should be doing that,' Maggie protested without conviction. ' 'Tis I'm cook, you know, and here we are with me knitting while you chop onions.'

Melissa smiled. 'Ah, but 'tis a remedy for my dear Thomas and I like to see to it myself. 'Tis foolish, I know. I daresay you think I mollycoddle him but since Oliver left I need someone to cosset. I'm like a mother hen with no chicks!'

Maggie gave her an affectionate look. The two women were very close friends. The suggestion that Maggie should move into Ladyford had proved highly successful to all concerned.

'Now,' Melissa went on briskly, 'I'll strain that when the onions are soft and add another spoonful of honey. Minnie made it last winter and 'twas most effective. Another quick stir—' She sniffed it critically and then nodded, apparently satisfied with its progress.

Maggie reached the end of a row and held the knitting up for inspection.

' 'Tis coming along well,' said Melissa. 'Beatrice will be astonished.'

Maggie held it to her cheek. ' 'Tis not as soft as I'd like,' she said dubiously. 'I hope 'twill not irritate.'

'Beatrice will not put it skin close,' said Melissa. 'Never fear. 'Twill go over the linen sheet so don't fret on that score.'

Another bout of coughing from upstairs held her attention for a moment and she went to the bottom of the stairs and called up, 'I've a certain remedy for that cough, Thomas. I'll be up with it directly.'

His reply was lost in a further paroxysm of coughing

and Melissa tried to hide her concern as she hurried back to the simmering pot and stirred it vigorously, in an attempt to hasten its completion.

For a while neither of them spoke, then Maggie glanced out of the window. 'I thought I heard a voice,' she said and went to the window to peer out. 'Can't see a blessed thing, but I could swear I heard someone.'

She just had time to resume her knitting when there was a loud rat-tat on the front door. They looked at each other in surprise.

'You were right,' cried Melissa. 'Who can it be – with Thomas upstairs in bed and Jacob loaned to Heron until tomorrow?'

'You'd best answer it and find out,' said Maggie with another tug at her wool, and Melissa went through into the passage and along to the front door.

A dark-eyed woman stood outside holding a young child in her arms. She was poorly dressed and her shoes were worn but she smiled cheerfully. Her dark hair was covered by a shawl and her skin was a dark golden brown. The child, who looked about a year old, was wrapped in a coarse blanket. She, too, had dark hair which curled over her head but her eyes were grey. The woman put a finger to her lips and shook her head and then pointed to a wedding ring on her left hand.

'What do you want?' Melissa asked, at a loss to know what to make of them.

The child muttered something unintelligible and held out her arms trustingly towards Melissa.

'Forgive me but I don't understand,' she told the woman. 'Who are you and what do you want?'

Again the woman put a finger to her lips and the child copied the gesture, laughing as though sharing a joke.

Melissa considered them. They didn't look like gipsies, she decided. Most probably beggars. But then what was the significance of the wedding ring – unless to prove that she was a respectable woman now fallen on hard times? And why pretend to be dumb? It was such an old trick, popular with such unfortunates. And yet there was something appealing about the woman and there was nothing humble or subservient in her manner.

'Wait here,' said Melissa and went quickly back to the kitchen.

' 'Tis a woman and child,' she told Maggie. 'Come and see for yourself. 'Tis really most strange.'

Intrigued, Maggie put down her knitting and followed Melissa to the front door. The woman, seeing a new face, smiled broadly and again repeated the little mime, putting a finger first to her lips and then to the ring.

'What's your name?' Maggie demanded loudly and clearly. 'Say something. Tell us who you are.'

'Do you think she's a gipsy?' whispered Melissa.

Gipsies were notorious rogues and cheats and Melissa had no wish to fall for one of their many confidence tricks. It was said they had magic charms which could pull silver out of a purse without opening it.

'I don't know. She's shabby but not in tatters. They usually dress in gaudy rags.'

They looked at the woman and her child who both stared back amiably.

'I'll give them some food,' said Melissa, 'and send them on their way. 'Tis miserable weather to be traipsing the countryside but what more can we do? Will you watch them? We don't want her stealing while our backs are turned.'

In the kitchen she collected together a half loaf, a spiced sausage and half a cold chicken. She wrapped them in a cloth and poured a large mug of milk. These she carried back to the front door.

'I'm blessed if I can understand it,' said Maggie. 'She's pointing into the house and then to that blessed ring but the child's a bonny little mite.'

'Mayhap she's not dumb,' said Melissa, handing her the glass of milk and indicating that they should both drink. 'Maybe she's from foreign parts and knows no English – Drink it,' she prompted, for the woman hesitated and then shook her head. The child had no such qualms, however, and snatched the mug, drinking greedily. Melissa watched them uneasily. She wanted desperately to invite them in and warm them by the fire, but times were dangerous and no one was to be trusted if the stories currently told in the markets were to be believed. Only a week ago an old woman was swindled of ten gold sovereigns in return for which she was promised eternal life . . . and died the very next day! In Tavistock they told of a rich but lovesick maid who paid a gipsy woman handsomely for a love philtre and while the transaction took place at the back door, the gipsy's husband broke in at the front and stole a silver snuff box and a set of gilt spoons. Melissa did not condone such crimes and had no time for those who chose a life of crime, but she felt sympathy for those poor wretches who, thrown out of work, had somehow to survive and often resorted to such trickery when honest means failed.

She longed to take them in and feed and comfort them but she knew Thomas would never approve.

'Eat!' Maggie told the woman, but she shook her head, smiling broadly and pointed to her ring and then back along the path by which they had come. The child, exploring the contents of the cloth, seized the bread and began to eat it hungrily.

Nervously Melissa looked along the path.

'Most likely the husband is following close behind,' said Maggie in a low voice.

'Why does she smile so?' said Melissa. 'Surely a homeless beggar has little to smile about? And look – she still doesn't eat and 'tis all good food I've given them. The bread is fresh and the chicken cooked yesterday.'

'And the child has drunk all the milk.'

They watched the path, half-expecting to see the husband appear but there was neither sight nor sound of anyone. Around them the trees dripped moisture and the birds were silent, subdued by the unnatural gloom.

'Oh, this is impossible!' cried Melissa. 'I shall take them inside and warm them and—' She shrugged helplessly,

137

'And then decide what to do. How can I turn them away in this dreadful fog? I shall never sleep tonight thinking of them huddled under a hedge. Why 'tis enough to give them both a deathly chill.'

She looked at Maggie for her approval.

'And the husband?' Maggie asked. 'If he should follow?'

Melissa hesitated. 'He can sleep in the stable. No! He might steal the horses. Holy St Katharine! What's best to do? If he comes then they must *all* go. Aye, that's best.'

Maggie nodded. Knowing Melissa's generous nature she was already resigned to the outcome of the encounter. Melissa touched the woman's arm. 'Come inside,' she said and beckoned them to follow her – which the woman did most willingly. Maggie closed and bolted the front door and joined them. Having made her decision, Melissa proceeded to make the visitors welcome. Smiling, she took the child on to her lap, unwrapped the blanket revealing a worn gown. ' 'Tis a little girl,' she said and then handed her to Maggie. 'Cuddle her by the fire,' she told her. 'Her poor little hands are frozen.'

She turned to the woman who was removing her shawl and took it from her. 'Sit by the fire,' she said. 'Warm yourself.' And she upturned a log for her to sit on. 'I'll mull some wine. That will bring the colour back to your cheeks.'

Melissa bustled happily between the fire and the larder, talking cheerfully, aware that the woman watched her closely but made no attempt to sit down. They heard Thomas cough again and the woman glanced up, pointing in the direction of the sound and nodding delightedly.

'That's my husband,' Melissa told her. 'Thomas Benet and I am Melissa Benet and—'

Suddenly the woman seized her hand, kissed it and pressed it to her cheek affectionately. Over her head, Maggie and Melissa exchanged astonished glances.

Maggie said excitedly, 'She seems to think she knows you. Mayhap she has mistaken you for someone else. D'you think she has come to the wrong house? Or was she making for Heron – a friend or relative of one of the servants?'

Melissa sighed. 'Well, if she cannot speak we shall likely never know. She may be at the wrong house but she's welcome to stay the night. The fog may lift by morning and she will—'

She broke off for the woman had snatched the child from Maggie's lap and now thrust her into Melissa's arms. Then she pointed from the ring to the child and from the child to the absent husband.

Melissa's eyes widened. 'Sweet heaven!' she whispered. 'It surely cannot be and yet—' Her eyes met Maggie's and comprehension was dawning in her eyes also. She looked at the woman who, sensing her new understanding, nodded delightedly.

'They are Oliver's!' cried Melissa. 'Dear God! They are Oliver's! It must be so – and I almost turned them away. Oh, my dears!'

She kissed the child passionately and then held out her free arm to the young woman who moved eagerly into her tremulous embrace. Tears of joy streamed down Melissa's face and Maggie, watching, wiped away a few tears of her own. At that moment there were footsteps outside and the kitchen door was flung open and Oliver was home.

The next five minutes were a time of great confusion. Melissa, Maggie and Oliver all talked at once and hugged each other and asked a dozen questions that, in the excitement, were never answered.

'Oliver, you are so *changed*!' repeated Melissa. 'I would scarce have recognized you. Isn't he changed, Maggie? Oh, I cannot believe you are really standing before me. Tell me 'tis no dream, Oliver. You are really home? And with a wife and child? Oliver, how could you keep them from us for so long? Wait 'til Thomas learns you are home! He's in bed with a chesty cold but there's nought to fret about. 'Tis not serious, but the weather was so inclement – Oh, come here, little one. Come and kiss your grand-mama. You are so like your papa! The same neat chin and oval face – but your mother's eyes. But she is so light! Like a feather. We shall fatten you up, little one. Maggie shall make you some of her best pies. D'you like gooseberry tart, eh? And quince flan – or little mutton pies with a frilly edge to the pastry? Maggie will make you some. Maggie, you hold the little lamb – Go to Maggie, my pet.'

Oliver threw back his head and laughed aloud. 'Mama, you will smother them with kindness.'

'Oliver!' said Melissa. 'I shall go up now and take Thomas his linctus. I shall break the news to him gently that you are here and then you shall go up and see him.'

'Break it to him gently?' cried Oliver. 'You'll do no such thing. *I'll* go up – I want to see his face. Don't fuss, Mama, no one dies of happiness. You shall not rob him of the excitement. Here, give *me* the linctus and I'll surprise him.'

And, ignoring her protests, he took the jug and spoon and hurried upstairs. Melissa ran out after him and listened at the bottom of the stairs to Thomas' shout of joyful recognition then, unable to resist seeing his face, she ran upstairs and into the bedroom. Oliver knelt by the bedside and Thomas was patting his head as one would a dog. He glanced up at Melissa and his smile was radiant.

'I thought never to see him again,' he confessed. 'I never spoke of it but I thought it often and the thought tormented me. Oliver! See how you've changed. Look at him, Melissa.' She took one of her husband's hands in hers and together they regarded their son. 'How broad he's grown – look at his shoulders – and how fair. The sun has bleached it, I daresay. What happened to our young lad? He's a man now—'

Oliver said, 'And with a wife and child, Papa. They are downstairs.'

Thomas' jaw dropped. 'A – wife, d'you say?' He stared at Melissa. 'And a child?'

Melissa nodded.

'You are a grandfather,' said Oliver and Thomas gave a roar of delight.

Then he threw back the bed covers. 'A daughter-in-law and a grand-child and here I am lying in bed like an invalid. Get me my clothes, Lissa. What will they think of me?'

Pushing aside the proffered linctus he scurried around the bedchamber on his long thin legs. Oliver was secretly dismayed by the change in him. In his absence his father had become an old man. The blue eyes had faded. Gone were the brown curls to be replaced by grey. The once firm hands trembled slightly and the voice was huskier than he recalled. He watched as Melissa helped him into his best brown velvet and he nodded as Thomas turned to him for approval.

'Will I pass muster?' he demanded. 'A daughter-in-law and a grand-child! I must look my best.'

'They will be most impressed,' Oliver assured him. 'Nina will not speak to you, Papa. She is dumb – from what cause I know not – but she will hear and understand you. You will love her as I do.'

'Dumb?' Thomas was stopped momentarily in his tracks. 'No speech at all? Poor soul! But we won't touch on it, will we, Lissa? Come along now. No, Lissa, don't hold my arm. You will make Oliver think I am an old man!'

When all the introductions had been made and all the tears shed, Maggie set to work to prepare a meal of roast pig and onions and a pan of honeyed plums. While she worked the whole family crowded round the kitchen fire so that Maggie, too, should hear the telling of Oliver's story. He had seen them last seven years ago and, up to that time, been engaged on various ships that sailed from Plymouth, plying to and fro across the Channel, across to the Netherlands, or round the coast of England.

'And 'twas very dull,' he told them. 'I considered seriously that I might quit life at sea and come home to shear sheep or plant turnips! But then I thought how much duller *that* would be.' His laugh was unforced, with his head thrown back and his legs sprawled comfortably towards the fire. 'So I took up piracy!' he said as casually as he could and was rewarded, as he expected, with a stunned silence.

'Piracy, eh?' said Thomas at last, looking up from the child on his lap. He looked at Melissa for a lead on how to react to this piece of news. Maggie had paused also, the dish of plums halfway between fire and table and she, too, glanced at Melissa.

'Piracy?' said Melissa. 'But that's dishonest – and dangerous!'

'Aye, Mama, 'tis both of those things,' he told her, 'but 'tis also profitable and I've no wish to die a poor man when there's riches for the taking. I jumped ship and joined a privateer by the name of *Rockalleen*, a sweet little ship seized from Flemish traders a few months earlier with a cargo of wines.'

None of his listeners could think of a fitting comment when he paused and he laughed again at the look on their faces.

' 'Tis not so wicked,' he insisted. 'In truth, Mama, fortunes are being made every day on the high seas. You cannot imagine. The whole world is opening up. The high seas are full of ships of all nationalities and all loaded with rich cargoes. Where they go, pirates go! Drake has reached Panama and has seen the Pacific. The world is changed, Mama. 'Twill never be the same again. Gentlemen pirates grow wealthy on the proceeds, and even the Queen is not averse to foreign gold if it fills her coffers.'

'The Queen!' cried Melissa, finally spurred to protest. 'You'll not tell me, Oliver, that the Queen goes pirating or encourages such – such deeds!'

'Oh but she does!' said Oliver. 'She pretends grave dismay and wears a disapproving face in public and condemns piracy to the world, but she has frequently helped fit out the self-same vessels with her own money. Aye, and takes a good percentage of the prize money. 'Tis well known.'

142

'He's right, Lissa,' said Thomas. 'I've heard the same report.'

'But you don't look like a rich man, Oliver,' said Melissa. 'Your clothes are faded and your wife and babe like two waifs. Where's your good percentage of the prize, then?'

'We lost it all again,' he said cheerfully. 'We took a fine prize off the north coast of Spain – a squat little ship sixty feet long with a heavy top hamper. And could she roll!'

They had taken the ship, he told them, and abandoned the crew on an isolated stretch of Spanish coast and had sold the cargo in Portugal. With the profits they had re-provisioned the captured boat and partially refitted her to make her suitable for longer voyages. The two boats had then set sail for the Bay of Biscay in search of rich cargoes, but had run into foul weather and storms had shredded the rigging, so they had been forced to run her aground and make such repairs as they could. The time thus lost left them short of food and what they had was rapidly becoming inedible. The biscuits rotted and the beer turned sour in the heat.

'And you with your stomach!' Melissa marvelled. 'When I think how you jibbed at your food when you were so high—' She held out her hand. 'You could scarce keep down an egg at times – There's no cause for you to laugh behind your hand, Thomas. 'Tis the truth.'

'An egg would have been a luxury,' said Oliver, grinning at his father, 'but the poor hens in their wicker cages had gone to a watery grave, worked free of their lashings and washed overboard in the first storm. So – back we came again and lost a prize on the way, for we passed a Spanish galleon on the horizon but had too little sail to come up with her. Even if we had we'd scarcely a dozen men left well enough to stand, let alone fight.' He shook his head regretfully at the thought of their loss. 'So we put into Portsmouth and I left them and took passage on the *Rose of Taw*. Oh that was a ship and a half! The beautiful *Rose of Taw* was bound for the West Indies.'

Maggie, listening enthralled, worked on, refusing to let

Melissa help, insisting that she should feast her eyes on Oliver. Eventually, the meal was ready and they all sat round the table and Maggie watched proudly as they enjoyed the good food and wine she had set before them. What a home-coming! She thought how much better it was to be part of a family and no longer sole mistress of a bakery and, with the baby on her lap sharing her dinner, she ate with a good appetite and a happy heart.

Towards the end of the meal Melissa could no longer hold back the questions regarding Oliver's wife. She had told herself that she would wait until they were alone – at least until the girl was out of earshot. But the strain of knowing nothing of the background finally proved too much for her.

'Oliver,' she cried, 'tell us how you met your wife and her name. We do not even know that!' She smiled at the young woman as she spoke and received a friendly smile in return. 'How d'you *know* her name if the poor soul is dumb?'

It was Oliver's turn to smile, not at all embarrassed by the directness of his mother's questions.

'I don't know her real name,' he confessed, 'but I call her Nina. It seems to suit her and she likes it.' Nina nodded. She obviously understood the direction of their conversation. "Tis a simple story, how we met, and I'll tell it simply. The *Rose of Taw* was coming back from the West Indies when she met up with some scurrilous pirates!'

There was a roar of laughter.

'The biter bit!' said Thomas and Melissa tried to hide her trepidation.

'Aye, and most cruelly bit! They took our cargo and so damaged our ship that they thought we would never make it to shore.'

'They left you to sink and drown?' cried Melissa.

'Aye – and we'd have done the same in their shoes. And no doubt will if we ever meet up with them again. I'd give a lot to watch those wretches sink beneath the waves!'

Melissa looked at her husband, dismayed by Oliver's

aggressive talk, but Thomas gave her a sly wink and she was somewhat reassured.

'But we survived,' said Oliver. 'At least some of us did. The *Rose of Taw* went down and a lot of good men with her. Most of the crew couldn't swim. A few of us could and some of those that could reached dry land. A very few. I was one of them but I didn't know the fate of the other survivors. I was thrown up, literally, on a beach in Portugal and would surely have perished. I was barely conscious and my left leg was badly torn on the rocks. I had lost a great deal of blood and was very weak. Too weak to tend my wounds or find food and water. I lay on the beach all night and was quite resigned never to see the dawn.'

Melissa put a hand to her mouth to hide her emotion. She tore her eyes from her son and glanced at Nina, who stared at him with such a look of pure adoration that Melissa's heart went out to her in that moment. The child lay asleep in Maggie's arms, but Melissa fancied she could detect a likeness to her son.

'Don't fret, Mama,' said Oliver gently, seeing the tell-tale movement of Melissa's hand. 'You can see that whatever dangers I've encountered heaven has seen fit to preserve me. As I say, I thought I would die and most surely would have done so, but a dark-eyed girl appeared like an angel from heaven. She brought a pony and helped me on to it. Then she led me home to a rude little hut where she lived alone. Why I know not. She can't tell me. I only knew she had no man of her own for she wore no ring but of her father or brothers – or any family – I could learn nothing. My dear little Nina is a mystery and will probably remain so.'

Thomas shook her head slowly, marvelling at the story. 'But you are wed?' he asked. 'And the child is yours?'

'Most certainly! How could such a beautiful child have any other father? No, we are wed and little Della is my firstborn. The second born—' He paused, waiting for the significance of his remark to sink in.

145

'Another child?' cried Maggie. 'Nina is expecting another?'

There was an excited clamour of congratulations. He laid a gentle hand on Nina's abdomen and she nodded and smiled.

'But when?' said Melissa. 'She looks so trim.'

'June of next year most likely. There is plenty of time for you to get to know each other. I shall leave her in your capable hands.'

'Leave her? Oh, Oliver, you are not going away again? Say you will not leave us again.'

'But I must go, Mama. I am a poor man but determined to be rich. All we have at present is in the stable. I sent Nina and Della ahead to find you while I took the pack pony to Jacob. He has unloaded it by now and there is precious little. A few trinkets, pots and pans, a blanket or two.'

Thomas leaned forward. 'Finish your tale, Oliver. 'Tis not quite done and my head grows heavy with sleep. I don't wish to miss a single detail. 'Tis all so daring and I am so proud of you. I have had so few adventures in *my* life that I am doubly enjoying yours.'

There was a chorus of agreement and so Oliver finished his story. The dark-haired girl had cared for him as well as she could. Their food was frugal – fish from the sea, a few birds' eggs from the cliffs and milk from the goat. His recovery had been slow, but in all that time he had seen no other living soul, so remote were they from civilization. They had fallen in love and Oliver had determined to bring her back to Ladyford. They had followed the coast for many months, until at last they came upon a small fishing village where they begged a passage on one of the boats in return for Oliver's labour. From there they had sailed to a larger port and Oliver had joined the crew of another privateer, agreeing to ask no wages if Nina could accompany him. They landed up at Calais and then it was a comparatively simple matter to cross the Channel. They

146

were lucky enough to make Ladyford at Plymouth and had bought an ancient pony for their few items of baggage.

There was a long silence when he finally ended the story of his adventures.

'We stopped in Plymouth just long enough to be wed,' he said. 'She is very brave, don't you agree? To follow a perfect stranger to a foreign country and all with no language. She is an exceptional woman and very dear to me. I think she is Portuguese, yet she understands a few words of French but I want you to teach them both English. Nina must understand it even if she cannot speak it.' Melissa sighed deeply and looked at Thomas. They exchanged a glance of complete understanding and Melissa stood up.

'Enough talk for one night,' she said gaily. 'Thomas must go back to his bed and Maggie and I will make up beds for the rest of you. Set your heart at rest, Oliver. Your bonny family will be in good hands and will be most welcome to stay at Ladyford for as long as you wish. I don't need to tell you they will be greatly loved. As for you, you must come back safely and claim them. If you *must* go back to the sea then we shall do nothing to try and dissuade you. But dearest Oliver, you have been so long away. I beg you, do not leave us again too soon.'

The dark mists of November gave way to a cold, clear December. The gardens were white with frost each morning until the sun warmed them, but underneath dense shrubs the heavy frost persisted all day. The air was still and so sharp that it caught at the lungs of the careless and made them gasp and fall to coughing. The horses twitched restlessly in their stables and their breath formed small clouds of vapour with the cold air. Jon took every opportunity he could to light bonfires which Lorna and Piers attended. They roasted chestnuts and toasted bread on long-handled forks and then fed it to a family of ducks which had left the freezing water of the river and adopted the riverside garden at Heron as their temporary home. Thin ice formed overnight on the slow-moving pools around the tree roots, but the current shattered it each morning when the winter sunshine shone through the bare branches and thawed it. Squirrels returned to their nests and were rarely seen and any wild creatures that did venture out moved cautiously over the frosted earth.

James Ballantyne wrote to his daughter every week, although his letters did not reach Heron with the same regularity. Nevertheless they were a constant reminder to Maria and Hugo that Eloise's father was determined to safeguard his daughter's happiness.

Eloise's frequent replies kept her father informed of the situation.

He was told of Oliver's return to Ladyford and Allan's frequent visits there to talk or ride out with the cousin he had always admired. For nearly two weeks Allan had spent most of his days at Ladyford until Maria, in her role as peacemaker, had privately pointed out to him that he was neglecting Eloise. The latter, however, did not object to Allan's visits to Ladyford, but she did resent not being included.

She had met Oliver once only, when Allan had first introduced her as his bride-to-be. Oliver, she told her father, had been charming. He had kissed her hand and he had laughed a lot and told endless stories to amuse them.

On that occasion Eloise imagined that she read in his eyes a grudging admiration and hoped that he envied Allan. The dumb girl was scarcely competition, she thought, and yet the handsome sailor was obviously devoted to her and the child. Even Eloise could not pretend otherwise. She thought it likely, however, that as Nina's pregnancy developed her attractiveness would be diminished by a thickening figure and a certain loss of mobility. Eloise was appalled by what she considered Oliver's foolishness in marrying the girl, but she was careful to keep her opinion to herself. She wished he had come back to England fancy-free and allowed her imagination to dwell

148

on the possible consequences. She saw herself being admired, wooed even, by Allan, Martin *and* Oliver.

These fantasies were allowed rein whenever Allan left her to her own devices. She imagined how it would be if Oliver declared his love for *her* instead of the Portuguese peasant he had chosen. What a handsome couple they would make! It was true Allan was good looking in his own way, with his slim build, fair colouring and delicate bone structure. Martin was a contrast with strong dark looks, but Oliver – Ah, he had the edge on them both with his tall muscular body and those large grey eyes. Surely Oliver found her attractive? All men did . . . And then Martin came home for the holidays. Three handsome men to pay court to her beauty, she thought, and was looking forward to it more then she cared to admit.

Eloise contrived to be alone at Heron when Martin arrived. She had feigned a slight indisposition and kept to her bed. If Maria suspected she said nothing. She had promised a length of woollen cloth for a new gown for Della and had finally finished it. She rode over to Ladyford with it, intending to return in time to greet Martin. Hugo and Allan had gone to the mine. Only Minnie and Ellie remained at Heron and both were busy in the kitchen making a fresh supply of candles from the last of the tallow.

By mid-day Eloise was hungry, for she had refused breakfast as part of her deceit. She therefore dressed carefully and went downstairs to the kitchen.

Ellie looked up, glad of an excuse to stop what she was doing. 'Good morning, ma'am. Are you recovered?'

'I think so,' said Eloise. She moved carefully and sat down on a stool beside the table. 'I feel a trifle light-headed but—' She let her sentence die and put a hand to her temple.

Minnie clucked sympathetically. 'Probably an empty belly, ma'am,' she said. 'Begging your pardon, but you

149

should eat something. An egg lightly coddled or a little broth? Ellie shall get it for you.'

Ellie was off her stool in a flash and halfway to the larder.

'An egg then,' said Eloise. She was wondering what time they could expect Martin but, knowing how shrewd Minnie was, she wanted to phrase her enquiry carefully.

'I wonder what has befallen Martin,' she said. 'Maria will be fretting I don't doubt.'

'Fretting?' said Minnie.

'Aye. He was expected yesterday evening but—'

'No, ma'am, 'tis today he's expected and not before noon, he said in his letter.'

'Ah, how foolish of me. I was beginning to wonder if he had come to some harm.'

'Not Master Martin!' cried Ellie. 'He has a charmed life, they say.' She watched impatiently for the egg. 'Always in scraps, he was, as a little 'un, so my ma tells.'

Minnie nodded. 'Never knew what he'd be about – and usually something as was forbid! I pity the masters at that school of his.'

They laughed.

'And what of Allan?' asked Eloise casually. 'What sort of boy was he?'

'Why, real strange—' began Ellie eagerly, but was silenced by a warning cough from Minnie.

'He was a sweet lad,' said Minnie defensively. 'Quiet and gentle . . . the way he is now. And he had a way of looking and listening. Very deep, he was, and he adored Master Oliver. They were more like brothers than cousins, those two.'

Ellie brought the egg to the table and Eloise thanked her with a nod and began to eat hungrily. She did not want to interrupt Minnie who liked nothing better than to talk about 'bygone days' and who could be relied upon to know all the gossip.

'Master Allan was—' Minnie searched for the appropriate word.

'Strange?' offered Eloise pertly and Minnie shrugged.

'Well, I dare say that *is* the only word that properly describes him, but he was strange in a good way, if you take my meaning.' She glanced at Eloise who nodded again. 'He was somehow in tune with nature. Animals trusted him and he could mend a bird's wing or cure an ailing dog. And he spent hours on his own, listening to the trees, he once told me. And he had no fear of storms, or deep water, or such like. Once they say he let a hive of bees swarm round him and they didn't harm him. Not one of them.'

Ellie shuddered dramatically and Eloise smiled briefly as Minnie went on. 'Another time he went dowsing for tin, up on the moors with a queer old man. Oliver went too but he found nothing. 'Twas Allan had the power, you see.'

At that moment the dogs began to bark and Eloise jumped to her feet. 'That might well be Martin,' she said. 'I'd best go and greet him since there's no one else. Bring him some hot refreshment to the Hall but give him time to change his clothes. He'll be weary no doubt.'

This way she managed to ensure that she went out alone to stand on the front steps, arms outstretched in welcome. Martin had already dismounted and Jon had run out from the stables to shout a greeting and lead his horse away. The dogs leapt ecstatically as Martin climbed the steps.

'I'm afraid my greeting will have to suffice for the present,' said Eloise. 'There is no other mistress of Heron here.'

They embraced briefly and their eyes met.

'And will you one day *be* mistress of Heron?' he asked softly, for no word had reached him of a decision on the proposed betrothal.

'I will,' she said.

'So I am too late!' His tone was mocking but his gaze was direct. He had grown taller and she realized with a thrill that his thoughts were not those of a schoolboy, but of a young man faced with a desirable woman. The game they had started when they last met was to be continued. He would play the not-so-secret admirer. He would make up the triangle and would act as catalyst in the relationship between Eloise and Allan.

'Too late?' she echoed, pretending ignorance of his
.meaning.

'Too late to woo the fair damsel.'

She laughed, tossing her head with a provocative movement of her hair. 'Too late or too young?' she teased.

'Too late, I fear.' Martin glanced round hurriedly but
failed to see Ellie ensconced behind the door. Gently he
put a finger beneath her chin and tilted her head back. He
looked intently into her eyes and said, 'Do you believe me
too young? Then you are no judge of a man and I am
disappointed in you.'

He let his finger travel over her chin and then traced the
line of her lips, which parted eagerly.

'Then you *are* betrothed?' he insisted.

'Aye. The marriage contract is being drawn up.'

He exaggerated his dismay and she laughed again.

'But—' he whispered, 'suppose I will not cease my
wooing? What then?'

'What indeed?' said Eloise, enchanted with his persistence.

'Shall we fight a duel for your hand, sweet lady?'

'That would be delightful,' she said, adopting the same
mocking tone.

'So shall it be,' he said. 'But where is my fortunate
brother? And Maria and Hugo?'

She told him as they mounted the steps and went into
the house. Ellie, looking rather flustered, appeared with
the hot mulled ale and cinnamon cake and Eloise glanced
at her suspiciously.

'I said wait a while,' she reminded her, but Martin said
he would drink and eat and change his clothes afterwards.
A huge fire burned in the hearth in the Hall and more logs
were stacked alongside.

'Where are the children?' he asked as he ate ravenously,
scattering crumbs which the dogs licked up greedily.

'Spending two days with Beatrice in Exeter,' said Eloise,
'and so excited. But they will be home tonight so you will
have no peace.'

She sat opposite him and the firelight warmed her face and softened the gleam in her eyes. It shone also on Martin's blond head and they watched each other with silent satisfaction. They continued to converse wordlessly, exhilarated by their mutual attraction until the dogs, leaping up once more, announced the return of Hugo and Allan and Eloise was forced to relinquish him to the family.

A week before Christmas, the lake froze. It lay between Heron and Ashburton and frequently did freeze over. When that happened, people converged on it from both directions to skate and slide and generally enjoy themselves. This year was no exception. As soon as Matt reported that it was freezing over there was a concerted rush to find suitable footwear and Maria sent him down to Ladyford to pass on the good news and to invite them to a 'skating party' that very evening.

He returned with the message that Thomas would not join them, as his chest was still paining him and Melissa would stay at home with him. He had not been out of bed since the night Oliver returned and Melissa was in daily consultation with his physician. But Oliver, Nina and Maggie would be there – little Della was too young and would stay at home in the care of her grandmother.

'And don't you go tumbling over,' Melissa warned Nina then, remembering that she might not understand, she repeated her warning to Oliver. 'We don't want any accidents and falling on to ice is not going to do the unborn babe much good. You take care of her, Oliver, or you'll have me to reckon with!'

And Oliver, grinning broadly, gave her his most solemn word on the subject. So Maggie, Nina and Oliver rode over to Heron just as the light was fading and arrived to a cheerful welcome from Maria, who was checking the contents of two large baskets.

'I'm taking plenty of spiced ale,' she told them, 'and

Matt and Jon will light a fire beside the lake. Where is Jon?'

She shouted for him and he appeared in the doorway, his arms full of kindling wood.

'I'm here, ma'am.'

'Jon, don't forget to take some sheepskins for us to sit on. They're in the big chest in the barn. If they're damp you must dry them off by the heat of the fire. Oh – and a small barrel of cider. Ask Minnie. Has Jack got the pony ready? Do go and see. I thought we'd forgo the fish this year,' she said. ' 'Twas Martin, I think, last year, got a bone in his throat. 'Tis too dark, even by fire light, to see properly – Ah! The torches. Jon! Come back!'

He reappeared, sighing audibly and muttering that his arms were growing cramped.

'Stop grumbling,' said Maria, 'and tell Matt to prepare a few torches. Three or four will do, for there'll be others there and 'tis a clear night. The moon will be shining later. And Jon! Bring the bellows. We may need it for the fire.'

Only then did she pause in her organizing to kiss the visitors, with an especially warm kiss for Nina. She rubbed her hands together, blew on her fingers and said, 'Cold!'

Nina nodded, copied her actions and silently mouthed the word.

'Well done!' said Maria. She turned to Oliver. 'Will this poor girl *ever* regain her speech, I wonder? Not that it seems to distress her. She has a sunny disposition, thank the Lord, but we must pray for her recovery. Now, where was I? Bread, butter, cheese – Oh, we must remember to take a spit or we shall dine off raw chicken! Ugh! I'd best see to that, since Jon has removed himself. Ah, here's Eloise. You look bonny, my dear. That deep red becomes you. Doesn't she look lovely, Allan? Now, the spit—' And she hurried out, leaving them all to make their 'hellos'.

The cavalcade that finally set off was a large one. Maria and Hugo led the way at a walking pace, with Allan and Eloise close behind. Oliver and Nina rode together as did Lorna and Piers, and Maggie rode with Martin. The servants followed on foot with Jon leading the well-loaded pony and Matt, Minnie, Jacob, Ellie and Ben bringing up the rear. As they came in sight of the lake and were recognized, a cheer went up from people around it, for the Kendals were well liked and everyone was curious to see Oliver's new wife. Nina gasped as the scene unrolled before them. The frozen lake glistened with the light of the bonfires already burning, and brightly dressed skaters slid and slithered over the ice, shrieking and laughing excitedly. A spit turned over each fire and the smell and crackle of roasting fish filled the air and mingled with the smoke and sizzle of pork and mutton. A few torches had been stuck in the ground immediately around the lake and the flames illuminated the skaters with a ghostly flickering as they circled and swooped. Some skated, with bones strapped to their shoes. Others ran and slid, arms outstretched with the effort of balancing. Here and there a child crouched and was pulled along by his friends. A boy towed two little girls on a wooden toboggan. The Tucker family were also there. Maria and Hugo waved to them and exchanged a few pleasantries as they rode past, but the two families were no longer close.

'Who are they?' Eloise asked Allan.

'The Tuckers? Oh, they were once our neighbours. They lived at Maudesley.'

'The big empty house you showed me?'

'Aye. 'Tis a shame to let it fall into disrepair but they built a new house further away. I hardly know them, but they were once connected to us by marriage. They also mine for tin. Joseph Tucker married my great-grandmother after her husband died and his daughter, Blanche, wed one of the Kendal sons – Matthew, I believe it was.'

'But where are their descendants?'

'There are none living. They had one daughter and she was never wed. Martin, Piers and I are the sole survivors!'

She laughed at the expression. 'And you are the sole *true* heir.'

'Aye.'

Eloise nodded with satisfaction. 'So I must give you plenty of sons.'

'One, at least!'

Oliver came alongside and the two men dismounted and began to talk to several of the Tuckers who had walked over. One was an elderly woman and the other a middle-aged man, neither of whom interested Eloise. She was annoyed that Allan had not helped her dismount, although all the other women in the party seemed to be managing quite well without assistance. Maggie and Maria were already unpacking the basket and Jon and Matt were preparing the fire. Eloise glanced round and saw Nina slide from her horse – a hired mare – but then suddenly Martin was standing beside her. With a flourish he took off his hat.

'Sweet mistress, allow me the honour to assist you,' he said and his eyes glinted with mischief. 'Don't fall,' he warned as he held up his arms but he winked as he said it. Accordingly Eloise allowed herself to fall clumsily and gave a little cry of pretended alarm. His arms closed round her instantly. For a few heady moments she was imprisoned within his arms and his lips brushed hers in the briefest kiss.

'I have caught you,' he said. 'You are quite safe.' He released her but his eyes did not leave her face as he added softly, 'But I doubt *I* am!'

'My ankle!' she murmured. 'I fear I twisted it as I fell.' She met his bold look with one of wide-eyed innocence and then as he hesitated, lowered her voice and said, 'Won't you please examine it for me? I would take it most kindly.'

'Would you? Then I will.'

She steadied herself with a hand on her horse's saddle as she raised her right foot. Martin knelt down, lifted the hem of her skirt and kissed her ankle, sending a thrill leaping through her.

Suddenly Allan's voice broke the spell. 'What's this?' he snapped, his voice harsh with suspicion. 'Martin? What's happening, I say?'

Martin looked up calmly. ' 'Tis her ankle. She slipped as she dismounted.'

'I think 'tis twisted,' said Eloise. In her excitement she did not trouble to disguise the lie. 'Martin was kind enough to—'

Martin said quickly. 'Put your full weight on it. Try it.'

Allan was no longer looking at them but at her foot. Eloise did as Martin instructed and grimaced slightly as though in pain.

' 'Tis not as bad as I feared,' she said.

For a moment no one spoke then Allan said, 'You had best not skate then, with a twisted ankle.'

'Oh, but—'

'Mayhap you would like to return home and rest it.'

'No, Allan—' she protested, trying to conceal her dismay. It was all a game, she knew. Allan had not been fooled, but they would protest their innocence if he challenged them and he could prove nothing.

Martin stood up and she gave him a furious look. She did *not* want to miss the skating *or* be sent home! He avoided her eyes.

'I think if you rest it a little,' he suggested mildly, 'there is no real damage. You can skate later.'

She nodded. Allan seemed about to argue the point but then he changed his mind, swung on his heel and abruptly rejoined Oliver. Eloise saw that Nina stood nearby, watching the little scene, and wondered how much the girl had seen and understood. Impossible to tell, for the girl's dark eyes stared impassively into hers. Eloise was disconcerted but not for long. The girl might well have seen and understood but she was dumb.

Just then Lorna came running up. 'Eloise! Come and skate with me and hold my hand.'

'I'll help you,' added Piers.

Lorna shook her head. 'He'll let me fall. I know it. Eloise, *you* come with me.'

Martin said loudly, 'Eloise has hurt her foot and must rest it awhile. Here, take my hands. I'll skate with you.'

Jon glanced up from the fire as they passed. 'Don't go

into the middle,' he warned. 'They say 'tis very thin. Keep to the edges and you'll be safe enough.'

Matt, skewering chickens on the spit, laughed boisterously, his eyes gleaming. 'I'll be skating afore long, you see if I don't!' he shouted. 'I'm a rare one for skating, I am. You'll see.'

Maria smiled at him affectionately. 'You're a "rare one" at everything, Matt,' she teased. 'Just finish the chickens and baste them and then join the others. Maggie and I are quite content to stay by the warm fire. We'll watch the food for a while. Do you want to skate, Jon? Then go, but keep an eye on Piers, will you? He's much too bold and will take foolish risks. And light the torches and take them with you to set at the water's edge.' She turned towards Eloise, who was spreading out the sheepskins – 'Aren't you going to skate?' she asked in surprise. 'Allan and Oliver are down there, and Martin.'

Eloise repeated the lie about her ankle and was thankful that Maria accepted it without question. She sat down and Nina joined her for a while. Then Oliver returned for her and, promising to take care of her, led her towards the lake.

There were more people now and the skating area was ringed with torches. Above them a full moon shone, cold and white, and the dark sky was speckled with stars. Time passed and finally Allan came to ask Eloise, sarcastically, if she was fit enough to skate. She said she would rest a little longer and he left her again without a word. A few moments later Nina came back and settled herself on the sheepskin, indicating to Maria that *she* would watch the chickens if Maria and Maggie wanted to skate. Maggie replied that they did and dragged Maria with her, leaving Nina and Eloise. Nina gave the spit handle a turn and Eloise, watching her, was struck by the girl's calm manner and serene expression. She almost envied her. She had an adoring husband and was with child and was being petted and pampered by all at Ladyford! She had good reason to be pleased with her lot!

'Will you skate with me?'

It was Martin. Eloise was tempted to refuse him also,

but that way she would be the loser for she would get no skating. By way of answer she held out her hands and Martin pulled her to her feet.

'Will Allan object?' he asked as they walked to the edge of the lake.

'He may,' she answered sharply. ' 'Tis of no interest to me.'

He looked at her in the light from the torches and marvelled at her beauty. The warm glow hid the hard expression in her eyes and softened the haughty line of her jaw. Her long lashes shadowed her eyes, making them dark and mysterious, and her lips were slightly parted to reveal her even teeth, which showed palely in the gloom. She wore red and the material, catching the light, gleamed where it curved over her breasts.

'Eloise!' The word was drawn from him. He had not intended it. Nor was he aware of the desire evident in that one word. He knew only that his blood pounded and his heart hammered against his ribs. Eloise, too, was aware of his excitement and her own body seemed to spring into life and vibrate with a dangerous passion. She had aroused him and the knowledge quenched all her anger, leaving her at the mercy of her own emotions. He is so young yet almost a man, she thought.

'Eloise! You've recovered I see.'

Allan's voice was as cold as the ice on which he stood. He held out his hand to her but she could not, would not, take it.

'Shall we skate as a threesome?' she suggested lightly.

'No,' he said. 'You will skate with me.'

Allan saw her as an enchantress – her lips pouting seductively and her eyes promising ecstasy. He glanced at his younger brother and saw the desire which Martin made no attempt to conceal.

'Or mayhap you will skate with me?' said Martin coolly.

Both men waited for what seemed an eternity.

'I cannot decide,' she said at last. 'Suppose you make the decision for me. I propose that you skate across the lake – straight across . . . and I shall skate with whoever reaches the other side first.'

Eloise knew that the ice was dangerously thin in the middle of the lake. She did not know how deep the water was, but she did not care. If they were both so determined to partner her they must prove themselves worthy. And the best man would win.

'Supper's ready!' called Maggie and there were answering shouts from the skaters. Allan and Martin continued to look at Eloise. Race, she urged them silently. Take up the challenge if you are so besotted. Men are such fools!

Now Maria was calling to them and Oliver passed, laughing and out of breath, with Minnie puffing and panting behind him and Piers and Lorna declaring that they were starving.

'The food is ready,' Piers told them and Eloise nodded her head to show that they had heard.

Matt lumbered by, boasting of his prowess on the ice, and Ellie and Ben danced after him, wildly exaggerating their own exploits.

Eloise, Allan and Martin were left behind and suddenly it seemed that everyone was eating or relaxing on the grass and the lake was quite deserted.

'Well?' said Eloise with a slight lift of her eyebrows.

Allan cursed her, then turned and began to skate across the pond. Martin followed him, a few yards behind. She watched breathlessly and her heightened senses throbbed with sudden fear. From behind her a cry went up and she recognized Jon's voice calling a warning.

The cry was taken up on all sides of the lake but her attention was riveted on the two figures mid-way across the grey expanse. Allan was now past the middle and miraculously the ice held. He was slimly built and skated at speed. Martin, heavier and less sure, reached the middle a few yards behind his brother. But Allan's weight had already strained the ice and now a sharp 'crack' was heard and a thin dark line spread across the ice as it parted under Martin. He threw up his arms soundlessly and was gone. There was a scream from Maria and then Allan turned and Eloise, seeing the horror in his eyes, felt a wave of panic which robbed her of all movement. She stood as though rooted to the spot and stared at the black water which spread slowly over the ice. As though in a nightmare, she watched Allan fling himself down on to the ice and begin to edge his way forward towards the spot where Martin had disappeared. Everywhere men ran forward, shouting to one another. A rope was produced and flung across the ice and Oliver and Allan edged forward from opposite sides towards the centre. As they went they beat at the ice ahead of them, and at last a large sheet broke free and for a moment Martin's head bobbed into view, only yards from Oliver's outstretched arms. Oliver slid forward and grabbed Martin by the hair and then the ice broke again and they were both in the water. Matt and Jon and another man hauled on the rope and drew the two cousins towards the thicker ice. Somehow they were pulled up on to it and out of immediate danger.

Martin was barely conscious but he opened his eyes almost at once and allowed Maria to force hot mulled wine between his chattering teeth. Oliver was also chilled through and they were both taken back to Heron as quickly as possible. Maria, Maggie and Hugo rode with them, but they insisted that the rest of the party should finish their meal. The excitement died down and the crowd at the lakeside dispersed. It was no longer possible to skate on the broken ice and a promising night's sport had been ruined. The disappointed people made their way home and within the hour there was no one left. The moon shone on the dying fires as a solitary dog made his way among them, snapping up any scraps of food that remained. The ice cracked as it settled and the sound alerted him but, sensing no danger, he finished his rounds and trotted slowly away.

CHAPTER EIGHT

Devon, May 1576

Hugo rubbed his eyes tiredly and began to straighten the papers and books that littered his desk. It was nearly eleven o'clock and at any moment the bell would go to end the morning shift. Then the tinners would start coming up to the surface, swaying in their leather 'bucket' as the windlass men winched them into the daylight after their seven hours' labour underground. It was hard work and they were hard men. Theirs was a labour of unrelieved effort in uncongenial conditions, but they took a perverse pride in their profession – they were proud people. A hundred fathoms or more under the ground, they sweated and swore together, hewing the tin ore with their picks, loading it into the trucks, hauling it back along the tunnel to the shaft bottom where it would be raised by others. They worked in semi-darkness, the blackness broken only by the light of their oil lamps, and frequently stood in pools of muddy water which never drained away fast enough, in spite of all their efforts. As they cut into the veins of tin, the water trickled down the rock face and their long leather boots were soon sodden and uncomfortable. Add to these discomforts the hazard of roof falls, flooding and the noxious sulphur fumes which sometimes seeped from fissures in the rock – in all it was a wretched existence. The money they earned was never enough to pay the physician when years of gritty dirt finally ruined their lungs and choked them into early graves. It was a grim existence. But, thought Hugo ruefully, tell them that existence was about to end and there would be a violent outcry.

He stood up and eased his back. He had been sitting

there for the last two hours, studying the facts and figures which he knew by heart, trying, even at the last moment, to find another solution. With no success. Some of the men would have to go and he could no longer delay telling them. He sighed deeply then shouted for Barlowe, the mine manager. Barlowe would stay. He was a truculent, violent man, but he was by far the most experienced man on the payroll and Hugo valued him. He was respected, too, by the other tinners, and there were few who would dare go against him. Hugo had given him a hint of the impending changes so he, at least, would not be entirely surprised.

'Aye, sir?' He appeared at the door already dressed for the next shift.

'Keep the next shift on the surface, Barlowe,' said Hugo. 'And don't let the last lot disperse. I must speak to all the men in the yard twenty minutes from now. The women, also, from the washing shed.'

He saw Barlowe's eyes narrow and waited for the question, but the man thought better of it and merely nodded and withdrew. The Heron mine employed twenty women and young girls. In the washing shed they sorted the rough ore which came straight from the trucks, washing off the mud and separating unwanted soil and rock fragments before it went into the crazing mill to be crushed. They were mostly wives and daughters of the miners, almost as tough as the men themselves. They came miles across the moors each day, mostly on foot and, apart from one or two troublemakers, they were a cheerful crowd. Hugo looked distractedly round the hut which served as both store and office. The womenfolk would not be cheerful much longer, he thought. Hell and damnation, he muttered, I wish to God it could be otherwise!

Through the window he could see the line of miners waiting for the next shift. Barlowe was talking to them and he could read the apprehension on their faces. As the manager left them and crossed to the windlass man to repeat the message, the line of men broke into small groups and their talk was agitated. Men coming off-shift handed in any oil which remained in their lamps and joined the others. Hugo waited nervously. Only half a dozen men had come up so far. There were another nineteen waiting below in blissful ignorance. Barlowe now made his way to the washing shed and within minutes the women came swarming out like angry bees, some talking among themselves, others making for their menfolk. Ten minutes later Hugo was standing on an upturned barrel and nearly a hundred faces, lit by the warm sunlight, were upturned towards him.

' 'Tis never easy to impart bad news,' said Hugo bluntly and a ripple of dismay swept through his audience, 'but I won't insult your intelligence by pretending otherwise. I've delayed it as long as I was able but to keep the facts from you any longer would be sheer folly. The Heron mine is no longer making enough profit to support us all – you've probably guessed that for yourselves. The men know how little ore we've taken over the last nine months. Maybe they've told the womenfolk, maybe they've kept it to themselves. No one cares to bear ill news and I'm no exception to that.'

He paused and swallowed. Their silence, after the first murmur, unnerved him. He cleared his throat and tried to remember the carefully chosen phrases he had prepared with which he meant to soften the blow, but they had all deserted him. 'I've paid the wages as long as I dared but there's no longer enough money to meet the bill. The mine is not producing enough tin. The tin we do produce fails to earn enough money. The little money we have no longer pays for oil, for your lamps, wood to shore the tunnels, tools to dig.'

He paused again. Still that awful silence and those impassive stares. What were they thinking? he wondered uneasily. He let his gaze travel over them and one woman in the front now lowered her eyes and scuffed the ground with the toe of her worn shoe. She looked undernourished and her dark hair was scraped back in an unbecoming knot. He could not put a name to the face.

'The situation is bad,' he went on. 'I won't pretend 'tis otherwise. The men know that of the three veins we're working one is run out, one is giving poor quality ore, and the third and most recent one is not yet fully proven. We have lost three of our best customers in one year – the two London pewterers and the Flemish company.' At last there was a response – a low, shocked murmur. 'They have gone elsewhere for their tin and we are helpless to stop them. We will never win them back. The Cornish mines are thriving while we in Devon – Oh aye, Heron is not alone in her plight – while we in Devon dwindle and fail. 'Twas not always so, but tin is fickle stuff and now it eludes us.' They were suddenly fidgety and Hugo decided the time had come to tell them the worst, before their mood changed from grey to black.

'Some of you will have to go,' he said. The murmur grew and a few voices were raised above the rest. 'Those that do will each have a week's wages and the promise that when . . .'

'We can't live on promises!' shouted someone at the back of the crowd.

'. . . that as soon as 'tis possible – if *'tis* possible – they can come back to us.' The muttering grew louder and Barlowe shouted to them to listen to what was being said. They fell silent again and Hugo went on. 'I'm going to get rid of a third of the men and half the women . . .' There was a fresh outcry and the shouts were definitely hostile now. 'Be thankful 'tis not *all* of you!' he shouted. 'Next month or the month after it may well come to that.'

The voices trailed into silence as the extent of the disaster was understood. 'I've thought this out most carefully and I've tried not to lose more than one wage earner in each family. More than that I could not do. I shall read out the list presently, but before I do I've a word of hope and I trust you'll hear me out. The Heron mine needs modernizing if 'tis ever to pay its way again. We need new methods and new machinery – Oh aye,' he raised a hand to silence their protests, 'I know you care little for change. 'Tis always so. But let me tell you this – without modernization this mine will be closed forever within a year. That's no idle threat but stark reality. And if the Heron mine goes we *all* go!'

Somewhere in the middle of the crowd a woman began to sob and the sound provoked a fresh protest, but one in which their previous hostility was touched with fear. A man stepped forward from the front row and shouted, 'Read the list!' but Hugo shook his head firmly.

'The list is last,' he told them. 'I've more to say yet and I want all of you to hear me and understand the reasons for my plans. Many of you may recall my absence earlier in the year.' There was a chorus of 'ayes'. 'I went abroad to take advice from a company that mines at a profit and most likely always will. The name of the company is of no significance, but I saw there the new methods of working that I spoke of and new machinery which *we* should be using.'

'Where's the money coming from?' shouted one of the men. 'If you've no money for our wages then you've none for fancy machinery!' A great roar of approval greeted him and it was some time before Hugo could regain their attention.

'I don't know where the money will come from,' he told them. 'I'll try and borrow it. If not we'll have to make the machinery with wood from our own trees. To do that I need someone with more knowledge than I possess – and with more knowledge than any of *you* possess. Don't misunderstand me. You are all skilled men and proud of it, and rightly so. But we need someone with new knowledge and new skills and I have found such a man. Hans Bucher is his name and he comes from Austria.'

A fresh outburst greeted this remark and he let the buzz die down before continuing.

'Hans Bucher is a mining expert – a consultant engineer with eleven years' experience. I've offered him a job at

Heron and he'll start as soon as he arrives at the end of the month. In a month or so, I may be able to offer more work to some of you. I say maybe. 'Tis by no means certain. If all goes as planned another three months and more of you should be re-employed. But – I can make no promises. And now I am nearly done. Remember, all of you, that without Hans Bucher we are probably finished. He is our best chance of survival. His coming could make a difference to the lives of each one of you. We need him. Heron needs him and we need his experience. He has spent the last six years in the most modern mine in Austria. With his help we could be the most modern mine in the West Country. Bucher deserves your respect and your support. For all our sakes I welcome his coming.'

Then he unrolled the list and immediately the shouting died away as the faces turned back to him and fear silenced all but the beating of their hearts.

'The women first – Marion Shorne, Sylvia Haddon, Bess Lovell, Rita Carp—' As he read on, he was aware of the shocked faces and whispered prayers and it was all he could do to keep his voice steady. His wildest imaginings had not prepared him for the feeling that he had betrayed these loyal workers – men and women who not many years since had danced at his wedding, or named their children after him and Maria. He wanted to throw down the list, run away from those accusing faces and hide. Instead he read on steadily. 'And now the men – Thomas Betts, John Green, Sam Tiddons, Alec Boord—' He glanced up. One by one the unfortunates bent their heads or covered their faces, hiding their shame and grief from their fellows. Somehow Hugo finished the list. 'If these people will attend at the office they'll receive their money,' he said. 'I'm sorry 'tis come to this. Much sorrier than you can guess at—'

'Not as sorry as us, though!' cried a voice and Hugo could only bow his own head in mute reply. He stepped down and strode into the office. He supervised Barlowe's distribution of the money and waited until the crowd dispersed, some to go home, others to go down for the afternoon shift.

Then he too went home, the taste of defeat strong in his mouth. He stopped his horse as he reached the brow of the hill and looked out on the moor where people straggled homeward, some of them thanking God for their deliverance, others cursing the devil for their loss. 'They are my people,' he whispered, 'and I must help them. Hans Bucher is our only hope.'

And he turned his face homeward and rode on with a heavy heart.

Alec Boord went home with murder in *his* heart. He was a small swarthy man in his fifties and already his lungs were diseased and this breathing was stertorous. He could no longer sleep in a horizontal position but sat up all night, propped against the wall and dozed fitfully. His wife Annie was a tall gaunt woman with large bones and a sour disposition. They had had five children. The first had died at birth, the second lived three years and was run down by a turf wagon. The third and fourth, twin boys, lived a few months before succumbing to an attack of dysentery and the fifth, a girl, was now eighteen and had run away from her loveless home and married a tinker. The Boords had never seen her again and had no wish to. Their life was a succession of days and nights. They quarrelled often and both drank to excess whenever they could afford to. Now they could not afford to. Alec Boord had lost his job. Annie, crippled with rheumatism, had not worked for the past seven years. They were bitter, lonely people and Alec's dismissal was the last of a series of disasters from which, it seemed, they would never escape.

'A week's money?' echoed Annie as her husband slammed down the handful of coins. 'Just that?'

'I'll kill him!' said her husband. He sat down heavily on a stool and stared at the small fire over which a black kettle hung.

'Who?'

'Kendal, the bastard! I'll kill him. I swear I will. A week's money and a lot of sweet talking and barely a thank you.'

He kicked the log further into the blaze and it sent up a flurry of sparks which disappeared into the roof. 'Forty-one years I've sweated for him and this is what I get!' He spat derisively and his wife watched him, letting him rant on, her thoughts busy with the immediate problems of food and warmth. Thank God summer was on its way!

'Hans Bucher!' he told her. ' 'Tis him we've to thank for this. Hans Bucher, a so-called expert. A so-called engineer. He's being brought over, no doubt at great expense, to take the work from men like me. What does a so-called expert know about mining? Damned foreigner! I'll warrant he's never sweated a seven hour shift, gasping for breath, shivering with cold—'

'You and who else?' snapped his wife. 'Who else is sacked?'

'Oh, there's plenty to keep me company. Tiddons has gone, and Tom Betts, Green, Simmons, old John Jenkins – and him with seven mouths to feed. He's a poor worker, granted, but he's older than most and he's never missed a day's work in his life, poor sod!'

'No more have you.'

'Aye. No more have I but it comes to the same thing. God's mercy, I could kill him with my bare hands.'

'Don't talk so wild, Alec Boord.'

'You'll talk wild when *that's* spent!'

'We won't starve,' she said. 'We never have.'

'I've never lost my job before,' he cried.

'You'll manage. Catch fish or a rabbit. There's ways.'

'Or a pheasant or a lamb! Want me to hang, do you?'

'Don't talk so soft.' Her fear sharpened her tongue. 'If you've lost your job you must find another. Not sit there on your arse, moaning. *If* there's any other work to be found it'll go to the first that asks.'

He gathered up the coins and flung them suddenly across

the room. 'Hans bloody Bucher! I'll kill him, too! He'll wish he'd stayed in Austria. I'd wring his neck till his eyes start out of his head!'

She got up slowly, moving with difficulty, and began to collect up the money. 'Have you talked to the others? What've they to say to it? I'll wager Simmons'll not take it lying down, nor Betts neither.'

'I talked to no one but I will. Aye, we'll put our heads together.'

'Well don't come up with any crack-brained notions, Alec Boord. If you hang, what happens to me? They'll not give me a bunch of flowers and shake my hand, that's for certain. What about the Tuckers' mine – Maudesley or whatever they call it? There's maybe work there.'

'Maudesley? God woman, the Maudesley mine is miles away! Twice the distance to Heron. By the time I'd walked home 'twould be time to go back.'

She straightened up with an effort and put the money into her apron pocket.

'On the table with it,' snapped Alec. 'That money comes back to me and no arguments. I'm in no mood for it.'

'It stays where 'tis,' she said defiantly. 'If this is all we've got I'll not have you drink it away.'

He leapt to his feet and struck her across the side of the face. She fell backwards off the stool and he stood over her as she fumbled for the coins. When she held them out, he struck her hand from underneath so that the coins flew again. He leaned over her, threatening her with his clenched fists, muttering a string of obscenities, then strode to the door. He slammed it and stood outside, amazed that the moor was so beautiful while life was so hideous.

'Hans Bucher is it?' he muttered. 'Bloody foreigners!' Having found a scapegoat, he felt a little better, a little more in control. This was not the end. It couldn't be. There had to be a way. Scowling, he whistled and a small terrier appeared, its head well down, its tail between its legs. Boord hesitated and then set off towards Simmons place, the dog trotting warily a short distance behind him.

*

170

Lorna wanted to cough, but she dared not for fear of disturbing the fish which, at any moment, would snap at Nat's line. Instead she swallowed hard several times. She stood quietly behind Nat who sat under a willow, his gaze fixed on the cork which floated a few yards from the water's edge. Beside him was a stone jar full of water in which several minnows swam. She leaned forward and whispered, 'What will you catch?'

'A perch,' he answered.

'How do you know 'twill be a perch? It might be a pike.'

' 'Twill be a perch.'

She looked around. 'Where's Brin?' she asked.

'Off about his own business, little monkey, but no doubt will be back when his belly rumbles.' He glanced up at her, squinting into the sunlight. 'And where's that animal of yours?'

She scowled. 'Gone otter hunting with the others. They said I was too young.'

'So you came to plague me, is that it?'

'Do I plague you, Nat?'

He smiled. 'Reckon I can bear it,' he said, 'as long as you don't frighten the fish.'

Lorna sighed. 'I wish *I* had a rod,' she said.

'But you haven't, so sit by me and tell me softly what news of Heron. I haven't seen you for more than a month – Ah!' He pulled on the rod and a small fish came into view. Lorna giggled but Nat lowered it gently into the water again.

'Was that a perch? 'Twas very small,' she said innocently.

He grinned. 'That was the bait, as well you know! The perch will see the minnow and snap it up and then *I* shall snap *him* up.'

'Is a perch much bigger than a minnow?'

'Much bigger. You'll see.'

She settled herself on the grass beside him and stared earnestly at the cork which moved slowly over the surface of the water. 'And what if it doesn't snap at the minnow?' she asked.

'Then I shall try another bait. A brandling worm or maybe a small frog. Or even a small girl!'

She gave a little scream and glanced at him anxiously. 'A fish won't snap at a girl,' she said. 'Will it?'

He laughed. 'The perch is a very bold biter,' he told her. 'I knew a man once dabbled his toes in the water to see how cold it was and snap! The perch had him by the toe and in two shakes of a lamb's tail had tumbled him into the river and pulled him away so fast that he was never seen again.'

Lorna thought about it and then shook her head. 'I don't believe you,' she said.

He shrugged by way of answer and continued to study his cork. 'How's that brother of yours – young Piers?' he asked. 'Gone away to school yet?'

'Not yet. He goes in September and a good riddance. He teases me and Mama scolds him.'

'You'll miss him when he goes – Ah! Another bite. Now stay still . . .' Deftly, he began to play his fish, guiding it into the shallows. 'The net!' he told her. 'Take up the net and put it into the water – Oh! he's gone again. Slipped away, and look, he's taken the minnow! I told you he was a bold biter. And strong too. That was a big fish. But this time we'll try a frog.'

He pulled a grimy cloth from his pocket and carefully unwrapped a small green frog.

Lorna watched fascinated as he slipped the hook through the loose skin of the frog's leg. ' 'Tis still alive!' she screamed, seeing the frog wriggle.

'Aye. He must be, then he'll swim up and down in the water and the perch will say "minnow for dinner, frog for dessert".'

'Will he?'

'Aye, he will. You'll hear him if you listen hard.'

When the frog was fastened to his satisfaction he swung it into the water with hardly a splash and the two of them settled down again to watch and wait.

'And what of the baby that's due at Ladyford?' asked Nat. 'Is that born yet?'

The little girl shook her head. ' 'Tis soon though and Nina is so fat! I shall have a baby when I grow up.'

'You'll need a husband first.'

'I shall wed Martin.'

Nat laughed. 'He's your half brother. You can't wed *him*!'

'Oliver, then. He has gone back to sea but when he comes home again.'

'He has a wife already!'

Her face fell then brightened suddenly. 'Then you, Nat! You haven't got a wife.'

'No, I haven't. Nor like to. Nought but a trial, women. I'd sooner stay single.'

'Then I'll wed Hans Bucher,' said the little girl. 'He's a good man and Papa says he is sharp as a needle. Papa says he has a brilliant mind. He is only thirty-one and I shall ask him to wait for me. He has a small beard that tickles and he smells of lavender water.'

'Does he indeed!'

'Aye. He and Papa are going to build a big machine. They will have to build it down the mine for 'twill be too big to go down the shaft. And they will have a pony to turn the wheel.'

'A pony?' Nat turned to stare at her. 'A pony down a mine?'

'Aye. He will live down there and have a comfortable bed of straw and they will take his dinner down.'

'A pony down a mine! And this is Master Bucher's idea?'

'Aye.'

'And what do – Ssh! Keep very still and quiet!' he whispered. 'Here's another. He liked the frog! And this – time – I'll *have* him!' With a swift smooth movement he landed the fish and it lay floundering on the grass behind them. It was over a foot in length and its deep body was covered in thick, dry scales. Two large fins stood up from its back and sharp teeth were visible inside the large mouth. Quickly he extracted the hook and slipped the fish into the net.

'Feel how heavy it is!' he told her proudly. ' 'Twill cook very sweetly for my supper. So, will you catch one now? I'll bait the hook for you.'

She hesitated. 'I'd best go home,' she said. 'Or they'll send Matt again to search for me.' She sighed.

He twisted the net to make his fish secure. 'I'll walk with you to the stepping stones,' he offered, 'if you promise not to wed me.'

She stared at him, laughed and ran away. Then she flung up her arms and turned a cartwheel with a flurry of petticoats. She fell and sat up laughing and tousled, jumped up, ran ahead and turned another one.

Thomas lay in the bed at Ladyford. His eyes were closed but he was not asleep. He was conscious of Melissa's hand holding his and felt the brightness of sunlight against his eyelids. He was very ill, he knew. Weak and ill and so very tired. It would be so easy to fall into a sleep and to slip from there into the longest sleep. There were times when the idea almost appealed – when his body burned with fever, and his mind grew dark with strange fantasies or his chest pained him beyond all tolerance. The physician had prescribed a draught that took away the pain, but it sent him to sleep also, and into such horrid nightmares that he woke in a sweat of fear and cried for Melissa to comfort him. Usually it was her sweet face he saw when he opened his eyes. Occasionally it was Maggie's. He preferred not to take the draught and now felt that he drifted like a rudderless ship somewhere between life and death. He wanted to stay alive to be with Melissa.

Her fingers stroked his hand, gently and rhythmically and occasionally she bent forward and lifted his hand to kiss it. Sometimes she murmured his name and he would move his fingers in return, to show that he was still conscious – still with her. When she sighed, he wanted to put his arms round her and comfort her, but he had no strength left. If she wept it was silently and he knew she did not want to distress him. Once he heard a choking sob and managed to make a small inarticulate sound in his throat that was meant to be 'Melissa'. She had flung herself onto the bed in a paroxysm of passionate weeping and he had lain powerless to help her, until Maggie happened into the room and he heard her homely voice comforting and sensed that Melissa was being led away to rest.

The door opened and Maggie entered the bedchamber.

'I've brought hot milk,' she said cheerfully, 'and I've stirred a good spoonful of honey into it and a generous drop of brandy. Shall I feed him while you stretch your poor legs?'

Melissa hesitated, wanting to do everything for her husband, but she recognized Maggie's need, too. She had no one in the world to call her own and she valued the opportunity to care for Thomas.

Melissa stood up. 'Try him with it, Maggie, while I just take a turn around the room. I confess my limbs grow stiff. You will hear my bones creak.'

Eagerly Maggie sat down on the vacant stool while Melissa watched from the window.

'Now then, my dear,' said Maggie cheerfully. 'Here's Maggie with a drop of something warming. Milk, honey and brandy and I don't know what else. Oh, and a pinch of nutmeg. A few sips of this and we'll have you well again in no time. You'll be leaping about the room like a frisky horse, I'll warrant. Open your mouth, my dear – a little wider and I can slip the spoon in – So! There, 'tis good and nourishing and light for the digestion. Never been known to fail, has this. Now, let's see if you can do it again – wait. I'll mop your chin. In goes the spoon! I could do with a drop of this myself. Make a new woman of me and not before time . . . Ah, Melissa! He's opening his eyes! Quick, come and see!'

Melissa needed no second bidding and flew across the

room to the bedside. Thomas *had* opened his eyes and he turned his head slowly towards her.

'Oh my dearest Thomas!' cried Melissa. 'How splendid. You are awake and taking nourishment! 'Tis a very good sign, isn't it Maggie? Oh do say 'tis a hopeful sign.'

'Why, 'tis most certainly,' Maggie agreed, equally thrilled. 'We shall have you up and about in a week or so, perky as a cricket. In goes another spoonful – Ah, Melissa will wipe your chin. What a fortunate man you are. Two devoted nurses, one on either side of your bed. There's plenty of men would be in your shoes, Thomas Benet, I'll be bound.'

And so they continued, chiding, teasing, encouraging him until he'd taken all the hot milk and a warm soothing glow spread through his body, giving him an illusion of returning vitality while the two women exchanged hopeful glances across the bed.

Downstairs, Nina sat by the fire spinning. Through the window, when she glanced up from her work, she saw Jacob chopping wood with regular swings of the axe. The chips of wood flew thick and fast and fell like rain over Della, who crouched nearby watching and laughing. She saw the child straighten up and point and Jacob turned to see two horsemen appear. Nina watched, her usual calm expression on her face, and saw that one of the visitors was Hugo. The other man she did not recognize at all. They dismounted and Hugo swung Della into the air, caught her again and kissed her. Nina smiled and went to the door to open it.

'Nina, this little one of yours grows more like her father every day!' He kissed the child again and swung her to the floor where she ran to hide behind her mother's skirts.

'I have brought a friend to meet Melissa and Maggie,' Hugo went on. 'This is Hans Bucher who is in England for the first time. Bucher, this is Nina Benet, my cousin's wife.'

Nina dropped a curtsey and the stranger bowed with an elaborate sweep of his hand. He was very slim and his movements were effeminate. His pale face was downy, his mouth small and his large eyes a very pale blue. He looked very young and ill-at-ease, and he smiled nervously from one to the other. His clothes were rather flamboyant in colour and the cut was not English. He was wearing perfume and Nina noticed that he wore no dagger at his belt.

She smiled at him and, in mime, indicated that the other women were upstairs and she would fetch them. Hugo thanked her and she made her way upstairs.

Melissa looked up as she came into the bedchamber. 'Thomas is awake!' she cried. 'He looked at us and recognized us. Come here and let him see you. Thomas, here is Nina come to see how you are.'

Thomas made a feeble movement with his right hand and tried to smile. Nina went forward and kissed his cheek while Melissa beamed on them both. Then Nina pointed downstairs and mouthed Hugo's name and raised one finger for his companion.

The other women were rapidly learning her simple sign language and Melissa said, 'Hugo and another? I'd best go down. Maggie shall stay here with you, Thomas, and I will be back directly. Now I wonder who 'tis?'

Downstairs, Hugo introduced her to his companion.

'Master Bucher, welcome to Ladyford,' said Melissa. 'My cousin tells us you are a very wise man and Heron has great need of you. We all look to you to help us through this difficult time.'

'I shall be most willing,' he answered. His English was good but he spoke with a marked accent.

'We have just come from the mine,' said Hugo. 'Bucher has several new ideas which I think will solve some of our problems. If only the tinners will delay their judgements and give themselves time to assess the innovations fairly and without prejudice. They are so resistant to change of any kind.'

'They did not like me,' said Bucher regretfully. 'I read it in their eyes and heard it in their voices.'

Hugo nodded apologetically. 'They resent your presence because they do not understand.'

Melissa nodded, bustling about to offer them cinnamon biscuits and ale. 'They are frightened men,' she said. 'They see their fellows out of work and the fear infects their minds. 'Tis a sorry state of affairs to see your neighbours beg and steal from sheer necessity. But enough of such sad talk. We must talk of other matters.'

'May I enquire after your husband?' said Bucher. 'I believe he is – in poor health.'

'A little stronger today, I'm pleased to say. He drank some hot milk and is taking an interest in his surroundings. 'Tis very hopeful. But your own family?'

He shook his head. 'Alas, I have no wife as yet but I hope to wed one day. At present I am – how do you say it? – wedded to my work!'

They all laughed.

'Seriously, he is unrivalled in his field,' said Hugo. 'I hope most earnestly we can persuade him to stay in England for a year or more. If we can find the money, his ideas will revolutionize the Heron mine. We shall then recoup our losses and start to thrive again.'

'I do hope so,' said Melissa. 'From what little you have told us, 'twill need nothing less than a miracle.'

Hugo waved a hand towards his companion. '*Bucher* is our miracle,' he said.

CHAPTER NINE

Eloise stood beside her bed, her naked body bathed in white moonlight. She brushed her hair with long even strokes, admiring the soft curves of her breasts and the smooth taut flesh of her abdomen. Her thighs were sweetly rounded, she thought, and, raising one leg, she looked with satisfaction upon her slim ankle and well shaped foot.

Allan would have all this, she reflected, and he would have no cause for complaint. She was flawless and she knew it and derived an almost sensual pleasure from the knowledge. As she drew the brush through her rich brown tresses, she tried to imagine how Martin would react to her, if he could see her. He would not bother to hide his delight – or his desire! She wished he had not returned to school. It was exciting just to know he was around the house and aware of her. Or Oliver – Oliver admired her, she knew. He could not do otherwise. But had he desired her, she wondered anxiously? He had that strange wife, Nina. Eloise frowned slightly. Whatever had induced a man like Oliver to marry such a girl? He was too good for her by far. She had flirted with Oliver quite openly on several occasions and he had not responded. He seemed to find her amusing. On one occasion she had flaunted herself before them both in her new russet silk and he had complimented her on the effect. But when he turned to his wife Eloise thought he winked, although she could not be certain. Her cheeks still burned at the thought of it. Yet the thought that he mocked her made him more of a challenge. Still, he had gone back to sea. She sighed and shrugged, dismissing him.

There were footsteps on the stairs and she heard Allan and Bucher pass the door on their way to their respective beds. Bucher laughed and, soundlessly, she mimicked his reedy voice and took a few mincing steps across the room. Hans Bucher was very impressed with her charms and quite unable to pretend otherwise. Everyone knew that he stammered when he spoke to her and his command of English, usually so good, temporarily deserted him. She laughed as she recalled the look of embarrassment on his girlish face. A pity he was that way, she thought. It was pointless to inspire devotion in such a man.

She shrugged again and laid down the brush. What did Hugo think of her, she wondered? He was so deeply involved at the mine he was rarely at home, but when he was he treated her with respect and affection. He paid her compliments in a vaguely distracted way as though his mind was on other, more important matters. Yet he looked at her in an admiring way and possibly he compared her with Maria. In which case – Eloise ran her hands over her breasts, down to the curve of her waist and over her tight buttocks – Maria would rate a poor second, for she had had two children late in life and her figure would never recover.

There were more footsteps. It was Hugo and Maria, talking quietly together. One day they would both be gone and she and Allan would be master and mistress of Heron. She turned round slowly until the moonlight fell across her back and she imagined the silvery light glinting on her hair. Tossing her head from side to side she could visualize the rise and fall of the rich chestnut waves and sighed deeply. She thought of Allan and, covering her face with her hands, uttered a small despairing sound. He had never even touched her breasts; had never even *seen* them in their full glory! He had never explored her body, except with his eyes. She wanted him to desire her so passionately that, in spite of her protests, he would take her. They were betrothed, and it happened to others. Her sister Bridget had told her, with ill concealed delight, how her husband-to-be had ravished her two weeks before the wedding. But Allan kept his distance. Flinging herself on to the bed, she clenched her fists until the nails bit into her palms. Time passed and still she lay there, without moving, her anguished face hidden in the coverlet, her ripe body sprawled carelessly. She might just as well be ugly and deformed, she told herself bitterly.

Around her the house grew quiet. Everyone was in bed and downstairs the dogs snored by the dying fire. Somewhere in the wood an owl screeched and then another. Stubbornly, Eloise refused to get into bed as though by so doing she would be giving in to her unhappy fate. She grew cold and uncomfortable, but in a perverse way felt that her physical discomfort suited her emotional turmoil. If she was doomed to be wretched she would be unutterably so. A small voice whispered within her that she was being foolish but she ignored it, wallowing in her self-inflicted misery.

A tap at the door brought her to her senses. She sat up, then sprang to her feet and stared down at her nakedness as though it surprised her. She reached for a robe then hesitated and crossed to the door.

'Who is it?' she asked, her voice low.

' 'Tis only Allan. I must speak with you. Let me in, I beg you.'

She was startled and for another moment hesitated, then opened the door.

Allan's eyes swept her from head to foot.

'Come in,' she said quickly, fearful that he would even now change his mind.

He stepped inside the room and glanced at the bed. 'I thought you would have been sleeping,' he said, seeing that the bed had not yet been turned down.

Eloise picked up her robe, pretending modesty. 'Excuse me,' she murmured. 'I had best cover myself.' She waited for him to disagree but he merely nodded and she was forced to put it on.

She smiled demurely. 'What brings you to my room at this hour and with so serious an expression? Will you sit beside me on the bed and tell me?'

'No—' He looked ill-at-ease she thought. 'What I have to tell you will not be easy. I don't think you will . . .'

'Will what?'

He swallowed. '. . . will want me next to you.'

Her mind raced and she felt a different coldness to that she had known lying on the bed. Sweet Heaven, what was he going to say that could not be said in daylight? Why come to her room at this hour if not for her body? She was bewildered, torn between anger and fear. Allan moved to the window and stared out while she waited beside the bed, nervously twisting the cords of her robe.

'Tell me then,' she demanded. 'Face me, if you have the courage, and tell me this dread news.'

He turned to her and she could no longer see his expression, only the slim, well-shaped head silhouetted against the moonlit window.

'You are a beautiful woman, Eloise,' he began haltingly, 'and you deserve a suitable husband.'

Her pulse quickened. Dear God, he was going to retract! He was not going to marry her. She would never be mistress of Heron and she would go home in disgrace. Her thoughts swam and she almost swayed. Feebly, she put a hand to her forehead and he stepped forward at once and guided her to the bed.

'Forgive me,' he begged. 'I've no wish to shock you but I must say it. Then 'twill be your decision.'

'Mine? My decision?'

'Aye, you will decide whether or not you still wish to wed me.'

'I *do*, Allan! Nothing you can say – Dear God, 'tis another woman! You are in love with another woman!'

'Another woman? Eloise, no! Be calm, I beseech you, and let me tell it before my courage fails me. 'Tis the Kendal blood – *my* blood. Damnation! I am telling it badly. My father was illegitimate and—'

'Is that all?' gasped Eloise. 'I care nothing about such niceties. You are the Kendal heir—'

'Let me finish,' he interrupted fiercely and moved back

to the window so that she would not see his face. 'Isobel Gillis, my grandmother, was . . .' His voice dropped to a whisper, '. . . a madwoman and *her* mother . . .'

'What's that you say? I can scarcely hear you.' Her heart thumped painfully. 'A madwoman?'

He turned towards her. 'Aye,' he said harshly, 'and *her* mother was hanged.'

'Hanged? Sweet Heaven, Allan! Hanged for what crime?'

There was a long pause and then he said flatly: 'For witchcraft.'

Eloise sat as though turned to stone. For a while the shock dulled her senses and the conversation seemed unreal. The words drummed in her brain – Madwoman! Witchcraft! She felt choked, unable to breathe and gasped for breath like one drowning.

He was still speaking and she tried to concentrate on his words, but the sounds he made came to her as an unintelligible gibberish and she wished he would stop.

'—and as you see I am unaffected. There is no real danger. The physician has assured us. No risk at all and yet I felt you should know. I want us to be wed with no secrets between us. I want nothing to hurt you. You know that I want you Eloise. Mayhap you do not know that I love you. I want to protect you from all harm and yet I am the one who must hurt you if this matter is to be open between us.'

She was aware again and listening intently.

'You shall have time to think it over,' he went on, 'and then if you want to wed elsewhere I shall honour your decision and release you from our contract.'

'But why?' she said. 'Why did he marry this madwoman?'

'She was very beautiful. They were in love and she was pregnant. She was not mad then, only later. Their marriage was not legal. My grandfather was already betrothed, and he kept Isobel and her child secret.'

'Sweet Heaven!'

At last he went to her, sat on the bed and put his arms

round her. 'I want you to know,' he said quietly, 'that whatever you decide to do I shall always want you. I wanted to tell you so many times, how I feel for you, but – this knowledge has prevented me. I could not risk losing you.'

Her thoughts whirled chaotically. 'Harriet!' she said. 'Did she know what you have told *me*?'

'No. Hugo and Maria thought it unnecessary and I was younger then and let myself be advised by them. They still do not think it necessary for me to speak of it but I determined to do so.'

'Gillis—' said Eloise slowly. 'That name is familiar. The first night I was here – Gillis! I'm sure of it. Your sister's pup came from a Gillis! So *that* was why you looked so strangely.'

'Aye. 'Twas a shock to hear the name after so long and at such a time. It seemed like an omen – that the day *you* arrived the dreadful name was thrust at me like a dagger.'

His arms were round her, holding her close, and she was suddenly aware that only a thin robe separated his hands from her flesh. They had never been so close. He had never held her that way, had never come to her bed chamber. Nor had he ever said that he wanted her with such conviction. More than anything, she wanted to take his hands and place them over her naked breasts and watch the expression on his face as his desire for her grew into passion. And then she longed to satisfy him. But now there were these other terrible facts to consider.

'Eloise, you may wish to discuss what I've told you with your parents.'

'No! I dare not. They will make me leave you. They must not know. 'Tis for me to decide and me alone. Promise me you won't speak to them, Allan.'

'I promise.'

Eloise knew that if she did not marry him someone else would. There would be plenty of women willing to take a chance for such a husband – and such an inheritance. The bad blood was a long way back. Three generations. She would take her chance – but she would not tell him yet.

'When shall I give you my answer?' she asked.

'When you have reached it,' he said. 'I shall not hurry you.'

Oh, but I wish you would, she thought. I wish you would hurry me now to make a decision and it would be 'Aye'. Then you could take me in your arms and I would take you into my bed and we would lie together until dawn and then I would truly know this man who is to be my husband and he would know the delights of my body and *then* I would see such desire in his eyes at all times!

He stood up. 'I must go – if you are over the worst of the shock. You have been very brave and very kind.'

'It was hard for you, also.'

'Eloise—'

She waited.

'You have never said it – that *you* love *me*. Mayhap you cannot but I thought—'

He looks so young, she thought, so very vulnerable. It was in her power to give him pain or joy and the thought thrilled her. The desirability of her body gave her the power over him – over most men. She wanted to laugh aloud. But in another moment he would be gone, back to his own bed chamber and her long-awaited chance would have been wasted. As he hesitated, she made up her mind. Slowly she unfastened the robe and let it fall to the floor. For a moment he did not speak. Eloise looked at him steadily, exulting in the fact that it was *his* turn to be shocked and confused. How neatly she had turned the tables on him! His eyes narrowed as his whole body tightened. He almost recoiled from her as though in fear.

'Eloise! Sweet Jesus, you are perfect!' he whispered. 'Quite perfect!' He made no move to approach her, but his eyes caressed her voluptuously.

She moved slightly, shifting her weight to her left foot, tossing her hair back so that it no longer obscured her breasts.

'Do you think you will enjoy me – if I stay at Heron?' she asked softly, and saw his throat tighten as he tried to answer but could not. She twirled gracefully so that her long hair flew out and then wrapped itself round her neck and shoulders. 'Will my body please you? Will you have any cause for complaint?'

He shook his head and she waited impatiently for him to cross the few yards that separated them, longing for the touch of his hands and the warmth of his breath and the strength of his body drowning in her riches.

'Oh God,' he whispered. 'What are you doing to me? Why now?'

By way of an answer she lifted her arms and gathered up her hair, twirling it into a loose rope. Then she piled it on top of her head and held it there, both arms upstretched to steady it, the tip of her tongue delicately busy along her top teeth. She shifted her weight again and let the angle of her hips change smoothly, turning slightly to one side so that her right breast, pale in the moonlight, would be outlined against the dark wall.

With a hoarse cry he covered the gap between them, took her into his arms and threw her backwards on to the bed. His weight pressed down on top of her, but at once she wriggled beneath him with a small cry of distress.

'No, Allan!' she begged. 'Forgive me. I was wrong. I—'

But her false protest died. She could not pretend. Instead she watched every movement he made as he stood up and undressed. At last he, too, was naked.

'Allan!'

She was kneeling on the bed facing him and now she backed away, stepped down on to the floor and went round to stand before him. She looked at the pale shoulders, narrow chest and slim waist. She put out her hands and touched his nipples then slid her fingers down over the narrow hips and down the thick thighs, down to his feet. As she straightened up she let her hair brush against his body and heard him gasp. His fingers tightened on her shoulders and the pain shot through her, adding to the clamour within her. Then he was pushing her back on to the bed and he lay beside her. His hands, his tongue, his teeth were all over her body, which cried out silently never to stop. Time and again she rolled over, twisted away from him. Always he caught at her wrist, her ankle, her hair, and held her gently captive. At last, when she thought she would die of ecstasy, he thrust deep inside her, smothering her scream, and let his own passion spend itself in the dark warmth of her body.

When it was over he stood up, picked up his clothes and went back to his own room without another word or look. Eloise, her eyes closed, let him go. Tears trickled down her face. She put a trembling hand between her legs as though to comfort her body. He had taken her wildly raging, regardless of her pleas. His hard body had battered and bruised her flesh. She wondered – had her power over him gone? She was terribly aware of his power over her. Because, despite the pain and the fury, she knew her body would soon be crying out for more. She would wed Allan Kendal despite his background. But she must never let him guess her terrible need of him. She must be clever, she told herself desperately. She would tease him, provoke him, even quarrel with him. Somehow, anyhow, she knew she must try to recover the power she had just surrendered.

June brought brilliant sunshine and with it an upsurge in their fortunes. Thomas made a slow but sure recovery, until he was declared out of danger by his physician and allowed to sit outside for an hour each day to 'take strength from the sun's rays'. On the twenty-eighth day Nina gave birth to Jason, a healthy boy, weighing nearly nine pounds. It was a short, straightforward delivery and within a week the mother was fit enough to leave her bed. Nina insisted on feeding the baby herself and Melissa gave in graciously, finding it impossible to argue with her determined smile and the persistent shake of her head when the wet nurse was introduced and her function explained. Thomas declared himself well pleased that the new addition to the household was male, for he had suffered the ministrations of *three* women and now looked forward to seeing some of their attentions transferred to his grandson. Melissa and Maggie were in their element and Ladyford fairly buzzed with cheerful activity and happy chatter.

The otter hunt in late July was in Bucher's honour. It was Hugo's idea. He, Bucher and Allan had developed a good working relationship and, although they were all very different in temperament, they had become firm friends. Hugo greatly admired Bucher's professional competence and drew heavily on his expertise, accepting his advice on many occasions and trusting to his judgement when considering most of the innovations that were to be introduced. To avoid clashes with the tinners, the mine was closed down for ten days while the three men explored it together, making drawings and discussing and devising new machinery that might profitably be installed. The tinners were paid for their absence and Hugo hoped there could be no further excuse for ill-feeling. Engrossed in the project, they spent long hours underground, rarely stopping to eat until they returned to Heron each evening in time for supper. Bucher threw himself wholeheartedly into the scheme, and by the time they were finally satisfied with the outcome of their labours they were all exhausted. Hugo reasoned that the hunt would provide them with fresh air, exercise and excitement, all of which had been sadly lacking in their lives for the past weeks.

They assembled on the river bank and then split into two parties. Maria, Hugo, Piers and Matt formed one group and Allan, Bucher and Eloise and Jon formed the other. Melissa had been invited but declined. Martin had not yet returned from his final term at school.

'I wish Oliver were still at home,' said Allan. 'He would have enjoyed it.'

Bucher stood beside him, his spear clutched awkwardly in his right hand. He had never hunted before and the prospect daunted him. The spears were wickedly sharp and he was sure in his own mind that he would never bring himself to plunge a weapon into an animal. He had no idea what to expect from the afternoon and, despite Allan's reassuring grin, awaited events with trepidation. The hounds seemed to sense his nervousness and growled menacingly whenever he ventured close to them. He had never seen an otter, but had learned from Hugo that a large dog otter had been seen along the stretch of water where a fish pond was under construction. The dam was already being built and when it was finished it would hold back enough of the river water to form a large pond which would then be cleaned, prepared and stocked with breeding fish. Eventually, it would supply both Heron and Ladyford with all the fish they required. A voracious otter would make large inroads into the fish population. A successful hunt would put an end to the problem and would, at the same time, provide an afternoon's sport.

'We must spread out along each bank,' Hugo told them. 'Then we beat along each bank. He's likely couched up under the roots of a tree. Keep a watchful eye for his seal.'

Bucher looked confused and turned to Eloise for enlightenment. She laughed ruefully and shook her head.

'I'm no wiser than you,' she confessed. 'Allan! We are none the wiser. Will you explain?'

'The seal is the footprint,' he told them. 'He has no heel to his foot, only a small round pad. 'Tis quite distinctive.'

Hugo led them all towards the wooden bridge where he and his party crossed over with two of the four dogs.

'Now,' said Allan, 'we work our way along the river bank and the dogs should flush it out. We'll keep an eye on the water. Loose the dogs, Jon!' he called. 'Go Bouncer! Go Dido! Seek!'

The two hounds lunged forward as soon as they were released and set off at a fast zig-zag pace. On the opposite side the other two dogs, Jewel and Spanker, were already at work, their tails waving enthusiastically, their heads well down after the scent. The two parties followed, keeping abreast with the river between them. Bucher took a deep breath and followed Eloise, who in turn followed Allan. Their spears glinted in the sunshine and the dogs ahead of them whined eagerly. Eloise carried hers over her shoulder like a musket, but Bucher found this too martial and carried his like a walking stick, grasping it a few inches below the head. Eloise turned to smile at him.

'Look more cheerfully!' she teased. ' 'Tis in your honour, this expedition. Aren't you enjoying it?'

'I am. Indeed I am,' he lied hastily. 'I hope I shall acquit myself well. You – er – you look greatly at ease, if I may say so. And that plum colour suits you most admirably.'

'Why, thank you, Master Bucher.'

'Call me Hans, I beg you.'

She smiled, flattered by the admiration evident in his eyes.

'You enjoy hunting?' he asked.

She shrugged elegantly. ' 'Tis part of the Heron way. We are country people and hunting is part of our lives.'

He fell in beside her, enchanted by her sure footedness across the hillocky grass, and by the slimness of the little hand that lifted her skirt clear of the grass as she walked.

'And,' he said, lowering his voice, 'you will soon be part of the family. I fear I shall miss the wedding, for in August I plan to return home for a few weeks. My father's health is poor and my mother begs me to visit them before too long.'

'We shall miss you,' said Eloise. She smiled brilliantly at him and a pale flush of embarrassment tinged his pale cheeks.

'Oh!' Eloise tripped suddenly and he put out a hand to steady her. At that moment Allan turned to see if they were keeping up. Bucher snatched his hand away and his colour deepened.

'Are you managing?' Allan asked.

'Hans is looking after me. I am in good hands,' Eloise answered. 'You go on ahead if you wish.'

Bucher began to splutter out a protest and immediately

quickened his pace. He heard Eloise laugh. He began to hope the otter would appear and distract everyone's attention. But it was some time before his wishes were met.

'Go Jewel! Go Spanker!' cried Maria and Matt began to halloo, his large hands held to his mouth in a parody of a hunting horn.

'Master Otter has seen us coming!' laughed Maria. 'He is probably a mile ahead of us by – Ah! What have you found?'

Jewel, the little bitch, was whining eagerly and Hugo called, 'She has picked up a scent – and here's a seal – and another! Go Jewel! Go with her Spanker.'

The two dogs were used to working together and in seconds had flushed out a large otter from the bark of a rotting willow which overhung the water. With a howl of pain Spanker sprang back, a long gash spurting blood from his muzzle. At the same time the large dog otter leapt for the safety of the water and vanished under it in a swirl of bubbles and a circle of widening ripples. The dogs began to bark shrilly, some racing up and down the bank, while Hugo and Maria stared down into the green depths, searching among the weed for signs of movement.

'Quickly,' cried Allan, calling his party together. 'He may make a break this way. Have your spears ready.'

They lined the bank, spears raised. There was no sign of the otter.

'We have lost him, I fear,' said Bucher thankfully.

'No, no,' said Allan. 'We have him on both sides. He will go up or down river. The dogs will find him.'

Eloise gave a scream and threw her spear into the water. 'He's there! I saw him. Look there. He's your side!'

A frenzied barking broke out as the otter surfaced suddenly just below Maria, and before the startled dogs could collect their wits he was away, streaking for cover across the grass. Hugo, Maria and Piers set off in pursuit, while Matt waded gallantly into the water to retrieve Eloise's spear.

'Thank you, Matt,' she said and he grinned sheepishly and waded back to join his own party.

The otter was old and wily and led the two dogs a fine chase. Finally it doubled back and headed once more for the safety of its natural habitat. Splash! He was in again and this time Bouncer leapt in to the attack. Before the otter could submerge to a safe depth, the dog was upon it and a fight ensued. The otter made no sound but the dog barked hysterically, occasionally yelping as his adversary's sharp teeth caught him. The second dog, Dido, went in to aid her partner, but she was too late. The otter seized Bouncer by the throat, and with a gurgling cry the dog was dragged under the water and out of sight.

'He'll drown!' cried Eloise. 'Allan, *do* something. I see them – no they're gone again! Oh poor Bouncer, you must help him!'

Allan and Jon were already wading into the water, their spears held aloft. Hugo and Matt prepared to follow them if needed.

'If you see them, take care,' cried Hugo. 'I saw a dog once speared by mistake. 'Tis easy to make an error.'

'I must go in,' Bucher told Eloise. He had gone very pale and hesitated on the edge of the bank. Eloise was too concerned for the dog to pay him any heed.

'Beyond that boulder!' cried Allan. 'No, 'tis only the mud they have stirred up. Where *are* they, in God's name?'

Suddenly, with an uprush of water and broken reed the two animals surfaced, no longer together. The dog gulped desperately for air and Hugo dragged it, howling, to the bank. It was badly mauled, one foreleg bitten right through to expose the pale bone. It gulped greedily at the air. The otter swerved away from the men and dogs in the water and dived and went downstream. Then it scrambled out on Allan's side of the river and once more set off at a great speed in the opposite direction. The remaining three dogs followed it, baying hysterically. They spread out, out-ran it, and it doubled back straight towards Allan who threw his spear, missed it and cursed roundly. By that time the otter was heading for Bucher who waited, spear upraised. In his nervousness he threw too early and Eloise threw too late. The otter weaved between them and went back into the water for the third time – and there they lost it. The dogs hunted in vain, but were finally recalled. Matt was sent back to Heron with the injured dog and the remaining hunters sat down to rest and regain their breath.

'We may find another further up,' said Hugo. 'We'll watch for this one – he should show his nose if he's here. He must come up for air. If not we'll move on and most likely flush out another.'

'Then this one will continue to haunt the fish pond,' Maria reminded him. 'This one is our arch enemy. I would sooner despatch the devil we know than seek out a new one.'

'We'll try. We've plenty of daylight yet. We'll see who has the most patience, him or us.'

They sat there for nearly half an hour with only a few false sightings to break the monotony of the vigil. Hugo was on the point of suggesting a move when one of the dogs growled and sprang forward. In the middle of the water a dark snout broke the surface and a sleek head emerged. The dark eyes took one look at each bank where the dogs and hunters were recovering from their surprise.

'Go Dido! Spanker! Jewel! After him!'

The dogs needed no urging. They were already in the water and encircling the otter whose shape could just be discerned below the surface.

'This time they've got it!' shouted Jon.

'They've got it! They've got it!' yelled Piers.

A life and death drama was being enacted in the middle of the river as first one and then another dog tried to close in for the kill. But the otter was not prepared to surrender and put up a tremendous fight, snapping at the dogs, diving below them and trying every trick to evade his tormentors. Bucher, determined to prove himself willing, began to wade into the water but Hugo called him to keep back.

193

'It could go for your legs,' he shouted. 'They've a most fearsome bite.'

Bucher turned at once and waded out, giving Eloise a disappointed look that in no way deceived her but she said kindly, 'We must return you to your homeland in one piece, Hans. You were wise to take Hugo's advice.'

'I thought to have him then,' he said with a shrug and stood beside her to watch the struggle that continued in mid-river. The otter was more than a match for the three dogs. He managed to wound Dido, tearing a flap of skin from her shoulder. The river was at once coloured with blood and the sight and smell of it maddened the dogs still further. One of them – no one could see which one – sunk his teeth into the otter's flank but a blow from the powerful tail half stunned it and it swam to the bank and staggered out, dazed and trembling. Piers ran to comfort it.

' 'Twill make a break soon if it's going to,' Hugo warned and the spears were once more raised. His instinct was correct. The desperate otter dived to elude the dogs and suddenly emerged at the water's edge. Eloise threw first and missed by a foot or more. Allan pinned it by the shoulder, and as the dogs scrambled out after it Bucher's spear flew wild of the mark and struck Jewel. The spear pierced the neck at the front and drove deep into the lungs. It was an unlucky but fatal blow and the little bitch, already exhausted and bleeding, sank down without a sound and gazed pathetically at Eloise who ran towards her.

'Oh no, no! Dear little Jewel. Oh sweet heaven! Bucher, you fool, you've killed her! Killed her, d'you hear?'

The dog gave a deep sigh which suddenly bubbled obscenely and faltered. The bright eyes glazed over. Jewel was dead. The otter's end was not so swift. The two remaining dogs set upon it and tore it to pieces. Hugo and Piers waded across the river, but by the time they arrived it was all over. All that remained of the prey was a mangled and bloody corpse. Eloise sobbed over the body of the plucky little hound while Bucher, ashen-faced, vomited a short distance away.

There was no more hunting that day. They returned slowly to Heron. Eloise was distraught; Bucher, pale and trembling, apologized again and again. Piers was resentful that he had missed the final drama which had taken place on the opposite side of the river. Jon, carrying all the spears, led the two surviving hounds. Allan carried Jewel and Maria kept pace with them on the far side of the river. It was a subdued hunting party which finally returned to Heron and Matt, greeting them, was secretly thankful that he had returned when he did. The afternoon was an unqualified failure and not one of the hunting party had the heart to pretend otherwise.

Minnie, stood at the table, a large sacking apron round her waist, her sleeves rolled up above her elbows. Beside her on the scrubbed table lay four eels, two large and two smaller. On the opposite side of the table Martin sat, watching her. He had drawn her, skilfully and without rousing her suspicions, on to the subject of her childhood. To her they were the years she spent at Heron as a girl, with Luke Kendal as master of Heron. Luke had rescued her from a brutish drunken grandfather.

'Bought me, he did,' she told Martin, her knife poised over the longest of the eels. 'Bought me with a bag of gold. Mind you, he tried to send me back to the old buzzard but I wouldn't have it. I refused to go home and just kept following behind him. Oh, he was a handsome man, your grandfather. A very handsome man. Even as an old man – even as he lay in his coffin – he was handsome.'

She sighed as she plunged the eel into a bowl of salt water. 'Young Nat brought us these,' she told Martin. 'A gift, he said. Gift, my eye! Most likely poached from our own river, but what matter. Hugo likes a bit of eel and the mistress is not averse to it.'

Martin smiled and gave her a saucy wink. He knew now

that his time spent with her would not be wasted. He would learn all that he wanted to know. At fourteen he looked sixteen and his charming manners won him friends and admirers with very little effort on his part. He was making it his business to discover all the facts relating to the Gillis family, with particular attention to Isobel and Marion. What he would *do* with the information was not quite clear to him. Tell Eloise, perhaps, or even Allan! It pleased him to think that his knowledge would give him a weapon. The accident of birth which made him second in line to the inheritance could not be overcome. Allan would always be heir to Heron, but Martin felt the injustice deeply. He had better blood in him than Allan, he was more handsome than his brother and he was altogether a more attractive personality – or so he believed. Allan would have Heron *and* the beautiful and desirable Eloise and Martin envied him both. He was helpless to change the natural order of things. Allan stood to gain all that Martin coveted – but if Martin could not stop him, at least he need not make life easy for him. Allan must inevitably win, but let him fight for his prizes. Martin did not hate his brother but neither did he love him. He knew of the deep friendship between Allan and Oliver and that hurt him, too. While he had been at school it had been possible to put such thoughts aside, but the holidays had never been easy to bear. Now he had left Winchester and would be 'banished' to Romney House. He was admittedly more fortunate than many second sons in that respect, but it was still a far cry from Heron.

'Luke must have been a fine looking man to have two wives,' he said innocently. 'Did you ever see Isobel Gillis?'

Minnie shook her head. 'I was a bit too young to know what was going on. Mind you, I listened at doors—'

'I'll warrant you still do!'

Minnie laughed. 'I shouldn't tell you if I did,' she said, 'but I got my ears boxed many a time for that. Oh, I heard a lot, don't you fret, but as to seeing Isobel, no. I never did. She never did come to the house – at least not to my knowledge – but they did say she was a rare beauty and most men would have died for her. But there, 'twas her that died, poor soul. All I can say is if Luke loved her then she wasn't a bad woman, not by a long chalk.'

She patted the eel dry, laid it on the board and cut off the head. Then she pulled back the skin and scooped the guts into a bucket which stood on the floor beside her. The stuffing was already prepared in a stone bowl and Martin, pulling it towards him, sniffed it appreciatively.

'Cinnamon,' he said, 'and nutmeg and something else.'

'Anchovies – and all mixed with butter the way the master likes it.'

'Shall I add the salt?'

' 'Tis done. Leave it be, Martin. You always did have meddlesome fingers.'

She grinned to soften the rebuke, but he was not really interested in the stuffing. He leaned his elbows on the table and cupped his chin in his hands.

'I bet you didn't see Marion ducked,' he said slyly.

Minnie hesitated, torn between the desire to tell all that she knew and the knowledge that she had been forbidden to go to the river on that fateful day. She began to fill the empty belly with stuffing and then drew up the skin again and tied it where the head should have been.

'Well, I did then,' she said. She slashed the eel five times along its back and pressed stuffing into the cuts. Laying it aside, she reached for the next one and plunged it into the salt water. 'I saw it all. Wormed my way to the front of the crowd and saw everything. Oh, she was a witch, no doubt at all. No matter what they did to her up she came again, bobbing like a cork tho' the water was deep and fast. Cursing she was, you never heard the like! She cursed them all, the master, the constable, even the minister! They had a rope strung right out across the water from one bank to the other – down below the bridge, 'twas. I could show you the very spot. And she was tied in the middle of it and her hands and feet tied, too. How could she *not* drown without magic? That's what they all said.'

'So they knew she *was* a witch?'

'Oh, aye. 'Twas proof, wasn't it?' The next eel was beheaded, gutted and stuffed, and she reached for the third. Martin put a finger into the bowl of stuffing and she tapped his hand sharply with the back of her knife. 'Fingers out, young Martin! Aye, they knew she was a witch and they hanged her the next day.'

'Did she confess it?'

'Aye, and to all the terrible disasters that had befallen folks in the past year. A woman who'd lost her child; a man took in a fit; three horsemen drowned in a mire – she confessed to it all. And she had a familiar in the shape of a dog. A big black dog. I didn't set eyes on the dog, nor ever wanted to for they're part of the devil himself. His messengers, they do say, with special powers. If that dog had so much as looked at me I'd likely not be here now.'

'What happened to it?'

'I don't rightly know. They say it howled by the gibbet where Marion was hanged, but I kept well away from that mournful place. There, that's done and a right messy job but so tasty. They'll roast a treat, they will.' She began to clear away scraps and utensils.

'Did Isobel have any other children?'

'Not that I heard of.'

'Any sisters or brothers?'

'I can't rightly say. 'Twas a long time ago. Now move your elbows – thank you kindly. She had a father but he moved away after his wife was hanged. Got too hot for him, I reckon. He took Isobel and they went to Tavistock. I don't know about any family.'

'But if the father took another woman then Isobel might have had half-brothers or sisters.'

'I dare say.'

'Or the father might have had a brother or sister. There might have been cousins, uncles, aunts.'

' 'Tis possible.' She looked at him sharply. 'You're mighty interested, all of a sudden. Why all the questions?'

198

He shrugged again and smiled disarmingly. 'Curiosity kills the cat, I know! 'Twas just a thought.'

She eyed him suspiciously. 'All that's in the past,' she said, 'and all over and done with. No one'll thank you to go stirring up muck. You mind what I say, Martin, or there'll be no good come of it.'

He stood up and pushed back the bench. 'Now would I do that, Min? You know me better, I hope.'

'I know that you only call me Min when you're up to some trick or other. It was always so. You called me Min the day you turned up here in the middle of the night, run away from school! *And* when you lost all that money at cards.'

He laughed. 'Your memory is *too* good at times! Well then, Minnie, I'll be out from under your feet – before you throw me out. I promised Piers I'd take him hawking and try out his new bird.'

He gave her a quick peck on the cheek and was gone before she could say more on the sensitive subject. She watched him go, her face suddenly serious, and then carried on with her cooking. But her expression was thoughtful. She had the uneasy feeling that she had not heard the last of the matter and wished some of her reminiscences unsaid.

CHAPTER TEN

There were seven people under the Boord's roof. Alec and Annie, John Jenkins, Rita Carp, Jake and Alfred Gillis – two of Annie Boord's brothers – and John Greer. They sat on the straw which covered the earth floor and each one held a mug of ale in his or her hand. Their mood was surly and it showed on their faces, lit by the faint glow of the smouldering fire. They had all tasted the humiliation of unemployment and had given up trying for new employment. The Maudesley mine was not looking for new labour – in fact the rumour was spreading that soon the men would be laid off there also. It seemed more than likely, for although the quality of their ore remained high, the quantity was falling with every month that passed. It was now late August, and the summer would soon be over. Autumn and winter would come and they would be cold and hungry.

'Bucher!' hissed Greer and spat derisively. 'What an apology for a man! Have you heard what happened a month or so back? Killed one of their hounds by mistake! Speared it instead of the otter!'

There was a roar of delighted laughter.

'And the way he walks!' cried Jake. 'Mincing along on his toes like a damned wench! He's soft, that's what he is. More woman than man.'

'And he comes to England full of fancy ideas, to tell us how to run a tin mine!' Alf Gillis's tone conveyed his contempt for the man. 'And Kendal tells us he's going to better things and what's the first thing that happens? They close the mine down for ten days. A fine start!'

Alf Gillis was short and swarthy and had lost an eye ten years earlier in an underground accident and the closed eyelids were badly puckered and made him ugly. He had a temper to match but that had been an accident of birth. He had left mining and now cut turf for a living. His brother Jake was ten months younger and taller but his face, with its small dark eyes, wore the sly look of a fox. He was a water carrier in Ashburton and had no quarrel with Heron, but his sister Ann had wed Alec Boord and *he* was now out of work. The Gillises stuck together and when Alec sent word to them, they came willingly, and though nearer fifty than forty, were both eager for the fray. Rita Carp was a widow with three small sons. Her husband had been a tinner all his life and had died in a brawl on the way home from the morning shift. She had asked Hugo for her husband's job – he loaded the ore into the wagons at the face. Hugo had refused but had put her to work in the washing shed. But she was a born troublemaker and many of the ensuing arguments and fights had been started by her slanderous tongue, so he had taken his chance to be rid of her troublesome influence.

John Jenkins was older than the others, nearing sixty, and a very sick man. His third wife had just given birth to a son and he had six other children, four by his second wife and two by the first. The youngest children had all arrived at intervals of less than a year, but his two eldest, twin girls, were sixteen and worked in the fields. They would be gleaning after the harvesting and that would mean a sack or two of grain, but apart from their meagre wages there was no money coming in. Hugo had sacked him reluctantly, but he had long since failed to give a fair day's labour in return for his money. Barlowe had reported that the other men resented him, complaining that he was no longer fit and yet was paid the same as the rest.

'But he's paid them for the ten days,' said Rita. She had no respect for Hugo Kendal, but even less for Alf Gillis who was scum in her eyes. Everyone knew the Gillises'had bad blood in them and could be taunted for it, but it was never wise to go too far with them just in case the evil eye had been passed down through the blood. Their father was the son of Rob Gillis who was cousin to Isobel.

'They've paid them for this ten days,' Alf agreed, 'but what about next time? I'll wager 'twill be different next time.'

'You reckon 'twill happen again?'

'I'd swear to it. You mark my words, there'll be others following us before the month is out.'

Alec held out his empty mug and Annie refilled it.

'But do we want to wait another month?' he asked. 'Do we want to wait another week? Every day that passes is another day's mischief hatched. I say Bucher should go now!'

There was a chorus of 'ayes'.

' 'Tis all very fine talk,' said Rita, 'but how does it come about? Do we all go up to Kendal and say – we don't care for your mining man, so would you send him home? He'll die laughing.'

'Aye,' said Annie. 'He'll not see reason, and likely not even listen to us.'

'There's ways and means,' said Jake. 'The mincing man might—' he shrugged expressively, 'disappear? Or he might trip and fall down the mine shaft. Accidents *do* happen.'

'Not to bloody Bucher, they don't,' said Greer.

'Someone might poison him,' said Alf. 'What a terrible thing that would be!'

'Oh, terrible!'

They all laughed except John. 'Wait a bit,' he said nervously. 'We're going too fast for my liking. Poison and accidents? I don't like the sound of it. Too high a price if we're found out. I've no wish to hang.'

Annie, Alf and Jake looked at him as one.

'There's nowt to be ashamed of hanging,' said Annie, 'lot of good folk has died that way – and noble.'

'And innocent, I dare say?' Alec jeered.

'Aye, and innocent!' roared Jake, his fists clenched.

'Is that so? Then if 'tis only good, noble and innocent folk as hang we should all be as wicked as we know how! That way we'll escape the gibbet!'

'Being wicked'll come easy to you, Alec Boord!'
Annie flung her half-empty mug straight into Jake's face and caught him across the mouth. 'Don't you miscall my husband under his own roof!' she screamed. 'You're no saint, Jake, nor ever have been. I know things about you you'd rather forget.'

Rita shouted, 'Quiet, you' rabble. I'm not here to listen to you settling old scores. If we're not talking about Bucher then I'm off home. I've an ailing mother and two babes to tend.'

The small commotion died. Annie's mug was retrieved from the corner and she refilled it with a surly look on her face. She looked into the pitcher and said pointedly, 'And that's the last of it. There's no more and since no one else brought any . . .'

'Let it go, Annie,' said Alec. 'They've brought nowt because they've *got* nowt so hold your tongue. Rita's right. Our purpose is to talk about Bucher so speak up if you've anything to say.'

'Are we all agreed he's got to go?' asked Alf.

They were.

'And by fair means or foul?'

It was agreed reluctantly.

'And we want the others to join us?'

There was a silence.

'I say not,' said Alec. 'If 'tis foul means then the less that knows the better.'

'A knife round his throat on a dark night!'

'Drown the runt!'

'Kidnap him, tie him up and leave him somewhere to starve.'

'String him up to a tree. They'll think 'tis robbers if we take his gold.'

John Jenkins held up a hand. 'Too fast again, by far,' he insisted. 'You won't give a thought to fair means, but must all risk your necks. Why not *frighten* him into leaving England. I'll wager he's the kind that jumps at his own shadow. Send him a letter threatening his life. 'Twill most likely be enough for such as him.'

'A letter?' cried Alec scornfully. 'God's teeth, man, who's going to write it? Can you write? For I can't even write my name!'

'None of us can,' said Rita. 'If a letter's the best you can come up with, John Jenkins, then foul it must be.'

'A message by mouth then,' said John Greer. 'Send one of the lads with a message – Leave England or live to regret it.'

'Send a lad?' It was Annie's turn to groan aloud. 'Send one of yours, then, shall we? Let him get hauled off to a constable? Eh John?'

John shook his head slowly. 'I don't rightly know,' he said, 'but I don't have a mind to kill a man.'

'You couldn't if you *had* a mind!' cried Rita. 'But I've no mind to do the deed and Annie's no use. That leaves Alec and the Gillises.'

'Oh that's fine that is!' cried Annie. 'That leaves *my* husband and *my* brothers! My thanks to you, Rita Carp! I'll have no family left if you have *your* way!'

The three men concerned then rounded on Rita and Alec bellowed for peace and quiet and they then turned on him. Rita stood up defiantly and glanced round.

'That's it, then,' she snapped. 'I've had a belly full of your snapping and snarling. You're like a pack of dogs. I've better things to do with my time than waste it with the likes of you! Count me out of your fine schemes and I hope you all rot!'

She scrambled over and round them and, ignoring their protests, made her way out into the rain and departed for her own hearth.

'And good riddance,' said Alf somewhat sheepishly. 'We're better off without that silly little whore.'

'You should know!' said his brother and suddenly they both guffawed.

'Not you and her!' cried John.

' 'Twas a long time ago,' said Alf. 'She was fourteen and

almost handsome in the dark! Almost but not quite! And she hasn't improved with age!'

Now they all laughed, eager to break the tension and dispel the gloom. They talked again until the light faded and the last of the wood burned to ashes. Annie went outside to relieve herself, moving slowly on cramped legs and the men were left alone.

'So are we agreed?' Alec asked for the third time. 'We go for his house – burn it down and him with it. But we go in a crowd – as many as possible. They'll never hang us all. Never put us all in gaol – there'd hardly be room. We need a mob of men. We must get the rest of them, whether they be working or not.'

'And we must make it soon!'

'The sooner the better.'

'Are we agreed on it?'

They cried 'Aye' and 'We are'!

'We'll give him bloody Bucher!' cried Jake.

'He won't mince when we're done with him!'

John Greer looked at them wearily.

'And if it goes awry?' he asked. 'If the plan goes awry?'

'We've got nothing *now*,' said Alec harshly. 'So what do we stand to lose?'

The afternoon was a mild one but dark clouds showed along the horizon, hinting at rain. The hay and most of the corn was already in, but one field remained. Eloise and Martin reined in their horses for a moment to watch the harvesters at work. An attractive sight as the wagon moved slowly along the rows, pulled by two heavy shire horses, one a dark chestnut, one a piebald with a light mane and tail. The men followed it and forked up the stooks, tossing them up to the men on the wagon who pulled them into place to keep the whole load stable. As the wagon moved on, the women scratched among the stubble, gathering the ears that had fallen from each stook and stowing them into whatever sacks, bags or baskets they had. Some of the grain would feed chickens, some be ground into a coarse flour. This field was one of Heron's, part of the small home farm that supplied the family with vegetables, grain and fruit. One of the girls glanced up at the two riders and, recognizing them, waved cheerfully. Martin made her a small bow and Eloise raised her hand in greeting but neither spoke. Eloise was thinking that they made a handsome couple. Martin was wondering if the ride would end in the way he had planned.

'There'll be a big supper tomorrow evening,' he told her. 'We'll go if you've a mind.'

She hesitated. Allan and Hugo were away in London on business, trying to raise the finance necessary for the new work at the mine.

'But if Allan and Hugo are still in London,' she said, 'I think 'twould be unwise for us to appear together in their absence.'

'You are too cautious. No one shall dare to doubt our integrity.'

'I think we should not risk it. Let's wait until tomorrow and hope they'll be back.'

'You will break my heart by your coldness,' he told her with mock earnestness. 'But if you do not accompany me I shall still go.'

She smiled. 'I'm certain of it! And flirt most fondly with these wenches!' She indicated the gleaners. 'That one waves and smiles at you as to a familiar friend.'

'Friend, mayhap, but familiar – no. I would remember it! She has a certain boldness in her eyes.'

Eloise laughed lightly to hide her true feelings.

'Do you admire boldness in a woman?' she asked.

'It can be exciting.'

'I'll grant you that. Boldness in a man has the same effect.'

'God forbid you shall look for it in Allan!' cried Martin, then, fearing he had gone too far, he turned his horse and called, 'Come, we have far to go.'

She rode after him and, catching up with him, said, 'Far

to go? Why, where are we going? I thought we were just taking the air and exercising the horses!'

'So we are,' he agreed quickly. 'But if we dawdle over every pleasing view we shall hardly exercise them at all for we are surrounded by beauty.' He stared into her face as he said this and she blushed delightedly.

'You could charm your way out of a barrel!' she said. 'I shall miss you when you leave for Romney House.'

' 'Twill be a mutual sadness. I shall have to console myself with Felicity and if she won't have me – why then, 'twill have to be the cook.'

They rode on, amused by their conversation, enjoying the splendid views and the warmth of the sun on their faces.

'I will show you the true Dartmoor,' he promised. 'The sweep of the hills, the purple heather, yellow gorse and orange rowan. There to your left, below the bridge – an old moor house where the tinners used to live while they were streaming tin. Further over the old ruined priory . . . beyond that Maudesley, now empty and decayed. A pity! They say 'twas a fine house once . . . There, just completed, Bucher's cottage and to the east of that you can just see the Heron mine.'

'And all this is Heron land?'

'Aye, even the priory tho' 'tis of no value now. We rent out the fields to sheep.'

'And if the mine fails?' she asked seriously.

Martin shrugged. 'Then Allan will be a poor man,' he told her. 'He'll be forced to sell land or rent it. Or go in for sheep, himself.'

'But it won't fail.'

'I trust not.' He held up crossed fingers. 'Here's to their success in London.'

'I second that!'

Another half an hour passed and they diverged from the main track and took what Martin described as 'a prettier road'. After another half an hour he professed himself 'unsure of the direction' and later still he admitted that they were lost.

'Lost?' echoed Eloise. 'But I thought you knew every nook and cranny. Or so you boasted.'

'And now I'm proved wrong – but we've plenty of daylight left.'

'I trust there is, Martin Kendal. I've no plans to spend the night cold and dark in a moor house.'

He winked at her impudently. 'You might find my company compensates for the dark and, as for the cold, why, I would keep you well warmed.'

'Another boast! You are quite incorrigible.'

'And you are very desirable,' he said softly. 'Mayhap I shall steal you from Allan on the very eve of his wedding and gallop away with you into a golden land where—'

'Martin, we are lost and you spend your time rhapsodizing! May we, I beseech you, search for a path of some kind or a familiar landmark.'

Martin assumed a deeply injured expression which made her laugh again. 'But you are right,' he told her. 'We'll ride on with the sun over our right hand – or is it left?'

'Martin!'

'Follow me and all will be well. Now 'tis rather steep here. Let me take the rein and lead your horse.'

Five minutes later they rounded a bend in the overgrown track and found themselves outside a rough hovel. The old walls were cracked and the turf roof sagged alarmingly in the middle. There was a hole in the wall and a low doorway. Outside two children played on the bare earth. A skinny goat wandered freely and a sheep, tethered by its hind leg to a post, had no grass within its reach, having eaten its immediate circle bare. A small terrier ran out of the doorway, barking·furiously, and the oldest child threw a clod of earth at it and missed. A woman appeared with a baby sucking at her breast. Her hair was wild and tangled and she was very dirty. She looked at Eloise and Martin with a mixture of suspicion and loathing. The child cried fitfully and she pulled her other breast free of her blouse and offered it to him.

'Who *are* you?' she demanded. 'What do you want with me?'

'This is Eloise Ballantyne and I—'

'Aren't you one of those dratted Kendals?'

'Aye – and proud of it,' he said coldly.

'And you have the impudence to show your face around here.'

'Why not?' Martin asked.

Eloise backed her horse slightly, embarrassed by the woman's hostility.

'Because 'tis you Kendals is making beggars of honest folks!'

'I deny it. What is your name?'

'Joan Gillis.'

'And your husband is – ?'

'Jake Gillis, if 'tis any of your business.'

At the name Gillis, Eloise moved back further but she could not tear her eyes away from the woman and child. This creature was a Gillis. This wretched scrap of humanity was related to Allan – and would soon be to her! Her stomach knotted with a revulsion which was touched with pity.

'And he does what?' asked Martin peremptorily, all his banter gone.

'He cuts turf,' she told him sullenly. 'He's an honest man.'

'I doubt *that*,' said Martin. 'Who was his father?'

'Donald Gillis but—'

'And he does what?'

'He's dead. He was a tinner at the Maudesley mine.'

'And his father?'

'How do I know?' She was becoming nervous under Martin's questioning and his brusque manner frightened her.

'You know.'

'I have forgotten,' she muttered.

'Then we shall wait here patiently until you remember.'
Her face hardened. 'My husband'll be home.'

'Not yet awhile. Now – your father's father? Who was he?'

She swallowed and her hands tightened round the child. 'William.'

'What was he to Marion Gillis, the witch?'

The woman's eyes widened with fear as she thought she understood the line of his questioning. 'I'm no witch!' she gasped. 'I've never harmed anyone. I've never so much as miscalled a living soul. You ask folk.'

'Hold your tongue and answer my question. What was William Gillis to Marion?'

'I don't know.'

'Cousin? Brother-in-law?'

'I swear I don't know! For pity's sake, leave us alone. Haven't you done the Gillises enough harm. We're despised and feared. Even now, after all these years, folk use us spitefully.'

'I have done you no harm,' said Martin. 'In God's name stop whining.'

'What d'you want with us?' she pleaded. 'Don't touch my children, I beg you. They're innocent of anything but a bad name!'

Eloise could bear it no longer. She now saw with great clarity the purpose of the ride and saw how cleverly it had been accomplished and she was very angry. Suddenly she urged her horse forward. 'We're lost,' she said. 'That is all. We came to ask directions. We've no quarrel with you or your children. Which way to Heron?'

The woman stared at her, began to speak and changed her mind. She pointed and mumbled something which Eloise did not catch but it was not important. Martin knew the way home. He had always known it.

'My thanks to you,' said Eloise. She took a few coins from her purse and tossed them on to the bare earth where the children fought each other to pick them up. Without another look at Martin, Eloise turned her mount towards Heron and urged it into a canter.

Martin rode after her and, putting out a hand, took hold of the reins of her horse.

'Eloise, I beg you. There's no need—'

Her eyes blazed with suppressed fury as she turned to him.

'That was despicable!'

Bringing up her riding crop she slashed at his hand with all her strength. He winced with pain and snatched his hand away. She rode furiously but he kept pace with her and so they continued, side by side, until they reached Heron. Despite Martin's attempts to make amends, Eloise did not utter one more word.

Later in the day Maria found Eloise weeping in her bedchamber and insisted on knowing everything that had taken place. She, too, was furious and a stormy scene followed between her and Martin. It ended with Maria's decision to ride at once to Appledore taking Martin with her. He had finished at school and could take his place at Romney House for the time being. More and more young men in his position were being sent abroad to finish their education, and Hugo and Maria had been considering the idea for some time without reaching any firm conclusions. To travel France or Spain for a year was not expensive for a young man - eighty pounds would cover his own expenses, but if he took a servant and a house the figure would be nearer a hundred and fifty. That would allow for clothes and entertainment - even fencing lessons - but the Heron fortunes were at a low ebb and there was nothing to spare. All their resources were needed if they were to save the mine and Martin's year abroad would almost certainly be delayed or sacrificed entirely.

Maria told Martin in no uncertain terms that this behaviour had been inexcusable, and since he was obviously determined to make mischief between Eloise and

Allan he must stay away from them, at least until the wedding, which had been set for the last day in September. At Appledore Martin could 'cool his heels' and reflect on his disgraceful conduct.

Matt went with them and the first day passed in an uncomfortable silence. Maria and Martin had nothing to say to each other and Matt's attempts at conversation were met with ill-concealed irritation. Finally, he, too, fell silent and rode behind them, muttering disconsolately to himself from time to time. Fortunately, on the second day they overtook a large family returning from a wedding and in their cheerful company it was impossible to remain churlish. Matt and Martin were immediately drawn into their lively conversation and only Maria chose to ride alone, busy with her thoughts.

As they neared Sevenoaks they passed a lone rider. Among other things, he carried a letter from Felicity to Heron with news of Ruth's death, but they were unaware of this. They therefore reached Romney House much earlier than Felicity had dared to hope, only hours, in fact, after the old lady had closed her eyes for the last time. Maria was immediately plunged into preparations for the funeral. There was so much to be attended to. Friends to be notified; a date fixed for the funeral; a coffin to be measured and made. The family lawyer was notified; a small funeral feast was prepared and the black ribbons and drapes which had served Harold were once more brought out of the chest. Matt and Martin wore black ribbons on their sleeves. Maria and Felicity went into Tenterden and seven yards of black silk was purchased and hastily made up by a local seamstress.

Felicity's grief was very real. She had grown fond of Ruth and had found a kind of fulfilment in caring for her, almost as a mother cares for a child. The old lady had been dependent on her and Felicity had enjoyed the knowledge that she was needed and had a purpose in life. Suddenly, that purpose had been taken from her and she felt lost. The tears she cried for Ruth were partly for herself also.

Her grief was sincere and her dark despair made her vulnerable. Maria comforted her as well as she could and kept her busy in an effort to distract her thoughts, but the grim reality of death could not be ignored and Felicity suffered deeply. Martin, genuinely regretting his cruelty towards Eloise, tried to make amends by treating Felicity with great kindness and consideration. Maria, seeing this, was grateful, for it allowed her more time for the many pressing matters requiring her attention. Martin could be gentle, understanding and sympathetic and Felicity clung to him for support during the days that followed. He felt protective towards the shy, grief-stricken girl and it pleased him to help and comfort her.

At the funeral they stood together and his arm was round her shoulders. During the meal that followed he made her eat, although she insisted she was not hungry. He fetched wine for her and talked cheerfully when her eyes filled with tears and his nearness made the day bearable.

'She is with her beloved brother,' he told her. 'She had a long life and a happy one. She adored Harold and now they are together, and at peace with God. You must be happy for her – for both of them. And you can rest easy in your mind for you made her last years happy.'

'Oh, I do hope I did!' said Felicity.

'But you did, most certainly. You fed her, read to her, talked with her—'

'I was impatient sometimes.'

'But did you let her know that?'

'I tried not to.'

'Then I dare say she was quite unaware. But even if she knew 'tis of no importance. I'll wager she was sometimes impatient with you!'

'Aye.' Felicity smiled faintly. 'At times she was.'

'And did you love her less for it?'

'No. I understood the reasons for it.'

'Then wouldn't she also understand *your* reasons? I warrant she did. None of us is perfect. Not you, not me, not Ruth. You need not fear your conscience, Felicity. I believe you were a kind and loving companion to her. Without you she would have been very lonely.' He smiled gently. 'I know you must mourn for her, but don't reproach yourself needlessly. She would not wish it. She loved you in her own way. I'm certain of it. Now, another glass of wine to put some colour back into your cheeks. You are so pale. No, I'll brook no arguments so waste no words. Another glass of wine – there we are – and mayhap a cinnamon biscuit?'

The will was read at ten-thirty the following morning. Samuel Hessop read it very slowly in a deep mournful voice and Maria, Felicity and Martin sat along one side of the table and the cook, the gardener and Matt sat along the other. This, Samuel Hessop had assured her, was the proper way to do it. He stood at one end of the table so that he was silhouetted against the bright sunlight – a short stout figure with a floppy velvet hat covering his balding head.

'February the third, one thousand five hundred and seventy-six—'

Maria marvelled that she had left the writing of the will to so late a date. Only a few months before her death.

As if reading her mind, Hessop looked up at her. 'This will was originally drawn up in fifteen fifty-four and has been revised and amended several times since that date.' She nodded and he continued:

'In the name of God, Amen. I, Ruth Cummins, being still in my full wits and of sound memory do hereby amend my will to read as follows and to be witnessed by one Samuel Hessop and later to be read out by the same after my death. To my dearest Maria Kendal I bequeath with love my jewelled pin and the carved oaken coffer which stands beside my bed. Romney House is bequeathed to her already by my brother Harold and so with my death it passes into her possession. And for the love I bear her, I bequeath also fifty gold crowns that she may live the more joyfully by it and think of me kindly. To Matthew—'

Maria saw Matt start in alarm and nodded to him reassuringly.

'—I bequeath my quill and ink pot and the small bible bound in red leather which I was given as a girl by my father, God rest his soul. To Matthew also the sum of five gold crowns to be spent—'

Matt rose to his feet, his eyes like saucers. 'Me?' he gasped. 'Five gold crowns for me? From the old lady?' He was at once astonished and delighted and a broad grin spread over his face. He did not see Samuel Hesslop's disapproving look, nor did he take note as the lawyer cleared his throat, indicating that he wanted to continue.

'Five gold crowns, Maria!' he cried. 'And I thought she—' He shook his head, bewildered and the lawyer tried in vain to attract his attention. 'I mean, she scolded me that many times—'

'She was fond of you, Matt,' said Maria. 'You know that.'

'Well, I did hope so, but I were never certain sure. And she would call me Matthew and not Matt—'

Maria smiled. 'She still does, you see, even in her will!'

Felicity smiled at him. 'I think she missed you, when you went back to Heron.'

'Missed me? Did she truly miss me?' He shook his head again. 'But five gold crowns! I wish as I could thank her.' He glanced hopefully upward but Samuel Hessop took advantage of the brief pause to continue reading and Matt sat down again, still marvelling at the old lady's generosity.

'And to Felicity Carr whom I love as a daughter, my bed and linen that she may have always a place to lay her head—' Felicity caught her breath and the tears welled up in her eyes, 'and all my garments, that they may be cut and fit to size, and as well as this my silver-topped walking stick to be sold for whatever it will fetch, and twenty-five gold crowns towards her dowry that she may marry as well as is possible and in which estate I wish her lasting joy and comfort.'

Samuel Hessop paused and took a sip of wine while he

waited for Felicity to compose herself. Matt still murmured excitedly over his five gold crowns and the lawyer gave him a reproving glance which went unheeded. At last he cleared his throat again. 'To continue, if I may have everyone's attention – *everyone's* attention,' he added and Matt was nudged into silence by the cook.

'To the cook, Meg Forbes, I bequeath one gold crown and my silver hairbrush and comb also to be sold for whatever they will fetch, and to the gardener, though I believe him to be an idle fellow, one gold crown.'

Maria repressed a smile and the gardener blushed furiously.

'She left me *five*!' crowed Matt, leaning forward to enjoy the man's discomfiture. 'Five gold—'

'Sir!' thundered Samuel Hessop, 'May I remind you that the reading of a will is a solemn occasion and ask you to show your respects to the dead in more seemly behaviour!'

All eyes were suddenly on Matt and it was his turn to blush and the lawyer took several deep breaths in order to compose himself for the rest of the reading.

'If there be anything remaining after these bequests, I charge that it be used to buy bread for the deserving poor—' Samuel Hessop glanced up. 'She has underlined the word "deserving",' he told them, 'the deserving poor of the parish of Appledore so long as they shall utter up a prayer for the safe passage of my soul to Heaven. My blessing and love be with those I leave behind and I pray you remember me oftimes with affection and do beseech my Heavenly Maker that he will pardon my transgressions and hereto I command my soul into His keeping.' He laid down the will and glanced around the assembled company. 'Are there any questions regarding this document?' he asked. No one answered and Maria stood up.

'I think 'tis all very clear. Ruth has remembered us all with great clarity and doubtless we appreciate her various bequests. She had faults, as we all have, but there is not one of us here who will not remember her frequently and with love or respect.'

There was a murmur of agreement and the lawyer gave a polite nod to show his approval of the timely sentiments.

'The bequests will be delivered as soon as practicable,' Maria told them. 'If anyone has a problem regarding the will after Samuel Hessop has left us, I pray you come to me straitly. And now may I ask that we all raise our glasses and drink to the memory of our mutual and very dear friend, Ruth Cummins.'

They pushed back the benches, stood up and joined her in the toast. Matt's bequest had gone to his head. He drunk his wine in one gulp and cried, 'And I say let's have a cheer for the old lady!'

And Samuel Hessop quietly gave up on the whole proceedings.

Maria stayed a few days longer then returned home with Matt to acquaint Hugo of all that had happened. He had already received Felicity's letter so he knew that Ruth was dead. Maria was undecided how best to deal with her own part of the legacy and wanted to talk it over with Hugo. She left Martin at Romney House on the understanding that if he had no further message from her, he was to ride back to Heron in time for the wedding, at which he would act as chief bride-knight. Romney House seemed very empty without her and Felicity spent the rest of the day mending the linen, deep in her own thoughts. Martin, for want of something better to do, spent what remained of *his* day in critical inspection of the garden. Ruth's unkind comment on the gardener had not been forgotten and Martin wanted the man to know he had a new master to reckon with. The two of them toured the rambling garden and Martin tried his best to convey a knowledge of gardening which he did not possess. He enquired about the pruning of the plum trees and suggested they purchase a new plum tree and maybe also a pear. He found fault with the herb garden, pointing out the numerous weeds, and ordered that the holly hedge, nearly seven feet high, be lowered to five and a half. Some of the rose bushes were dead and should be replaced as soon as possible. Lastly, the small pond, containing nothing but rank water and dead leaves, should be restored and stocked with gold fish. When Martin went back to the house for supper he left the man scowling moodily.

That evening, after supper, Martin and Felicity stood by the water and stared at the spot where Mark Wynne had met his end.

'You are always here,' she said suddenly to Martin, 'when I need someone. You were here when Mark Wynne came back and when the mistress died. Your presence is very reassuring. I wanted you to know that.'

'That pleases me greatly,' he said, surprised by her remark. 'I should not like to think of you alone and in distress.'

'I want to thank you,' she said, 'but I don't know how.'

'There's no need for thanks.'

They watched a moorhen working its way through the rushes.

'Once there were three of them,' she told him, 'but one night a fox came. It killed five of the chickens and two of the moorhens. One chicken it took away, the rest were left with their poor heads half-bitten off. 'Twas a dreadful sight. I didn't understand why the fox killed all the others, if not for sport.'

'Nature can be very cruel.'

'Aye. Mark Wynne spoke once of a cock fight. The birds wore spurs and they clawed and pecked each other until one of them dropped dead with fatigue and the other was declared the winner. It made me sick to hear of it.'

'Your heart is too soft,' he said and his voice, in the growing dark, caressed her.

A deep happiness filled her and she closed her eyes. If only she could die, now, with Martin beside her she would be content. She would consider her short life well spent and would envy no one!

Vaguely, he was aware of her emotions.

'So,' he said, to change the subject, 'you now have a dowry! How does that feel?'

'Incredible!' she laughed shakily. 'Now all I need is a husband!'

'They will find a good man for you, you'll see.' He wanted to look at her face but knew what he would see there.

'Will anyone wed me – for a mere twenty-five crowns?'

'If you had nothing men would still desire you – would still want to wed you. You are an attractive young woman.'

'Am I? Or are you being kind – sparing my feelings?'

'I speak truly, Felicity. You have a quiet charm. Look at me and I shall convince you. Now let me see. You have beautiful eyes, a soft mouth, delicate cheek bones—'

'Oh no! I beg you!'

She tried to turn away, confused, but he pulled her back.

'Let me finish!' he said softly. 'If you are nearly a woman and still don't know that you are desirable, why then, no man has ever told you so and that's a pity.'

'Martin!' she begged, but he only pulled her closer.

'I *shall* finish and you *will* listen to me. Your hair is soft and smells sweet and fresh. You have a slim neck, creamy breasts – Ah, but I *have* seen them. When I came to your room that night.'

'Oh!' She was staring into his face, trying to read the thoughts behind his bantering words.

'A neat waist . . .' He slid his hands lightly down her body, 'And no doubt shapely legs to complete the picture. Are they shapely?'

'Don't ask me,' she cried, half laughing at his earnestness.

'If you don't answer I shall be forced to see them for—'

'Aye! They are shapely – I think.' He dropped to his knee and plucked at the hem of her gown. She jerked it from his fingers. 'They *are* shapely. I confess it!' she cried.

'And no man has seen them?'

'Don't, I beg you!' the exhilaration had left her.

Martin stood up. Her expression had changed and, subtly, her mood also.

'Felicity?'

'Don't ask me!'

'Was it Wynne?'

'He didn't touch me – not that way.' She was suddenly terrified he would find her distasteful. That Mark Wynne's hands had sullied her for ever.

'How then? You must tell me.'

'Why? Why must I speak of it? I want to forget it.'

'I want to know,' he insisted.

'But I can't bear the telling of it!' she cried.

Aware of the panic in her voice he drew her into his arms. 'Then I will make it easier for you,' he whispered. 'We will sit together in the old boat – No, lie together. You shall lie in my arms and I will keep you safe. 'Twill not seem so terrible, I promise you.'

Felicity wavered. The prospect of lying with Martin was a tempting one. It was more than she had ever dreamed of – but the price was high. She had no wish to relive the nightmare, of which she had never spoken . . . not even to Maria.

Martin took her prolonged silence to be an assent and pulled the boat in to the bank. He stepped in and helped her into it. The boat was old and creaked protestingly. There was a sheepskin and cushions in it for Maria and Felicity had sometimes used it to while away an hour. Felicity laughed softly. 'I used to imagine Ruth as a young woman, sitting in this boat under the willows, but when I asked her she said 'I never had time for such nonsense'. That made me very sad for her.'

'She was happy, I dare say, in her own way.'

They sat down carefully, trying not to rock the boat, watched by the curious moorhen. Martin arranged the sheepskin across her knees and smiled.

'Tell it,' he said softly and closed his eyes and she began, reluctantly, to speak of it.

Ruth had sent her into the fields one day in search of

Wynne. He had not reported to the house for nearly five weeks and Ruth had no idea whether or not he had attended the sheep market and, if so, to what profit. She no longer had any clear knowledge of the make-up of the flock – the relative number of rams, wethers and ewes, the ratio of lambs to tegs or the number of sheep per square acre. She dimly understood the importance of such figures, for Harold had been at pains to explain it all, but he had told her, also, to 'leave it all to Wynne – he's an honest man'. Wynne's reports on the flock had gradually become less detailed and as she grew older the occasional irrelevancies had puzzled her, but she had relied on Wynne's reputation and concerned herself less and less with the management of the flock. All that she asked for was a monthly report and the profit of any transactions. These dwindled until at last she *did* begin to query his accounting and his reports then became even less regular. Sometimes five weeks passed, sometimes six, before he would put in an appearance.

'I saw him in the distance,' said Felicity. 'He was lying in the shelter of a large outcrop of rock. The sheep were all around him, grazing. He had no dog then to warn him of my arrival. When I reached him I could see that he was either asleep or cupshotten – there were several empty pitchers nearby.' She faltered, seeing him again in her mind's eye, spreadeagled against the turf, breathing heavily. She saw the thick stubble round his jaw and the slack mouth from which a trickle of saliva ran. He smelt of sour ale and urine. His clothes were filthy and stained. 'I stood looking down at him and dreaded waking him. At last I coughed but he didn't stir. I spoke his name and he still didn't move. I thought he was still asleep but when I called him louder and he still lay there I began to think him ill – or even dead! I looked around but there was no one else in sight, so I knelt beside him and touched his arm. Then I put my head down to listen to his heart and—'

Martin's arm tightened round her as she broke off again, biting her lip. A fierce shudder swept through her as she recalled what happened next, as she felt his arms clamp her and his raucous triumphant laughter rang in her ears. He held her in a vice-like grip and pulled her down on top of him. She struggled wildly, too frightened and breathless to scream out and well aware that no one would hear her if she did. He rolled over until she was beneath him.

'I couldn't move under his weight,' she whispered, 'and the smell of him choked me. He was trying to kiss me and I couldn't fight him off so I bit him. He swore and then laughed and said – he said he'd tame me. We were on a slope and he rolled us both down so that I was dizzy when we stopped. I was crushed and bruised and my whole body ached. He knelt over me, so I was trapped between his legs.' She swallowed hard and Martin could feel her body trembling. 'He started to loosen his clothes with one hand and with the other he tugged at mine. I held my bodice together and pushed him as hard as I could. He lost his balance and I wriggled out from under him. As I scrambled to my feet he caught at my skirt and held on, trying to steady himself. As I tugged myself free my skirt tore and I left most of it in his hand. I ran from him – how I don't know, for I was breathless and so terrified that my legs seemed to have no strength in them at all. He ran after me, laughing and roaring and shouting that I'd "got his blood going", and saying what he would do with me when he caught me.'

'And did he catch up with you?' Martin asked after a long pause.

'No, he didn't. He slipped or tripped – I did not see what happened, but when I looked back he was on the ground, nursing his ankle. He didn't follow me and I came back to the house. No one knew what had happened and I couldn't bring myself to speak of it. I hid in my chamber until I had recovered, then I changed my gown. I told the mistress I couldn't find him. He came limping in the following day with his report and I kept out of his way. The dress was quite ruined. I burned it piece by piece.'

'And you told no one?'

'I've told you. I welcomed his death and yet I feel I should think kindly of him now.'

'And you don't.'

'No. If I had the power to bring him alive again I wouldn't use it. Is that a terrible thing to say?'

He shook his head. 'My poor little Felicity. Have you never known a man's love?'

'Never. There's only Jon and we feel nothing for each other.'

'Don't judge all men by Mark Wynne,' he said.

'I don't. I've met you and you treat me with kindness.'

He kissed her on the side of her forehead. 'I shall see to it personally that your husband is all that you desire,' he told her lightly. 'Tell me your requirements and I shall seek out the perfect man.'

'My requirements? Oh no, Martin, I—'

'Tell me!' he insisted. 'Describe your perfect man.'

She was silent. If she described Martin he would guess her secret. If she described anyone else it would be false.

'Eyes?' he prompted.

'Brown with flecks of grey.'

'Hair?'

'Dark.'

'Age – do you like older men? Allan's age, mayhap?'

'Allan? How old is he?'

'Nearly twenty-three.'

'No, too old.'

'Your own age, then?'

'Not that either. A younger man, mayhap a year younger.'

Now he knows, she told herself, and the idea was at once sweet and terrifying.

'And what height should you prefer?' he asked calmly.

She drew away from him slightly and turned to look at him.

'Don't!' she said quietly. 'Don't play this game with me, Martin. I believe you know how I feel about you. I won't pretend.'

Her directness confused him and for a moment he blustered, denying the truth of what she said.

'Stop Martin, I beg you. I'm not ashamed of my feelings for you. I will never be your wife, I accept that. I would not presume to be more than I am. My twenty-five crowns will not buy me a Kendal—'

'Felicity! Don't—'

'Let me finish what I have started, Martin. I cannot unsay it even if I would. No, this is the time for speaking the truth. For me, if not for you. You have treated me respectfully and with kindness. I don't deceive myself that you feel anything more for me—'

'You are wrong, Felicity. I—'

'I know how you feel for Eloise. You have spoke of her with love in your voice.'

He was silent, astonished by her perception and she went on:

'You must marry well and you will not marry me. But that doesn't stop me from loving you, Martin, and I do. I don't ask anything in return for my adoration. I am content that you are near and we are friends. I want to be allowed to love you in my own way. I expect nothing from you.'

Martin felt an unutterable sadness at her words. He also felt guilt. He had been aware of his effect on her and had enjoyed her admiration. There was nothing wrong in that. But he had drawn from her a confession of her feelings and for that he must accept responsibility. But for her gentle, passionate declaration he felt guilt. He had thought to play with her emotions, perhaps even amuse himself at her expense. Not unkindly, but without consideration for *her* feelings. Now she had expressed her own love and his knowledge of it. She knew that he had enjoyed her esteem and he was vaguely ashamed of his behaviour. He recalled the glowing picture he had painted of Eloise, and cursed himself for an insensitive fool. He had smiled at Felicity, letting his eyes express more than was in his heart. He had tried to enchant her and he had succeeded. To one of his looks and charm it had been all too easy.

'Forgive me,' he said. 'I'm not worthy of your love but I doubt I will convince *you* of that.' He wanted to be as honest as she had been but that would hurt her. Her honesty at worst could only flatter him. His honesty might well destroy her.

'I am honoured by your affection,' he said, choosing his words carefully, 'and touched by your honesty. You say I will never marry you and that is true. I must look elsewhere for a bride as the family sees fit. My circumstances demand it. But you say I do not love you and I must argue with that.'

'Martin! You—'

'Hush, little one! Let me have my say. I feel a kind of love for you, not quite brotherly yet not lustful either.'

She laughed shakily but did not interrupt him. 'Eloise *is* very beautiful. She is also hard and I think greedy. But to speak of her that way is ungentlemanly. All I mean to say is that she appeals to the baser instinct in me and you appeal to the finer. Do you understand at all?'

'I think so.'

'I cannot wed you, Felicity, but I love you for your gentle spirit. If I am to stay in Appledore and not travel, as seems likely, I should like you to stay on here. Will you be my loving companion? Would such a position appeal to you?' His voice had resumed its bantering tone but he had said enough of love to satisfy Felicity's needs.

She nodded and her eyes shone with a new brilliance. He was all that she had hoped and he had said he loved her. Not lustfully and for that she was relieved. She was not ready for that. But a loving companion was precisely what she craved. She sighed with happiness, unable to believe her good fortune. As she slid down into the boat with him, to lie chaste and safe in his arms, she knew he had only to command it and she would follow him to the ends of the earth.

CHAPTER ELEVEN

The celebration supper was normally provided for those workers involved in bringing in the harvest, and it included all who worked on the home farm and the house and stables staff at Heron and Ladyford. It was held in the Hall at Heron, which simplified all the preparations. This year, however, Maria and Hugo were keenly aware of the plight of the out-of-work miners, and so they had decided to extend the range of the supper. They invited all the tinners and their families – those working as well as those unemployed. Some of the most needy among the latter had been taken on temporarily to help with the harvest, and thus did qualify for inclusion in the supper. A few worked willingly, others resentfully. The tinners were a proud people and farm work was considered very inferior and not worthy of their skills, but few of them could afford to turn down the opportunity of earning a shilling or two to buy food for their families.

Maria had intended to preside over and supervise the supper, but changed her mind when the trouble between Martin and Eloise flared. Melissa willingly offered to take her place as supervisor, but felt that Eloise, as a future Kendal, should sit at the head of the table in Thomas' absence. Eloise was easily persuaded to do so. The day of the supper dawned hazily, but with a brightness that promised fine weather when the morning mist finally dispersed. The Hall would not hold the increased numbers, so the largest barn was pressed into service and soon after cockcrow Matt and Jon were at work, pushing and pulling sacks of grain, ploughs and barrels to the far end, to make room for the tables. They moved armfuls of rakes, scythes, and flails, collected buckets and pails, coiled ropes and stacked an assortment of ladders neatly in a corner. The barn itself was high and wide with whitewashed walls, and dark rafters supported the sagging thatch. It smelled dankly of wet straw and rats and leather, and as soon as a sufficient space had been cleared the men set to with brooms to sweep up the earth floor. Within seconds the air was thick with dust and Jon began to cough and splutter.

Matt wrinkled his nose disparagingly. 'Stinking stuff! 'Tis to be hoped they'll put down a few herbs to sweeten the place.'

'They will – or rather, *we* will. There's to be fresh straw and lavender. We'll open all the doors and windows to let the air blow through.' He peered down at a number of rat holes revealed by his sweeping. 'I reckon we shall need Nat Gully again before long. The rats are back again. Nothing gets rid of them for long.'

'Aye,' said Matt. 'That first sack I shifted was leaking corn like water! Little varmits!'

They swept out the stale straw and left the barn for half an hour for the dust to settle and the clean air to do its work. They had to collect trestles, boards and benches from various places – Ladyford had offered two and there were several stored at the mine. Another small trestle was fetched from the buttery. As they collected them, they were stacked outside the barn and shortly after Melissa appeared to inspect their work.

'There were a hundred and ten at the last count,' she muttered, 'not counting ourselves. There's how many boards – seven and a small one? That's ten to a board and six to the small one—' She looked hopefully at Jon and Matt, but the former shook his head regretfully.

Matt, however, considered what she had said. 'Aye,' he said, 'I reckon that's about it.'

Melissa looked vaguely surprised. 'Is it?'

'Aye,' said Matt. 'What you said about the tables and there being seven and all that.' He glanced at Jon to see if he was impressed, but Jon was hiding a grin and did not meet his eyes.

Melissa did a rapid calculation on her fingers. 'No,' she

said. 'I think not quite enough. Seventy and six – we're short by twenty or more.'

'That's what I said!' Matt protested. 'Leastways 'tis what I meant to say.' He looked accusingly at Jon. 'You're not much help, any road. Not saying nowt, are you?'

Jon shrugged good-humouredly. 'Mayhap we could make up a table with an old door,' he suggested. 'Set it on four barrels.'

'Oh, that's well said,' cried Melissa. 'I'll leave you to see to it, Jon. See what you can find. Now, Matt, I want you to take the shears and cut a good quantity of greenery to decorate walls and tables. Eloise will see to the arranging later. Put it in water until 'tis needed. Oh dear, my head will never save my feet! I've left the candles at Ladyford. Mayhap I can send young Ellie over, or Lorna – if I can find her. She is always gadding about with that young Nathaniel. She'd best have been a boy, that one!'

Matt disappeared into the wood with the shears and Jon went off in the opposite direction. Melissa stood for a moment, deep in thought, then went inside the barn and began to consider where the tables should go. Just then Eloise joined her, looking very businesslike with an apron over her skirt.

'We'll need a dozen torches,' Melissa told her, 'Jon can fasten them along the walls and we can use that raised platform for the fiddlers.'

Eloise nodded. 'And the family – where shall we sit?'

'At the far end, do you think?'

'I think so. Minnie wants to know how many loaves to bake. She has forgot.'

'Loaves? Ah, Maria said twenty, but now I think on it 'twill be too few. We will feed a hundred or more and they will be very hungry. Times are so hard for them, poor souls. Tell her forty if she has enough flour. If any is left over the most deserving shall take it home.'

'And if there is *not* enough flour?'

Melissa sighed distractedly. 'Then Ben can ride to the mill and fetch back another small sack. No, wait. I have some at Ladyford. He can ride for it if necessary. Maggie will know where it is.'

Eloise hurried off and Melissa was left alone once more. There was so much to do. If only Maria had delayed her visit to Kent. Maria had not confided in her, but Melissa guessed at the reason for her hasty departure and sympathized. Sons could be a great trial, she reflected, and was thankful that Oliver was happily wed. Still, she envied Maria in one respect, for at least she had her sons around her and knew that they slept safe in their beds at night. But that was a foolish way to think, she reproached herself. She had a daughter-in-law and two fine grandchildren and a good friend in Maggie. Her dearest Thomas had recovered his health. There were so many things for which she was thankful it would be churlish to complain because her son was at sea. Especially as he promised to return a rich man. She allowed herself a smile but then marshalled her wandering thoughts. There was work to be done. The bare earth floor of the barn caught her eye and she raised one finger to tap her lips. 'Clean straw and lavender,' she said briskly and went to see what Ben had done with it.

Allan and Hugo returned from London to find the preparations well under way. They were in high spirits, for their journey had been a fruitful one. They had promises for the financial help they sought and the future of the Heron mine was beginning to look distinctly healthy. With Bucher's expertise and the additional finance, they could begin work on two new drifts and, with the installation of the new machinery, re-employ most of the men they had thrown out of work.

Hugo was a little puzzled and disappointed to find that Maria and Martin had already left for Romney House, but soon after mid-day the messenger arrived with Felicity's letter, informing them of Ruth's death. Hugo realized then that she would have gone anyway on receiving the sad news. It seemed they were destined to hold the harvest supper without her.

Allan was pleased to find Eloise in a more cheerful frame

of mind. The preparations for the supper were keeping her busy and for the time being the Gillis family were forgotten. She greeted him warmly and was obviously enjoying herself – and greatly looking forward to the evening when she would grace the head of the table. For the first time she would act as mistress of Heron and the idea thrilled her. She threw her arms round his neck and hugged him. The news of their success in London pleased her, too, and she clung tightly to his arm as they went up the steps into the house. She was glad that Martin had gone. She now had Allan to herself. Allan, who in a month's time would be her husband and Heron her rightful home. Stretching before her she saw a delightful succession of harvest suppers with Eloise Kendal as queen of ceremonies. She saw herself engaging staff – a suitable tutor for their children; maybe a dancing teacher for herself. Just as easily, she pictured herself dismissing unsatisfactory servants – she would be firm, polite and implacable.

'Later we shall decorate the barn with green boughs,' she told him excitedly, 'and Maggie is bringing some coloured ribbons and baubles for the tables, but do not look into the barn until we are quite finished. I want to surprise you. Oh – and I have planned a short speech.'

'A speech?'

'I thought it proper that I should, Allan. I thought to apologize for Maria's absence and thank them for their efforts. Do say you approve.'

'If it pleases you to make a speech—'

'Oh no, Allan. Is it seemly?'

He laughed. 'Of course it is. A nice gesture. Tell them also that I love you!'

'Allan! I don't dare, though I wish I could. But mayhap you should give the speech instead of me? I might be too bold.'

'No, no, they will love to hear it from you. Give your speech and I'm certain you will do it prettily. Now I must change and persuade Minnie to give us some refreshment. I cannot wait until the evening and nor, I wager, can Hugo!

We stayed overnight at an abysmal inn and the meat was scanty and over-cooked. Tell me when all is ready and I will come and admire your barn.'

By seven o'clock the transformation was complete. The barn was ablaze with lights from the burning torches along each wall. Green branches hid the stained walls and formed a graceful awning over the top table, which was set at right-angles to the others. The tables had been covered with sheets and long strands of ivy trailed down the centre of each with, here and there, a glass bauble or a cluster of ribbons tied in bows. A sheaf of corn made of bread was suspended over the centre of each table and two stooks of real barley held the barn door wide open. Each table groaned with dishes of apples and nuts, with which the hungriest could blunt the edge of their appetites before the arrival of the main dish. From one of the rafters a solitary ginger cat watched the proceedings with, now and then, a suspicious flick of his tail.

Allan and Hugo looked round with obvious pleasure and announced themselves duly impressed.

'You have all done exceedingly well,' said Hugo. 'My thanks to all you good ladies – and men – who have wrought the miracle. The old barn even *smells* good. Is there any lavender left within a mile radius of Heron?'

They all laughed and after a little more conversation they retired to put on their finery and reassembled just in time to greet the three fiddlers hired to play throughout the evening's festivities. They were three brothers named Dan, Sam and Willie Crocker and were in great demand at all functions, for they were rightly judged the best in the neighbourhood. The three musicians joined the family in a toast to the evening's success, then took their places and struck up the first tune, so that the first visitors to arrive would not find the barn silent as well as empty.

Allan wore green and gold with a golden feather in his cap. Hugo wore dark brown trimmed and slashed with white. Melissa was in blue, Maggie in a slate grey with orange lace and Eloise wore a striking gown of purple silk, cut very low and decorated with red and gold braid.

'Here comes the first couple!' whispered Maggie as an elderly man and woman walked towards them. She looked very frail but her face was tanned by the sun and Allan thought he had seen her working in the fields. Most of the labourers worked until the day they died unless struck by infirmity. It was a hard existence and the feast days and celebrations were, for most of them, the only excitement in their lives. Allan hoped they would enjoy themselves.

'Come right in and find a seat,' Melissa urged them. 'Matt shall give you a drink – Ah, here comes another. Good evening to you and welcome . . . And Nancy Fookes, I remember you – and here's a whole cartload arriving! We'll be rushed off our feet soon!'

She darted off to see that the food was ready, leaving Hugo, Allan and Eloise to greet each new arrival. They came shyly, the men uncomfortable in the best clothes they possessed, the women with flowers, ribbons or feathers stitched to their gowns or worn in their hair. Most came smiling but a few nodded stiffly, their resentment written plain on their faces.

Whenever they could, they addressed their visitors by name in an effort to make them feel welcome. Gradually the tables filled up and the chatter, once drowned by the music, now threatened to overwhelm it, but the three men drank heartily and played harder than ever.

There was cider and fresh brewed ale for everyone. The pitchers were set along the tables and replaced as soon as they were empty. Trays of veal pies and mutton pasties arrived – Maggie had excelled herself – and two pigs, cooked the previous day, had been carved ready and piled high on the trays, beside hunks of chicken and thick slices of spiced sausage – Melissa's speciality. Ellie ran to and fro, with bread, cheese and beetroot pickles, her face glowing, her hair tied back with a red ribbon and a few ears of barley.

On the top table sat all the Kendals with the exception

of Martin and Maria. Melissa was there with Nina who, in a bright red dress and coloured beads, looked more gipsy than ever with her swarthy skin and dark flashing eyes and black hair. Thomas had remained at home with the little ones and Nina and Melissa, with Jacob, would ride home as soon as the meal was over. Nina had not long recovered from the birth of her second child and was still feeding him herself.

The Crocker brothers played with great enthusiasm and the lively music echoed among the rafters of the old barn. As drink loosened the tongues, they wagged more freely, and between mouthfuls of food people sang snatches of the well loved songs, punctuated by bursts of laughter as jokes were exchanged and riddles explained to the growing satisfaction of everyone. Hans Bucher sat between Allan and Melissa in an outfit of pale green brocade. It made his face look paler than usual and he looked ill-at-ease. He drank sparingly of the cider, for he had tried to bolster his courage earlier by a glass or two of madeira and now the two liquids mingled unhappily in his delicate stomach. He was by nature a timid man and large noisy gatherings exhausted him.

'More pork, Master Bucher?' asked Melissa. 'You eat so little – it would not keep a flea alive! Will you try a veal pie? They are Maggie's speciality – or mayhap a slice of sausage? No? Are you unwell, Master Bucher?'

She looked at him with concern but he merely shook his head and smiled feebly. From the other end of the table there were giggles from Lorna and a burst of excited chatter from Piers who sat beside her. Ellie, Maggie and Minnie were rushed off their feet, removing empty dishes and bringing in new ones. There were custards and junkets to be served, and tarts to be cut up. Maggie carried a large bowl of fruit which she ladled out generously and there were seven large fruit cakes waiting to round off the meal. Maria had decided that the meal should be filling rather than fancy. It might be the only good food many of them would have.

233

At the end of one of the tables Hugo saw Barlowe, the mine manager, and raised a hand in greeting. Once they had been enemies – they had even fought. Now Barlowe was loyal to him and Hugo trusted him. He was a hard man but he did his job well and the tinners respected his authority. Halfway down the table Hugo recognized Tiddons and Boord with Annie Boord beside him, and at the next table Rita Carp sat with John Jenkins and his family. There were other faces – Green and Lennard and a man whose name he could not recall. He saw that they ate well and said little and was surprised that they had accepted the invitation to attend.

Matt, Jacob and Jon were kept busy replenishing the pitchers and Ben ran to and fro between the barn and the kitchen, where a great pile of dishes and bowls were waiting to be washed up. They would start on that job as soon as the feasting was through and hopefully would eat their own supper, prudently reserved, and get back into the barn in time to join in the merrymaking which would last until midnight. As the evening progressed into a harmonious blend of laughter, music and the occasional belch, at last it was deemed time for Eloise's speech. She stood up while Hugo banged on the table with the hilt of his knife and Matt bellowed a demand for silence.

'The mistress wants to speak,' he shouted and Eloise's heart warmed to him. As she looked round at the rows of flushed faces, the fiddlers finished their tune and rested their instruments, and the chatter died away until a small boy hiccupping was the only sound in the room. All eyes turned to Eloise, and no one could deny her beauty. The excitement had touched her cheeks with a warm glow and her eyes sparkled. The torchlight on the walls behind her gave her face a flattering softness, and her neck and shoulders shone creamy-white in the light from the candles set at intervals along the table.

'Good friends,' she began and there was a delighted murmur of approval from her listeners. 'Hugo has asked me to speak to you in Maria's absence and I am pleased to do so. Maria has to attend a funeral and we are all sorry she cannot be with us tonight, but on her behalf and on behalf of all at Heron and Ladyford we welcome you to this harvest supper.' Her initial nervousness vanished and her clear voice carried easily to the far end of the barn. 'There are many here tonight for the first time and to those we give a special welcome. Our thanks to all those who prepared tonight's feast—' There was a clamour of approval and a burst of applause, 'And our thanks to God also for a bountiful harvest. You have all worked long and hard and tonight is your due reward. We want you to enjoy yourselves. When the food is finished we shall clear away the tables and the fiddlers will play until the stroke of twelve. So, from all of us to all of you, our blessings and God go with you.'

She sat down to tumultuous applause and stamping of feet and even a few ragged cheers. Allan gave her a kiss and Hugo leaned forward.

'That was splendidly done, Eloise. Maria will be very pleased.'

An hour later the room was cleared and the dancing was in progress. The Crockers had managed to keep the music going without a break. One would fall out to eat and drink while the other two played on. Now they were all replete and could give their whole attention to their music, with only the briefest pauses to wipe the sweat from their faces or gulp large mouthfuls of ale. Among all this jollity, Hans Bucher was not at all happy. His stomach heaved and his head ached and the room swam before him. Melissa, Nina and Jacob had already returned to Ladyford and Eloise was dancing with Allan, so it was left to Maggie to realize what a sad state he was in.

'Would you care to go to bed, Master Bucher?' she asked him kindly. 'You look so tired and the best part of the evening is over. We could find you a bed in Heron or someone will go with you if you wish to sleep in your own bed.'

He turned in his seat and regarded her blearily. 'My

own bed?' he repeated. 'Go home to bed?' He shook his head. 'Who says I must go to bed, eh?'

' 'Tis I, Maggie, from Ladyford,' she told him. 'I don't say you *must* go only that I think you are very tired—'

'I am indeed tired. Aye, I am tired . . . Aye, 'tis true good lady, I am very tired.'

'And will you sleep the night at Heron? You will be most welcome to do so.'

'No! Not at Heron . . . No, no. I must sleep in my own bed.'

'Then I'll send Jon with you to see you safely to your door.'

'To my door? Oh aye, my door . . .'

Maggie spoke quickly to Hugo who looked at his guest with some amusement. 'Aye, send him home,' he told Maggie. 'Our English hospitality has proved too much for him, poor man.'

Jon cursed inwardly at being forced to relinquish even half an hour's entertainment, but he helped Bucher outside as discreetly as possible and set him on his horse. He rode alongside him as they moved at a walking pace and, when necessary, put out a hand to steady his companion when he swayed. When they reached the cottage he helped the little man down from his horse, saw him safely inside and lit his candle for him.

'Will you manage the stairs?' he asked. 'Shall I help you?'

'No . . .' Bucher waved his hand in a shaky gesture of dismissal. 'Go . . . leave me.'

'I'll tether your horse behind the cottage,' Jon told him.

Bucher had slipped down and was sitting on the bottom stair with the candle on the floor beside him. Jon hesitated then, with a shrug, left him. He tied the horse to a tree at the rear of the cottage and then remounted his own. As he rode back towards Heron he passed two men walking towards him. They kept their faces averted and muttered no greeting in answer to his own, 'A safe night!' Jon thought them ill mannered, but wasted no more time on them. Spurring his horse, he cantered back to the harvest supper where Minnie was waiting impatiently to dance with him.

Hans lay propped against the stairwell, his head lolling forward on his chest, his eyes closed. Outside, the wind had risen and gusted the first autumn leaves against the shutters. The house timbers creaked a little, but otherwise there was no sound save his own heavy breathing and an occasional groan whenever he moved his throbbing head. His bladder was full and he would have to relieve himself, but he doubted if he could crawl to the door. Slowly, he let himself topple forward until he was on all fours, but as he reached for the candle he fell sideways on to it and extinguished it. He cursed weakly, then continued his erratic progress to the door. He managed to open it and somehow found himself outside and on his feet. A handy shrub served his purpose and he staggered back to the door. As he did so, he thought he heard a whispered voice very near him in the darkness.

'Hold! Who . . . Who's there?'

Swaying, he clung to the door for support and stared into the darkness. Another sound, like a muffled laugh, caught his ear and he turned towards it. At any other time he would have been afraid. Now he just felt too ill to care. After a moment's further hesitation, he stumbled back inside and, closing the door, leaned back upon it. Somehow he had to get upstairs and into bed, but it was a daunting prospect and one that worried him. A wave of nausea swept through him and tears of self-pity welled up in his eyes. He was ill and he was alone. With a supreme effort he propelled himself forward and up the first two steps, then his legs gave way under him and he was forced to make his way up the rest of the stairs on his hands and knees. At last he reached the small neat bed chamber and suddenly he heard the sound of footsteps below his window. A prickle of fear touched his spine then blurred into a vague disquiet.

The nausea had eased temporarily and he stumbled to the window and opened the shutters so that he could look down into the garden. Dark shapes of trees and shrubs swam together.

'Who goes there?' he asked and was suddenly aware that his voice was slurred. The knowledge shamed him and he lost interest in the footsteps and withdrew his head. He went to the bed and fell carefully on to it, face downwards. A wonderful feeling of relief seized him. He had reached his own bed. He was safe.

The number of men lurking outside the house grew steadily as, one by one, the men concerned slipped away from the harvest supper and made their way through the darkness to meet their fellows. Some carried unlit torches, others a bundle of rags soaked in tar – anything that would conceivably burn. They spoke in whispers, crouched in the shadows, their voices blown by the wind, their faces harsh and strained. When eleven men had assembled there, they were ready.

'He'll be sleeping,' Boord told them, 'for he's had a bellyful tonight. Cup shotten is our mincing man, so we'll get no trouble. He'll wake up burned to a cinder and never know what happened!'

There was a rumble of muted laughter.

'Let's be done with it then,' said Alf Gillis. 'We're wasting time.'

'Aye, let's get it over.' That was John Greer.

Boord scowled. 'You're an impatient bastard, Alf Gillis. We'll do it when I say so and not afore. Now we all know the plan – we set it alight then scatter *fast*. Don't linger to enjoy the blaze or we'll have the constables after us. If they catch one of us then likely we'll *all* hang. There's to be no one here when help comes. No one!' There was an impatient nodding of heads. 'And remember, we were all at the dancing and none's to know otherwise. Stick to the story, every man jack of you, or by God's teeth we're done for.'

'Cut the talking and start the doing!' growled Jake Gillis. 'We all know the plan. Light the torches.'

From the first torch they lit all the others, and soon the little cottage was ringed by a circle of flames as the men crept up on it from all sides. At a whispered signal they hurled the flaming brands – a few landed on the new thatch, others were thrust against the wooden doors and in at the open shutters. The thatch took a moment or two to catch alight, for the reeds were densely packed and slightly damp, but they smouldered in several places and then, simultaneously, the fires burst out with a fierce crackling sound. The doors were scorched and thick smoke drifted from the wood, but they did not flare immediately. Inside the room, the burning rags set fire to the rushes that covered the floor, and in no time at all the flames had spread across to the bottom of the stairs and were licking hungrily at the wooden risers. Smoke filled the room, swirled by the gusts of wind blowing in at the window, but upstairs Hans Bucher lay in a drunken stupor oblivious to the danger.

Hugo and Maggie finished their dance and returned, breathless and laughing, to their seats. There they found Barlowe waiting.

'May I speak with you?' he asked Hugo, who obligingly walked a few paces with him until they were out of earshot of the rest of the family.

'It may be my suspicious mind but there's a few faces missing,' said Barlowe. 'Suddenly the Gillises are gone, Boord, Jenkins – a lot of mean men—'

'Gone?' said Hugo. He had drunk a little too well and his mind was slow to grasp what Barlowe was suggesting.

'Aye, sir. One minute they was all here, now there's a good number missing. And Master Bucher's home alone.'

'Bucher? Dear God! Do you think they mean him some harm? No! I won't believe it.'

'I wish you would,' said Barlowe grimly, 'because time's passing and I wouldn't trust any of them. They're up to some mischief together I'll be—'

'I hope you're wrong,' cried Hugo, 'but we'd best go and see. Jon! Fetch the horses man, quick! It might be life or death. Matt! Allan! Come quickly.'

As they came running, a few curious faces turned towards the commotion, but there was no time to spare feelings or consider the party atmosphere.

'We fear for Bucher's life. Fetch weapons. Jon is saddling the horses. Every minute counts!'

Faced with a possible emergency, Hugo's head had cleared and within minutes the small group of men were mounted and galloping towards Bucher's cottage. As soon as they rounded a bend in the highway they could see the glow in the sky that told them Barlowe's guess had been correct.

'My God, I'll hang them all with my own hands if they've harmed him!' muttered Hugo.

The cottage was ablaze by the time they reached it, but the smoke had finally entered Bucher's lungs and made him cough. Dimly, he had become aware of the fact that his home was on fire and he had the presence of mind to stagger to the top of the stairs, only to find them burning fiercely and offering no escape. His peril was very real and fear sobered him.

He lapsed into his native tongue, and began to pray. As he prayed, he ran to the window and looked down. It seemed a long way to the ground and there was nothing to break his fall. Looking up, he saw the blazing roof and was seized by another fit of coughing as the wind blew the thick white smoke towards him.

'Help me!' he screamed. Terror gave added power to his thin voice, which was heard by the approaching group of horsemen. Behind Bucher the flames had reached the door and flickered under it and around the edges. From below him came the dull roar and the room was uncomfortably hot. Wisps of smoke found their way through the planking of the floor and he stared at them hypnotized, like a rabbit before a snake. Despairingly he fell on his knees beside the bed and resumed his prayers, his eyes closed against the smoke, his hands covering his ears, blotting out the awesome crackle of the fire. With a crash, the stairs collapsed and the sound jerked him into a fresh paroxsym of fear and a heightened sense of his helplessness. He knew he was going to die as surely as though he read the words. With a moan, he ran to the window to take a last look at the sky and from there to rail at his cruel God, who thus abandoned the innocent.

To his astonishment he saw a group of men ride up to his gate. They were shouting to him urgently, but he could not make out what they said. He leaned out, a wild hope forming in his breast that God, in his infinite mercy, had relented.

'Jump!' shouted Hugo. 'As soon as the horses are in position. D'you hear me? Jump on to the horses. They will break your fall.'

'I can't!' cried Bucher. 'I know I can't! God help me but I can't.'

'You must!' shouted Hugo, and already the men had dismounted and were pushing the horses together. There were five animals and their backs made a broad if insecure platform.

'Jump, you fool, before 'tis too late!' urged Jon. The extreme heat was affecting the horses nearest to the house. They whinnied shrilly in alarm and fidgetted sideways.

'Jump, damn you!' shouted Hugo. 'If not, then you'll burn. We can do no more for you so *jump!*'

Awkwardly, Bucher climbed out on to the window ledge and closed his eyes. The ceiling behind him collapsed in a fierce tangle of burning reeds and a whirling mass of sparks. He actually fell out of the window, and his scream of fear was abruptly ended as he landed heavily among the backs of the horses and all the breath was knocked from him. The horses reared as he slipped down between them, and a hoof caught him across the back of the head. With a final agonized shudder he slipped into unconsciousness and was carried back to Heron in the same state.

★

No words from Hugo could reassure him or persuade him to reconsider his decision to go home. He was not a brave man nor a foolhardy one and he was convinced that, having failed the first attempt, his adversaries would try again. The prospect terrified him and his one aim was to put as many miles as possible between himself and Heron. He was breaking his contract by going, but remained unimpressed by all the arguments put forward to keep him in England. The shock of his ordeal had seriously undermined his health both physically and mentally. His hands shook visibly and his eyes had a haunted look which revealed his inner turmoil. He had lost weight and could not eat without nausea. A sleeping draught was recommended by the physician but he refused to take it, afraid that another attempt would be made on his life while he slept.

All the men believed to be involved in the attack were rounded up and detained for questioning by the justices, but they could not be shaken from their alibis – that they were at the harvest supper and had gone home early. They insisted stubbornly that they went straight to their homes and knew nothing of the fire until the following day. No one believed them and it was only a matter of time before one of them would back down and confess. So far it had not happened and no action had been taken to convict and punish them. Hugo was deeply incensed by this failure and his bitterness grew as Bucher remained adamant on the question of his return home. The entire success of the innovations at the mine depended on him and the prospect of losing him was unbearable. Jon was questioned about the two men he had passed on his return from Bucher's house but he could not identify them. He was secretly glad that he could not do so, for he was convinced he would be marked down for harassment if he did. He was not a coward, but he had a wife and family and the tinners were hard men who could be very vindictive – as they had already demonstrated. Jon had no wish to cross them.

On the Thursday following the attack, Hugo stood in the Hall with Allan. 'If only Maria would return,' said

Hugo wearily. 'I don't know what she could do but she is very shrewd. She might even charm Bucher into staying with us. He likes her well enough. They have become good friends.'

'I doubt if anyone could persuade him,' said Allan. 'Eloise has tried to no avail. You have tried and so have I.'

'Hell and damnation! Something *must* be done. I cannot let him go. He will never return and we will never find another to equal him. I know he is an odd fellow – they call him mincing man – but I'd give my eye-tooth to have half his skill. He is a brilliant man and we are going to lose him. Oh, why did Maggie let him go home? She should have insisted that he stayed at Heron.'

'Poor Maggie. She reproaches herself daily, but how could she know what would happen? She's not at fault. The blame rests squarely with the perpetrators of the crime.'

'I know. I know.' Hugo pressed a hand over his face and sighed heavily. 'Dear God, I'll crucify those bastards if I can. I swear I will. So much at stake! So much to lose! By God, they'll know my wrath. They'll know how it feels to cross a Kendal! But what good will it do if Bucher is lost to us?'

'Revenge is sweet,' said Allan.

'Aye. So they say. And defeat is a bitter pill to swallow. They say that, also. If Bucher goes we may hang the villains but we'll have lost. What a sorry mess. Ah, here comes Minnie.'

Minnie came downstairs with a tray and shook her head.

'Not a bite!' she reported. 'I've cajoled him and sweet-talked him but he wouldn't touch it. A nice coddled egg, I said, and a fine slice of ham. Very soothing for the nerves, eggs, I told him, but he said he had no appetite and was there any news of a riding party he could travel with to Harwich!'

'Hell!' muttered Hugo.

'Poor little man,' said Minnie. 'He's wasting away and his eyes have sunk right back in his head. I doubt they'll recognize him when he does get home. And his fingers keep twitching at the sheet, never still. He took a sip or two of milk, though.'

'He did? Did he drink much?' asked Allan eagerly.

She shrugged. 'A few sips. See, here's the beaker. He took less than half. I don't know how he'll get to the coast the state he's in. He'll be that weak.'

She went away and the two men regarded each other dejectedly.

' 'Tis the Gillises,' Allan said. 'The damned Gillises.'

Hugo looked at him sharply. ' 'Twas not them alone. Boord, Greer, Jenkins.'

'But they were behind it, I know it in my bones. Working out the curse after all these years.'

'Don't talk that way! 'Tis folly and you know it.'

'Is it? I wonder. Perhaps we have been doomed ever since they hanged Marion Gillis.' He spoke calmly but he avoided Hugo's eyes. 'She cursed the Kendals, so they say.'

'Stop it! You rant on like an old woman!'

'Mayhap we kick against our fate but cannot escape it.'

'You play into their hands, then, by such fancies. Don't speak this way again, Allan, d'you hear me?'

Allan turned to look at him and his face was haggard. 'These accursed Gillises are my kin,' he said. 'All mad or bad, Nat said.'

'I won't stay here and listen to you!' Hugo stormed. 'Those Gillis brothers are far removed from you.'

'And Annie Boord. She's another of them.'

'They're an evil brood, but in Heaven's name you are a *Kendal*. You were never a Gillis. Annie was born to a Gillis father. You were more fortunate. Your father was more fortunate. His was a Kendal father. There's a world of difference and you'd do well to – Ah, here's Eloise.'

She came up smiling cheerfully and slipped her arm through Allan's. 'I refuse to be sick at heart,' she said. 'A few more weeks and we shall be wed. Come, Allan, smile for me.'

But he pulled his arm free and strode away without a word.

'Forgive him,' said Hugo. 'This wretched business has played havoc with our spirits but we must not give up hope.'

But his optimism was ill-founded. Maria returned three days later in time to witness Bucher's departure. Hugo's mood was one of black despair as they made their farewells and watched him ride away to join his party.

'Someone will pay for this!' he whispered bitterly.

Maria was shocked by the change in him. She had never seen her husband so angry and was suddenly fearful.

CHAPTER TWELVE

Hugo sat on a grassy mound, his elbows resting on his knees and his mouth pressed against his clasped hands. The mound on which he sat had once been a wall of the old Harben Priory, but it had long since crumbled and many of the stones had been taken away for use elsewhere. From where he sat he had a good view of the rest of the ruins and, beyond them, the gardens which had once been so lovingly tended by the monks. Andrew had been among that devoted band and Hugo found himself wishing his spirit might somehow return to advise him. Andrew was Elizabeth's brother and Elizabeth had wed the first Kendal to live in Heron. So long ago and so promising a start, Hugo thought joylessly. Now where were they, this proud line of Kendals? The mine was closed: doomed in Hugo's eyes. They were living on borrowed time. Without the precious tin, Heron would surely dwindle and die. There was a great bitterness in his soul and his heart was heavy. A month had passed since the outrage, during which time much had happened and none of it good. Bucher had returned to his native land with a half promise – reluctantly given – that he might one day come back to England and finish the task for which he had originally been engaged. Hugo knew in his heart that he would not do so, although for Maria's sake he pretended to believe it.

Hugo had given the tinners an ultimatum. If the perpetrators of the deed confessed he would reopen the mine. If not he would close it forever. Those suspected – the men missed from the harvest supper – were held in custody awaiting charges, but there was no real evidence to connect them with the firing of the cottage. Jon had not recognized the two men he had passed that night on his return to Heron and all the men had alibis. There was someone to vouch for each one, to say that they were safe at home or on the way home in the company of friends or family. The ranks of the tinners had closed round the would-be assassins and time was running out. No one had come forward to confess to a part in the attack and no information had been laid before the justices which could bring about a conviction. The suspected men remained in gaol and Hugo's vengeance fell upon the others. After an extended deadline there was still no response and he had closed the Heron mine for an indefinite period. A notice was posted outside to the effect that the planned alterations could no longer go ahead, since they were now without the expert advice needed to further the scheme. Hans Bucher would not return to England while the attack on his life went unpunished.

Maria had tried to remonstrate with him. It distressed her that the innocent were suffering along with the guilty, but Hugo argued with some justification that by concealing the identity of the guilty men they all shared responsibility for the crime and must thus be considered accessories to it. By refusing to betray the criminals they were giving tacit approval to their actions, and Maria was unable to argue with the ultimate logic of his argument. The plight of the tinners' families disturbed her deeply, for she had always prided herself on a genuine interest in their welfare. Now she knew that the children would go hungry and in a few months' time the elderly would be at risk from the winter cold. She would have helped them had she dared, but Hugo was adamant and she knew she must support him in the matter, however her humanitarian instincts might dictate to the contrary. All work at the mine ceased and the tinners and their families were left to endure the ensuing hardships.

For Hugo it had been a difficult decision. His loyalties were also divided to a great extent. On the one hand, he felt a natural responsibility to his work force. The Kendals were accounted good masters who treated their workers fairly. On the other hand, he felt a moral obligation towards Bucher who had come to England at his instigation. Hugo was deeply ashamed at the way his visitor had been treated. Whatever their imagined wrongs the men had gone too far. They had overstepped the limits of peaceful protest and had stooped to murder. There could be no relenting. Hugo was determined to maintain the pressure until they cracked under it. Justice must be done and all his thoughts were directed to that end.

He was thankful that Maria had other matters to occupy her thoughts. She had the wedding to prepare for and the household at Appledore to manage. The latter presented no real problem. James Moore had generously offered to undertake Martin's initiation into the mysteries of sheep farming, and he had already started work with Frank Innley, one of Moore's best shepherds. After a year, Martin should have a fair grasp of the basic principles of successful sheep farming. He would have experienced the various seasonal activities and he would have some idea of market procedure, feeding, breeding, lambing and doctoring. Not until then would Maria buy the new flock. When she did, one of James Moore's younger lookers would be permanently engaged to help Martin. Hugo was very hopeful of the outcome of this venture. He would be pleased to see Martin with a means of livelihood. The only problem would be financing the flock. A little of the money remained from the sale of the previous flock, but more would be needed. If the Heron mine did not reopen they would be hard-pressed to find the money.

The wedding preparations were Maria's most urgent problem. Allan and Eloise seemed more content with each other after their earlier discords and Hugo felt a little more hopeful of the success of the alliance. Allan must master his moods and Eloise her roving eye – but a family would soon take up all her energies. Her first son would provide Heron with a new heir – but what would remain for him to inherit if the mine failed? It was a bleak prospect and one which increasingly occupied Hugo's thoughts.

He sighed deeply, stretched himself back against the

springy turf and closed his eyes. He reconsidered the action he had taken in respect of the mine and wondered, if Simon had lived, would *he* have acted in the same way. He covered his face with his hands the better to recreate Simon's image. What would Simon have done in his place? Simon, blond and blue-eyed, with only a hint of the Kendal arrogance. Simon Kendal alias Betts . . . His death had dropped the plum of Heron into Hugo's lap. Was he now throwing it all away needlessly? He thought not, but there was a small doubt which persisted in spite of his declarations to the contrary. He sat up again and stared round him at the decaying masonry and weed-filled crevices, all that remained of the priory. Slowly he stood up and eased the tense muscles in his shoulders. He would waste no more time on doubts, he told himself. The die was cast. All he could do now was follow the course of action to the end, however bitter that might prove. He had taken a firm stand and he would not weaken. Come what may, he was determined Hans Bucher's ordeal should not go unavenged.

Maria decided to invite Felicity Carr to the wedding and wrote to Martin suggesting that they should ride to Devon together two days before the wedding. She was fond of Felicity, but her real reason for the invitation was one that she scarcely cared to admit even to herself – that she hoped Felicity's presence would distract Martin's attention from Eloise. She dreaded another clash and had seriously considered not inviting Martin to come home for the event. But Allan wanted him as chief bride-knight so she had no alternative. Now she crossed her fingers for luck and prayed nothing would go wrong.

Eloise was not pleased to learn that Felicity was coming with Martin but she kept her feelings hidden. Martin had described the girl in flattering terms whenever he had wanted to arouse her jealousy and Eloise did not relish the prospect of a rival. She had hoped for the undivided attentions of both brothers, but it was done and there was nothing she could do about it. It was merely another source of irritation to her. As it was, the conflict between Hugo and the tinners had cast a gloom over the occasion. The large crowd of anticipated well-wishers would doubtless not now materialize. In addition, Hugo and Maria had decided to make the actual service as short as possible and omit the procession, so that any troublemakers could be kept away. One day *if* the mine reopened, Allan and Eloise would be mistress and master. It disappointed her that the families of the tinners would not recall their wedding day with joy. In many ways she wished they were not marrying at this particular time, but there was no way she could bring about a change in the plans. Eloise felt that Fate was using her unkindly, but she tried to put such disagreeable thoughts aside and greeted Felicity and Martin, when they arrived, with every appearance of pleasure.

Her heart gave an unexpected leap as she saw Martin, but her radiant smile went unheeded as he slipped from his horse and turned at once to help Felicity from hers. Eloise saw his hands linger round her waist once she was safely on the ground and she bit her lip in vexation. Was he trying to make her jealous, she wondered, or was he truly enjoying the companionship of this nobody? It was hardly likely, but she would certainly not give him the satisfaction of seeing her discomfiture. She hurried forward, arms outstretched to take Felicity's hand and kiss her cheek. The girl smiled shyly at her.

'You must be Felicity,' said Eloise. 'I'm pleased to meet you at last and am glad you could be here for the "great day".'

'I was so hoping to be invited,' said Felicity with disarming frankness. 'I have prayed for fine weather for you.'

Eloise had to admit to herself that the girl was attractive and well mannered. But low born, she reminded herself. How she must envy the new Mistress Kendal! She, Eloise, could afford to be generous.

Martin leaned between them, his face a picture of pretended dismay. 'Don't I qualify for a kiss of welcome?' he asked. 'I am to be chief bride-knight and have ridden many miles over rough terrain—'

Eloise laughed. She wanted to kiss him to show Felicity the closeness of *their* relationship, but she would not give Martin the satisfaction of such a kiss. Also, Allan was already on the step behind her, so instead she turned and put her arm through his.

'Here is Felicity,' she told him. 'Say "Hello" and then I shall take her under my wing. We have so much to talk about and none of it fit for your ears!'

She smiled at Felicity, who seemed unsure how to take this remark, but Allan kissed her briefly.

'You look remarkably fresh after your long journey,' he said.

'Do *I* look fresh?' asked Martin. 'Will no one pay *me* a compliment?'

'Martin has taken excellent care of me,' said Felicity. 'Will that suffice, Martin?'

Maria now came out of the house and Jon arrived to lead away the horses. Maria hugged both new arrivals and apologized for Hugo's absence.

'He is out somewhere,' she told them. 'The Bucher affair has affected him deeply and he prefers often to be alone. I think my chatter about food and clothes and gifts is more than he can bear at present, but he will be back soon, I'm sure, and is eager to see you both. Eloise, you take care of Felicity. I crave a few words with this young man.'

As the two young women disappeared upstairs she led Martin into the Hall, her arms about his waist.

'What have I done now?' he protested.

'Nothing, to my knowledge,' said Maria. 'Nor will I trust. I want only to ask you not to rile Allan while you are home. No, let me finish. These last few weeks have taken their toll and our tempers are easily frayed. Martin, whatever grievances you bear each other lay them aside, I beg you, for these next few days. I want nothing to mar the wedding. There is no need for anything to go amiss. Think twice before you speak and try not to provoke your brother.'

'And if he provokes me?'

'Why should he do so, Martin? He is to be wed in three days' time to a beautiful bride. He deserves to be happy and 'tis right that he should. Your turn will come later. For my sake, Martin, try to behave as a loving brother and . . .' She hesitated, '. . . keep away from Eloise.'

'Maria! How can I—'

'Oh I know that look of injured innocence, Martin, but you well know that a word or a look will call forth a pert answer from her and Allan will take it the wrong way. I do not find fault with you—'

'Indeed you do!'

Maria rolled her eyes despairingly and counted to ten. 'Then I do not mean to,' she said placatingly. 'I merely ask you to try and avoid any ill feeling. No one is perfect. Eloise can be provocative and Allan can be touchy and you can be maddening. Oh, you can. Don't deny it.'

'Then I must sit in a corner all day and twiddle my thumbs and answer with monosyllables if spoken to—'

'You see! You are being maddening now! I'll say no more but trust to your good intentions.' She smiled suddenly into the handsome but sullen face. 'How are you enjoying your time with Innly? Is he as good a teacher as was promised?'

Fortunately, she had touched upon a subject dear to his heart. He was thoroughly enjoying his time with the capable shepherd and was quite happy to talk of their mutual experiences. The other less acceptable topic was put aside and no further reference made to it.

Meanwhile Eloise had shown Felicity to her own chamber, which they were to share for the next few days. She left the girl to refresh herself and then, after a decent interval, rejoined her in the little room which would not be hers for much longer.

Felicity was admiring the bridal gown which hung

against the wall. It was of heavy cream brocade and the head-dress was of pink and gold with creamy lace.

' 'Tis exquisite,' she said, turning as Eloise entered the chamber. 'And 'twill be quite perfect with your rich auburn hair. Martin told me you were beautiful and he did not exaggerate.'

Her candour impressed Eloise and she eagerly began to show off the other items of finery – the delicate lace mittens and dainty satin slippers.

'And Allan has not seen the gown?' asked Felicity.

'Why, no. That would be bad luck.'

She showed Felicity the petticoat she had scalloped and the fine white hose. 'And this necklace,' she said. ' 'Tis Allan's gift to me. I have given him a silver knife with an ivory handle. My parents are giving us a chest full of blankets and – but forgive me. I prattle on so. But you will wed one day and then you will understand and excuse my excitement.'

A slight shadow passed over Felicity's face but she made no answer and Eloise regretted her tactless remark. Presumably the girl had no dowry and would not easily find a husband.

'Ellie, my maid, is as eager as I am for the day to arrive,' said Eloise, changing the subject clumsily. 'And her mother, Minnie, the cook. She's busy baking from dawn to dusk. She has only just recovered from the harvest supper and now she has to start again! But she loves it and Maggie is helping her. What shall we do now? You must not let me go on so.'

Felicity protested that she was not in the least bored by the conversation but Eloise *was* and she led the way downstairs again to rejoin the menfolk. Hugo had not returned and Maria was elsewhere. Only the four younger people remained in the Hall. Allan suggested that they walk awhile in the garden and they did so, eventually making their way down the steps to the riverside garden.

' 'Tis beautiful!' exclaimed Felicity.

'You outshine it,' said Martin.

Eloise glanced at Allan, hoping he would make an equally flattering remark about her, but he merely nodded.

'No·wonder Martin spends so much time in Kent!' he joked.

Felicity, seeing Eloise's face tighten, said hastily, 'I swear I can smell almonds.'

'Indeed you can,' said Allan. ' 'Tis the small white flowers that grow on the surface of the water. They are almond-scented.'

'We'll take some roots back to Romney House if you wish,' said Martin. 'No doubt 'twill grow on the pond there.' He reached over the water to pull out a few strands and Felicity gave him a steadying hand in case he overbalanced. It was a very natural gesture and spoke of their relationship without words. Eloise felt a pang at their obvious closeness and wondered anew how they behaved towards each other in the privacy of Romney House. Was Felicity still a paid companion and, if so, to whom, for Ruth was dead? Or had she assumed the role of cook or housekeeper? No, there was a cook. Her eyes narrowed slightly. She would drop a careless word to Maria when next the opportunity arose. The girl did not deserve the attentions of a boy like Martin. Was it possible he would waste his time with her? She reached out her own hand and took Martin's.

'I haven't shown you my new mare,' she told him gaily. ''Tis a gift from Hugo and Maria. We can leave these two to become acquainted. They will not miss us for a few moments.'

Martin allowed himself to be led away to the stable with Eloise's arm casually linked through his own. Felicity watched them go then she and Allan looked at each other. Allan saw in her eyes the love she felt for Martin and she read in his the doubt and pain he could never express.

' 'Tis only three more days,' she said simply.

He continued to regard her with the same vulnerable look, then he sighed and nodded and they walked back to the house without speaking further.

★

The following day Melissa invited Felicity over to Ladyford to meet 'the two bonniest grandchildren ever a woman was blessed with' and Felicity accepted with alacrity. She was aware of the tension slowly building between Allan, Martin and Eloise, and knew also that her own presence was not helping the situation. She therefore asked Maria if she could stay at Ladyford overnight and make herself useful there. She was not a visitor in the true sense of the word and felt that in her position she should contribute something, particularly as there was so much to be done. Maria was quite agreeable and Melissa took her back to meet Nina and the little ones, and Felicity found them all charming. She and Nina managed to understand each other without too much difficulty and Felicity divided her time happily between caring for the children and helping Maggie with the cooking. Although she was sorry to be away from Martin, of whom she was too fond by far, she could not enjoy his company at Heron under Eloise's watchful eye. The cheerful affectionate household at Ladyford was much more suited to Felicity's gentle temperament. She relaxed among her friends and began to enjoy herself.

And so it was that Eloise had the bed chamber unexpectedly to herself that night. She was awoken in the early hours by soft footfalls in the room and sat up sleepily to see a figure beside the bed. As she opened her mouth to scream a hand covered it firmly and she heard Martin's voice whispering urgently to her to make no sound.

' 'Tis Martin. I mean you no harm.'

'Martin? Sweet Heaven, what *are* you about? To come to my bed chamber . . .'

'Hush. I must speak with you and this is the only time we can be sure of secrecy.'

'Dear God, I hope you're right, for if anyone should see you here 'twill be my undoing!'

She sat up, hugging the sheet around her, trying to make out the expression on his face in the darkness. She was alarmed by his temerity, but greatly exhilarated by the fact that he was in her room and had 'urgent' matters to discuss. She thought she could guess what they were and she would refuse him – but she would have the satisfaction of his declaration. It would be their secret, a bond between them that nothing could break.

'I think you know what I have to say—' he began. 'I have seen it in your eyes – the feeling you have for me.'

'*My* feeling?'

'Aye. 'Tis no less than mine for you. Eloise, we love each other. Do you deny it?'

'I do indeed,' she gasped. 'Why, I am to wed Allan the day after tomorrow. I shall be another man's wife.'

' 'Tis not seemly that you should! You do not love him. You know it, and so does he. 'Tis you and I, Eloise. *We* are the lovers. Ever since we first set eyes on each other. Confess it. I have seen it in your glances. You cannot pretend 'tis otherwise.'

'Martin how can you expect me to confess such a thing at this time?' He was standing beside the bed, looking down at her. With a trembling hand she lit the candle and in its glow she saw the passion in his eyes. She set the light on the other side of the bed.

'Sit beside me,' she whispered, 'so that we can speak more softly. If anyone finds us together—'

'I care not if they do!' he said fiercely. 'We *should* be together. 'Tis not too late. Be my wife, Eloise. Allan does not care for you enough nor you for him. 'Twould be a shallow union. In God's name, Eloise, confess your love for me and say you will wed me, for I swear I shall not leave your bedside until you do.'

'Martin! Don't speak so wildly,' she begged. 'Oh, what have I done to bring this about? I have given you no word—'

'I did not need words. I saw your true feelings in every glance.'

She saw his gaze travel along the outline of her body revealed by the light coverlet, and the candlelight revealed the desire he felt for her. She almost wished that Allan could discover them together. Then he would see that other men coveted her wholeheartedly. He had been so distressed recently by the Bucher affair, and before that he had been engrossed with the mine. She had taken second place when she ought to have been first and foremost. There were only days now before the wedding, but still he would ride off to be 'alone with his thoughts'.

'My true feelings?' she repeated. 'Oh no, you must not talk that way, Martin. You must not ask me to compromise myself by such a declaration. 'Tis not worthy of you. Allan is your brother.'

'What matter? He might be the Queen's consort for ought I care! He is not the man for you, Eloise. I am. Will you not admit you love me?'

'I dare not.'

'That says it loud and clear!' he cried triumphantly. He took her hand and held it to his lips and the sheet slipped down to expose her full breasts. 'Oh what sweetness!' he whispered. 'Let me kiss them.'

As he bent his head she retrieved the sheet with a half-hearted protest.'

'You must not! For pity's sake.'

'Then say you love me or I will kiss every inch of your body! I *will* hear those words from you, Eloise.'

'I – I am fond of you—' she faltered.

'Don't speak of fondness but of love!' cried Martin. The nearness of her naked body inflamed him. His body stirred and stiffened and his voice was hoarse. Suddenly Eloise realized that the adventure might not end the way she anticipated and felt the first stirrings of unease. What if he took her unwillingly? What if he proved too strong for her and would accept no denial? She drew back, holding him at arm's length.

'I cannot speak of love,' she insisted. 'You must not ask it. You must leave me.'

'I have told you I will not go without those words.'

'And if I give them?'

'Then I shall never let you go! You know I love you, Eloise. You have always known it.'

'But Felicity?' she murmured. 'I have seen how you look at her. I quite thought you felt some passion—'

'Felicity Carr? Are you mad? She is nothing to me. I am kind to her, no more than that.'

'I have seen her look at *you* with love.'

'I do not return it, then.'

'You live under the same roof,' Eloise persisted, 'and you will not deny she is attractive.'

'No, I'll not deny that but I have eyes only for you. Don't waste words on her. We are talking of *our* love and *our* future.'

Eloise sighed. 'We have no future, Martin. Whatever I might feel for you I cannot betray Allan. He is my betrothed and cares for me in his own way.'

He stood up' suddenly, unable to bear the proximity, and moved away so that his face was hidden from her. He put out a hand to steady himself against the wall and bent his head. His other hand slid down to his loins to comfort the throbbing that threatened to overwhelm him. Seeing the gesture, Eloise felt an answering thrill and longed for him to come back and lie with her. Suddenly she wanted to explore and experience love for a second time. Her body demanded attention from his and it was all she could do not to call him to her. She sat hugging her legs, drowning in the sweet feelings that spread to every part of her body. She wanted him to make love to her. But a small urgent voice warned that the penalty for such bliss would be severe – if it were discovered. And Martin would not remain silent, she was sure of that. If she yielded to him he would never give her up.

He turned slowly back to face her. 'Then tell me you do not love me and I will go,' he said evenly.

She stared up at his ardent face and was greatly tempted to say, 'I love you. Take me'.

He said again, 'Tell me you do not love me. Say you do not want me.'

'I – Oh Martin, I beg you.'

He took a step nearer and her own desire flared at his approach. 'Marry me, Eloise, and come to Romney House. We will be happy there, I swear it. Say that you love me and we will go tonight – now! We will steal away and be wed secretly. No one need know until we are man and wife. You want me, I can see it in your eyes, and this nearness torments me.' He moved forward and knelt beside the bed. 'I am pleading with you, my sweet Eloise. Do what your heart tells you is right. Wed the brother you love. Wed *me*, Eloise. Give me an answer or I swear I shall take you here and now, in this very bed, and then there will be no argument. I could do it if I had a mind – but I will not threaten you. Do not look at me that way. I would not hurt you. But do not play with my feelings any longer. Give me an answer.'

She still hesitated and at last he raised his head. His expression had hardened and his eyes were suddenly cold.

'If *I* were to inherit Heron,' he said, 'would *that* change your mind?'

Eloise caught her breath. The shock of his question, so near the truth, was like a douche of cold water. She began to stammer an answer but her voice trembled.

'I see,' he said.

'You don't!' she cried. 'You don't begin to understand. 'Tis not that I would not wed you—'

'If I were to inherit Heron you would *still* refuse me?'

'Martin, I—' She fell silent.

'So that's it,' he said softly. 'You are marrying Heron, not Allan. Dear God, I pity him.'

'Don't!' she cried. He stood up and moved towards the door. 'Don't you dare say such terrible things. Don't you dare leave me this way. Martin, you can't believe that. How dare you accuse me. You come uninvited into my room and then insult me.' She was furiously angry. It was the only way she could cope with the painful truth of what he had said. She had not expected him to see her motives so clearly and could not tolerate his lowered opinion of her. She could not bear it to end this way, with this cold rejection of her. She sprang out of bed and crossed the room to him. She was naked and her body glowed warmly in the flickering candlelight.

'Martin, think kindly of me,' she begged him. 'What can I say that will convince you that my intentions are honourable? I don't wish us to part this way. If you love me as you pretend you do, then how can you revile me so? Or treat me so harshly? Martin, listen to me. Hear me out.' She put a hand on his arm. 'If I lay with you this once, will that suffice? Will you be content? If I give myself to you to prove my love, will you never speak to me again of marriage – and of what has passed between us? Oh Martin, I am yours for the taking. Allan need never know.'

His eyes darkened in his pale face. 'You would give yourself to me and then wed Allan to gain Heron? Is that what you mean?' With a muttered oath she struck out at him, but he caught her hand and thrust her back. 'I decline your offer,' he said. 'Allan is welcome to whatever you have to give.'

And he pushed her away and went out, closing the door softly behind him.

Eloise stared in shocked disbelief at the closed door. She wanted to scream, run, fight – do anything to relieve the fury that threatened to choke her. She was tensed like a spring without the means to uncoil. A deep groan escaped her and she threw herself face downwards on the bed, pummelling the pillow in an agony of frustration, unable even to put into words the pent-up anger and shame which filled her. If Martin had reappeared before her, she would have killed him without a moment's hesitation. Her deepest despair came from the knowledge that she had brought about her own downfall. She *had* encouraged him, but she had not intended it to end this way. She had wanted him to go on loving her. Then she would have won in the game they played. Now she had lost ignominiously and the bitterness was real. She had a sour taste in her mouth, and rage in her heart. She could never undo the shame he had inflicted upon her but – could she serve him as cruelly? The thought gave her the first ray of hope, the first glimmer that some of her wounded pride might be salvaged from the disaster. Or if not salvaged, then at least avenged. If only she could even the score she felt she would not suffer so dreadfully. Perhaps her humiliation would not be so complete. She felt tarnished by the events that had just taken place and longed for comfort and reassurance that she was not as bad as Martin would have her believe. But there was no one to turn to. No one to whom she could recount the sorry story and expect sympathy. The blow to her self-esteem and the matters which led up to it could not be shared. Somehow she must deal with it alone. If only she could weep, she thought, desperately, but she remained stubbornly dry-eyed and there was no relief from tears.

Throughout the hours that followed, Eloise tossed and turned in a torment of unexpressed emotion and turned the burning rage inward upon herself; her nerves, in fact her whole body suffered from the repressions of her energies. The adrenalin produced more energy which found no natural outlet and remained in her body like a poison. The desire for physical release from her anguished thoughts played on her imagination and her mind grew dark and fearful. As the night wore on she dozed fitfully and was a prey to horrid dreams in which violence and fear played equal parts. Her waking moments afforded no relief and the hours became a fevered succession of fantasies, in which she stood ridden with guilt and utterly despised by those who had formerly professed to love her. Not one tear passed her eyelids throughout the long dark hours.

When she did not come down to breakfast, Maria sent Ellie to fetch her but the little maid ran back down again her face pale.

'She's not well, ma'am!' she told a startled Maria. 'She's in bed still, tossing and turning and doesn't know me! 'Tis I, Ellie, I told her but she stared at me as if I was a ghost and gave a little moan. She looks that wild, ma'am.'

Maria left her breakfast at once and hurried towards the stairs. Hugo stared after her, a look of concern on his face. Martin lowered his eyes hastily as Hugo turned towards him. 'I hope the child is not unwell,' he said. 'With the wedding tomorrow and everything arranged. It would be most untimely. All the visitors already on their way. Has she been in contact with any contagion, I wonder?'

Martin shrugged, trying to hide his alarm, hoping that her sudden ailment was not connected with the events of the previous night. She had seemed in perfect health when he last saw her. From upstairs they heard Maria call Hugo and he, too, hurried up to Eloise's bedside.

'Her eyes is all staring,' Ellie told Martin. 'And her voice is funny. Stared right through me she did, as if I was a apparition. Awful, she looked—'

When Hugo reappeared he told Ellie to send Matt for the physician. 'She seems to burn with a fever,' Hugo told Martin. ' 'Tis all very sudden and Maria is seriously alarmed. Eloise is quite delirious and somewhere between sleeping and waking. She does not know Maria but tried to push her away. Is Allan come down yet?'

'He is already gone out,' said Martin. 'He said he was going to the mine, though for what reason I cannot guess since there is no work in progress.'

'Poor Allan, he has taken the closure very hard and the place still holds a strong fascination for him. Will you ride over and tell him of Eloise's sickness? He should know without delay. She may grow worse.'

Martin tried to think of a reason why he should not go but finally nodded. He could compose himself on the way to the mine, he told himself, and Allan need never know of his disquiet. He must behave as normally as possible and hope that Eloise would not reveal in her delirium what she would never reveal in more rational moments. Martin went out to the stable in a very subdued frame of mind. He wished with all his heart that he had not gone to her room and that he had not left her so abruptly. But it was done and wishing would not undo it. He would keep silent on the matter and hope that Eloise would do the same.

When she was once more alone, Eloise relaxed a little and congratulated herself on a fine performance. She felt no remorse for the deception, for she had made up her mind to punish the entire family for what she considered Martin's duplicity. During the night she had come to regard all the Kendals with the same hatred and was determined, in the absence of a champion, to redress the wrong in her own way. Only Martin might guess the truth, but he could never prove it without confessing his own part in the affair. That, she was certain, he would not do. She had had a tormented night and it was not difficult to exaggerate the disorder of her mind into a state approaching frenzy. Whatever the physician prescribed she would fail to recover in time for the wedding. All the visitors would be sent home – she felt no compunction for them – and the food would no doubt be given to the poor. She closed her eyes with a weariness that was not feigned. She wished them all to Hell! If it had not been for the lure of Heron she would have refused Allan altogether.

There was a tap at the door and Ellie came in with a pitcher and a plate of biscuits. Eloise sat up so abruptly that the maid jumped and splashed the contents of the pitcher.

'Who's there?' Eloise stared at her wildly.

' 'Tis only Ellie, ma'am.' The maid looked at her with a mixture of fear and fascination. 'I'm sent up with these.' Keeping a wary eye on Eloise, she poured ale into the mug that stood on the bedside chest and, holding it at arm's length, offered it to the patient.

Eloise flung out her arm with a groan and sent the mug flying, then turned over and lay down with the sheet hiding her face. She heard Ellie's hasty movements as she mopped up the spilt liquid, then the door closed behind her. Eloise sat up again. Maria had closed the shutters and the room was dim. She got out of bed and crossed the room to where her wedding gown hung against the wall and stood staring at its softly draped folds. With an unexpected rush of regret she reached up and stroked the smooth fabric and, taking it down, hugged it to her. Suddenly she was crying and the hot tears fell unheeded, wetting the dress. Loud sobs racked her and her whole body shook with the depths of her despair. At last, through eyes blurred with tears, she replaced the dress and stumbled back to bed. She hid beneath the clothes like a wounded animal and sobbed unrestrainedly until she was exhausted.

When the physician finally arrived, Eloise was sleeping deeply and he was reluctant to disturb her. Sleep heals, he told them, and it would be foolish to wake her merely to examine her. He would call again the next day, he promised, unless she took a turn for the worse. The wedding? She would be in no fit state to attend the ceremony. It would have to be delayed. Eloise must remain a Ballantyne for a while longer.

CHAPTER THIRTEEN

Martin's nocturnal visit to Eloise was to have far-reaching effects. The relationship between Eloise and Allan was strained almost to breaking point after her 'recovery'. They quarrelled bitterly when, for no apparent reason, she refused to agree a new date for the wedding. Martin felt doubly threatened by possible treachery on Eloise's part and by Allan's growing suspicions. He therefore announced that he would shortly return to Kent with Felicity, since there was no immediate prospect of the wedding. Allan was convinced that Martin had somehow contributed to the disaster, but this feeling was based purely on intuition. He had no positive proof to link his brother with Eloise's rejection but he noticed, as others did, that her relationship with Martin had also undergone a change. He tried to put aside the notion but finally resolved to ask Eloise outright. She flew into a rage and Allan lost control of himself and struck her. In retaliation, she told him a version of the scene which had taken place in her bed chamber, although she was careful to omit the true ending. Instead she substituted one in which Martin tried to force himself upon her and she resisted. As she had anticipated, this sent Allan in search of Martin, demanding an explanation. Martin's version was also a concoction of half-truths in which Eloise invited him to her room and tried to seduce him. From these two accounts, Allan was able to make an educated guess at the real cause of events and, sick at heart, he flung out of the house and made his way to the old priory. There he wandered aimlessly for several hours, seeing nothing, and feeling only a desperate mixture of hatred and loathing for the two people who had caused him such exquisite pain.

There, in the twilight, Felicity came to him. He was

sitting amid the crumbling remains of the priory and he did not turn as she approached, although he heard her footsteps. For a wild moment he thought it was Eloise come to ask his forgiveness but that hope was shattered when Felicity drew level and stood looking down at him.

'Was it Martin?' she asked simply.

He recognized the voice and opened his eyes as he nodded.

'I'm sorry,' she said.

For a moment they looked at each other, each recognizing the suffering in the other's eyes.

'You love my brother?' asked Allan and, without waiting for her answer added, 'Then may God protect you!'

Felicity sighed. 'They are both young and foolish.'

'There is no excusing them. She will not wed me now. I know it.'

'But you still wish it?'

'Aye. 'Tis folly, I know, but I still wish it. She says she must have time to think – that the Kendals have used her ill. She will doubtless write to her father and he will take her away.' He looked at her with an expression of deep misery. 'Eloise will never be mine. I should never have allowed myself to believe it. 'Tis not my fate to wed such a beauty.'

Felicity sat down on the ground in front of him.

'And is that where your whole happiness lies? With Eloise? Are you so sure?'

'Why do you ask?' His tone was sharper than he intended, but she kept her grey eyes fixed upon his face.

'You do not speak of love,' she said gently. 'Only of your loss. Do you truly love her?'

The question startled him. 'I want her,' he insisted. 'She is my betrothed. Mine, not Martin's. Do you want Martin? If so, then you will feel as I do. You will not relish the prospect of losing him to another.'

She gazed at him and her face in the grey light was pale and ghost-like. A troubled ghost, he thought.

'I love him enough to wish his happiness,' she said at last. 'If Eloise is his happiness—'

'You would let him go? With your blessing?'

'I want his happiness,' she repeated. 'Isn't that love?'

He looked at her wearily. 'I confess I do not know,' he said. 'I am wretched, angry. I feel betrayed. I do not see as clearly as you. I do not have your compassion. All I feel is a desire to put them both from me. Never to see either of them again. Perhaps what you say is true and what I feel for Eloise is not love. How shall I know? How can I find out the truth when one look from those beautiful eyes and I am weak with longing for her. She dazzles my senses.' He shook his head and she stood up.

'I must go,' she said. 'I have said too much. Forgive me.'

'Wait!' He stood up. 'Tell me how you came by here. Did you come in search of me?'

'Aye.'

'For what purpose? To persuade me to free Eloise so that she could wed Martin?'

'No, Allan.'

'Then why, Felicity?'

She hesitated lowering her eyes. 'To give you comfort,' she whispered, 'if that were possible. Now I see 'tis not and I have intruded on your privacy.'

'Comfort?' he repeated. 'You suffer also but you seek to comfort me. That's kindly meant. I thank you.'

She gave a slight nod and then was gone quietly, leaving him to his solitude. Only after her footsteps had faded did it occur to him that he had not tried to comfort her.

He stayed at the old priory until it grew dark, then made his way home. Martin and Felicity were no longer at Heron. They had made a hurried and unexpected leave-taking at Martin's insistence.

Later that night Allan also rode out and he did not return. He left a brief note that he was on his way to London and would let them know later of his whereabouts.

He would stay in London, he told them, until he had made up his mind upon the matter of the betrothal.

Eloise was beside herself to find the tables so neatly turned, but she dared not write to her parents for advice. They would insist on her return to Rochester and she could not face the humiliation. She would await Allan's return, which she prayed would not be too long delayed. Then she would affect a reconciliation and they would wed as quickly as possible. In spite of everything, Eloise had not abandoned her intention to become mistress of Heron.

Hugo, however, had little time to spare for Simon's errant son. New developments were taking place regarding the attempted murder of Hans Bucher. Rita Carp, having fallen foul of Annie Boord, turned informant and told the justices all that she knew about the attempted murder. In exchange for the information, she was pardoned for her own small part in the conspiracy and the trial went ahead with her as the chief witness. On her evidence, Alec Boord and the Gillis brothers were convicted and subsequently hanged. The rest were detained for an indefinite period. Hugo took some comfort from the verdict and wrote at once to Bucher, but his letter went unanswered and the mine remained closed. Hugo had no heart for it. Bucher was gone and so was Allan. Maria grieved for him but there was little she could do. His spirit was broken and he no longer cared. The atmosphere at Heron was heavy with defeat and, for the first time, Minnie found herself wishing that she was back at Ladyford.

Maria took up her pen to write briefly to Abigail:

'You must on no account blame yourself for the trouble between Alan and Eloise. You recommended her to us in good faith and we were equally impressed with her. We can only pray that they will be reconciled. At least I can rest easy that Martin is returned to Kent where he seems content. We must be thankful for small mercies. Last Sunday the sermon was of Life as a boat upon the river. If that be so, then surely we at Heron have reached our white water and must steer through the rocks as best we can. I try to remain in good spirits for Hugo's sake, but there are times when I almost crave the peace I once knew at Arnsville. But no more of this sad talk. I still hope that matters will mend and I ask your prayers to support us through these dark days. My best wishes to your husband and all your family. I envy you your grandchildren. But now I must go about my work and will write again when the news is brighter. God be with you all, Maria.'

The lowering December sky cast a gloom over the marsh, darkening the green of the turf and dotting it with grey sheep. Frank Innly whistled as his knife slid expertly over the wood, gouging here, smoothing there, chipping it into the shape of a bird with outstretched wings – a hovering sparrowhawk. Martin envied him his agile fingers and his accurate eye for detail. He envied him also his calm cheerful nature and his placid acceptance of his place in society. Frank Innly would never be anything but a shepherd. He would never own a flock of sheep but would call another man 'master'. Yet he was a respected shepherd and James Moore was a good man to work for. He had much more to be thankful for – a wife and five healthy children – all girls! But, he told Martin, the good Lord would have it so and Frank Innly was not a man to argue with the Lord. A son would have pleased them but it was not to be. He began to sing softly:

'Away my brown linnet
My gaudy wood-pigeon
Away and aloft
My merry wood lark
Sing not of my wooing
And hush your brave cooing
My maiden is sleeping
In yonder green park . . .'
*

269

Martin glanced sideways at him and Frank met his gaze with an impudent wink.

'Frank! I have told you, 'tis not that way at all!'

'No?'

'Not at all.'

'I believe you but you protest too soon. I said nothing to the contrary.'

He concentrated again on the bird he was carving, his head bent. He was a small man with handsome brown eyes in a tanned face. His dark hair straggled untidily over his head and met his beard, and his thick moustache was untrimmed. He had a ready smile and a deep hearty laugh which lifted slightly at one corner where a scar ran from his temple to his chin.

'You said nought but you looked volumes – and that song! I've heard it before.'

'Have you now?' said Frank innocently.

'Aye. Whenever Felicity is around! I think you have an eye for her yourself!'

'I do indeed! What man surrounded by feckless sheep wouldn't have an eye for a pretty maid? She brightens my day – and your night, mayhap!'

He laughed at the look on Martin's face as he continued to deny that he and Felicity were lovers. Martin denied it reluctantly for they *were* lovers and he wanted to shout it to the whole world. He wanted to tell Innly and see the envy in his eyes. He wanted to write to Heron with the news and seek out Allan in London and boast to him also. But he dared do none of it. If he did she would most certainly be sent away. She was not a suitable bride for the master of Romney House and a Kendal at that. One day he would be offered a worthy bride, but in the meantime Felicity Carr adored him and her body was given most generously whenever he wanted it. Did Frank Innly really suspect, he wondered? And hoped that he did.

With a slight nod of his head Frank indicated that she was approaching, picking her way across the flat water-logged turf and shivering despite her thick shawl. She carried a basket covered with a cloth and waved cheerfully as soon as she saw them watching her.

'What a bonny sight!' said Frank. 'I wonder what's she's brought you today. Spoils you, she does.'

'A cake, most likely.'

'Ah, I'd take a bite of her cake!' he said. 'Some folks has all the luck.' He raised his voice. 'Hey up, beautiful! Brought me a cake, have you?'

She looked up, laughing, and her cheeks were pink from the cold wind for they were nearly a mile from Romney House.

' 'Tis for Martin,' she told him, 'but no doubt he'll share it.'

'By God, I wish he would,' said Frank and Martin nudged him sharply, hoping Felicity had not noticed the hidden meaning.

She was out of breath and her face had a pinched look about it. Standing arms akimbo she laughed down at them.

'Look at you! Idling the time away. Frank with his carving and you, Martin, with nothing to do. 'Tis a fine easy life being a shepherd.'

Frank squinted up at her silhouetted against the dark sky.

' 'Tis not so easy when the snow's on the ground and there's foxes about and your dog's maybe gone lame.' He gave the sheepdog a push with the toe of his boot. 'Go and say a greeting to your friend, then, and she'll likely spare you a crumb or two.'

The dog bounded forward joyfully and she bent to fondle him.

'You look cold,' said Martin. 'You shouldn't come so far in such weather.'

Felicity smiled radiantly at him and Frank, seeing her eyes also, knew that he had guessed correctly. Well, they were both young and 'twas none of his business, but there'd have been no such goings on if the old lady was still alive. A tartar, she was, so he'd heard.

Felicity cut the cake into three, a small piece for herself.

271

She loved her daily visit to Martin in the fields and often walked much further in search of them. Frank Innly, she thought, was an honest man and she was pleased that Martin had him for a teacher. His wife, Jenny, was a nice woman, forthright but well meaning. She had had five children and all surviving. She would be a good person to talk to if – But no! Felicity shut her mind to the small doubt.

'Here boy!' She held out a handful of crumbs and watched the dog gobble them noisily. Suddenly she became aware that Frank was staring at her.

'You should eat it all yourself,' he told her. 'You look a bit on the skinny side.'

'Oh?' Alarm flickered in her eyes for a moment. ' 'Tis nothing. My appetite's deserted me this last week or more.'

'Has it now?' he said slowly.

Martin glanced at him sharply, but Frank was pushing the last of the cake into his mouth and his eyes were on the furthermost sheep.

'I like my women plump,' he said. 'Loss of appetite. Tut, tut. 'Tis a pity, that. My wife suffered from it more than once. Five times, to be exact.'

There was a long vibrant silence. The colour fled from Felicity's cheeks. She opened her mouth to say something then changed her mind and stood up abruptly, spilling the knife and cloth from the basket.

'I must go,' she said and her voice trembled slightly.

Martin handed her the knife and cloth. 'So soon? You have only just come.'

'I've – I'm busy today.' She looked at Martin. 'Will you be home tonight?'

Occasionally, if there was reason, the lookers slept out in one of the shelters but Martin nodded. 'Aye. About dusk,' he told her.

They watched her go back across the marsh, a slim figure in her blue gown and black shawl. Once she turned and waved briefly, then she was lost to their sight as she followed the track round the lower edge of the hill.

Frank began to whistle then stopped and looked at Martin.

'Is that right?' Martin asked, low voiced.

'Aye. 'Twas with my Jenny.'

'Damnation!'

'So it might be?'

'Aye. It might.'

'Don't look so down.' He laughed. 'Proves you're a man!'

'Maria will kill me!'

'But why? You're a mite young but you've a place and a living. She's a bonny girl. You could do a lot worse.'

'A servant? No, it won't do.'

'Get rid of it then. Send her to my Jenny. She knows ways. We'd have had eight, else!'

Martin looked at him doubtfully. 'I don't know—'

'Well, you don't know for certain, any road. Don't count your chickens, lad.'

'She's said nothing.'

'No, they don't. Not that kind of girl. You'll have to ask her.'

'Damnation!' said Martin. 'Out of one mess into another!'

'How's that then?' asked the shepherd, but Martin could not bring himself to say more. Frank resumed his whistling and whittling and Martin sat beside him, stony faced, until the light no longer filtered through the heavy cloud and the marsh vanished into the darkness.

When Martin plucked up courage to speak to Felicity about her condition she denied it flatly. He tried to ask her more delicate questions about the state of her body, but she laughed gently and said there was nothing at all to worry about. He was agreeably surprised but happy to accept her reassurances. Weeks passed and she certainly did seem in better health. Her eyes sparkled, her skin bloomed like a peach and her appetite returned with a

273

vengeance. She went about her work with a serene expression on her face and the subject of a child was not referred to again.

For a few days Martin had slept in his own room, but he was easily persuaded to go back to Felicity's and their love-making continued. By the time Maria made another visit Felicity was four months pregnant and there was no hiding it from her. She had had children of her own and the signs were unmistakable.

'Aye,' said Felicity when Maria asked. ' 'Tis four months gone. I would have told you by and by.'

Maria's jaw dropped and she shook her head helplessly. 'But why did you not tell us before? You must have known. Surely Martin suspected. Is he blind?'

'No,' Felicity's manner was polite but firm. 'He *did* ask and I lied to him. I knew he would want me to give up the child. To lose it or give it away. I will not do that, Maria. I made up my mind as soon as I knew. I want Martin's child more than anything in the world and no one is going to rob me. I know Martin will not wed me – I'm not suitable to be a gentleman's wife. But I have my dowry still intact. I can care for it, feed it. I don't need a husband. I can go away—' Her voice broke suddenly at the thought of leaving Martin, but she recovered and went on. 'Don't ask me to regret what I've done, for I don't nor ever will. I have loved Martin with all my heart and we were happy. If I never have another happy hour, I shall consider myself well blessed.' She took a deep breath and Maria swallowed.

'I don't know what to say,' she began. 'That little speech—'

'I've practised it. I knew you would come one day and see what has happened. I don't expect you to understand but — I'm proud to be carrying a Kendal child.'

There was a silence between them while Maria struggled to adapt to this new Felicity. The timid girl had gone and in her place was a strangely confident young woman.

'And Martin doesn't know?' she asked.

'No. He's very young still and there was no need for him to know so soon. I didn't expect him to share my joy.'

'And does he love *you*?'

'No.'

There was no bitterness in her voice and she looked at Maria with untroubled eyes. 'I won't ask your forgiveness for I doubt if you can give it. You have problems of your own, I know, but – will you at least try to understand? You have had children by the man you love. I wanted that, too. My child will be a love child, that's the difference, but I will make it up to him. Martin's son will never lack love.'

There was a lump in Maria's throat as the girl's expression softened with the words and she put her arms round Felicity and hugged her.

Felicity promised not to tell Martin about the child until Hugo had been told. Seeing Felicity every day he was less aware of the change in her and it did not occur to him that she would withhold such information. Felicity's body had developed, but he had not noticed the gradual thickening of her waist and the extra fullness in her breasts. His early excitement in the relationship had given way to a contented acceptance of the situation. Felicity was always there, willing to satisfy his needs – eager to do so in fact. He enjoyed her adoration and triumphed inwardly because he had a woman of his own and Allan, the firstborn, presumably did not – although what he was doing in London no one knew. But Martin, not yet sixteen, had a mistress and the idea pleased him enormously.

Maria busied herself at Romney House after writing an urgent letter to Hugo. She sent it to Heron with Matt on the pretext that he was needed there to help in the rebuilding of the buttery, which was threatening to collapse imminently. Maria visited James Moore and his wife and also called on one or two people who had been friends of Harold and Ruth and whom she dimly remembered. She felt it was important that, since Martin was to inherit

Romney House, the ties between him and various neighbours should be strengthened. Young men were headstrong and careless and she doubted if Martin would take the trouble to renew old friendships or create new ones.

She therefore invited eight people to dine at Romney House one evening but it was nearly her undoing. She made it clear that she and Martin would be host and hostess. Martin insisted that Felicity should be included, but Maria was adamant that no one should be given the idea that she was anything more than Ruth's companion who was still given a home at Romney House. Maria argued that if he was to take a bride eventually it would not do to encourage scandalous talk. It must be established, she told him, that there was no close bond between himself and Felicity. He gave her a strange look and she thought he was going to confide in her but he said nothing. Felicity added weight to Maria's argument by insisting that she would feel uncomfortable with such visitors and Martin let the matter rest.

The evening was pleasant enough. The visitors were James Moore and his wife; his brother and sister-in-law; their younger son and his bride of six months and two elderly spinster sisters – Marion and Jessica Galloway – who lived together in a rambling manor on the far side of Appledore and who were distantly related to Ruth. The talk ranged from local affairs to matters of state and the current rumour that the Queen would marry Francis, Duke of Anjou. They spoke of the plague which was ravaging Cornwall and then the explorations that were taking place in further parts of the globe. Felicity served at table so that the cook – still troubled by her teeth and with a swollen jaw – need not appear. Martin tried several times to catch Felicity's eye but she kept them resolutely downcast and he finally gave up. The young bride, a homely girl with red-gold hair, stared at Felicity when she thought herself unobserved and Maria wondered anxiously whether she had recognized the girl's condition.

The only awkwardness occurred when James' brother

Lionel congratulated Martin on acquiring such an excellent property and urged him to find a wife to share it. He could recommend a young woman, he told him. At that moment Felicity's hand shook and she let a handful of spoons fall back on to the table. In the ensuing good-natured teasing the topic was forgotten.

Hugo's letter, when it arrived, was furious and unequivocal. In no circumstances would Martin marry Felicity Carr. She had no money and no connections. Romney House needed a mistress with both. The mine was finished and Heron would soon be forced to sell its land if the Kendal family were to survive. Allan, totally irresponsible, had vanished and was contributing nothing. Their young son Piers had somehow to be kept at Winchester, the tutor must be retained for Lorna. If Martin also chose to behave recklessly he, Hugo, could only despair . . .

Maria sighed as she read the letter. The handwriting was scrawled and she could imagine the suppressed anger that had propelled the pen across the page. The ink had splattered and the paper was sharply creased. She could see his heavy thumb pressing the folds. She was very glad she had not experienced his anger at first-hand. The letter ended forcefully. Martin *must* marry well if Romney House and Heron were to survive. His bride must have a large dowry and she must come from a well-respected family. Martin must be told and the child must be fostered. If Maria had not made satisfactory arrangements within the month he would join her at Romney House and see to it personally.

There was no greeting at the head of the letter and no fond farewell. Slowly Maria refolded the letter. No, it was not a letter, she thought. It was a bitter communication from one human being to another. She put the letter to her lips and kissed it. 'Oh my dearest Hugo,' she whispered! 'What is happening to us? We must not let circumstances come between us.' She would write back to him, she decided. It would be a hopeful, loving letter. Of course she could make satisfactory arrangements for Felicity and the child. This was one burden he should *not* have to take on his own shoulders. She would be home as soon as she could. Christmas was nearly upon them all and mayhap Allan would come home to surprise them. They would start 1577 with fresh enthusiasm and Fate would be kind to them! She wanted to write the letter at once but first she must speak with Felicity. When Felicity had told Martin, then she, Maria, would talk to both of them. She re-read the letter and nodded. Trying to assume a confidence she did not feel, she went in search of Felicity.

The following morning Felicity waylaid Martin on his way out. She had risen earlier than usual and stood outside feeding the chickens, halfway between the house and the stables where she was sure they would not be overheard.

'What are you doing up so early?' he asked cheerfully.

Felicity stood in the midst of the clucking hens, an apron tied strategically over her swelling belly.

'I've something to tell you,' she said quickly, fearful in case he rushed past her. ' 'Tis most urgent, Martin. I pray you wait awhile.'

Martin looked at her, disconcerted by her manner.

'Good tidings or bad?'

'For me, good,' she answered. 'For you? I think you will be angry. I *am* with child, Martin.'

The expressions that chased over his face spoke volumes. Shock, disbelief, belief and dismay. Perhaps she had hoped for more but she had not expected it.

'But you said—'

'I lied to you,' she said carefully. 'But with good reason. No, please hear me—'

'Then 'tis mine for you've lain with no other man to my knowledge. A child!'

He could scarcely keep the triumph from his voice. 'Does anyone else know of this? I hardly know what to say – 'tis so sudden. Our child! Felicity—'

'You will be angry, Martin, but you must hear me out. I deserve your wrath. I kept it from you these four months because—'

His eyes widened. 'Four months? Felicity, do you know what you're saying? Four months gone. Then in five months more—'

He took her by the shoulders, and his eyes lit up as he let out a whoop. 'Allan will never forgive me! A child for me and him in his twenties and still childless! Ah, what I'd give to see his face when he knows. I shall scour the streets of London in search of him and tell it to him myself!'

For a moment he had almost forgotten her and she watched him, feeling strangely dispassionate. He was still a child himself, she marvelled. An excited boy who has won a race with his brother! The look in her eyes brought him down to earth.

'The child is mine,' she repeated. 'Hugo has decided that we should not marry and I do not wish it.' That was a lie but she felt it necessary in the circumstances. 'You must marry well for the sake of Heron and I understand that. Maria will help me – find me somewhere to live. A position where I can keep the child. Allan will have nothing to fear. The child will not be a Kendal.'

'Not be a Kendal? By Christ! I shall decide that!' Martin's face worked furiously. 'Who else shall decide the fate of my child? He *will* be a Kendal – if I decide so.' He broke off and she could see his thoughts racing. 'I *shall* wed you!'

'No! 'Tis impossible. You know it and so do I.'

His mood changed and he was bewildered. Felicity pitied him.

'If we don't wed,' he said slowly, 'then I could adopt him when I do. He shall be legitimized.'

'No!' she cried, suddenly passionate. '*I* shall bring him up. *I* am his mother.'

'But he is a Kendal!'

'No, not without marriage. He is a Carr. You will have other sons. *They* will be Kendals. This one,' she put a hand protectively to the slight swelling that was the child, 'this one will be a Kendal only in my eyes.'

Martin shook his head wonderingly. 'And all this time you knew and you didn't share it with me.'

'I was afeared. I thought you would want me to rid myself of it.'

'Aye, that would have been—' He checked himself hastily. 'So Hugo knows. When was he, told? Before me?'

'Aye, but 'twas Maria that told him in a letter.'

'Matt! I can see it now.' He shook his head again. 'I thought it odd that he should leave so soon, and looking so ill-tempered.'

'Poor Matt.'

'Matt is not to be pitied!' he shouted, shaking her roughly. ' 'Tis I who deserve your pity – Oh, forgive me! I forgot!' He released her guiltily. 'You should have told me!' he said. 'You would have had all the love and comfort you wanted. You would have had a wedding ring. Aye, we could have wed and told them after.'

'And borne their rage? They might well have cast us off and you would grow to hate me then.'

'Don't say such things! Oh Felicity – my sweet Felicity. What's to be done? If you go away when will I see my child?'

'And when will I see you?' she whispered. 'I love you, Martin. No, don't pretend you return it for I know 'tis not true. You are too young to love anyone but that's to be expected.'

'I'm not too young to father a child!'

'No, but I beg you Martin, don't let us part enemies. We have been loving and pleasant together and we have a child. Let it be a secret joy to you and not something of which you are ashamed. I confess I did wrong to keep it from you, but I wanted so desperately to bear you a son. I shall never regret it. Tell me you will think kindly of us both.'

'I will. Indeed I will. Felicity, the child – does it move yet?'

'Not yet. Another month, I think.'

'And will you still be here?'

'I don't know,' she said simply. 'I am content to put myself into the hands of Fate. Whatever is in my stars, so shall it be.'

In the evening they sat round the fire. Felicity and Martin on one side of it and Maria on the other. Felicity was very pale and she fidgeted with the braid on her dress. Martin sat close to her but not touching, and although Felicity touched his hand lightly he did not take hold of it. He stared into the fire, his legs stretched out, a defiant expression on his face which made him look his age and very vulnerable. Maria tried to speak briskly and without emotion but it was difficult. Felicity's quiet manner evoked her sympathy and Martin's occasional blustering irritated her. But she made allowances. It was a distressing matter and they all reacted in their own ways according to character. Maria began by reading Hugo's letter aloud so that there was no doubt in anyone's mind that the measures she was going to suggest were necessary and for the general good.

'Our good?' Martin interrupted her. 'Or the child's good?'

'Everyone's good – as well as it can be,' said Maria. 'One love child cannot be allowed to bring down Heron. Allan's inheritance cannot be used to support this household. In fact, it cannot do so for there is very little money and we can only sell plate. After that all we have is land and without that all is lost.'

It was a sobering admission and Martin and Felicity looked at her in alarm.

'I propose,' said Maria gently, 'that we ask Frank Innly to take in the child and . . .'

'Not without me!' cried Felicity, her eyes blazing.

'. . . and you.' Maria finished the sentence. 'Your twenty-five crowns would pay for your keep and you could help care for the children or even the sheep. Martin should finish his year with Frank and—'

'But surely Felicity can stay here until the child is born!' cried Martin. 'There is no need to banish her like a criminal. Innly is a good man but they are peasants!'

Maria went on as though he had not spoken. 'Martin should finish his year with Frank and mayhap, if our financial position is better, could then spend a year in Italy.'

'We are both to be banished!' he cried.

Felicity gave him a quick glance which said that he should restrain himself. 'I beg you, be patient,' she said.

'By this time,' said Maria, 'you will be nearer eighteen and we can begin negotiations for a wealthy bride. 'Tis no use to protest, Martin. You have always known that Romney House can scarcely survive on sheep alone. Harold had his own fortune, but there is nothing left of it. There is not enough land to graze more sheep and not enough money to buy more land.'

Felicity wiped away a silent tear but said nothing. Martin put an arm round her shoulder and Maria looked away unable to bear the tenderness in his eyes.

'With a wealthy wife you can buy land, sheep, raise a family and you will be self-supporting. If necessary, you will be in a position to help us at Heron if we find ourselves in desperate straits. If you wish to adopt Felicity's child at a later date – if for instance Felicity became ill or died – you could discuss it with your wife. The child would not inherit but—'

Felicity looked up. 'But a love child cannot expect anything but charity,' she said bitterly. 'I accept that.'

'But if Felicity weds?'

'Then the child will take her husband's name. That can't be avoided.'

They were all silent, thinking.

'One question is,' said Maria, 'is it sensible for you two to be so near each other? Does that put too great a strain on you both? Will it put a strain on Martin's marriage? His wife will have to be told the truth. I think we must wait and see. Take one step at a time. Now we must find a good family to give a home to Felicity and the child – for two years. When Martin returns from Italy – supposing that he goes – we can reconsider. Felicity's husband, if she weds, may wish to take her further away from Romney House. 'Tis all ifs and buts and maybes. We must not expect to solve all the problems at once.'

A deep sigh shook Felicity but she merely nodded. 'I will do whatever you advise,' she said quietly, 'with Martin's approval. Boy or girl I swear I shall be a good mother to Martin's child and I will make no trouble and cause no embarrassment. But no one, now or in the future, will part me from my child.'

CHAPTER FOURTEEN

Nat Gully was hidden behind a log, covered with leaves and branches. He groaned as he saw Lorna's small figure approaching along the river bank. Then he smiled affectionately and resigned himself to the inevitable meeting. Beside him, Brin strained his neck eagerly in an effort to see her, but dared not move until Nat gave the word. As she came on, Lorna called Nat's name and turned her head this way and that in search of him.

'Nat! Where are you, Nat?' she called. 'I've something for you. A Christmas gift. Nat Gulle-e-ey!'

She stood still and, with her hands on her hips, stared round, surveying river, field and wood with an impatient stare. She walked on and, suddenly breasting the small slope, came upon the heron which Nat had tethered close to the net. He thought of the care he had spent on his trap and the time he had spent behind the log, cramped and chilled. Ah well, 'twas the season of goodwill, so they said! He smiled as she regarded the bird warily. The heron observed her solemnly and when she waved her arms to drive it away it remained where it was flapping and struggling. Then she saw the cord round its leg.

'Nat!' she called again. 'Here's a bird on a lead.'

If she went any further she would step on to the net. With a grin Nat threw back his head and gave an imitation of a fox barking and Lorna jumped visibly. Then he hooted like an owl and she looked skyward. When he grunted like a hog, her expression changed and she stamped her foot.

'Nat! I know 'tis you! Where are you hiding, you wretch?' She looked round her again, eyes narrowed. 'You shan't have my gift,' she warned him. 'Show yourself, Nat Gully – or I shan't marry you!'

He burst out laughing at this threat and at the same time

released Brin, who ran forward barking excitedly, giving the clue to Nat's whereabouts.

'Don't move,' cried Nat, 'or you will rob me of my Christmas dinner!'

As she patted the dog, he stood up and went out to greet her. She flung her arms round him and he kissed her warmly.

'Merry Christmas, young Lorna,' he said.

'Merry Christmas *old* Nat!' she replied.

He pointed out the net spread carefully over the grass and led her round it and back to his hiding place.

'Who are you hiding from?' she asked.

By way of answer he held up the end of a cord which ran through the grass towards the net. 'I am up early to catch a plump bird for my Christmas dinner,' he said. 'The net is sprinkled with grass and the bird won't see it. At least I hope he won't. When he comes along I tug this and—'

He rolled his eyes expressively and she gave a squeal of excitement.

'I'll catch him for you, Nat.'

Nat laughed. 'I doubt you could keep that tongue of yours still enough for long enough. And you'll be missed. Fancy sneaking out on Christmas morning in all your finery! You'd best not snag it on a bramble or there'll be something said – and it *won't* be Merry Christmas!'

'I don't care. I've brought you this. I made it and if you laugh I shall take it back and give it to Jon.'

'Laugh?' he protested as he unwrapped the gift. 'I'd cut me throat first! Ah, now look at that. Why 'tis real handsome, that is.'

'Do you like it?'

'With all my heart,' he said, wondering what it was.

' 'Tis a pochette to keep handkerchiefs in. Are you sure you truly like it? See, your initial is stitched in red against the yellow cloth and this button is pearl. Minnie gave it me.'

She looked at him anxiously. 'Put your handkerchief in it,' she prompted. ' 'Twill fit neatly, you'll see.'

Nat had never possessed a handkerchief in his life, but he made a pretence of searching for it.

'Well I'm jiggered!' he exclaimed. 'Must have lost it.'

'Oh Nat!' Her tone was reproachful.

'But I've another at home,' he said hastily. 'And 'tis a fine clean one so I'll pop it into this – what is it, d'you say?'

'A pochette. 'Tis a French word.'

'My, my. A French pochette. I swear I never had a finer gift. My most hearty thanks, young – I mean, Lorna.'

Brin wriggled closer to her as they sat in the hide and she patted him absentmindedly. Then she sighed.

'Sighing on Christmas day?'

She frowned. ' 'Tis scarce like Christmas at all,' she told him, 'with so many long faces and Allan gone away. Mama is sad without him and Papa is cross and doesn't smile. Eloise wouldn't come with us to church this morning for she says she is "shamed" to hold up her head with all eyes upon her and everyone wondering where her betrothed has gone.'

'Oh? Don't she know?'

Lorna shook her head. 'To London, is all he says, but Mama says London is a big place and mayhap he is lost and will find the way shortly.'

'She told Eloise that?'

'No, she told me.'

'Never you fret. Folks is queer but they're all we got.'

'Where's your folks, Nat?'

'All gone.'

'And so you spend Christmas all alone?'

'But I like it that way. No scowling faces, no sad ones. *I'm* as happy as a lark.'

'But you've no dinner!' Her eyes sparkled mischievously.

'I'll be happier when I've caught a nice fat quail or mayhap a partridge. Then I'll stuff it with an onion and a sprig of thyme.'

'Minnie is roasting a goose because Beatrice is partial to it. She's come with Mark and the little one. I don't like

Mark. He calls me Tiddler as if I was a child! And Martin laughs.'

'Martin is there also? You have a full house. 'Tis to be hoped the walls are strong. I heard of a house once, just about as big as yours, and so many folk went crowding in it fell down with a great roar of dust and timber! 'Tis to be hoped no one else arrives.'

Lorna swallowed nervously. 'Felicity Carr is come also,' she whispered.

'Lordy! Then you'd best get along home before it falls down!'

She hesitated.

'Mayhap I will . . .' She stood up and brushed down her skirts. 'Nat, why do you keep that heron? He has mean eyes. I don't care for him at all.'

He laughed. 'He's my decoy. When a bird sees him there standing so still he thinks it quite safe to come and gobble up the worms I've scattered. Then when he is near enough and intent upon his dinner – Whoosh! I pull the cord and the net closes around him.'

'You could eat the heron,' said Lorna hopefully.

'No, no. He is worth a dozen dinners, I tell you, but you'd best be off before they all come looking for you with those long, sad faces. Wish them all the season's greetings from me. And enjoy yourself.'

She began to walk away, giving the bird a wide berth. Nat watched the small figure until it was out of sight then settled down to wait once more with Brin beside him. The little terrier whined softly for attention and nuzzled Nat's hand.

'We've got each other,' Nat told him, fondling the small silky ears. 'What do we need with folks?'

No one else at Heron had been told that Felicity was pregnant. Hugo and Maria thought it best that as few people knew as possible and only Martin regretted the secrecy. He was immensely proud of the achievement and would have enjoyed the drama. Felicity was content to follow Maria's advice and if anyone at Ladyford suspected anything from her appearance they kept their own counsel. Eloise, wrapped up in her own tragedy, noticed nothing and, slightly to Felicity's embarrassment, chose her as confidante and constantly tried to arrange for the two of them to be alone together. She wanted sympathy, and that Felicity could give. She did not know her well enough to judge her, and Allan's desertion had shocked her.

Eloise's feelings towards Felicity were ambivalent. She resented the fact that she was treated like a guest instead of a servant, and she noted jealously the consideration which Martin showed her. She was also incensed by Felicity's obvious affection for Martin, which he did nothing to discourage. But she needed someone to talk to – someone who would not argue or condemn. Felicity, knowing so little of the events leading up to Allan's defection, would be ideal. Eloise therefore waited until Christmas dinner was over and then suggested a walk in the garden to stretch their legs and settle their stomachs! Felicity understood the reason for the invitation, but agreed nonetheless. Eloise's problems might help her to forget her own.

Martin, Hugo, Matt and Jon had gone hawking. Maria rested in her room. Beatrice, as promised, took the children to spend some time at Ladyford with the Benets. Tomorrow all those at Heron would dine at Ladyford, but Melissa wanted a few quiet hours so that Beatrice's child could get to know Nina's. They were cousins, Melissa insisted, and should grow up with affection for each other. She believed privately that the world was a dangerous place and she considered a close-knit family to be a form of insurance.

There was a thick frost which the sun had not dispersed and the autumn leaves crackled underfoot, but the two young women were well wrapped against the cold air. The dogs had followed them out and now circled them happily, sometimes chasing each other, sometimes tumbling in front of Eloise and Felicity and threatening to trip them up. Without thinking where they were walking, they found themselves in the riverside garden, looking down into the dark swiftly flowing water. The almond-scented flowers of summer had gone. A rat scurried into the water at their approach and they watched it swim strongly, to land up on the far bank.

'You've no idea what I have had to endure,' Eloise exclaimed as soon as she was sure they would not be overheard. 'Allan has dealt with me so unkindly, 'tis almost beyond belief. It has all been a disaster. To go off without a word. To leave me in this uncertainty. I wonder I am still sane. You heard, no doubt, that he is in London?'

'Lorna spoke of it. I didn't ask. It was not my place.'

'Indeed not. But doubtless all Ashburton has heard the sorry tale by now. I think I could cheerfully strangle him! Oh, the humiliation. You cannot imagine.'

'But I can. I feel for you, Eloise.'

'I have been deceived from the very first.'

Felicity heard the bitterness in her voice.

'They did not tell me of his background. His dreadful link with that terrible family! Two more were hanged recently for their part in a murder. You heard of that?' Felicity nodded. 'Allan has bad blood in him – but I would have borne that. Even when I knew, I was prepared to wed him. Would you have been so loyal? Would any girl in her right mind? I was a fool. Such a fool.'

She picked up a stone and tossed it into the water without any interest. 'When I think that I refused better men than him. Can you believe that?'

'I believe you if you say so. Of course I do.'

'There was a man loved me – in Rochester. His name was Steven – Steven Kennet.' She did not mention that he would have been quite unsuitable. 'He loved me desperately and when he knew I was betrothed – he was beside himself. Oh, I could have wed elsewhere. Even Martin.'

Felicity went pale but Eloise was too absorbed in her narrative to notice. 'He begged me to wed him but I would not. And he's a fine looking man – with his dark colouring.

And such eyes! I found him better company, too. Allan is so strange at times. So dour and pensive. It was Martin's persistence that made me ill so that we could not go ahead with the wedding. Why do you stare so? Did you not hear of it? I feel the whole of Devon knows of my sufferings.'

Felicity lowered herself to the steps and pulled up her cloak hood in an effort to hide her confusion.

'Are you cold out here?' asked Eloise.

Felicity shook her head and Eloise sat on the step beside her. 'But *I* shall have the last word,' she said. 'I have written to my father. When he realizes the humiliations I have borne he will take me away. I shall go with a thankful heart. There is nothing here for me now but painful memories. Allan will come home to find me gone. Gone to a man who will appreciate me.'

'To Steven Kennet?'

'Steven? No – he has wed elsewhere,' she invented hastily. 'But I shall take my dowry and my father will arrange a new match. Heron has lost its charms for me. The mine is failing. Hugo is in a black despair and there is no money. What is there for me here? I shall be well rid of them all.'

'You say your father will come for you? Does Maria know?'

'Most certainly not, and you must not tell them. They would try to dissuade me and I am quite determined. Promise you'll say nothing.'

'Of course I do. 'Tis no business of mine.' She spoke mechanically, still digesting the disturbing news about Martin which Eloise had disclosed so innocently. Had he really wanted to wed Eloise? It seemed possible. Even probable. She was a beautiful girl and her dowry had no doubt been a generous one. If what she said was true then Martin had turned to her, Felicity, after his rejection. She did not relish the thought, but tried to convince herself that now it was of no significance. Nothing could take away the child she carried and, whether or not Martin loved her, she loved him. That was enough. She would not let Eloise's remarks distress her. It would be harmful to the child. A blithe mother bears a blithe child.

'I said, wouldn't you?' Eloise was staring at her. 'Your thoughts are miles away,' she accused.

'No, no. I heard you. Aye, I would.'

The dogs began to bark then and they raced up the steps to greet Minnie who was coming towards them, wiping her hands on her apron.

'There's a sight of food left,' she told Eloise. ' 'Tis usual to go round the cottages and give it to the poor, but the mistress is resting and I don't wish to wake her. Shall I parcel it up and send it off? Ellie or Ben can take it.'

Felicity looked at Eloise. 'We could take it, mayhap?'

Eloise hesitated. She did not want to lose her audience so soon.

Felicity got to her feet. 'If you parcel it up and tell me where to take it—'

Minnie smiled. 'That's well said. Come with me then. Ellie can go with you. She knows folks and you don't.'

Felicity looked at Eloise, who stood up with as good grace as she could manage. 'I'll come with you,' she said. So the two girls made the rounds together.

That night Felicity's heart beat loudly as she waited for Martin to open the door. Eloise had talked well into the night until Felicity had finally pretended sleep herself. The door opened and Martin drew her inside. It was the bed chamber he shared with Allan, but now he had it to himself.

'I thought you were never coming,' he said. ' 'Tis nearly two o'clock.'

' 'Twas Eloise. She would not sleep – but what is wrong? I should not be here.'

'I had to speak to you before tomorrow. Hugo and Maria have decided to keep you here until—'

'Stay here? Oh Martin, no! Let me return to Appledore, I beg you.'

"Tis their decision and I can see their reasons. If we are together too much and then the child is ever discovered—' He shrugged. 'I shall ride back to Appledore the day after tomorrow and so this might be our last night.'

She was ashen and he put his arm round her. 'Don't take it so hard. You knew we would have to part.'

'But not so soon. I did not know 'twould be so soon.'

'I wanted to sleep with you this last time, Felicity. Will you stay?'

'Of course I will. Our last night! Oh Martin. Forgive me. I've tried to be so brave. I'll be myself again in a moment.'

'Come to bed, little one. Let me love you and all your fears will melt away. I promise.'

She allowed him to lead her to the bed and climbed in beside him. Sleeping with him seemed the natural thing – they had been together so often – but the room was unfamiliar and Felicity felt tense with the misery she was trying to conceal.

He put his arms round her and comforted her as well as he could.

Felicity tried desperately to put aside all her fears and regrets so that she could respond to his caresses and make this last love-making happy and memorable. She was amazed to feel Martin grow hard against her thigh and wondered that a man could so control his body that sorrow could not interfere with its working.

' 'Tis for you,' he whispered. 'See how ready I am for your warm sweetness? I have missed you these last few nights.'

'And I you.'

His hands slid over her, touching her ears, throat, shoulders. She felt a slight thrill and prayed, 'Let me make him happy this last time. Let it be the best time, dear God.' He was feeling for her nipples and the thrill came again, intensified. If only her body would take over from her mind. His hands moved to her abdomen and he stroked the taut skin, then kissed her thighs, and between her legs.

'Martin! Oh Martin!'

He took each hand and licked the palm. It was unbearably sweet and she moaned, knowing that her love sounds increased his own excitement; knowing that he liked to linger over her, saving the greatest thrill until much later – like a child with a cherry cake, she had teased him. She wanted him to reassure her – to tell her that no other woman would satisfy him so well. But it was not his way. Now he would make love to her almost without words. He could rouse her with his fingers and tongue. He rolled her over and began to trace her spine with his fingers. As she sighed she opened her eyes but saw the outline of the unfamiliar window and closed them again.

'I'll never forget our loving,' he whispered suddenly and she was surprised and turned over to see his face.

'I mean it,' he told her urgently. 'I want you to know you are my first woman and that is unforgettable.'

'And you are my first man.'

She wanted to add: 'and you have given me your child'. But she could not do it. This night was for lovers. Already it was too good to share. He moved until he was above her and his weight crushed her. Tonight there would be no delaying. His entry into her was fierce, greedy – almost triumphant. And yet, she thought, so very sad.

Minnie looked at her daughter, thunderstruck.

'Felicity Carr? 'Tis not possible,' she asked. 'Did you see it with your own eyes?'

'No, but I saw her coming out this morning. 'Twas very early and she was on tiptoes, wearing only what she was born in! 'Tis true, I tell you. Why should I make up such a story?'

'Why indeed? Then I'm sorry for doubting you.' Minnie frowned at the carrots she was scraping. 'Have you told anyone this?'

'Only you. Do you think they were—' She giggled. 'You know?'

'Well, if they weren't, I'm a monkey on a stick! Why else should a girl go to a young man's bed chamber? Dearie me! Felicity Carr! Who'd have thought she'd dare such a trick? Mind you, I'll wager she's been encouraged. She'd not go to him otherwise. Young Martin and Felicity Carr! I can hardly credit it. And mother-naked, too! She must have known what they'd be doing.'

'She had a shawl round her,' said Ellie reluctantly.

'A shawl? 'Tis not what you said before.'

'She was naked *under* the shawl.' Ellie wriggled uncomfortably under her mother's gaze. 'The rest was all true.'

'I hope so for the sake of your soul, my girl.'

'I swear it.'

'Hmm! And she didn't see you?'

'No. She had tears in her eyes and her hand up to her mouth – so.' Ellie put a hand to her own mouth in a gesture of distress and Minnie's heart was instantly softened. Her earlier disapproval vanished. Felicity was no longer a wanton hussy but a wronged woman.

'Poor little girl,' she said. 'I wonder how long that's been going on? I wonder . . . Mind you, I did think it strange, sending young Martin down there but then again, he's only a lad. At least—'

'He's sixteen!' said Ellie. 'He's old enough!'

Minnie shook her head and began to slice the carrots into a pan. She realized suddenly that Ellie, opposite, was leaning on the table doing nothing useful and she pushed pan, carrots and knife across to her.

Ellie grimaced but began to slice, while Minnie went into the larder and collected two hares and began to skin them with quick practised movements.

'D'you reckon she'll have a baby?' asked Ellie. 'If she did – you know—'

'Sweet Heaven, don't speak of it!' Minnie's dismay was almost comical. 'Not that nice girl! Oh, that *would* put the cat among the pigeons!' She *knew* the griefs of an illegitimate child, for Ben, her eldest, had been born out of wedlock and Minnie preferred not to remember the miseries and hardships she endured at that time. True, she was partly to blame for she had run away from Heron and all those who would have helped her. But her innate stubbornness – cussedness Jon called it! – had prevailed, and she gave birth to the child alone. Unable to care for it, she left the baby on the doorstep at Heron and disappeared. Now her eyes darkened as she recalled the degradation she had undergone and the depths to which she had fallen.

A deep sigh did not escape Ellie who looked at her curiously.

'Do you pity her, Ma? Martin be handsome enough. I'd creep to his room if he asked me – Ow!'

Minnie's hand caught her across the face and she half fell from the stool. 'Don't you do no such thing!' cried Minnie. 'Unless you want a good hiding from your Pa – and another from me. Creep to his room indeed! He's not so handsome as to wed you, that's for sure.'

Ellie ignored the blow. 'Why then, won't he wed Felicity?'

'Most likely not, young rogue. They'd not let him if he wanted to, for she's a church mouse and Heron needs money. Times are hard. Poor girl. Poor foolish girl. But there, we will do these things and then there's the reckoning.'

Her own reckoning had been immediate and she did not envy Felicity the road ahead if she *was* with child, although the family would surely provide for her. They were good people, the Kendals, and Maria was the best of them all. Since Luke's death Minnie had transferred her devotion to Maria, for it was she who had finally saved her from her own folly. It was to Maria she had run, at the Arnsville convent. There she had queued with the 'poor' at the kitchen door, waiting for the scraps left over from the nuns' supper. Maria had recognized her and taken her in. She had fed her, washed her, cared for her – and she had given her love as well as the reproaches. Then she had taken her back to Heron and Jon had wed her and Ben, her child, had been handed back to her. She had been more fortunate than she deserved. Felicity's path might be harder.

'He'll never wed her,' she said. 'Poor Felicity. If she's with child she'll have a hard row to hoe!'

Outside the kitchen door Eloise halted incredulously. She caught the last few words and the shock sent the colour from her face. The words rang in her ears but for a moment she would not believe them. It could not be Felicity Carr of whom they spoke. It was not possible. Ellie's next words, however, dispelled her doubts.

'Then Martin's a pig! I shan't smile at him ever again. I shall keep my face so straight he'll know. He'll know what I think of him.'

'Will you, then?' said Minnie.

Eloise turned, her heart hammering under her ribs, and fled back to her room.

Hugo finished reading the letter and handed it back to Maria. He looked defeated and utterly dejected.

'So she wrote to them,' he said. 'We should have expected it – and yet it didn't enter my head that she would want to go. We have nothing to offer her – not even a husband – and yet I didn't think she would want to leave us. Was that very vain of me? The Ballantynes are very angry and who can blame them?'

'I can,' said Maria, 'and I do blame them. If Eloise had wed Allan on the proper day she would be his wife. There would be no running away then. She would have taken the good and the bad with the rest of us.'

'Mayhap 'tis well she didn't wed him. To turn her back when things go ill with us! We must let her go, of course, and the dowry goes with her. Oh Maria, I'm so weary of it all. What's to be done? We are bedevilled on all sides. The mine, Allan, Martin and Felicity and now this.'

Maria did not answer. She was reading James Ballantyne's letter for the second time. Its tone was uncompromising:

'A letter from my beloved daughter disturbs me greatly and you will understand my horror when the full extent of her predicament is revealed to me. 'Tis greatly to her credit that she has borne in silence for so long the indignity heaped upon her by the disappearance of her betrothed. Your son, Allan, in whom we placed such trust, has deceived us all and there can be no valid excuse for his cruel behaviour. You did not inform us of his departure and we take that most unkindly, considering you to have a duty to us in all such matters. My daughter speaks also of certain revelations regarding your son's forebears. The Gillis strain would seem to be an evil one, combining madness with the black arts, and those facts should have been revealed to us during our earliest negotiations. 'Tis most certain we should then have terminated all arrangements for the union, desiring our daughter to wed an upright man of wholesome descent.

We are determined that Eloise shall return to Rochester at the earliest opportunity and have instructed our solicitor to travel to Ashburton in one week's time and bring her home. During his visit to your home he will also serve upon you documents authorizing the return of the dowry in full. This letter is intended to forewarn you of this fact, so that you may make these preparations as are necessary to raise this sum and give Eloise time to prepare for the journey home.

I will speak no further of the disillusionment we feel towards the Kendal family. Abigail and Adam Jarman have been our friends for many years, but we must reluctantly consider them party to the deceit you have practised upon us, and our feelings towards them have undergone a change. When our daughter is once more under our roof we shall sever all Kendal connections . . . James Ballantyne, this first month of the year fifteen seventy-seven.'

'He is right, Hugo,' Maria said slowly. 'We *were* at fault.'

'There is nought wrong with Allan!' shouted Hugo. 'He

is a fine—' He could not finish. 'Let us say that there is no trace of madness nor black arts. I don't pretend he is perfect – but is any man? Irresponsible, aye and moody. Unpredictable, even. But nought else. Upright and wholesome! The man's a pompous fool! I misjudged him utterly.' Maria agreed. Wrath was preferable to dejection, she thought. 'But when I set eyes on him – Allan, that is – I shan't mince my words. To bring such shame upon us!'

'Poor Abby,' said Maria. 'She was so proud of having recommended Eloise and now feels so badly. Ah well, 'tis done and we must all come to terms with it. Who will tell Eloise?'

'Mayhap you should,' said Hugo. 'I may say something I'll regret. She has a week, tell her, and Ellie can help her pack. *I* must see what can be done about the money.'

Maria folded the letter. 'And poor Allan – when he comes home she'll be gone.'

'Poor Allan? The young fool has only himself to blame.'

'That's not quite so, Hugo. He is not to blame for the Gillises.'

'You are right. But without Isobel Gillis his father would not have been born and neither would he. In a way he owes his very life to them. He should think on that!'

And he stormed out, leaving Maria to consider the point. It was a new slant on a vexed question and she thought about it with some eagerness, wondering if it might reconcile Allan to the otherwise unacceptable branch of his family. Then, with a dismissive gesture, she put the idea aside and went in search of Eloise.

Martin paused at the stable door and took a last look at the familiar scene. He had the feeling that he was seeing it for the last time and yet he knew that was not so. Romney House was his home but Heron would always be here. He would visit. He would always be welcome. His present transgression would be forgiven and he would ride in again through the familiar gates and Jon would run out to take his horse and welcome him back. So why, he asked himself irritably, did he feel this remorse? As though he was closing the last page of a book. He shrugged mentally and opened the half door. His horse neighed at the sight of him and tossed his head eagerly. Jon had saddled him already and it only remained for Martin to strap on the bundles. He ran a hand down the smooth dark neck and patted the broad back.

'Come on, Sedge. 'Tis just you and I this time.'

Felicity had ridden with him on the outward journey. Now she would remain at Heron for a few weeks until final arrangements had been made for her. He tried not to recall her distress as she left his bed chamber. He had wanted the night to be happy for them both. He had planned that their parting should be a memorable one, but she had wept and it had turned sour. His pity for Felicity was mingled with a faint resentment that she had spoilt their last moments together.

He would miss her at Romney House, in fact, he could not imagine it without her. There was an emptiness inside him that was fast becoming a feeling of desolation. He tugged at the straps and rocked the bundle to make sure it was secure. The basket would go on the other side. As he moved round, the horse tossed its head and Martin saw Eloise approaching. She moved quickly and there was no smile on her face. His spirits fell further. Surely she did not know! He glanced round anxiously, hoping that Jon was nowhere within earshot. If Eloise was going to raise her voice . . .

'I hear from servants' gossip,' she said without preamble, 'that another bastard Kendal is on the way.'

Martin fought down a desire to hit the beautiful mouth that spoke so harshly. Instead he closed his eyes and did not answer.

'Did you hear me?' she demanded.

The warm rose-coloured gown contrasted with the pallor of her face and her eyes were green and cold.

'You shouldn't listen to gossip,' he said and bent to examine the horse's legs and ankles.

'Is it true?'

' 'Tis not your affair.'

'I think differently. I think 'tis the affair of the whole family if you have gotten a servant with child.'

'Felicity is not a servant.'

'So you admit it?'

'I said she is not a servant. I do not admit nor deny anything. And how does it concern you? I hear, through more reliable channels, that you are leaving for Rochester at the end of the week. You'll no longer be a member of the family so why are you so interested?'

Her eyes glittered and he saw her mouth move convulsively. She was struggling to control her feelings, but he knew that it would not take much to make her lose that control. God's wounds! he thought angrily. Not more tears! Women were desirable creatures, but they could be the very devil when crossed. He had been hoping to slip away while Hugo was at Ladyford with just a quiet farewell to Felicity and Maria. A quarrel with Eloise was to be avoided if possible. He must try to moderate his tongue.

'You know why I am interested!' she snapped. 'Because, if you recall, 'twas not long since you were declaring your passion for me! 'Twas me that you loved – or so you would have me believe. Was that all false? Were they lies?'

'In faith I don't recall it well. If you say 'tis so—'

'You – you pretend not to remember? Oh, what nonsense. You recall perfectly but are ashamed to—'

'I'm ashamed of nothing!'

'Then more's the pity for you *should* be, Martin. You should be ashamed of trifling with my affections and of toying with a servant! No doubt you told *her* you loved her and the poor little fool believed you. Did you promise to wed her? You slept with her and yet—' She broke off, choking back words she did not want to say.

Martin was fast losing his temper. If she was determined to goad him she would regret it. What did it matter? He had already blotted his copybook and was surrounded by disapproval on all sides. He no longer cared for their good opinions.

'You mean I bestowed my favours on Felicity instead of you,' he said. 'I chose her bed and not yours. Her body instead of—'

'Don't! Don't you dare compare me with her. 'Twas you wanted it – you that begged, saying that you loved me.'

'Saying that we loved each other. Aye, I'd have wed you but you were too greedy. Felicity is not greedy. She asked nothing in return. Nothing. I won't compare you for there is no comparison. Felicity is worth two of you! There, you wanted the truth. Now you have it.'

Her bosom heaved passionately and she was gasping for breath. Martin thought dispassionately that she had never looked more beautiful with her flushed cheeks and wild expression. A pity she was such a shrew. Eloise stared at him furiously, but a similar thought intruded into her consciousness. His body still appealed to her animal senses, and if he offered her one crumb of comfort she would take it readily and the way would be clear for a reconciliation. If he touched her she would flame with desire. But no! She had forgotten Felicity. That damned strumpet! And the child! That would always be between them. No. Martin Kendal's body might cry out and hers might answer but Felicity had effectively come between them forever.

'You are worse than worthless, Martin Kendal,' she told him. 'You are arrogant, selfish, unscrupulous, shallow. And your Gillis brother is no better. A plague on the Kendals! I shall watch your ruin with great pleasure. I shall—'

He had swung himself into the saddle and sat looking down into the glorious face that spat so venomously. He had no desire now to make any farewells.

'And God be with you, too, ma'am,' he mocked and, spurring his startled horse, cantered across the stable yard and out through the gate.

Eloise, incensed beyond all bearing, ran after him,

stumbling precariously on the uneven cobbles and screaming vengefully, but by the time she reached the gate he was out of sight and the sound of hoof beats was fading. She would never see him again.

The store behind the chandler's was a poor exchange for the splendours of Heron, but Eloise Ballantyne knew she would die rather than admit as much to Steven Kennet. He sat opposite her, sprawled across a pile of ropes, his eyes fixed upon her face. She had told him about her disastrous alliance with the Kendal family and her determined efforts, from the very first day, to free herself. Sitting on a new wooden sea chest, she looked as beautiful as ever with her blue eyes flashing fire at the memory of the indignities she had suffered. The long fair curls rested on her softly rounded shoulders, and she twisted a strand of hair as she spoke, occasionally releasing it so that it sprang back among its fellows.

'If 'twas so terrible,' he said, 'why did you stay so long? You had only to write to your father and he'd have taken you away. Lord knows, he dotes on you enough. You only have to lift a finger—'

'I had no wish to distress my parents,' she told him. 'They were content, believing that I was happy. They thought Heron a fine place.'

'And so 'twas, you were just telling me.'

She frowned impatiently. 'I said 'twas a large estate and a big house—'

'And a tin mine. Don't forget the tin mine.'

Eloise looked at him suspiciously. Was he playing with her? No, he would not dare. He would not risk her displeasure. He looked at her still in that certain way and there was unfinished business between them. She wondered anxiously if he remembered the day she had rejected him. Probably not, she thought. Such men do not suffer.

'Aye, and the mine,' she added. 'But 'twas not thriving.

They had mismanaged it all and the fortune was gone. Sad to see a fine inheritance lost by such folly.'

'So you were misled,' he persisted. 'Your parents were fooled by these Kendals.'

She hesitated, unwilling to admit that her family could be duped so easily.

'I don't think you properly understand,' she said at last.

'Nor ever will if I explain it a dozen times or more. Let us just say 'twas an unfortunate period of my life from which I am glad to escape.'

He laughed. 'So here you are, back in Rochester and your fond father is no doubt arranging a new match for you.'

'He is . . . But enough of me, Steven. What are you about these days? I thought to find you wed by this time.'

'Mayhap I haven't found the right woman,' he suggested. 'Maybe I'm pernickety who I marry. I don't have a doting father to arrange my future for me, but I've had my share of comfort, don't you fret. A young man like me doesn't need a wife. There are plenty of willing beauties in Rochester and I've found a fair number of them.'

Eloise bit her lip, restraining a caustic comment. 'I don't doubt it,' she said with an attempt at lightness. 'You always did have a winning way, Steven Kennet. I still remember the touch of your lips upon mine, brief though it was.'

'Do you? Now I've forgot that.'

Damned liar, she thought. He *did* remember. She forced a smile. 'If your luck holds out I might remind you,' she said with a provocative toss of her blonde head.

'My luck?' he said. 'There is nowt wrong with my luck. 'Tis you that seems afflicted by bad luck. This Martin and this Allan you've spoke of at such length. Two fine handsome men and you couldn't land either one of them!'

Her eyes blazed suddenly but hastily she lowered her lids. 'I told you, I would not have them,' she said.

'Oh, they did want you then?'

She swallowed hard. He was going to make this as difficult as he could, but she would win. It might take all her cunning, all her guile, but she would not be rejected by Steven Kennet. She was still beautiful. No, she was more beautiful! He wanted her, it was written boldly in his eyes. But if he recalled her scornful treatment of him then he wanted his revenge. Was he worth her time, she wondered? She had almost decided to surrender to him, to restore her faith in her own desirability. And to experience once more the ecstasy of love which she remembered only too well. Her body and mind were ripe for love and while she waited for her father to negotiate another husband, she might well amuse herself with Steven Kennet.

If only he did not push her too far in his zeal for revenge. She wondered how he would take her – in a furious passion of delayed longing, no doubt. Her senses thrilled at the prospect.

'They wanted me,' she said carefully.

'But you teased them and ran away!' he said.

'That was spiteful,' she said, allowing her lips to tremble. 'I was much younger then – I was afraid.'

'Afraid, my eye!' said Steven. 'I saw the way you fluttered those lovely fingers up there, at that very window. Such a delicate "farewell"!'

She faced him squarely. 'I would have thought a man like you, with all the "comfort" you've had, would have easily forgot a young girl's foolishness.'

'You thought wrongly, then.'

'It meant so much to you? You wanted me *so* desperately?'

'I did.'

'And now you don't?'

'Have I said that?'

'You imply it by your insulting remarks and spiteful looks.'

He threw back his head suddenly and laughed. 'Well, well, a fine pair we must make, sitting here arguing if we will or we won't. I've learnt a lot while you were in Devon being made a fool of by the Kendals. A fair reputation I've got, I can promise you. No one makes a fool of Steven

Kennet and gets away with it – but I just might make an exception in your case. I say I might. Those wide blue eyes that speak so clearly to me – Oh they do! The message rings like a peal of bells in my ears. I know what you want, Eloise Ballantyne.' He stood up and crossed the small distance between them. Slowly, he put his arms round her and raised her to her feet. She began to tremble, unable to control the clamour of her body crying out for the attention it had lacked for so long. He pulled her closer, keeping his eyes fixed on her face, noting the flush that coloured her cheeks and the way she unconsciously parted her beautiful lips. Her chest rose and fell, hastening its rhythm. He let the fingers of one hand travel up her back until it touched the bare skin at the nape of her neck. Eloise gasped with pleasure.

'I might make an exception,' he repeated softly. 'Would you care to be the one exception to my rule, Eloise? How would you like to discover for yourself all that I've learned while you were away? Would that please your sweet body? Answer me, Eloise.'

Wordlessly, she nodded her head, as his fingers explored the lobe of her ear and the contours within it.

'Steven!' she gasped, feeling her whole body come alive with a great aching desire for his.

He ran his finger softly along her teeth. Then down went his hand to her breasts, first one then the other, feeling for the nipples which stood out stiffly through the material of her gown. She snatched at his other hand and held them both against her breasts. He raised an eyebrow and his eyes glinted with malice.

'So you *do* want me, Eloise Ballantyne. Say it then and maybe you shall have all that's mine to give. Maybe you'll have it more than once. I warrant you'll want it, Eloise. They all do and you're no different. Do you realize that? No different to any of them. They all want it, you see, and when they get it they want more—'

'Steven!' She clung to him fiercely, pulling his lips against her own, moaning.

He teased her and his hands fell to her waist and back and down past her waist to her thighs. She cried out.

'Tell me that you want me, Eloise!' he insisted. 'Say it! I want to hear it from those sweet lips.'

'I – Oh Steven—'

'Say it! I, Eloise Ballantyne want you, Steven Kennet.'

'No – I cannot—'

He put his mouth to her ear and whispered, 'Say it!' His tongue reached in. 'Say it, Eloise. You want me, don't you?'

She nodded again, aware of nothing but her body's overwhelming need for his. She would enjoy him. Oh, she knew it. He had promised. More than once, he had said. She would want him again and again.

'Say it, Eloise.'

'I want you, Steven Kennet. I, Eloise, I want you, Steven Kennet. I want you. I want—'

But he had stepped back, a look of triumph on his face. She tried to cling to him, gasping, imploring, but he pushed her away.

'But I don't want *you*,' he said. 'So don't wait around!'

And then, with a slight flutter of his fingers, he was gone and Eloise, broken and defeated, was left alone with the echo of his laughter ringing in her ears.

CHAPTER FIFTEEN

Frank Innly's wife, when approached on the matter of Felicity Carr, was sorely tempted to agree. Another pair of hands would be useful and so would the extra money. The girl, apparently, had twenty or more gold crowns that the old lady had left her and that was a lot of money. However, she resisted the temptation long enough to think it over carefully and finally said 'No'. Her reason was no secret. She told her husband plainly that a girl who would lie with a man who was not her husband would lie with any man and she knew Frank Innly! He would doubtless be the next. All his protests to the contrary went unheeded. Frank was still an attractive man. His work in the fields kept him lithe and lusty. His wife, on the other hand, had borne more children than was good for her figure and she had also eaten too well. She was shapeless and tired of nights. Felicity would be neither once the child was born. There was a short sharp argument and it was decided that Felicity would not be welcome. Instead, she approached her elder sister, Dorothy Waller, a widow of thirty-six whose husband had left her with five sons to bring up. In that household there would be no danger of Felicity corrupting the husband. If she chose to set her cap at the eldest boy no one would object. Lucas was eighteen and Felicity was a better match than he could expect to make.

Dorothy seized the opportunity gratefully and the Kendals were informed. Within a month it was all settled and Felicity moved in to the tiny cottage. She had her own bed chamber, although that meant that Lucas moved back into a room with two of his brothers. The other two younger boys slept with their mother. Dorothy was a feckless but good-hearted woman and she made Felicity welcome. She was genuinely pleased to have her there. The all-male houseful bored her and she was secretly hopeful of a match between Felicity and Lucas. He was a well-built lad with the physique of a wrestler and he was six feet tall. But his heart was gentle and his personality in no way matched his rugged frame. His mildly humorous eyes were blue and he had a curly golden beard. Of all the boys he was the only one to resemble Dorothy's side of the family, and she kept a special place in her heart for him, telling everyone that he would grow up the image of her father.

She was a fierce, wiry woman with boundless energy and she worked at the various big houses in the neighbourhood on a casual basis, helping out on washdays, spring cleanings, special occasions and the like. Twenty gold crowns sounded like a fortune, but Dorothy was not avaricious and would have taken her in for much less. Felicity's child was due in early May and, as Maria had hoped, the delay gave her time to settle into her new surroundings and get to know the family.

Sam was three years younger than Lucas, for two girls had been stillborn. Then there was Harry, fourteen, Davy, twelve and Robert, eleven. At first they were all very shy and quite abashed to find a pretty girl in their midst, but they soon found that her presence enhanced the home. Their mother was less aggressive towards them, for she no longer felt outnumbered by her family of sons. They ate as well as anyone in their circumstances – and a little better after Felicity moved in – and Felicity took over most of the housework, some of the cooking and she patched and mended the clothes. It was a simple, repetitive existence, but the boys' cheerful company amused her and Dorothy's courage inspired her. They were two women, each without a man, and they shared many secrets and much laughter, so that very quickly Felicity looked upon the older woman as half sister, half mother and was surprised to find that she was contented with her new life. The only shadow in this new-found happiness was the nearness of Romney House. It was less than a mile away and the knowledge that Martin was so close tormented her in the early days, but as time passed her new 'family' took up more and more of her energy and the memories began, imperceptibly, to fade.

One morning – it was the second of May – she was outside spreading the previous day's wash along the hedgerow to dry. She shook each garment free of the night's creases and draped it carefully, so that the thorns held it well enough to stop it blowing away if the breeze strengthened. There was a hedge alongside the cottage for forty yards or so and it provided the ideal drying ground. As she worked she hummed cheerfully. She was large with the child, for the birth was only a few weeks away and she moved awkwardly, pausing occasionally to straighten up and put a hand to her back where it ached. Her pregnancy had been almost trouble free and she counted herself fortunate. Her minor pains had been swiftly alleviated by Dorothy's infusions of motherwort. Her cheerful support had also helped greatly.

' 'Twill dry a treat today.'

Felicity turned to see Lucas on his way to work in the nearby smithy where his strength made him invaluable to the blacksmith, who was now nearly seventy and doubled up with rheumatism.

'Aye,' she answered. 'But you're early today, Lucas.'

She bent to pick up a pillowslip but he was there first and handed it to her.

'All that bending,' he said. 'It might well harm the little 'un.'

'I don't think so, but thank you. Shall you be busy today?' She had a sudden premonition of his purpose and fought to keep the conversation on mundane matters.

'I came early a-purpose to find you,' he said. 'I've summat to say. Summat important. Can't you guess what 'tis?'

She wanted to say 'No' but that was a lie. Her premonition was right and he meant to say it. Prevaricating would do no good. 'I think I do,' she said softly. 'Is it about – you and me?'

'Aye, 'tis that. I was wondering and thinking a lot lately that I'm eighteen and in work and I've no maid of my own. And here's you, with child, and no man. You're a bonny lass and—' he grinned. 'I'm a handsome man. We'd make a fair couple, I reckon, if you'd have me.'

'Oh Lucas, I—'

He put a large finger to her lips. 'Let me finish my speech,' he protested. 'I've spent that many hours on it! Where was I? Ah, that's it. If you'd have me. I'd not mistreat you and I'd care and love the little 'un like he was my own. That I promise. And I'd love you, Felicity, for I nearly do already and I've only just set my mind to it!'

Felicity's face relaxed into a smile and he put the finger under her chin and lifted her head.

'I'm not a gentleman,' he said, 'but I'm honest and I work hard and no one should ever harm a hair of your head if you was mine. Now was that all of it? No, I've forgotten a bit. But it's gone so what I've said will have to suffice. Ah, I know it – that you may have a notion to stay unwed and wait for your gentleman to claim you and the child. If that's what you want I'll wait a year for you. How's that for a speech? I must admit I'm proud of it.'

'And so you should be, Lucas. That's my first proposal and so well said! I'm proud of you. And beholden to you for asking.' She sighed. 'The truth is, Lucas, there's some truth in what you say – that I'd like the child's father to claim him. I don't think he ever will but mayhap he should have the chance.' Lucas nodded and she went on, 'I'd like to wait and think it over. You *are* a handsome man and you'd make a fine husband. If 'twas not for the child I'd accept your proposal but – the child should have a chance to be with his father if he's wanted.' She swallowed. 'I don't think he will be,' she said, 'and that's the truth, but I'll bide my time if I may.'

'Then can I kiss you?'

'Kiss me?'

'To show you I'm in earnest – and a fair kisser. Then I'll not plague you further.' She nodded and he drew her towards him. 'We'll not get very close!' he joked, but kissed her soundly nonetheless. 'How did you like it?'

'A very sweet kiss! I like you, Lucas. You're a good man.'

'Well, that's nice to hear.' He glanced up at the sun. ' 'Tis getting on. I'd best be on my way. We've a busy day ahead. I'm glad we understand each other.'

'Aye. Enjoy your day, Lucas.'

'I will – and you take care. You're in a delicate way.'

She nodded and watched him until he was out of sight then shook the pillowslip and spread it to dry with a heart grown lighter for his words. Lucas Waller *was* a good man. She could do a lot worse than wed him.

That night Felicity dreamed – a vivid dream which had returned again and again since the conception of her child – but there was no child in the dream. Hardly a week passed without the dream appearing in her sleep and in her waking moments she tried desperately to hold on to it and recall it in detail. But this she could never do. It slipped from her, leaving only the essence of the dream and the knowledge that it had a significance for her.

As soon as her eyelids closed and her breathing settled into its regular sleep pattern, the images rose crystal clear. In that last moment before the conscious mind surrenders to the subconscious she thought, This time I'll remember it, and then she was walking in a strange place, walking up to the doorway of a dilapidated house. A large house with gardens overgrown with weeds and nettles. The trees were large and shapeless and without leaves, and the bare branches and twigs brushed against each other with a sighing sound, although there was no wind to move them. Her hair was longer than it was in reality and reached almost to the ground. She was naked, but she was not aware of the cold although the garden was shadowed by a full moon. As she went up the steps to the front door it opened soundlessly and she went inside. Desolation met her at every turn of the passage which twisted interminably. Dead leaves had blown in through the cracked and broken windows. Cobwebs hung across the corners like massive grey drapes and there was no furniture in the rooms. Door after door presented itself and she opened them and peered inside. The rooms were shuttered but chinks of moonlight gave them an eeriness that did not frighten her. Then she realized that the dimensions of the passage were changing – it was becoming narrower and loftier and her journey though it was faster. Her feet moved more quickly until suddenly she was no longer running but floating along the passage, and she was so high she could no longer see in at the half open doors. She followed the passage, which took her upstairs and along another passage into a room at the end. There were no shutters and the moonlight streamed in. She opened her mouth to scream, for there was a figure sleeping on the floor amid the dead leaves and cobwebs. Although she made no sound, the figure stirred and sat up, staring at her. Martin, Martin, Martin she whispered, but it was not Martin but Allan, looking gaunt and ill. He held out his hands to her but she floated out of the window, up and up towards the moon. The grey moonlit moor passed below her, faster and faster, and there was a great rushing sound as a wind sprang up and swirled her giddily. Glimpses of the old house passed before her, growing smaller and smaller, until it finally disappeared.

Lucas stood with his back to the horse, his head bent over its hoof, which was tucked firmly between his knees as he pared the edge in preparation for the shoe. The horse, a large bay cob with a white blaze on its face and mild eyes, stood patiently while Lucas worked. It was hot in the smithy and sweat beaded the man's face. From time to time he wiped his forehead with the back of a hairy hand, and then wiped the sweat on to the split leather apron which covered him. Small trimmings of horn fell round his feet as he whistled tunelessly. When he had finished he nodded to the young lad, who watched him enviously, and the boy darted off to fetch the first hot shoe, which he carried carefully with a pair of tongs. It was handed over, tested for fit with a hiss of painless steam, and then Lucas plunged it into the water trough to cool it a little before reseating it and banging in the nails.

'They don't go straight in, see,' he told the lad. 'That'd hurt him. They go angled in – so – and the point comes out here.' The boy nodded. 'And in goes another and comes out here. See that? You bang it straight in and he'll likely kick you into eternity! You don't want that!'

The boy shook his head. At eleven years he was a runt of a boy, undersized and lame, and would never make a blacksmith but he haunted the smithy and no one had the heart to discourage him from his ambition.

. . . and in goes another and we're nearly done. Chip off the end of the nail, so, and clench it over. That's it. Then the next . . . Mind you, this old horse is soft as butter, but some'd lead you a merry dance. You have to know your horse. So – have you eaten today?'

The boy shook his head and Lucas tutted. 'Well, I'll see what I can find for you when Felicity comes.'

'Is she your woman?'

'She is and she isn't.'

The boy nodded. 'She's right bonny,' he said, 'but she's – big.'

Lucas roared with laughter. 'Aye, she's that, right enough,' he said. He straightened up and patted the horse's rump and began to lead her out into the yard. 'You like her?'

'Aye, but—'

'But she's big!' Lucas laughed again. 'You go up the lane and look for her, then. Find out what she's brought us.'

It had been Dorothy's habit to send Felicity along to the smithy each day to take him a flagon of ale and a bundle of bread and cheese or a piece of salt pork. It was a walk of a little over a mile and Felicity, although she guessed the older woman's motive, went willingly enough. She enjoyed the solitary walk, but for reasons which Dorothy would not have approved. The time spent going to and from the smithy was the time she allowed herself to dwell on Martin. Treasuring his memory, trying to imagine what he would be doing or thinking about his child – these thoughts were her luxuries. For the rest of the day she concentrated on the present and her new family. At night she slept as soon as her head touched the straw bolster and, apart from her recurring dream, her nights were peaceful and she woke refreshed.

She *was* big, as the boy had said. Dorothy hoped she would go into labour early, for she knew the birth of such a large baby could be difficult, even dangerous, but she kept these thoughts to herself. The child was not very active, giving Felicity none of the painful kicks and jabs which Dorothy had received from her own babies. A placid child, she told Felicity, and a girl most probably. But Felicity's thoughts were not on the baby, but on its father, as she moved slowly and somewhat heavily along the highway and then turned off along the lane. She leaned backwards slightly, to help her balance, and occasionally put a hand to her back when the strain of the child's weight developed from a discomfort to an ache. Her face lit up with a smile as she saw the puny figure approach with a step and a hop. The boy hated the sound of his left foot scraping the ground and gave a little hop on his good leg so that he could swing the other past it.

'Hey up, Ned,' she greeted him.

'Hey up.'

He kept his eyes above her waist in case his awe at her size was obvious.

'Did Lucas send you to meet me?'

'Aye. He wonders what you've brought.'

'And so do *you*, eh?'

He grinned.

'Then I'll put you out of your misery. 'Tis a cold bacon pasty and an onion.'

'Mmm! Will I carry your basket?'

'My thanks, Ned, I'd be glad of it.' He took it from her.

'And what's going on today?' she asked.

'Lucas is shoeing the Ellerdale's bay cob – and Jonas is fixing the wheel off Sutton's wagon. The wood's dried and shrunk and the rim came off.'

'And old man Jowitt?'

'Making horse shoe nails. I've been working the bellows and fetching and carrying – and I'm to take the Moore's cart horse when the new shaft is fitted. I'm going to sit up in the seat and drive the horse. Lucas says he'll likely give me a coin or two for myself!'

'Will he now? You'll be rich, then. And what will you do with them?'

'Give them to my Ma.'

'You're a good lad, Ned.'

Lucas came out to greet her and they stood talking for a few moments until Jonas shouted to him to take a bite while they weren't too busy. Then Lucas, Felicity and Ned sat on the bench which ran along the outside wall of the smithy. Lucas opened the cloth and broke off a piece of pastry for Ned and cut him a slice of onion to go with it. Felicity would eat on her return to the cottage and was content to watch the other two.

'Felicity made this pasty,' Lucas told Ned. 'What d'you think on it?'

' 'Tis good.'

Felicity smiled, pleased, then put her hand to her back with a sudden indrawing of her breath. Lucas paused in mid-bite to raise his eyebrows in an unspoken question. She shook her head, but almost immediately gave another gasp and this time her face twisted with pain.

'No, no,' she said quickly seeing his concern. ' 'Tis too early by a week or two. 'Twas just a twinge and now – aah!' She closed her eyes and the cry was jerked from her. Ned stared, wide-eyed, from her to Lucas. The next pain was not in her back and she bent forward, clasping her arms round her swollen body, her teeth clenched to silence any cry.

'Felicity! Has it started?' cried Lucas.

She nodded, unable to speak, but then it passed and she smiled at him. 'I'd best get home,' she said.

'Is my mother there?'

'No, but she told me to send word if I was taken sudden.'

'Then I'll come with you,' he said, 'and Ned shall go to fetch her. What day is today? Where will she be found? I'm all of a heap and can't rightly think!'

But Felicity had doubled up once more in silent agony and Ned swallowed the last bite of his pasty without tasting it. When she could breathe again she said, 'She's at Lumley House, the other side of the village. But there's no need to come with me.'

She spoke bravely, but she hoped he would insist on accompanying her. The pain frightened her, it was so fierce.

'I say I'll come with you. I'll tell Jonas what's up and he can tell the old man.'

He went inside and Felicity, to her surprise, did not have another pain.

' 'Tis over,' she told Lucas when he reappeared.

'And I say 'tis *not*,' he said. 'You'd best go home with me alongside and I'll wait with you until my mother comes. If you was took sudden like – I'd not forgive myself.'

He gave Ned a few directions as to the whereabouts of Lumley House then, leaving the basket and ale on the bench, took Felicity's arm.

'We could ride,' he said, 'but I think walking's more natural. 'Tis only a mile and I'll be – another one?'

She nodded, biting her lip. Unwittingly, her hand tightened on his arm and the slim fingers biting into his flesh gave him some idea of what she was suffering. They began to walk back along the lane, with Lucas talking cheerfully and trying to hide his concern. He recalled his mother's labour when the younger children were born and knew that the first pains should be at longer intervals.

These sudden fierce pains so near each other might mean something was wrong. Or it might not, he argued silently. Perhaps all women were different in such matters. He said nothing to alarm Felicity and hoped all would be well.

There were no more contractions until they were a third of the way home and then it was less severe. Felicity screwed up her face but made no sound. She had wanted to keep the child and the choice had been hers. However bad the pain, she had promised herself she would make no sound. The first few contractions had surprised her out of her promise, but from now on she would not complain. In a few hours she would see the longed-for child of the man she loved. Each pain brought that moment nearer and she tried to visualize the child curled up within her starting on his journey out into the world. It would not be an easy place, but she would love and cherish him.

There were a few more pains before they reached the cottage and the last two were severe. She wondered how much more severe they would be and prayed for strength to bear it. The cottage was empty and Felicity wondered how she would feel if she were on her own. Even Lucas's male presence was comforting.

'Shall you lie down?' he asked.

Felicity shook her head. The hours in the bed chamber would be long enough! She would stay in the homely untidy kitchen as long as possible.

He poured her some dandelion wine 'to calm her spirit' and she sipped it dutifully. 'You see what a comfort I am?' he asked and she nodded. 'I'll wager I'd make a good father with practice. You recall what I asked you, Felicity. The offer stands and I'm in hopes you'll have me.' He put a large arm clumsily round her shoulders and she smiled. Another pain caught her unawares, but she bit back the cry that came to her lips and bent her head.

'Should I rub your back?' Lucas offered.

' 'Twill do no good. Just talk to me, Lucas.'

'Ah, soon as you say that I'm tongue tied!' They both laughed. 'But I'll tell you a riddle that will make you smile.

Hmm. On second thoughts I'd best not. 'Tis not fit for a lady's ears.'

'Oh Lucas! I'm not a lady.'

'You are to me, Felicity. Another pain so soon? I wish my mother would come. Let me rub that back of yours, turn round on your stool.'

He began to move his large warm hand up and down and round over her back and, to Felicity's surprise, the action was comforting. 'It may not help *you*,' he said, 'but it makes me feel a sight more use. Now I'll sing you a song that old Jonas is always singing. 'Tis about a miller and his wife and the old parson. Now, let me recall how it goes.'

Felicity took another sip of wine and waited. She was trying to conjure up Martin's face but the wine and the pain were making it difficult for her to concentrate.

'Hmm. No, 'tis not a suitable song,' Lucas concluded regretfully. ' 'Tis a lively tune but the words are hot. Does my hand soothe your back a little? This is what my grandmother did for my Ma. Poor old soul, she's dead and buried now. She'd have soothed it for you. She was a rare old bird, my grandmother.'

He paused as another pain seized Felicity and he wished he could bear it for her. He wished it was *his* child she was carrying. If wishes were horses beggars would ride, he thought. Maybe the next child . . .

'My grandmother,' he went on, as soon as he felt her body relax. 'She was a fierce one. Even the men was scared of her, and her nearly seventy years old and so tiny. Like a feather she was, but she'd take up a broom and beat a man over the head if he said a wrong word. Broke up a fight, she did, one time—'

He waited but Felicity gasped, 'Go on! Tell it, Lucas. I'm listening. Oh I do hope your mother is not too long. But go on!'

'Er - aye, broke up a fight she did between two men. Giants they were too—'

'Like you!' Felicity smiled weakly. There was a sheen of

perspiration on her face and her eyes were larger than ever in her drawn face.

'No, they were bigger than me and fighting over a wench. They'd come near to murdering each other – they was bleeding like a couple of stuck pigs and the wench ran to my grandmother, screaming and hollering that they was going to kill each other. None of the men would go near 'em. I was only nine or so, but I'd have been afeared even if I *had* been growed! She snatched up the old broom – I can see her to this day – and marched out into the square. She yelled and hollered but they took no notice and then she whacked 'em both. There was a great crowd by then and they roared to her to let 'em finish, but she wouldn't. She laid about 'em with that old broom! 'Tis a wonder she didn't break the handle. Well, they couldn't get on with their fighting for this broom come at 'em from all sides, even round their legs and ankles, til they was nigh on tripping over it.' His booming laugh rang out and then he hugged her as gently as he could. 'Dear Felicity, wed me! Wed me!' he whispered, but then Ned rushed in and gasped out, breathlessly, that Dorothy was following close behind on a borrowed mare. They heard the clatter of hoofbeats in the distance and then she, too, was rushing in, her face beaming with excitement. She stood and surveyed them with her arms folded.

'What, no water on to heat?' she demanded, 'and precious little fire. Fetch some water from the well, Lucas and be quick about it – and you, Ned, fetch logs to make up the fire. Now, my chick, how are you? How many pains and how bad? Don't look so fearful, I'm here now and 'tis all going to go a treat. You must have nothing to eat but sip that wine as often as you like. It dulls the pain a little. Come into the bed chamber and lie down. I want to feel that baby of yours and find out where he is. Then I'll listen for a heartbeat. I can sometimes hear it. Oh aye, I've delivered that many babes you've no cause to fret. I'm a dab hand. I sometimes think I could have made a living as a midwife, but some folks will have their babes at awkward times and I do hate leaving my bed in the middle of the night to go traipsing off over the moor. No, I'll stick to my washing and ironing. You can do that at a respectable hour. Don't hurry, my chick. Breathe slow. Deep and slow. I'll find you a leather to bite on. That's the way. Come along. 'Twill all be over by the morning and you'll have your son in your arms . . .'

It was over much sooner than anyone expected. Felicity's labour was painful but mercifully brief and as the sun went down she gave birth to a boy, small but healthy. Almost immediately, a second boy made his way into the world. Smaller still, but crying lustily as soon as he opened his eyes. It was all over. Felicity was filled with an exhilarating joy and Dorothy laughed aloud with relief. Lucas came in and saw Felicity, tired but radiant, with a child in each arm and his heart was so full he could only stare at her while tears streamed down his cheeks and into his beard. At last he brushed the tears away and crossed the room. He stood looking down at her and he was filled with such powerful emotions he could only shake his head in wonder at the double miracle. Blinking back the tears, he tried desperately to think of something to say to the woman he loved who hugged another man's twin boys. He swallowed hard.

'Oh aye,' he said at last. 'That grandmother was a fierce old body. I can see her now laying about them with that old broom.'

Felicity, smiling, blinked back the tears in her own eyes because she understood.

CHAPTER SIXTEEN

The Marshalsea was no worse than any other prison in London. It was primarily used for the incarceration of religious offenders but Allan had been arrested for brawling in Southwark High Street and the Marshalsea was the nearest. He was thrown in to the poorest quarter where even the sick lay on the ground on dirty lice-infested straw, but as soon as he sobered up he bought his way into a better grade cell where only eighteen other inhabitants shared the intolerable heat and stench. It was July and the flies buzzed over the floor among the inedible scraps which remained from the meals brought in by friends or relatives of various prisoners. For the first few days Allan paid the gaoler for food to be brought in and paid two pence a night to share a straw mattress and filthy sheets. But his money was rapidly becoming exhausted so he was taken back to the meanest cell. There, compassionate passers-by dropped food to the prisoners through a rusty grating and the basket man called once a day with scraps collected from rich men's houses.

His cellmates were a fascinating collection – a rich man's son caught cheating at dice and another in debt to his tailor; a woman cook accused of poisoning her mistress and a younger woman who picked pockets at the bear baiting. Jenny was a whore and Hugh the pimp who controlled her – both accused of stealing from their clients. A man and his wife arrested on a charge of witchcraft were fettered while they awaited transfer to another gaol on the north side of the river.

Fortunately for Allan's health and sanity, a dozen mariners were brought in at the end of October on a charge of conspiring to mutiny. There was no room for all of them so the gaoler released a few of his less profitable prisoners – men like Allan whose money had run out.

Free once more, he had nothing to show for his stay in the Marshalsea except a few tricks with loaded dice which he had learned from an expert gambler. All kinds of false dice were made in the prison and a roaring trade conducted. Allan had purchased a 'fullam' – a dice weighted with quicksilver – in exchange for a silver ring. On his release he managed to earn enough with it to buy food and lodgings for one night and then make his slow way back to Devon, mostly walking but sometimes riding in the cart of a friendly farmer. From time to time he hitched a ride by clinging to the back of a wagon on which he had been refused a ride. He begged food, worked for it and occasionally stole it, he learned a lot about life during his stay in London and the long journey home. The Allan who finally came in sight of Heron was a very different man to the one who had left so many months before. He had longed for his first glimpse of home, but when at last he saw it, shame and remorse held him back. He had lost weight; his clothes were dirty and his hair unkempt. He had not shaved and a beard hid the lower part of his face. He was torn between his feelings of degradation and his longing to be accepted once more into the family.

For a long time he leaned against a tree, watching the peaceful scene before him. Smoke rose from the kitchen chimney and hens clucked at the back door. A dog barked and he heard a door open and close; footsteps carried in the still clear air. In his imagination he saw Minnie in the kitchen, homely and cumbersome; he saw Maria with her wise, concerned gaze and Hugo, defeated and disillusioned. Allan had passed the mine and knew that it was still silent. Heron, for all its peaceful exterior, lay under a cloud of misfortune and he had deserted it – had deserted them all at an ebb tide in their fortunes. How would they react to his return? Most probably with reprimands, he reflected, but he deserved them. He would have to bear it and prove himself worthy of their forgiveness. They would ask him about London and he would not lie.

The thought of Eloise caused him great anguish. As he stared at the house he rehearsed what he would say to her. She would be hostile, resentful. It was inevitable but it would have to be borne. But not yet, dear God, he whispered, his courage suddenly deserting him. For tonight he would lie up somewhere. The old priory! There, in the crypt, he would at least have a roof over his head. The decision made, he turned thankfully away and made his way to the ruins of Harben Priory. The old buildings were no longer habitable for the stones, door and shutters had all been stolen for use elsewhere and now adorned other more humble dwellings scattered over the surrounding area. The walls had crumbled and the roof had long since fallen in. It was a desolate place, but it held no terrors for Allan, for he had played hide and seek there as a boy with Martin and later with Piers and Lorna.

Slowly, he made his way down the stone steps to the darkened crypt where he knew every niche and archway. In the gloom he could make out the blackened remains of a fire and wondered idly who had been the last person to make the old crypt his home. Now it was his turn, but he was probably the least well endowed of them all, he thought ruefully, for he had no blanket, no fire and no means of snaring food. A smile crossed his lips – a failed vagrant! Could he possibly sink any lower? With a sigh he arranged himself wearily upon a long stone slab and closed his eyes. All he wanted to do was sleep. That way, for a few brief hours, he could forget his plight. But it was not to be. The cold chilled him through and as night fell his hunger distracted him. Small nocturnal creatures woke and moved round him. A bat winged its way over his head and there were rat-like scurries in the furthermost corners. The wind blew dead leaves down the stone steps with ghostly sounds and the drip, drip of water became audible somewhere above him although he felt nothing. He turned uncomfortably, drawing up his knees to conserve his body's heat but the chill reached through his flesh to his knees and he could not suppress bouts of shivering which made his teeth chatter. By first light he was stiff and desperately cold. His stomach was seized with painful cramps and his eyes felt heavy as lead. With an effort he pulled himself to a sitting position and blew on his frozen fingers. His mind seemed frozen, too, and his thoughts wandered. Easing himself upright, he moved around, stamping his feet and flapping his arms to restore his circulation and warm and loosen his aching muscles.

When he felt better he made his way up the steps and out into the early morning mist which lay like a shroud over the ruined priory and stretched as far as the eye could see, broken only by the tip of a shrub or bush or the occasional hawthorn. He walked and swung his arms and muttered to himself that he could not stay there.

'Nor yet go home . . . I cannot face them . . . all so dear to me . . . I cannot see the look in their eyes – cannot bear their pity . . . No, no, I must not, cannot, go home. Not yet awhile . . . later, aye, later when I am more myself . . . But not yet awhile. I must find another place to hide until I am myself again . . . Such pitying looks they'll give me. Eyes so full of pity and scorn . . . And Martin will despise me – laugh at me, even. No, no. I'll wait until I am myself again . . .'

He wandered on, unaware of his direction, forgetful of his hunger, oblivious to his discomfort. His mind had taken over from his body and all he knew were the rambling thoughts and confused emotions which drained the last of his energy. When he stopped he was standing on the steps of a large house and he put up his hand to tug at the bell rope. He heard it jingle in the inner recesses of the house and waited impatiently for the door to open. When it failed to do so he tugged again and then stepped back to examine the house more closely. The windows were shuttered and weeds grew round the front steps. No smoke rose from the chimney and all was silent. He stepped back further and dimly recognized it as Maudesley, the old house abandoned

324

by the Tucker family. He felt a great sadness, as though their absence was a personal betrayal.

The back of the house presented a similarly gloomy façade. Allan regarded it with dismay and then anger. He picked up a stone and threw it against the house. Almost before it fell he was reaching for another stone – and another. The stones flew towards the house with all the force he could muster then struck and fell. Suddenly he stopped and sank to his knees. The effort had exhausted him. He began to shiver again and his eyes would not focus properly. Vaguely, he was aware that something was not right. His only clear thought was that he must shelter in the house. Then in a few days, he would 'be himself' once more.

Stumbling around the house again, he discovered a shutterless window at the side and, after some difficulty, managed to clamber inside. He fell awkwardly and sat cursing and grimacing with pain as he massaged his right knee. When it was easier, he began a tour of the house and was delighted to find a couple of damp and faded wall hangings in which to wrap himself and a tinder box with which he promised to make himself a fire. But although he gathered plenty of dry leaves and straw and assembled them in the hearth of the largest room, he could not raise a spark, and, quickly discouraged, gave up the idea and curled himself up in a corner. Within minutes, he fell into a deep, troubled sleep.

There, the next day, Nat Gully's dog discovered him, delirious and in a high fever. At first Nat failed to recognize the Kendals' eldest son, but when he did he hastened to Heron to tell them of Allan's whereabouts. They were deeply grateful and Matt and Jon were sent over to Maudesley with a litter on which to carry him home. Three days later, when the fever broke, Allan opened his eyes to find himself at home.

They initially managed to keep the news of Eloise's

departure from Allan but Maria determined to tell him at the first opportunity. She wanted to wait until he was sufficiently recovered to be able to stand the shock, but she knew that the longer she waited the more likely it was that one of the servants or the children would let slip a careless word on the subject. On the third morning after his return she tapped on his door and on entering found him sitting on the side of the bed.

'Allan! The physician said a week's rest. What are you about?'

' 'Tis nonsense, Maria. I am not an invalid. You know 'twas no more than a severe chill and the worst is well past. I thought to try out my legs this morning or they will be too weak to carry me. I *must* speak with you of Eloise.'

'Allan, she has gone back to Rochester. You could not expect her to wait so long. She left soon after Christmas.'

'Gone!' he whispered. 'Aye, she would not wait. I thought to find her gone and yet hearing the words—'

He covered his face with his hands.

Maria gave him a moment or two to digest the information then went on:

'She finally wrote to her parents. She was distraught. We had no warning of what she intended to do until a letter came from her father. We kept it. You can read it later if you wish.'

'What did he say?'

Maria shrugged. 'Only the truth, as Eloise saw it. He said that she had not been happy and your desertion was—'

'Desertion?' he sighed deeply. 'I didn't intend to desert her. Only to put a distance between us so that I could think more clearly. Poor Eloise!'

'I think you have lost her forever, Allan,' she said firmly. ' 'Twas her letter to them, remember, that set the wheels in motion. From the tone of her father's letter she was adamant about leaving Heron. 'Twas most likely for the best.'

'For the best? Do you truly believe that?'

'I do. Did you ever really love her? Did she love you? I think the fault initially was ours, Allan, mine and Hugo's. When Harriet died we were too eager to find a new love. I feared it might be too soon, but Hugo was sure Eloise would make you happy. Abby spoke so well of her and when we met her—'

'Don't blame yourself, Maria. You meant it kindly, I know.'

There was a tap at the door and Minnie appeared with a tray of breakfast. She glanced at both faces and guessed what was being discussed but bustled in cheerfully.

'Out of bed, master Allan?' she said. 'You hop between those sheets and get some food into your belly before you go putting your feet on the floor.' She hustled him back into bed and laid the tray across his knees. 'There's two coddled eggs and plenty of toast and a dish of strained plums to clean your mouth. Eat every bit!'

When she had gone Maria listened at the door until she heard Minnie's footsteps on the stairs. Minnie's habit of listening at keyholes was well known. Satisfied, she went back to sit on the chest beside Allan's bed and watched him eat.

'Eloise was not the right woman for you,' she said quietly. 'I want you to accept that, Allan, and try not to grieve for her.'

He sighed. 'My grieving days are over,' he told her quietly. 'I know now that whatever I felt for Eloise it was not love. Felicity showed me that.'

'Felicity Carr?'

'Aye. But no matter. I have come to my senses at last.'

Maria nodded. 'Eloise wanted you for what you stand for - Heron! No, hear me out although 'tis distasteful. If the mine had not failed I believe she would have waited for your return.'

'The mine has *not* failed,' said Allan. ' 'Tis Hugo's obstinacy. We could reopen it - I have given it much thought while I've been away. The men would come back

327

willingly. We could find another so-called expert to carry out Bucher's plans. Bucher himself might—'

'There is no chance of that,' said Maria. 'I, too, have urged Hugo to reconsider without result. I love him dearly but in this you are right. He *is* stubborn and there *is* hope for the mine, but while Hugo is head of Heron his word is law. I wish it were otherwise.'

'You do not wish it more deeply than I do! 'Tis my inheritance he is throwing away.'

It was Maria's turn to sigh. 'We must pray for a change of heart,' she said. 'But we were speaking of Eloise. What will you do? Will you write to her?'

'I think I must. I owe her an apology and she shall have it. But I shall not ask her to come back. What of her dowry?'

'She has taken it.'

'That must have been hard,' he said.

She shrugged. 'Thank God we were able to raise it.'

'Then 'tis really all over,' he said slowly. He had toyed with his food, not eating it. Now he pushed the tray away. 'And Martin?' he asked. 'Is he still at Romney House?'

Maria nodded. She had told no one of Felicity's pregnancy. 'He is spending a year with Frank Innly, studying to be a sheep farmer.'

'So – if he thrives mayhap *he* will win the beautiful Eloise.' He spoke bitterly.

'I think not,' said Maria as lightly as she could. 'But I must go now and leave you to your thoughts. Think on it calmly, Allan, I beg you. 'Tis finished. A chapter in your life. Today is the first page of a new one. Meet it with hope, Allan, for 'tis all we have left.'

Maggie and Melissa rode side by side, conversing in a desultory fashion. The pack pony followed behind them, snatching a mouthful of grass or a few leaves from the hedgerow. It was laden with the day's purchases – provisions for the coming months. The two women enjoyed their outings to Ashburton. Melissa met friends in the town and Maggie took the opportunity to call in on the bakery and see that all was well. They had bought flour and spices, lemons and tallow, silk and braids and were well satisfied with their joint efforts. Now, as they frequently did when the weather was fine, they rode the long way home past Maudesley. It was Maggie who noticed it first. She broke off in the middle of a sentence about the bakery and pointed through the trees.

'The old house! There are men working on it.'

They stopped so abruptly that the inattentive pack pony nearly collided with Melissa's mount.

'So they are! But - why did they not tell us?'

'Who?'

'The Tuckers,' said Melissa. 'If they are moving back—'

'It may not be the Tuckers.'

'But Maudesley belongs to them. It has always been theirs. Mayhap 'tis for one of their sons. Let's ride a little closer. How very strange.'

They turned off the road and made their way through the sparse hedge and out on to the other side. From there they had a clear view of the house and could see that, indeed, a number of men were at work on it. Two men were on the roof tearing the thatch apart and throwing it down to the ground, where another man swept it up and carried it some distance away to a fiercely burning bonfire. A wagon loaded with bricks stood in the courtyard. There were several piles of newly cut timber and a stack of what looked like roofing tiles.

Maggie whistled. 'The Tuckers have come into a fortune by the look of it. A new roof - and what is all that timber for?'

'And the bricks! Mayhap they are going to enlarge it? Oh, I wish we knew what is happening. I've a good mind to ride up and ask one of them. What do you think?'

'There's nothing lost by it,' said Maggie. 'I doubt they would tell me but they will doubtless recognize you. Aye, do that, Melissa. Ride over and ask them. I'd best wait here with the pack horse. 'Twould be nice to have neighbours.'

'If 'tis the Tuckers, aye. If they have sold the house – then only time will tell. We must hope they are congenial folk. Then I'll ride down and find out whatever I can. I'll not be long.'

She urged her horse down the gradual slope until she reached the outskirts of the garden. There she tethered her mount to a gate post and went through the gate and into the courtyard. Several of the men glanced at her but no one spoke and for a moment she looked round at the scene of feverish activity. To her left the bonfire blazed and spluttered and wisps of charred straw floated in the air. Two men sawed wood over a newly dug pit and another was measuring the ground floor windows. The front door had been replaced with a new one, ornately carved. Two men were breaking out the infilling between the timber framing and a fine white dust hung in the air, making one of the men cough and curse. All the shutters had been removed from the windows. Melissa's astonishment grew. Surely they were not putting in *glass!* The cost would be tremendous. A new roof – she saw that the stack by the door *were* roof tiles. The Tuckers mine was also going through a difficult time financially. They could never afford such luxuries, she told herself. But if not the Tuckers, then who was responsible for the restoration, or conversion, of Maudesley?

'Mistress Benet, isn't it?'

She turned to find a tall elderly man beside her. He had piercing brown eyes and she recognized the voice instantly. He gave her a steadying hand as she stumbled.

'Henry Bullen!' she cried. He had worked on Ladyford when it was restored for her and Thomas to move into. 'I might have known you'd be here. Won't you ever stop working?'

He laughed. 'Not while there's breath in me body. And this place is a fair old challenge. I couldn't say no, tho' my

330

old woman ranted at me when she knew. You're nigh on seventy, Henry, she says. You should give up while there's still time. Put up your feet and tell stories to your grandchildren. But I can't bear to be idle, that's my trouble. And Maudesley! Why, there's plenty of younger men'd give their right arms for this job.'

'And you got first offer,' said Melissa. 'They know they've got the best man. Trust the Tuckers to come to you. They know a—'

'Tuckers? 'Taint the Tuckers,' he said. 'They sold it, the Tuckers did. Nigh on a month ago.'

'Sold it? Who to?'

He shrugged. 'Can't tell you,' he said, ' 'cos I don't know. A foreign gentleman, 'tis said, but then I don't listen to rumours. We started work a week ago.'

'Foreign!' Melissa's face fell. 'French, d'you mean, or German? Don't you know anything about them?'

'Not a thing.' He broke off for a moment to bellow at one of the workmen on the roof above them. Then he took Melissa's arm and led her in through the new doorway into the house. Here more work was in progress. The stairway had been demolished and the earth floor was being raked up and carted away in barrows.

' 'Tis all a mystery,' he told her eagerly. He kept his voice low and she had to lean towards him, straining her ears to hear.

'All I know is a lawyer from Exeter offered me the contract and gave me a free hand. He sent me a list of work to be done and, except for the men doing the glass windows, I chose the men myself.'

'But if you don't know who owns it, do you know who's paying for it?'

'No. I don't know nowt about it. The lawyer fellow sends me money as I present my accounts – and a good payer, he is, too. Prompt, he is. I've no complaints. I chose the best tiler and these tiles are worth a tidy sum. Hand-made of terra cotta, they are, and baked in a charcoal clamp. Local tiles, they are, last forever, I'm telling you and so they should at the price. But he can afford the best, this gentleman, whoever he is. And the floor – look at it.' He waved an arm. 'Three days it's taken them and they've another day's work afore they're done. Earth floor's no good, you see. Chestnut planking, it has to be, on wooden rafts, like upstairs. Much warmer, of course. And no need to straw it. They're having one of the upstairs rooms panelled in oak!'

'Panelled?'

'Aye, linen fold. That's going to look a treat. The old fellow that's doing it is tied up at the moment, finishing a rede loft at the church. But he'll be here before the month's out.'

Melissa shook her head in amazement. 'But why all the secrecy?' she said. 'I don't understand.'

'No more do I,' he said, 'but I've learnt to live with it. I get my money and that's all I care about. He can be from Timbuctoo, for all I care, and black as the ace of spades! He pays and I work.'

Melissa looked round. ' 'Tis certainly going to look very different,' she said. 'Sad in a way, for I liked the old place. I only recall it as a young girl but I've heard tell of it in the old days.'

'Aye. One of the Tuckers wed a Kendal, I believe.'

'Aye. Joseph wed Elizabeth – a long time ago. And the windows? I see the shutters are all gone.'

'Glass, as I've told you already, but upstairs he's having oriel windows.'

'Oriel?'

'Aye – they project from the wall, so.' He described it with his hands. 'And inside a seat under the window.'

'In the bed chambers?'

'Ah, no. The largest bed chamber is to be a withdrawing room for entertaining or receiving visitors. Oh, 'twill be very grand, I can tell you. Did you see them pulling out the old wattle and daub? 'Tis to be filled in with bricks set in a pattern. Aye, 'twill set a few eyes popping when 'tis all done, I can tell you. Oy!' he shouted. 'Mind how you go with that barrow. You're not ploughing a field, you know!' He tutted. 'Some of the youngsters! Not got the same dedication to the job as we had.'

Melissa said, 'I won't ask you to show me upstairs!'

'Ah, the missing staircase! All wood, the new one's going to be, and very grand with a pierced balustrade, whatever that may be. An old fellow's coming from London 'specially to make it. Arriving any day now.'

They walked out again into the sunshine and Melissa remembered guiltily that Maggie was waiting for her. She made a hasty farewell and rode back to pass on the fascinating details to her friend and the two women rode back to Ladyford in a state of great excitement.

Minnie accepted the letter from the messenger because Hugo and Maria had ridden over to Maudesley, on hearing Melissa's news, to see the transformation for themselves. Allan was resting and Ben and Ellie were busy – Ben in the garden and Ellie gathering in washing which lay drying in the orchard.

'From where has it come?' she had asked and been told only Appledore. But that was enough! She thought she recognized the handwriting as Martin's but could not be certain for he wrote so rarely, much to Maria's disappointment. It was *not* Felicity's. Of that Minnie was convinced, for she had written frequently while old Ruth had been alive. The question was – if it was from Martin – did it concern Felicity?

Carefully Minnie eased up one of the corners and 'hollowed' it out so that she might read a word or two. She saw the words '—without too much' and beneath them '—not to one but' and again below that 'and good spirits'. Did that mean what she thought it meant? It was very frustrating to hold the letter in her hand and know that it contained news of great import, or else why was he putting pen to paper. She took a knife from the box and separated the sheets further – 'this fifteenth day of' was quite distinct

333

but not very illuminating. Cursing under her breath, she took the letter to the window and held it, hollowed, to the light, and peered closely at it. Was that a capital 'F' for Felicity or was it February? Hardly the latter, for it would soon be June. Turning the folded paper and squinting horribly, she made out the words 'has asked for' and before that it looked like a word beginning with capital 'L'. Gently she prised the corners wider, but she put a little too much pressure and to her horror the seal parted and the letter fell open in her hands.

'Holy St Katherine! They'll slaughter me!'

She was now faced with a dilemma. If she stopped to read the letter there might not be time to repair the damage – if there *was* a way to make good the seal. If not, she must concoct a convincing story that would explain how it came to be opened.

The temptation was too great and she unfolded the letter and began to read. She was not a fluent reader, having been taught late in life, but she could manage most of the words. Certainly enough to understand the content to her own satisfaction. Felicity had given birth to twin boys! Someone called Lucas had offered to wed her. Martin had gone to visit her, so she was obviously no longer living at Romney House. The reason for that, Minnie concluded, was equally obvious. They were Martin's children. She refolded the letter clumsily, her fingers trembling with excitement. And Martin would be arriving within a few days of the letter. Phew! Minnie rolled her eyes expressively. Heron was in for a shock – unless they all knew already. Yet she was sure she would have overheard a chance remark here or there. No, there was a shock coming, she was certain of it. But now what was she to do about the seal. She would have to reheat it and press it down again – and quickly. She would have a lot of explaining to do if she was caught. Thrusting the poker into the fire, she tapped a foot anxiously while she waited for it. Then carefully she touched the seal. To her immense relief it softened but not enough. Back went the poker into the fire and this time she allowed a little longer for it to heat up. This time she was lucky and the sealing wax melted. She dare not let it bubble or the impression of Martin's ring would warp and there was no way to put *that* right. With a quick movement, she pressed a forefinger on to the seal, closed her eyes and prayed.

From outside she heard the distant clatter of hoofbeats and knew that Hugo and Maria had reached the stable. The letter was closed! Thankfully she ran through into the Hall and laid the letter on the table then hurried back to the kitchen. She was dismayed to smell burning wax and snatched up a cloth and fanned it frantically in the air to disperse the smell. I never will again, she vowed, if only they don't notice. Never again, as God is my witness. She tossed the cloth down as Ellie came in with the washing and dumped it on the table. The girl wrinkled her nose.

'Is something burning?'

'No, nothing.'

'I can smell something. 'Tis like—'

'Get on and fold these clothes,' snapped Minnie, 'and don't waste time on imaginings.'

' 'Tis no imagining, I tell you. I can—'

'Ellie!'

The girl looked at her mother and muttered something uncomplimentary under her breath.

'I heard that,' said Minnie untruthfully. As casually as she could, she opened all the doors and windows. Ellie watched her thoughtfully but said nothing. She was trying to identify the smell. At last she knew. It was sealing wax – which meant a letter! In a flash of inspiration she threw down the towel she was folding and raced into the Hall. A glance at the letter confirmed her suspicions and she flew back to the kitchen as Hugo and Maria entered by the front door.

'The letter!' whispered Ellie. 'You opened it! You did, I know it. Tell me what was in it.'

Minnie cursed – the girl was too sharp by far for her own good. But she was longing to pass on her ill-gotten

335

news. Swearing Ellie to utter secrecy, she whispered the contents of the letter and was pleased to see that the revelation made the impact it deserved.

'Twin boys!' Ellie gasped. 'And will we never see them? Do you think Felicity will—'

'Ssh! They're coming.'

Hugo came into the kitchen followed by Maria. They were full of the news about Maudesley and had obviously not been into the Hall. Minnie fetched a drink of lemon barley for them and mentally urged them to go into the Hall and find the letter. But they sat talking to Minnie and Ellie and finally it was Allan who found it. He came downstairs after his rest and brought the letter with him.

'This was on the Hall table,' he said.

'A letter?' said Hugo. 'Why, Minnie, when did it come? And why did you not tell us?' He broke the seal as he spoke and his eyes were on the letter or he would have seen the guilty expression on Minnie's face as she mumbled an apology, pretending she had forgotten it. She dared not look at him as his eyes raced along the lines.

'From Martin?' asked Maria.

'Aye – come into the Hall and you shall read it for yourself.'

With an effort he kept his voice normal and Minnie watched him go with relief. Now he had broken open the letter he would not suspect anything. She was safe.

'Allan,' said Hugo. 'Come with us, will you?'

Allan followed them out and Minnie and Ellie exchanged conspiratorial glances. Ellie winked and Minnie grinned sheepishly. It had all been too close for comfort.

On an impulse, she went to the larder where she kept a pitcher of orange wine behind the flour sack. She poured them each a generous mugful.

'A toast!' They raised their mugs. 'To two little Kendal boys,' said Minnie wistfully. 'God bless them wherever they may be.'

★

Martin arrived three days later in a defiant mood. He was prepared for a cool reception, and that is what he received. Maria was distressed by the knowledge that now there were two illegitimate Kendals instead of one. Hugo was incensed by his son's irresponsibility and the air of jubilation which he hardly bothered to hide. Martin was shocked to learn that Allan was back, but there was no meeting between the two brothers until the evening, for Allan had taken himself off to the deserted mine as soon as Martin arrived. At supper Allan spoke and ate very little and excused himself early and went up to his bed chamber. When Martin went up several hours later, Allan feigned sleep and there was no chance of conversation.

Next morning when Martin woke he saw that Allan's bed was empty and cursed roundly.

'I'm damned if he'll avoid me any longer!' he muttered and leapt out of bed. He splashed cold water over his face and dressed as quickly as he could then ran down to the stables. As he had guessed, Allan was there saddling his horse. He did not turn his head when Martin appeared and leaned nonchalantly on the lower half of the stable door. Allan continued to arrange the saddle until Martin coughed exaggeratedly.

'Am I invisible?' he asked lightly.

Allan ignored the remark.

'Are you suddenly deaf?' Martin persisted. 'Your prolonged stay in London seems to have done you no good.'

Allan paused and glanced at him. 'I've nothing to say to you,' he said, 'that you'd wish to hear.'

'Nothing to say to your own brother? No exploits to recount? No news to impart of the wicked city? You surprise me, Allan, and disappoint me. I thought you had gone to make your fortune and save the house of Heron from ignominy. It seems I misjudged you.'

Allan reached for the harness and slipped the bridle over the horse's head. As he fussed with the adjustment, his face was set but his ragged breathing betrayed his feelings.

'And the fair Eloise has departed,' Martin continued.

'What an unkind cut. Though some say, who can blame the girl? You *did* desert her.'

Allan looked at him briefly, but with a look of pure hatred. Martin registered it with satisfaction. He knew Allan did not want to rise to the bait but he also knew that he would.

'Still, doubtless 'tis all for the best. She was not the woman for you.'

'And she was for you?'

'I think so. I know what it takes to please a woman like Eloise. She needs attention, to be appreciated and flattered. She needs laughter and excitement. You two were like chalk and cheese, if I may say so without offence.'

Martin smiled, letting the malice show in his eyes.

'Everything you say offends me,' said Allan his voice rising. 'Your presence here offends me. The expression on your face offends me.'

'Oh come now. Such harsh words! What has happened to brotherly love? I expected you to seize my hand and congratulate me and all you . . .'

'Congratulate you? On what?' Allan gave up the pretence of adjusting the bridle and turned at last to face his tormentor. 'Tell me something decent, courageous or honest that you have done and—'

'Honest? *You* talk of *honesty* and decency? 'Twas not I that was flung into the Marshalsea and begged and cheated a way home. 'Twas not I that abandoned a wife—'

He broke off suddenly, realizing he had laid himself wide open.

'You treat women well then, do you, Martin?'

'I did not say I—'

'How would you rate your treatment of Felicity?' cried Allan. 'To get her with child and then turn your back on her! Is that decent or honest? How can you live with your conscience, Martin? I'd truly like to know. Two sons, Martin, and—'

'Aye, two sons and I am barely sixteen! What have you to show for your twenty-four years? Nothing. No wife and no family. Oh, don't remind me. You had a wife. I know. But she's dead and gave you no heirs. Heirs, that's what I have that you lack. And you envy me. Confess it, Allan. You are eaten up with jealousy and that is why you shun me. I have fathered two sons and you have none. You inherit Heron and 'tis worthless and I have Romney House and will be prosperous with my sheep. Oh, sneer at them if you will. 'Tis the fashion to do so. But when you are starving on your precious tin, I shall wax fat on my sheep. What, nothing to say? No answer to make? Because you *have* no answer. You know I speak the truth. You are Simon's son. You are the eldest. You are the heir. Well, as far as I can see you are heir to nothing.'

Suddenly Allan stepped forward and seized Martin by the shoulders.

Martin winced in pain but the furious fingers bit deeper as they faced each other over the door.

'What are you going to do about those two sons?' Allan hissed. 'They are yours. Your flesh and blood.'

'They'll be well provided for. Damn you, let go.'

Allan intensified his grip. 'By whom? Provided for by whom? This fellow Lucas? What is he – a blacksmith?'

'He's a good man. He loves her.'

'And does she love him?'

' 'Tis no concern of yours!' With an effort, he jerked himself free and took a step backewards, out of reach of the cruel fingers. Allan turned to the horse, his shoulders heaving.

'She could have rid herself of them if she'd wanted,' cried Martin. 'She wanted them. Now she's got them. She didn't tell me in time. 'Twas her intention to have a child. *My* child. She wanted my child because she loves me.'

'And you don't love her?'

'She's not suitable. Lucas will make her a good husband. He dotes on her and he'll give her plenty more.'

'And the boys will take his name?'

'Aye. They're not Kendals. They're Carrs.'

'They're Kendals and you know it!' Allan's hand shot

out and grasped Martin's hair and jerked him back to the door. Allan's control deserted him as he thrust his own face close to Martin's.

'Those boys are Kendals and you owe them your name, you miserable wretch! You know it. I can see it in your shifty eyes. You make me puke! Now get out of my sight before—' He could not finish. His fury and frustration welled up inside him and a blackness swam before his eyes. Taking another handful of hair, he began to force Martin's head down so that his neck lay across the top edge of the door and the wood bit deeply and painfully into his neck. Martin struggled helplessly then, fearful that Allan would succeed in choking him, reached for the small knife he carried and brought it up to slash at Allan's hands and wrists.

'Aah!' With a short cry of pain Allan released him, then in the same instant he brought up his foot and kicked open the door. It sent Martin backwards, stumbling and cursing, desperately trying to save his balance. He fell backwards over a mounting block and lay still, sprawled grotesquely across the cobbles. Allan fell onto his knees, exhausted and emotionally drained, his hands clasped against his bowed head. The half door creaked on its hinges and was still. Allan finally raised his head and looked across at his brother. He sighed deeply, pulled himself to his feet and crossed the yard to where Martin lay.

'Forgive me,' he said. 'You provoked me but – 'tis this damnable temper. Martin!'

The boy lay face down and Allan thought he was sulking as he had done when a child. Allan knelt and touched his shoulder gingerly, half expecting a sudden retaliation but Martin did not move.

'I ask your forgiveness,' said Allan formally and tugged at him to turn him over. He thought nervously that the boy had sustained a concussion but then he saw the knife. It was still held in Martin's hand and was embedded in his chest up to the hilt. Dark red stained his jerkin and there was a similar stain on the cobbles. Allan's mouth opened and his lips moved in a desperate prayer. 'Please God, I haven't killed him. I haven't killed him. Oh no, dear God. Say I haven't killed him.' He touched Martin's face and then his eyes. He picked up Martin's free hand and patted it.

'Martin! I beg you. Martin, open your eyes and tell me you are not dead. I do not want you dead. Only open your eyes, Martin, and I will love you. I swear it. I'll love you as a brother, Martin. We'll love each other. Oh dearest God, give him back to me, I pray you, and let me make amends.'

He was still kneeling beside the body when Jon came into the yard, his eyes bleary with sleep.

CHAPTER SEVENTEEN

It was considered too far for Felicity to travel, so soon after the birth of the twins, but a letter was sent to her telling her of Martin's death and she insisted on attending. Abby and Adam therefore travelled down from Rochester to Appledore in a hired wagon and took Felicity with them to Devon.

The circumstances of Martin's death had been reported to the appropriate authorities, but there was no question of charges being bought against Allan. No one doubted that it was an accident – it was obvious that Martin's own hand held the hilt of his own knife and Jon confirmed that Allan was unarmed. Allan confessed to the quarrel and to the push that ended so disastrously, but if anyone believed the death to be more than a tragic accident, he or she kept silent.

Allan, as was to be expected, blamed himself for the tragedy and no amount of persuasion could convince him otherwise, but apportioning blame was a useless exercise, as Maria told him in an effort to reduce his terrible guilt. It was an accident. It was a tragedy, but it had happened and no amount of self-reproach would change the fact that Martin was dead. They must all come to terms with it, she told him. They must all live with the grief and help each other.

Hugo took it very badly. He broke down and wept and Maria could not comfort him. It was the final blow in a series of disappointments which had dogged him for the past few years. After the first passionate outburst he became very withdrawn and rarely spoke and Maria found herself having to be strong for both of them. It fell to her lot to make the funeral arrangements and invite the mourners.

Maggie and Melissa prepared the food so that, at least, was one problem less with which she had to deal. Piers came home from school and Beatrice and her husband rode over from Exeter leaving the children with their grandparents. The funeral had been set for ten o'clock in the morning, so that most of the visitors would be able to return home in daylight. As they stood at the graveside Maria thought sadly how frequently the Kendals were reunited by death. She recalled Luke's funeral and that of Hannah. Luke had been buried here and Alison, and Simon. Of that line only Allan remained. She thought of Hugo and Simon and how close the cousins had been. Now Simon's son had brought about the death of Hugo's son and the thought of the Gillis curse flashed into her mind only to be rigorously rejected. She would *not* believe it.

As the coffin was lowered into the ground, it began to rain, adding to the misery of the mourners. Allan found himself next to Felicity and looked at her with passionate entreaty.

'Will you ever forgive me? I have killed the man you loved.'

By way of answer she took his cold hand in hers and put it to her lips. Her tears fell warmly onto his hand and suddenly she put her arms round him and they clung together as the first spadeful of earth fell on to the coffin. Maria watched them through eyes blurred with tears and Hugo's arm was around her shoulders as she, too, struggled for composure. Lorna and Piers, beside her, stared solemnly ahead, trying to withstand the concerted grief by which they were surrounded. Melissa stood with one arm round Nina, who held the youngest child in her arms. Little Della held Maggie's hand and Thomas stood beside them, a tall frail old man who had been so near death himself not so long ago. Now he wondered why fate had spared *him* and taken a young man in his prime. It made no sense, he thought sadly.

'. . . and so we lay to rest a young man of tender years, one Martin Kendal, late of this parish, the beloved son of

Hannah, deceased, and Hugo Kendal. His sojourn on this earth has been a short one and his departure sudden. But who are we, mere mortals, to question the will of God? He has seen fit in his infinite wisdom to take this young man from our midst and we must abide by his decision. We cannot rail against death but must endeavour to understand God's holy will. Martin was beloved by us, he gladdened our hearts with his presence and we are made desolate by his death. As we shared our love for him so we share in the grief at his going away from us. But our griefs are for ourselves, not for Martin. His soul is on its way to Heaven and everlasting peace. Soon he will be eternally at rest and will be reunited with those of his family who went before him. He will rejoice in God's boundless love. We who remain weep only for ourselves and our loss.'

The rain fell more heavily, hissing through the dark trees and into the sodden grass. It mingled with the tears on the faces of the mourners and Nina's youngest child began to cry fretfully – a thin sad sound.

'And so we take our farewell of this bright life. He loved us all in his own way as we loved him. We are none of us perfect but we live our lives as best we may in the image of Jesus Christ. Now the final blessing . . .'

As they turned to go, Hugo put a hand to his chest as a sudden pain gripped him. He tried to speak to Maria but the pain increased and drew a tight band around his heart. He stumbled against Melissa and she turned. Hugo put out a hand to steady himself but stumbled again.

'Hugo!'

Maria turned at the alarm in Melissa's voice and saw her husband fall to his knees, both hands clutching his chest, his face screwed up in wordless agony and she flew to him.

'Hugo! Dearest God! Hugo, what ails you? Speak to me if you can.'

All eyes had turned from the grave to Maria and thence to Hugo, who hugged his pain to him and could not utter a word. Maria knelt beside him.

' 'Tis his heart, I'm sure of it. Oh dear God! This cannot

344

happen. Hugo, my dearest Hugo. 'Twill pass. Be patient. The pain will pass.'

Everyone crowded round trying to help.

'He hugs his heart,' cried Maria. 'We must get him back to Heron. Bring one of the wagons, quickly. Hugo, can you speak to me? My dearest, they are gone to fetch the wagon. You will soon be home, safe in your own bed. Is the pain still bad? Oh Hugo! I cannot bear it.'

Allan knelt beside her. 'He will live, Mama. I know he will. Do not weep for him. So many tears!'

The wagon was driven up to the church yard gate and gentle and willing hands lifted Hugo from the wet grass and carried him to the comparative comfort of the wagon, which at least had a canvas hood over it to keep off the rain. As soon as he was settled with Maria and Allan beside him they led the procession back to Heron. Hugo had relaxed slightly and was able to speak to them. The pain had eased a little, he told them, and they must not concern themselves unduly. It was a cramp, nothing more. Maria did not believe him for a second and had already despatched Matt to fetch the physician.

Back at the house, Hugo was put to bed and Maria sat by his side, refusing to leave him.

'They can all manage without me,' she declared. 'There is a good fire and plenty to eat and drink. They will be well cared for and I shall stay with you, Hugo, until the physician tells me I can safely leave you. Oh my dearest, it has been such a terrible day – such a terrible year! But don't give up, Hugo. You must not give up the fight. We are so fortunate to have each other – but I talk too much and will tire you. No, you close your eyes and rest. I will sit here beside you and wild horses shall not drag me away.'

Minnie came in with hot milk for Hugo and mulled wine for Maria. She helped her out of her wet clothes and into a dry gown. Maria asked her if all was well downstairs and Minnie said it was going splendidly. Folk were drying themselves out and everyone sent Hugo their best wishes for his recovery. Maria nodded absentmindedly and grumbled that the physician took so long.

'Bring him up the moment he arrives,' she told Minnie. 'He may be wet through but no matter. He can dry out *after* he has seen Hugo. I want no delays, Minnie. 'Tis most urgent. And put another log on the fire. We must keep Hugo warm.'

Intuitively, she knew the seriousness of Hugo's condition. A pain round his heart, cramping his chest! She had heard folk speak of such seizures and knew they could be fatal.

When Minnie had gone, she saw that Hugo's eyes were fluttering. 'Doze a little,' she told him. 'I dare say the pain has tired you. Close your eyes and sleep until the physician arrives.'

An hour passed and still he did not arrive. Hugo slept but Maria fretted anxiously. Matt came back to report that the physician was not at home and he and Jon were sent out again to make what enquiries they could concerning his whereabouts. From downstairs came the sounds of the funeral supper – subdued voices, footsteps, the clatter of pewter, the scrape of furniture. Maria tried to concentrate her thoughts on Martin but Hugo's condition filled her mind to the exclusion of anything else. Martin had gone and none of their prayers could bring him back. She prayed God that he would not take his father with him into the grave. Just before five Maria was herself dozing when a strangled cry from Hugo roused her. His face was once more contorted with pain and his arms were clamped round his chest.

'Hugo! Sweet heaven! I'm here, my love. What can I do to help you? See, my arm is round you, I'll hold you safe. Don't be fearful. Your Maria is here. Is it so bad? Oh Hugo! What's to be done?'

He tried to speak but could not. He gasped for air and Maria felt weak with a terrible dread. For all her brave words she knew she could not help him. Only the physician might do that and he was not found yet. She shouted for

Minnie and stamped on the floor to make sure she would be heard above the babble of voices below them. Minnie ran into the room, breathless from the stairs.

'Is it the master, ma'am?'

'Aye and taken again with the same pain. I know of nothing we can do but send Melissa up – and Allan.'

'Oh ma'am!' Minnie burst into tears.

'Don't stand there bawling!' cried Maria. 'Send them to me at once!'

Within minutes Allan and Melissa had joined them and a moment later Abby hurried in and they all stood helplessly beside the bed. Hugo was still doubled up in agony and perspiration beaded his face. He made no sound except for an occasional groan which was forced from him. His eyes, dark with pain and fear, were on Maria. She looked up for a moment.

'We must do something,' she cried, 'or he will surely die. Think, I beg you. Abby? Melissa? What shall we do to save him?'

Abby knelt on the floor opposite her. 'We can only pray,' she whispered. 'If we all pray.' Allan and Melissa knelt also and put their hands together. Abby saw Minnie hovering in the doorway.

'Minnie. Go down. Tell the others what is happening. Beg them all pray for Hugo.'

Minnie sped off and they heard her voice above the clamour. Gradually the noise faded and there was a great quiet followed by the low murmur of voices. The door opened and Beatrice came in with Piers and Lorna and they knelt and began to pray. Maria gazed round at all the faces then turned back to Hugo. He had fallen back against the pillows, his face white and drawn, his jaw slack, his eyes rolling upwards. His mouth twitched soundlessly.

'Dearest God,' whispered Maria. 'Look down in your infinite mercy and spare our beloved Hugo. Do not take him from us, I beseech you. We all love him. We all need him. He is a good man and does not deserve to die. Sweet Jesus, be merciful and spare him. Spare him a little longer

to share our lives and comfort us. He is a good father, a
loving husband – Oh, I cannot bear it if you let him die.
What can I say to entreat you further. If I have sinned
forgive me. Forgive us all our faults and do not take Hugo
away from us—' Her voice trembled and she opened her
eyes to look at her husband.

'Maria! He is dying!' It was Beatrice.

Piers closed his eyes, unable to watch and Lorna flung
herself into Beatrice's arms and the two sisters clung
together tearfully. Allan put an arm round Maria but she
had eyes only for Hugo. His eyes were now closed and she
felt his hand go limp in her own.

'Hugo!' She screamed suddenly. 'Hugo! Don't leave me.
Don't! Don't! I love you, Hugo. Do you hear me? I love
you . . . I love you.'

But it was all over . . .

Hugo's body was laid to rest beside the son who had so
recently preceded him. The service was held early in the
day and there was no funeral feast. This had been arranged
so that the mourners, who had already extended their visit
to Heron, might make a start home the same day with as
much daylight ahead of them as possible. Only the Heron
and Ladyford households remained and they went their
separate ways. Adam, Abby and Felicity would return
home the next day. The grief was too deep for comfort and
intuitively it was accepted that the company of others
would not ease the despair. Each person had to live through
their own agony and come to terms with it in his or her
own way. Everyone craved the blessed oblivion of sleep
and most people at Heron retired to bed early that night.
Felicity was exhausted and went up at nine o'clock,
knowing that only Allan and Maria remained downstairs.
At last she heard Maria's footsteps and struggled to keep
awake until Allan followed. She was concerned for him.
He looked haggard and his eyes were red-rimmed with lack
of sleep. Still he did not come upstairs and at last she slid

out of bed and, pulling a wrap round her shoulders, went downstairs to the Hall. Allan was sitting by the fire, leaning forward, his face hidden in his hands. For a moment she stood watching him without speaking. The fire was low and the dogs had wriggled close to it, their noses reaching out for the last of the warmth. Felicity moved forward and set a small log among the glowing embers. The fire crackled and the dogs leapt back, glancing at her reproachfully.

Allan looked up at last but with no curiosity.

'I thought you would be sleeping by now,' he said. 'You should have accepted Minnie's offer of a sleeping draught.'

'I have no need of a draught,' she told him. 'I am so weary I shall sleep once I know you are safe.'

'Safe?'

'From yourself, Allan.' He shook his head but she continued. 'Safe from your horrid thoughts. I'm fearful of what you will do and I cannot allow myself to sleep.'

He looked at her in surprise. 'You are fearful for *me*? After all I have done to you?'

She knelt in front of him, feeling the warmth from the fire on her back. Gently she took his hands in hers and looked into his handsome face, which was now ugly with unexpressed horror.

'What *have* you done to me, Allan?' she asked. 'Don't tell me you have killed Martin, for that is not how it was. Oh, I have heard what happened. Was the knife in your hand, Allan? Did you plunge it into his body? Answer me, Allan.'

A shuddering sigh racked him.

'No,' she went on. 'It was an accident, a cruel trick of fate, the purest chance. You have nothing to blame yourself for except your temper and Martin provoked you beyond measure.'

'My temper,' he muttered dully. 'Aye, my damnable, murderous temper.'

' 'Twas not your temper that killed him, Allan. Maybe 'twas your temper that sent him back across the yard, but 'twas fate made him fall upon his own knife the way he

349

did. Listen to me, Allan. If I had thrust that door and he had fallen and was dead would you blame me? Or if it had been Maria, provoked beyond all bearing – would you call it murder?'

'No. I could not.'

'Then why deal more harshly with yourself? Can you not see, Allan, the reasoning is false?'

He glanced up and his face, in Felicity's shadow, was grey and drawn. 'I see,' he said, 'that you are determined to make a saint of a sinner. It cannot be done, but I thank you for trying. But go to your bed, I beseech you, and leave me with my thoughts.'

Felicity shook her head. 'I will not go, Allan. You must believe that I will not leave this Hall until I am satisfied you will go to bed also. I will kneel here by the hearth all night if needs be! I will not let you drown in your sorrows.'

Again he shook his head and tears glinted in his eyes. 'Maria also,' he whispered. 'It has killed Hugo – the only man she has ever loved.'

'Hugo is dead but you did *not* kill him!' Felicity clenched her hands fiercely round his to underline her words. 'A terrible accident killed Martin and Hugo's heart could not withstand the shock. Oh fate has been unkind. Most damnably unkind, I confess it. But an unkind fate that brings about two deaths – how are you to blame for an unkind fate? Dear Allan, forgive me if I bother you with my poor arguments. I know you wish only that I go away and leave you to your griefs and yet I cannot. I too am grieving, remember, but my grief began many months ago. I lost Martin when I moved in with Dorothy. I know what grief can do – if you allow it. My life has not been easy, but we have to face griefs and setbacks and overcome them. We have to survive, Allan. Believe me. I do not talk idly. I am not at all brave but I have learned what passes for courage and you must do the same. It takes courage to live when 'tis so much easier to die. You *can* do it, I tell you. You are stronger than you know.'

He pulled her up to sit beside him, saying nothing.

Together they stared into the flames which now flickered round the log. The dogs had returned to their dreams and the house was silent.

'You say I can be strong?'

'I do, Allan.'

'What makes you so certain? I have no such faith.'

'Think on it this way. A year ago in the face of this tragedy you would have blamed it on the Gillis blood. Oh, I know of it. Poor Martin had his faults like the rest of us. He was indiscreet and talked often of matters which were not meant for my ears. But you won't deny what I say, will you? That today you do not blame the Gillis blood or take refuge in the Gillis curse. You take the blame for the accident upon your own shoulders. Isn't that a sign of your growing strength?'

He did not answer immediately and she almost held her breath, praying that at last she had found the right words. Somehow she had to give him hope – a raft to cling to in those swirling waters of despair. She waited, afraid to say more. Her arguments were all used up and she was longing to go back to bed and close her eyes against the day's miseries. Then at last she felt a change in him. An imperceptible tightening of the careless muscles, a small but decisive intake of breath. And still she waited. She had said it all and now he must summon his own resources. Slowly he raised his head and straightened his back and drew a deep breath. He stood up and held out his hands to pull her to her feet. Felicity stood up. She was weak with exhaustion. The long journey and the violence of her grief so soon after the birth of the twins had drained her energy. Even as she tried to smile at him she swayed suddenly and almost fell. Allan caught her and lifted her into his arms, cursing his stupidity. Wrapped up in his own distress he had overlooked her obvious frailty. Half fainting, she made no protest as he carried her up to her room and laid her upon the bed. She murmured but he 'hushed' her gently as he covered her with the blanket. He watched her for a moment until he was satisfied that she was asleep then he bent to kiss her forehead.

'My thanks,' he whispered and, moving softly to the door, left her alone with her dreams.

Three days later Felicity returned to Dorothy's. After greeting her sons and seeing to their welfare, she sought out Lucas and told him all that had befallen.

'So Hugo is dead too,' she concluded. ' 'Twas his heart failed him. Melissa says the shock and grief were too much for him.'

Lucas shook his head. 'There's no luck in that family, seemingly. 'Tis like a curse—'

'Don't say that!' she cried.

'But 'tis one thing after another.'

'Aye . . . And Piers and Lorna. They are so young and now they have lost their father.'

'Mayhap Maria will wed again.'

'Maria? No, no. She'll never wed again. Hugo was the only man in the world for her. Poor Maria. She will stay alone. She lived for him.'

'A death at a funeral, eh? 'Tis a terrible thing, that.'

He watched her closely, hoping that the news would distract her thoughts from her own loss. The death of Martin had thrown her into a deep gloom but she had made strenuous efforts to dispel it, for the sake of the twins.

'So there were two of us widows in one week,' said Felicity.

Lucas frowned. '*You* was never wed.'

'Not in the world's eyes, no. But I told myself we were wed in God's eyes.'

'Not in his eyes, neither.'

'No. 'Twas just a comfort to me. Maria said she will come to Kent as soon as she is recovered from the shock. Romney House is to be sold by auction.'

Lucas tried to hide his satisfaction. He wished no man

harm but his feelings towards Martin had not been charitable. He planned to marry Felicity as soon as he could win her affection and he had not relished the idea that Martin Kendal would be living so close, having as he did a father's claim on the children. Now he had gone and, Lucas thought, a good riddance. A man who could abandon a woman with two small boys was no great loss. And now, if Romney House was sold, all Felicity's old memories would be swept away and she would settle more easily into her new life. She still had not agreed to wed him but he felt certain it was only a matter of time. These sad, unexpected events might well hasten her decision. But he would not press her for an answer. She must come to him in her own time. Lucas was a patient man.

' 'Twill fetch a good price, a house that size,' he said.

'Aye.'

'Shall you go to the sale?'

'I don't rightly know. 'Tis as well the mistress is in her grave, God rest her soul.'

'And old Harold.'

'I never knew him but Maria did, of course. Change – always change. How I hate it. I am faint-hearted, I know. Say it, Lucas. 'Tis true enough.'

He laughed. ' 'Tis no crime to be afeared of change,' he told her. 'Sometimes 'tis for the better, sometimes worse. There's no saying.'

'No – but Romney House!' she protested. ' 'Twill hurt Maria. She had such plans for Martin. Frank Innly said he would make a good shepherd.'

Lucas did not answer. It did not please him to know that Felicity had talked with Innly about Martin.

One of the babies cried out in his sleep and Felicity rocked the wooden crib with the toe of her shoe.

' 'Tis a fine crib that,' said Lucas, 'though I say it as shouldn't!'

He had made the crib large enough for two babies.

'The finest,' Felicity agreed.

'So,' said Lucas, 'they had a double funeral.'

'They buried him next day – in the same grave. All the mourners stayed on. It was very hurried.'

'Sad to be hustled into eternity, like that.'

' 'Tis all very sad. There's only Allan and Piers left now. Only two Kendal sons. I wonder if Allan will wed again? He must, I think. Piers is still only a child.'

She sighed heavily.

'You've nowt to fret about,' he said. 'If there was not a single Kendal left you'd be cared for. You know that. You know I'll care for you and the boys. You'll never lack a roof over your head and food for your belly while I'm caring for you. If they was all to die tomorrow—'

'Don't say such a thing!' She crossed her fingers hastily.

'I mean, *if* they was,' he persisted, 'you and the boys would still be safe. I swear to you I'll love them like my own. I do already.'

'I know, Lucas. I—'

'And we'll have a couple of girls to go with them. How does that sound? You'd like daughters, wouldn't you? And then I'll give you a couple more sons. Strapping lads like their father! Eh? We'd be a nice little family and go to church on Sundays. We'd take up half the church! Oh, Felicity, I'll make you happy, I swear I will. Cut my throat and hope to die – Oh! I'm sorry. I didn't mean—'

' 'Tis of no matter, Lucas. I know you mean well but – you did say you'd give me a bit of time.'

'I did. Aye, I did. And I will. We'll speak of it no more. I'd best chop a few more logs. Ma will be home soon and we'll both get a scolding! There's nowt you can do about other folks' grief so put it out of your head.'

Felicity nodded. What he said was very sensible but it was easier said than done.

Romney House was almost deserted. Only Jem remained to keep an eye on the property in case vagrants moved in to take up occupation. There were always plenty of homeless people and an empty house, fully furnished, was a great temptation. Maria found Jem in the empty stable - he had sold the horses on her instructions. He was lolling against a bale of hay with a flagon of ale beside him but scrambled quickly to his feet and grinned sheepishly.

'Good morning, ma'am.'

'Good morning, Jem. I'd like a fire in the kitchen hearth, please. Matt is with me but I have sent him to tell Felicity of our arrival. We shall stay for a day or two while I make arrangements for the sale. I've written to James Moore on your behalf and will see him while I'm here. I hope he will find work for you. I have spoken well of you and have said you are industrious. If you go to him I trust you will live up to my recommendation.'

'I will indeed, ma'am, and thank you kindly, ma'am. Er, 'tis a sad business, ma'am - the young master going like that and his father with him. I could scarce believe it when Felicity told me. I'm that sorry, ma'am.'

'Thank you, Jem.' For a moment her lips trembled but she made a supreme effort to control her feelings. There was so much to do. She had plunged into it all with desperate eagerness as a way of forgetting. Nearly a month had passed and she felt Hugo's loss as keenly as ever. When she felt her grief overwhelming her she thought of Felicity who had lost Martin after so brief and turbulent a love. At least Maria had had Hugo as husband and lover for many years. Now she straightened her back with an unconscious gesture and smiled faintly.

' 'Tis God's will and we must abide by it.'

'Aye, ma'am, but—'

'When did you last see Felicity?' Maria interrupted him hastily.

'A fortnight or more, ma'am. When you wrote to her. She came over and read the letter to me so I should know what to do with the horses and such like. I've the money safe by.'

'I'll take it later, Jem. Now I want to go through the house and decide what is and is not to be sold. 'Twill most

355

likely take an hour or so and I shall hope to find a comfortable blaze in the kitchen and some mulled ale.'

'You shall, ma'am. I'll see to it. The house is ready unlocked.'

He stoppered the flagon and stuffed it behind the straw before setting off at a quick pace for the kitchen. Maria watched him go then made her way towards the front of the house. She stood well back along the overgrown drive and saw the house exactly as she had seen it when she first arrived as a young bride-to-be so many years ago. Then Hugo had been Hannah's husband and she had despaired of ever sharing his life. Looking across the lawn, she saw the tree under which Harold had enjoyed the sunshine. Too weak to walk, they had tucked him up warmly and he had taught Matt to write. She smiled at the memory of Matt as he sat on the grass, bent over his slate with his face screwed up in furious concentration. And Ruth, calling him Matthew instead of Matt. Poor Ruth, thought Maria. How she must have resented Harold's new bride-to-be – a mere slip of a girl to be mistress of Romney House where she had reigned for so long.

And Harold, so frail and helplessly in love with Maria. He had adored her. Had felt for her in a way that was new to him even though Maria was his third wife. The others had been wives. Maria had burst into his life like a breath of spring or a ray of sunshine, gladdening his eye and making his heart race for joy. And yet she could not love him in return. She was kind to him most of the time and tried to hide her dismay at the prospect of marrying such an old man.

Always her heart had longed for Hugo, and finally she had confessed her love to him. She left him and went into a nunnery. Poor, dear Harold . . . Slowly she made her way up to the house and pushed open the front door.

Already the house smelt damp and empty. She drew a deep breath and went into the dining room. The tableboard lay folded against the wall making the room seem larger than ever. The old straw had been swept up and not replaced, she noted. Jem had done his best. The hearth contained ashes and a half burnt log. There were two benches and a chest stood against the far wall. Above it was the shelf which held 'the plate' – Ruth's pride and joy. A silver gilt salt cellar, two embossed plates and a solid silver sweet dish. They must go, she decided. She had already decided how the money raised should be spent and was determined to get every penny possible. There was no room for sentiment, she told herself. There was a painting on the wall which she had never liked. It showed Ruth and Harold as children, standing with their parents. It would have to go – unless Felicity should want it. Maria had made up her mind that all the kitchen equipment should go to Felicity when she set up home with Lucas. The pans and cutlery would fetch very little if sold but would save Felicity a considerable sum. Upstairs she went into the bedroom where Ruth had lived out her last days, bed-ridden and blind. The room seemed stiflingly small and air-less and impulsively Maria flung open the shutters to let in light and air. Then she regarded the room as unemotionally as she could. The bed had gone, bequeathed to Felicity. The chest and the stool – on which Felicity had sat reading to the old lady – could go to Felicity. A small piece of tapestry on the far wall caught her eye and she smiled. Ruth had made it as a wedding gift for Harold and his first wife. The second wife had not appreciated it and Ruth had taken it back! Maria decided to keep it. Ruth would not like it to pass into the hands of strangers.

The chest was unlocked and she lifted the lid. It was almost empty and a smell of musty lavender drifted from it. In the bottom lay a pair of satin shoes, with grass stains at the toes and a pair of walking shoes, well scuffed but clean. There was also a pair of gloves with the fingertips neatly darned. Slowly, almost reverently, she closed the lid and went out of the room.

The next bed chamber was Harold's, with its large four-poster bed. Had Martin and Felicity slept in it, she wondered, or had he gone along to her little room? It no longer mattered. And yet – a man and a woman had lain together as lovers and now there was a lonely woman with two small boys and they would grow up to be men. Each one would lie with a woman and more sons would be conceived. What *is* God's purpose, she asked herself suddenly? What *is* His plan? Of course the church had an answer to the questions, but the tragic series of events over the past month had shaken her faith considerably. But no, she would not doubt His goodness. Her earlier religious training would stand her in good stead. She whispered a few words of contrition and made up her mind to set aside a short period each day to consider and renew her beliefs. But now her task was to raise money by the sale of the house and furniture and with it to carry out her own plans. She could not day-dream over every room.

Felicity's room was almost bare except for the truckle bed, and a small carved chest which was empty except for a few faded rose petals. There was a rectangular mark on the wall where *her* tapestry had once hung.

Upstairs was the cook's room, downstairs was the kitchen. Jem lived over the stable but he, too, would soon be gone. New people would move in and there would be changes.

She blinked her eyes tiredly. Tonight she would sleep in Harold's four-poster. He would like that, she mused. Jem should bring up a few warm bricks to dry the dampness out of the sheets. Tomorrow morning the auctioneer would come to Romney House. It would seem so very final. In the afternoon she would go to see Felicity. They had so much to talk about, yet she dreaded the meeting for Felicity's grief would compound her own. But that was tomorrow. Now she could go downstairs and sit by the fire and remember Hugo.

Henry Strobert, the auctioneer, was an efficient man, small and plump and sparing with his words. Their survey of the house and its contents was conducted in a businesslike manner that left no room for sentiment. He went from room to room, listing the articles for sale and noting separately the size of the rooms. From outside he surveyed it from all directions and noted down relevant details which might affect the price. He then conferred with Maria and they agreed on a reserve price below which he would not sell. A date was arranged for interested parties to view and he mentioned two people in the neighbourhood who might wish to buy the property. He made no reference to the previous tenants and if he had heard of Martin's death he kept the knowledge to himself. If he noticed Maria's reddened eyes he asked no questions. For Maria it was a relief not to have to speak of her loss and her meeting with Henry Strobert refreshed her.

She left Matt and Jem to their own devices and rode, as arranged, to visit Felicity. Lucas waylaid her a few yards down the lane, out of sight of the house.

'She's over the worst of it I think,' he told her, his expression earnest. 'I've cheered her along a bit, best I could. She's a fine girl - woman, I mean. And the boys are that bonny, like their mother.' Maria opened her mouth to reply but he gave her no chance. 'I reckon she'll have me, ma'am, in time. She seems to enjoy my company and we laugh together. Leastways we did until - well, she hasn't laughed since *he* died, that is, him from Romney House but that's natural enough, I reckon, and she's only human. 'Tis hard to smile and be cheerful when someone like that dies. You'll understand what I'm saying, I know. And *your* man dying so sudden, she took that hard, too. He was a good man, she tells me, and I don't doubt it and my condolences to you . . .'

'Thank you—'

'But she'll get over it in time. I'll see to it, never you mind. It grieves me to see her so quiet and thoughtful, but to tell you the truth I'm so taken with her! I'd wed her tomorrow if she'd have me, but she's not said the word and I can't hurry her at such a sad time—'

'Lucas, I—'

'What I was thinking, or hoping, to tell it plainly, is that you'd put in a word for me if you thought me a proper husband for her. My ma is all in favour, if you should want her opinion on the matter. I love her, ma'am, and I'll not let a soul hurt her. She'll be safe with me—'

'Lucas!' Maria held up a hand and he stopped abruptly.

'Oh, ma'am. Forgive me. I was so wanting to tell you how 'tis.'

'I can see, Lucas, that you do indeed love her and have her interests at heart. You are a good man and I see you have a generous heart. If 'tis any consolation, I think you would make her an excellent husband and I dearly hope to see the two of you wed. The boys need a father and Felicity needs a husband—'

'And *I* need a wife!'

'Of course. I will speak for you, Lucas, but as you say she is very distressed at present and we must give her time to recover and collect her thoughts.'

'You've no objection to me speaking to you then?'

'Certainly not. 'Twas well meant and now we understand each other.'

'I'll be on my way then. I've work to do. Good day to you, ma'am.'

'God be with you.'

She watched him go for a moment and her heart went out to him. A kindly, honest man, she thought. Almost another Matt Cartwright but without Matt's disadvantage. He would be a loyal husband and loving father. Felicity was very fortunate. She forced a cheerful expression and went on to the cottage. There was no answer to her knock so she made her way round the side of the cottage and found Felicity collecting eggs from the hen coop. She straightened up as Maria called her name and, setting down the basket, flew into Maria's arms. The composure of both women gave way under the strain of the meeting and for a while they wept unashamedly. Each had lost the man dearest to them in the world and each understood perfectly the other's grief. But after a while, when the worst was over, they stood back and regarded each other and were forced to laugh, albeit shakily, at the dismal picture they presented.

Felicity said, 'We must not weep any more. Dorothy tells me that weeping ruins the eyes.'

'Does she indeed?' Maria smiled briefly. 'Then we'd best take heed of her advice. We don't want to ruin our eyes. We have enough problems without adding to them.'

She swallowed hard and wiped her tears while Felicity did likewise. Then they hugged each other again and drew apart. Felicity picked up the basket, found the last three eggs, and led the way into the house which was empty except for the two babies fast asleep in their crib. Fresh tears welled up in Maria's eyes as she looked at them and she wished that Hannah could see them – her first grandchildren. Even in sleep, with their eyes closed, she could see the difference between them. One had dark lashes and a fine covering of dark downy hair, the other sandy lashes and no hair. The dark boy was the first born.

'They are beautiful,' said Maria. 'You must be very proud.'

'I am.'

'I wish it had – been otherwise.'

Felicity did not answer but fetched ale for herself and Maria. They sat beside the hearth and talked about the future and Maria confided her plans. She spoke as calmly as she could but beneath the flat, unemotional voice, Felicity sensed the older woman's despair. Maria told her that she had no wish to continue at Heron without Hugo. She wanted, more than anything else, to return to the nunnery where she had spent some years before marrying Hugo. It was not possible to do that while Lorna and Piers still had need of her, but in a very few years she would leave them. She was quite adamant. Allan would marry again as soon as a suitable match could be arranged and Piers and Lorna would be put in their care. Heron was their home still and would be until *they* married and settled elsewhere.

'But they'll miss you!' cried Felicity. 'They need a mother.'

'They need a father, too, but he has been taken from them. The world is not an easy place and they must learn to stand on their own feet. How would they manage if I were to die? Allan would assume responsibility.'

'But – will you not marry again? In time, mayhap?' Felicity was distressed for her.

'Never. That is my real tragedy, you see. Hugo was the only one for me. I always knew it. No, there will never be anyone else in my life and now I crave the peace and security of that little convent. You have never known such tranquillity so you will not understand. You must believe me – 'tis the only way now that I can end my days. I have written to them explaining the situation and will visit them as soon as I'm able. Part of the proceeds of Romney House will go there to await me. Another part of the money will go to set up a trust for Martin's sons so that they shall never lack. He would have wished it. But the money will be for them alone and not for any children you and Lucas may have. I'm certain you will see the fairness of what I say. The sum will not be large enough—'

'I understand.'

The third part of the money was to refinance the Heron mine in an effort to get it back into production. Without the mine Heron would fail.

'The money will not be enough,' said Maria, 'but 'tis the best I can do. Allan must marry money to raise the rest and try again to raise a loan in London. It may not be possible. The last loan came to nought for without Bucher 'tis no longer such an attractive proposition. We shall see. Allan deserves another chance. He has had a lot to bear these last few years and it has not all been self-inflicted. My heart aches for him. He is a haunted man. Those damned Gillises will be his undoing if he cannot rise above his fears. If only Harriet had lived. Poor little girl . . .' She sighed. 'But regrets get us nowhere. We must look forward as hopefully as we can. I'm glad you are happily settled and now that the twins are provided for—'

'And if I should *not* wed Lucas?'

'Not wed him? But why not?'

'If, for any reason, I do not wed him, the money is still theirs?'

'Of course, but - Felicity, what do you mean? I thought—' She shrugged her shoulders. 'Lucas loves you. I'm certain of it. He spoke with me before I arrived. Oh, he will ask for your hand.'

'I know he will. But I may not give it.'

'Felicity!'

The girl lowered her eyes.

'The boys are Kendals,' she whispered.

'They are Carrs,' said Maria, her tone gentle. 'You and Martin were never husband and wife, Felicity. You cannot pretend otherwise. Lucas is a good man. You are most fortunate that he wishes to wed you.'

'I know. I do not say I will not accept only that I have not made up my mind.'

'Then I urge you to do so without too much delay,' said Maria and there, for the time being, the matter rested.

CHAPTER EIGHTEEN

Lorna sat at the kitchen table with four-year-old Della on the seat beside her. Nearly ten years old now, Lorna had grown taller and her features were those of her mother. She had Maria's slim neck and the same firm tread, but she had so far shown none of Maria's passion. Now that Piers was away at school, she spent as much time as possible at Ladyford, where she had taken it upon herself to teach the little girl to talk. She had rashly promised Oliver that by the time he came home again his daughter would know 'a hundred words, no less' and she worked diligently with that aim in mind. They sat close together, heads bent, and a selection of small articles was arranged in front of Lorna. A crab-apple and a thimble stood in front of Della. Maggie, busy at the fire, watched them surreptitiously, and smiled to herself.

'Now then,' said Lorna picking up a walnut. 'Nut. Say it, Della. Say "nut".'

The little girl looked at it solemnly and said: 'App-le.'

Lorna shook her head patiently. 'No, no. You've had the apple. See, this is the apple.' She showed Lorna the apple which stood in front of her. 'You've got the apple and the thimble. Now this is a nut. Say "nut" and you shall have *that*, too.'

Della regarded it with an inscrutable expression but said nothing.

'Nut,' Lorna repeated. 'N-u-t. Say it, Della. You can if you've a mind. Say "nut". Say it for me, there's a poppet.'

Della took a deep breath and said 'nu . . .'

'Well done! You nearly have it,' cried Lorna.

'Nu-t,' repeated Della.

Lorna clapped her hands and Della did the same.

'You've done it. So you have the nut.' Lorna put the

walnut with the apple and thimble. 'Apple, thimble, nut,' she said, naming them. 'Now this one is a spoon. Sp-oon – spoon. Say it, Della. Say "spoon".'

Della shook her head. She picked up the walnut and banged it on the table, trying to crack it.

'She wants to eat it, the little pet!' cried Maggie but Lorna looked at her sternly.

'She can eat it when the lesson is done,' she said. 'Now say "spoon", Della. Be a clever girl and say "spoon".'

Della threw the walnut across the table and it rolled on to the floor. The dog ran over to it but Maggie retrieved it just in time and put it back on the table. She marvelled at Lorna's patience.

'Spoon, Della,' the girl insisted. Finally Della repeated it to Lorna's satisfaction and the spoon joined her other successes.

'She's doing very well,' said Maggie. 'You're a good teacher, Lorna. How many words does she know now?'

'Eleven,' said Lorna.

'Eleven? Is that all? And how many more still to go to reach a hundred?'

'A great many,' said Lorna, 'but there is plenty of time. Oliver won't be home for ages and ages if he is gone away to foreign lands. I may even teach her a little rhyme. What are you making, Maggie? It doesn't smell very good.'

Maggie laughed. ' 'Tis not your dinner, but the chickens' food. If your lesson is over in time you can feed the chickens for me – *if* you tidied your bed.'

'I did.'

Lorna had stayed overnight. Since the deaths of her brother and father she found Heron a 'drodsome place', as she called it, and stayed there only on the days that her tutor attended, which were Mondays, Wednesdays and Fridays. Most of the rest of the time she spent at Ladyford, where Maggie and Melissa's cheerful chatter helped her momentarily to forget the recent tragedies and teaching Della to talk gave her an interest and kept her too busy to brood.

'Now, Della, what is this?' She held up a tortoiseshell comb.

'Comb,' said Della promptly.

'Well done! That is enough. You shall come with me to feed the chickens.' Lorna glanced up as Nina came into the kitchen with Jason in her arms. He was a little over a year old and a lusty child. Now he was fed and clean and he held out his arms to Maggie, who kissed him loudly.

'The girls are going to feed the chickens for me,' she told Nina who nodded and smiled. 'Melissa is weaving today and has gone over to Heron to use the big loom.'

Nina sat the boy in a tub lined with a sheepskin and gave him a wooden rattle to play with. Then she pointed first to herself and then to the back door and made two quick downward movements with the fingers of her right hand.

Maggie nodded. The gesture meant that she was going to milk the goats. They had all grown very adept at 'conversing' with Oliver's wife and a mutual sign language had evolved quite naturally.

'I'll keep an eye on His Majesty,' she told Nina and watched her drop a light kiss on each of the two girls before she went outside.

Maggie thought how changed she was from the bedraggled creature who had turned up on their doorstep nearly two years ago. Nina had blossomed into an attractive woman, her body rounded out into soft curves, her olive skin gleaming and a bright flashing smile that radiated her joy in living. Oliver would see a change in his bride, she thought, and uttered a quick prayer for his safety. They all shared the unspoken fear that they would never see him again, although all their talk was directed towards the magic moment when he would come back to Ladyford for good. Privately, Maggie disapproved of his 'gallivanting over the oceans', believing such a life suitable only for single men. Her view was that a married man with a family should stay home and care for them. But she did not voice her opinion to anyone else. In his absence, it was a happy enough household and she was grateful for her place in it. They teased Thomas unmercifully about his harem of three women but he declared himself a most fortunate gentleman!

She gave the pail of food to Lorna and watched the two girls go out, hand in hand, to feed the chickens. Jason dropped his rattle over the side of the tub and Maggie knelt to pick it up for him. As she did so, there was a piercing scream from the direction of the hen coop.

'Now what in God's name?'

She hurried towards the door, darted back to snatch Jason up, and went out into the yard. Nina was just ahead of her, heading in the same direction.

'Maggie! Maggie! Come quick! Oh, the poor hens. The poor, sad hens!'

A terrible sight met their eyes as they rounded the corner. Dead and dying chickens lay everywhere. There were headless bodies and separate heads and there were birds still alive but with no feet. A few that had survived pecked distractedly among the less fortunate, their heads nodding nervously. The ground was littered with feathers and one hen had been mangled out of all recognition. Della surveyed the carnage curiously but Lorna, her face white with shock, sobbed.

'Sweet Jesus!' whispered Maggie. 'We've had a fox, that's what we've had.' Nina turned away from the horrid scene, a hand to her stomach, the contents of which heaved uncomfortably at the gory mess. 'A damned fox!' cried Maggie. 'Senseless, murdering beast! Jacob! Where are you? Come here, lad. I've a job for you. Jacob!'

He came out from the orchard at a run, spurred by the urgency in Maggie's voice. He, too, drew up short at the grisly sight that met his eyes and his face wrinkled in disgust.

'Wring a few necks, Jacob,' said Maggie, 'and put them out of their misery. There, there, my lamb, don't take on so. 'Twas a cruel wicked thing to do, but the fox is an animal as knows no better. Dearie me, there'll be no eggs today! Whatever will Melissa say when she comes home! What a sorry mess.'

'What'll you do with the dead ones?' Jacob asked. He picked up one of the footless hens and twisted its neck and snapped it with a neat jerk.

'Eat them, I suppose. What else can we do – Oh, you needn't eat it, Lorna, if you've no mind to. Don't start to wail again. But we cannot waste so many fowls. 'Twill be chicken casserole, chicken broth, chicken pie 'til we *look* like chickens! Oh dear! I do hate foxes. They've become a sight too bold round here. Hush now, Lorna!' She switched Jason to her other hip and patted Lorna's head to comfort her. Nina ran forward to take a severed head from Della, who held it out to show her mother what she had found. Lorna screamed at the sight of it and Maggie turned.

'We'd best take them away,' she told Nina. 'Jacob can do whatever needs to be done out here.' To Jacob she said in a low voice, 'Leave them on the kitchen table and we'll pluck them later. Doubtless Melissa will send a few to Heron for we cannot eat so many. Eh dear, what a dreary business. That fox had a high old time!'

'Aye – and at our expense! Still, no use to cry over spilt milk. 'Tis a mercy we all enjoy a roast fowl and a bit of broth. We'll maybe stuff a bolster with the feathers. Poor dumb creatures. What a way to die and frightened the others half to death, no doubt. Foxes! Tut! 'Tis a wonder the dogs didn't bark. They usually scent them.'

'They did bark,' said Jacob, 'but I put my head out and saw nothing amiss. Around midnight 'twas. Went back to earth most likely and slunk back later. They're that cunning.'

'I've another word for 'em but I'll not scorch your ears with it!' said Maggie. 'Now, Lorna pet, do give over weeping. You'll wash your eyes out of your head and you won't look bonny then. Come on away and I'll find you a handful of currants if you stop grieving.'

'And some for Della?' said Lorna. 'She's grieving, too.'

'Some for Della, then, if you say so. And mayhap a few for me! I'm all at sixes and sevens.'

'And poor Jacob?'

'Lordy; at this rate there won't be a currant left in the house! But you can give Jacob a few if you've a mind. Now, come away from the horrid sight. All these feathers! Whatever Melissa will say, I cannot imagine, but there we are. A fox is a fox and grumbling won't make him mend his ways. More's the pity, for he's a handsome creature – but don't tell the chickens I said so!'

Over at Heron Maria went into the Hall where Melissa still sat at the loom.

'Click, clack, click!' she teased. ' 'Tis all I've heard all day! You'll wear out your fingers, Melissa! Are you nearly done?'

'Nearly. Another few inches will do it.' She rested the shuttle and rubbed a hand over her eyes. 'I was hoping to finish it but my eyes ache. What time is it?'

'Nearly supper time. Will you stay and eat with us? We've a nice mutton stew and plenty of it and apple dumplings. Your favourites!'

Melissa laughed. 'You're tempting me, Maria, but I'd best go back to Ladyford in case they wait supper for me. But thank you for the invitation.' She leaned forward and smoothed the blanket approvingly. 'It's made up very smooth. Nina's a fair hand at spinning, I must grant her that. Better than me, bless the girl. Yes, it's made up very well. I've promised her I'll teach her to weave when young Jason is older and the two of us can spend some time on it. She learns fast and she's nimble with her fingers. Another few inches and 'twill tuck in well. 'Tis for Della's new bed. That child grows so fast! She has outgrown her Sunday best and Nina is making a new one out of my old green brocade.' She stood up and straightened her back with a slight gasp of discomfort. 'Oh dear, I am getting old, Maria. I can't pretend any longer.'

Maria said, 'We all are.'

Melissa put a hand on her arm affectionately. 'You look tired, Maria. Are you sleeping? Maggie makes a fine draught—'

'Thank you but no. Minnie prides herself on *hers* and I wouldn't care to offend her. I doubt I would sleep with any draught. The bed is so large and empty. I wake up in the early hours, cold and lonely. 'Twill always be so and I am resigned to it.'

'Oh Maria, I wish I could comfort you but what good are words? They don't fill the void. I know how you suffer. I long for news of Oliver and yet dread the messenger in case he is lost at sea. It haunts me daily. But you still have Allan. You must take comfort in him. He needs your love.'

'He has never lacked it. But try as I will, I can't get close to him. He believes I blame him for Martin's death and in a way I do. Oh, I know 'twas an accident. I don't doubt it for a moment but that temper of his!'

'But Martin goaded him—'

'I know. I believe it happened exactly as Allan told it. But my heart says if Martin still lived Hugo would also. Oh Melissa, I know I am wrong to think thus and I pray morning and night for God to soften my heart and make me see it more clearly. I do Allan a grave injustice but he has robbed me of Martin who was like a son to me and my husband—'

Her voice broke and Melissa took her in her arms, murmuring soothingly.

'I must go,' Maria whispered. 'I must go back to Arnsville or I believe I will go out of my mind. I am like a puppet going through the motions of life. I am lost without Hugo. Utterly and irrevocably lost. I must go back to Arnsville because there I may find peace. I pray when the time comes no one will try to prevent me. Say *you* at least will understand, Melissa. Let me go, I beg you.'

'I will, Maria. I will. Don't fret so. We will understand if 'tis better for you.'

'When the children are older – or when Allan is wed. Oh

Melissa, how will it all come right? I cannot see a way. I am in such despair—' She broke off and straightened up as she heard Minnie's footsteps. 'She comes in search of me.' 'Tis supper time. You will not change your mind and eat supper with us?'

She was wiping her eyes and composing her features in an effort to hide her distress. Melissa had a glimpse of the terrible strain she was under and made her farewells with a heavy heart.

Over the mutton that evening Allan told Maria that he meant to bring Martin's twin boys up at Heron.

'As Kendals,' he told her. 'I shall give them my name. They will be my sons. No, let me finish, Maria. I have thought it all out most carefully since Martin—' he sighed. 'I cannot let my brother's sons be brought up by a blacksmith, even if he should be the best blacksmith in England and a kindly man. They belong here, with the family. I shall see lawyers and take advice on the subject of inheritance – though there is precious little to inherit, but that's of no consequence. If I ever marry, my *own* first son must inherit Heron but Martin's boys shall be like brothers and treated exactly as the others. I have thought of nothing else, Maria, since the accident. I don't know if you will approve or if Hugo would have given his blessing, but I am certain my own father would applaud my decision. He, too, was illegitimate and was reinstated. Otherwise I would not be master of Heron. Oh, I know that Heron has less to offer now and may fail entirely, but if the twins are Kendals they must take the rough with the smooth and share the Heron fortunes, good or bad. Now, I am asking for your blessing on the plan but – Maria, I shall do as I see fit, with or without your approval.'

Maria had made no effort to speak while Allan outlined his intentions. When he had finished she still did not speak. The suggestion had taken her completely by surprise and her mind reeled.

'You will be disappointed,' she said at last. 'Felicity will never let them go.'

'She will, Maria. I shall make her give them up. She will
do it for their sakes. I'm convinced of it. She will want
them to be Kendals. She will wed Lucas and have other
children. She will know the twins are where they rightfully
belong.'

'You do not understand, Allan, the way a woman feels
for her children. She will not part with them.'

'I think you are wrong, Maria. And if I prove you wrong
and she *will* part with them. Then what do you think of
it?'

'I think it most generous, Allan. 'Tis so sudden – you
must allow me time to think on it further—'

'There is no time, Maria. I shall leave for Kent tomorrow
at first light.'

'Allan! Why the haste? Surely 'tis better to reflect
longer—'

'And have a change of heart?'

She shook her head. 'No, I do not say that. But 'tis a big
step. I must tell you, Allan, that I will not be at Heron for
much longer.'

'Aye, you have spoke of it. You want to go back to the
convent.'

'You cannot bring up a family without a woman. You
must wed first, Allan, and your wife should give her
consent to the plan.'

'No, Maria. That is not the way. I shall bring the boys
back—'

'They are only babes, Allan! 'Twill be impossible to
bring them back so soon. You are much too hasty, I tell
you. 'Tis a serious step. Wait until I have found a suitable
wife and Heron is financially a little more secure. There is
the share of Romney House – that will be sold within the
month. Add to that a dowry and Heron will better be able
to support two more sons. You cannot ask a dowry to
endow another man's children! If they were *your* sons
'twould be a different matter.'

'They *will* be my sons, Maria. I do not intend to ask a
wife's permission to do what I know is right. They are

Kendal boys and Martin died – indirectly – by my hand. I won't argue with that and 'tis to my eternal grief but I cannot bring him back to life. All I can do is bring up his sons and I mean to do it.'

'But Allan, even Martin was not prepared to do so much. He was content to see Felicity happily wed and the boys financially secure. Mayhap you take too much upon your shoulders. Martin's death is not a debt to be paid. I beg you think about it further. I admire your generosity of heart, but 'tis always folly to act rashly and without careful thought.'

'Maria, I have *given* it careful thought – and I shall do exactly as I have said.'

Maria sighed. 'Then I'll say no more, Allan. I'll reason no further on the matter. If you are adamant – but, dearest Allan, prepare yourself for possible disappointment and do not take it too hard. I am utterly convinced in my own mind that Felicity will not agree to it.'

Allan rode the third and last leg of the journey in the company of three nuns and an elderly man and his son. The nuns kept to themselves, a few yards behind, and conversed in whispers. The two men had had a disagreement and were not on speaking terms. There was no one to distract Allan from his thoughts and he gave particular attention to how best to broach the subject to Felicity. Maria's conviction that she would refuse to let the boys go disturbed him. The problem had occurred to him only fleetingly and he had given the matter no serious consideration. As to their youth, that *was* a valid point. They must stay with their mother until they were weaned – unless a wet-nurse could be found for them at Heron. There was always a willing girl in the village glad to take on the job. As long as he could convince Felicity that the plan was in the boys' best interest and that their satisfactory welfare was assured, he was almost certain he could persuade her. Maria would stay at Heron for a few more years – at least until he had found a wife who would care for Piers and Lorna as well as the twins. Perhaps he could persuade Maria to settle the portion intended for the twins on Felicity and then she and Lucas could greatly improve the quality of their lives and that of their children? But no – that bordered on bribery or appeasement. That would never do. Felicity would feel she was bartering. No, that idea was *not* acceptable. If only he could find a solution that was beneficial to everyone. Lucas, surely, would have no objection to the idea. They were not his sons. Possibly Lucas would support his idea and help to convince Felicity that it was the proper thing to do. They were Martin's children and if he were alive . . . Of course, Martin's death and the circumstances of it, might also weigh against him. Allan knew that in Felicity's eyes he had killed her lover. Would she allow Martin's children into the care of the man who had indirectly caused the death of their father? Would Felicity even agree to talk with him? This new thought made him go hot and cold with a momentary panic but he managed to thrust it from him. He must wait and see. If she did refuse his proposals, he would *not* lose his temper, he told himself. He would give her a month in which to reconsider. He would be patient and understanding. At all costs he must not antagonize her. She must be persuaded of two things – that life at Heron was best for the boys and that Allan was attempting to redress the wrong he had done Martin. His intentions were entirely honourable and Felicity must be made to see the matter in that light.

In his subconscious mind, Allan was beginning to believe that in this way he could atone for all his past mistakes. Somehow his life, so dogged with misfortune, would take a turn for the better. A new and better life would begin. A clean slate would be presented to him on which he would write with love and hope. He decided, also, that it would not be ethical to approach Felicity without first speaking to Lucas. No one must accuse him of dishonourable behaviour. There must be no reason for anyone to fault him.

He therefore went to the smithy as soon as he had

refreshed himself at the local inn. He gave his name and enquired for Lucas and a moment later Lucas came out, his face already set in anxious lines.

'You're the brother?' he asked abruptly. 'Of him at Romney House?' He wiped the perspiration from his brow with his forearm.

'Aye.'

Briefly, Allan outlined the reason for his unexpected visit. Lucas's face hardened.

'She won't give them up,' said Lucas. 'And neither will I. You're wasting your time. Good-day to you.'

And he turned his back on Allan and went back to his work. Allan's face burned at the man's insolent manner but his heart sank at his words. It was going to be much harder than he expected. A young boy sat on the bench eyeing him curiously and from him Allen obtained directions to the cottage. He rode up to the door and heard a baby crying. A strange, and unexpectedly tender, emotion filled him. That was one of Martin's sons. A new generation and new beginnings. He dismounted, tethered his horse, walked up to the small front porch and knocked at the door. The crying continued and for a moment nothing happened. Then the door opened and Felicity stood there, a tiny child in her arms. Her face registered shocked dismay and Allan felt her hostility in tangible waves.

'I beg you, let me speak with you,' he began. 'No, I don't beg – I insist I talk with you. I have seen Lucas. He knows why I am here. Felicity—'

He stopped, his attention taken by the baby in Felicity's arms. The small face was tear-stained and the little body heaved with the passion of his weeping. Allan was overwhelmed. How could Martin have rejected the fruits of his own body – the children of his lover, Felicity? It was incredible. He was still staring when Felicity spoke.

'You'd best come inside.' No greeting. No friendliness in her voice. But what could he expect?

He nodded and she led the way into the kitchen where the other baby lay in a double crib, awake but not crying.

375

Allan looked down on it and saw the blue eyes waver uncertainly, trying to focus.

'They are fine boys,' he said. 'Martin—' He could not go on.

'Martin saw them once,' she said. 'I think he – approved.'

She indicated a chair and he sat down then, as she remained standing, rocking the child in her arms, he stood up again. Allan was astonished at her composure. She must surely hate him and yet she said nothing. She watched him, waiting, as he searched for the right way to begin. He had practised many convincing openings but now, faced with the little family, the words fled his mind.

'You spoke to Lucas—' she prompted at last. The child in her arms puckered his face and wailed tentatively and she lifted him briefly and kissed his head.

'Aye . . . I told him I came to – with a proposition . . . I told him I—'

She waited again, her face impassive. It unnerved him.

'I told Lucas – No, Felicity. There is something else I must say first. I – Martin's death, you must believe it was an accident. You must believe that or else—'

'I do believe it, Allan.'

'You do? Thank God! Oh, thanks be to God! I thought, at least, I feared – I dare not ask your forgiveness but I want you to know—'

' 'Twas an accident and there is therefore nothing to forgive. If I must forgive you your temper . . .' she shrugged, 'then I do. Your own remorse must be punishment enough. Indeed I pity you.'

He looked at her, astounded, but a sweetness touched his soul and her words were like balm on a wound. And yet her face remained mask-like; nothing of her emotions showed in her eyes.

'You loved him,' he stammered.

'So did you, in your own way. And he loved you.'

'He loved me?'

She nodded. 'In *his* own way.'

'I wish I could believe it. Indeed I do.'

Allan groped blindly for what he wanted to say to her, knowing that there was no way to spare the agony of mind.

'Martin,' he began, 'would have wanted the boys to—'

'No!' she said quickly. 'He did not want them. He was content to let me wed Lucas. It was his wish.'

'Yet he—'

'He did not want them.'

'Felicity, he certainly did love them. He—'

'Aye. Oh, he said he was proud of them but he did not want them. We must not play games with each other, Allan. We must speak plainly and only the truth.'

'You are right. Forgive me. What I want to say—' He stopped again.

'Say it, Allan.'

'I want to take the boys—'

'The answer's "no"!'

'Felicity, let me speak, I beg you.'

'The boys stay with me, Allan. They have no father now, and they are not going to lose their mother. There is nothing to talk about.'

'And you will not even *hear* me?'

'I am afeared to listen to you, Allan. I told you I would speak honestly with you. I am afeared that you will persuade me against my better judgement to do something I shall regret. Let *me* speak. Listen – I have two bastard Kendal boys and no husband. The Kendal father rejected them. Lucas loves them. He loves me. He wants to wed me and make a home for us. We will be poor but we will be loved and cherished. Have you anything better to offer? I doubt it.'

'Will you listen to my offer? Will you give me a chance?'

'I don't want to hear it, Allan.'

'For the boys' sake?'

'Say what you have to say.' She sat down suddenly and for a moment the mask slipped and he saw the fear and weariness in her soft grey eyes. He wondered how Martin had found it in his heart to abandon her to a man like Lucas. He sat down opposite to her and she was silhouetted against the window, a madonna and child. The idea moved him and he had to make an effort to redirect his thoughts.

'I propose,' he said, without looking at her face, 'that the twins should come to Heron when they are weaned to be adopted by me.'

'No!'

'I haven't finished, Felicity. You said you would hear me.'

'Go on.'

'I shall remarry shortly and my own sons would have to take preference with regard to the inheritance. But in all other respects they would be treated exactly as the other children – part of our family. They would receive a good education and marry well. They *are* Kendals, Felicity. You know it in your heart. You cannot deny them their birthright.'

There was a moment's silence. Her shoulders seemed to sag a little and her lips trembled.

'I knew you would try to twist me with your words,' she said, 'but the boys stay with me. Your offer is kindly meant, I don't doubt it, and I thank you for it. 'Tis more than Martin would—' He detected a trace of bitterness in her voice. 'I think their future happiness lies here. I love them dearly, Allan. You have no children yet and I cannot expect you to understand. But I could not part with them. It would break my heart. I have lost Martin and they are all I have left in the world.'

'You will wed Lucas, then?'

'Aye.'

'Do you love him?'

'No. I love Martin. I always will.'

He looked at her despairingly.

'And will you tell the boys, later, that they were born Kendals?'

It was a telling question and he saw the doubt flicker in her eyes.

'I don't know,' she said. 'I can't answer you because in truth I had not decided. Lucas will help me know what is best. It may set them apart from their brothers and sisters. It may not be wise.'

'Is it honest not to tell them?'

She hesitated.

'Will they resent what you have done, if they do learn of it later?'

'I cannot answer that, either!'

'*Do* you know what is best for them, Felicity? Are you *so* sure? Think hard before you commit them to this life. You can give them much more. I know Heron is not thriving but Hugo was so stubborn. He would not reopen the mine and I shall do so at whatever the cost. I shall *make* it thrive, if it takes the rest of my life to do it. No, I *will* have my say. I shall bring out tin again from that mine if I have to break it out with my bare hands. I have had enough of tragedy and disaster. I am turning my back on all my mistakes and the rest of my life will be very different. I confess to my past errors. I have as many faults as the next man but I will not let them ruin my life. The time has come to tilt the scales and today is the first step in the new direction. Felicity, you must accept—'

'I won't! I don't!' She bowed her head. 'Leave us out of your plans, do you hear me? Take your bright future and I wish you all good fortune. I even admire you for your determination to rise above your unhappy past. We all try and we all fail at times. All we can do is what we feel to be right and honourable. You ask me to give up my sons but I do not feel it to be either right or honourable. I must follow my conscience in the matter, Allan. If time proves me mistaken, I must learn to live with my remorse.'

The child in her arms, distressed by her behaviour, began to cry noisily and she stood up, greatly agitated, and began to rock him.

'Please go,' she said, without looking at Allan again. 'I thank you for coming but you have my answer. You are a good man, Allan, and I wish you only happiness. But please go.'

Allan hesitated and then stood up. He said, 'If you

change your mind, I am staying overnight at the sign of the Red Lion. I shall leave to go home at first light.'

'I won't change it, Allan.'

He went out and closed the door quietly behind him, muffling the child's cries. As he rode away he passed Lucas hurrying home. They eyed each other warily, each raised a hand, then went their respective ways without exchanging a single word.

CHAPTER NINETEEN

Allan was awakened next morning by a knock at his door. 'Come in,' he called, struggling into wakefulness. The room was still half dark and the disgruntled innkeeper's wife was glaring at him from the doorway.

'There's a young woman to see you,' she said. 'At this hour of the morning! 'Tis a downright liberty to wake honest folks from their rest and I told her so in no uncertain terms but she would insist—'

'Did she give her name?' Allan was struggling into his clothes as fast as he could. 'Is it a Felicity Carr?'

'Could be. I don't recall the name although she gave it. Said it was most urgent. It had better be, I told her.' She watched Allan with undisguised interest as he fastened his doublet and bent to pull on his shoes. 'Friend of yours, is she then? Looked most upset – eyes all red with weeping, by the look of it. About so high, with light brown hair tied back with a ribbon. Dark shawl. In the family way, is she? That's the usual way when a maid must see a young man urgently.'

Allan, ignoring this last remark, pushed past her and went down the stairs two at a time.

'I've put her in the front room – and I shall be about so there's to be no nonsense of any kind. This is a respectable inn—'

Felicity was waiting for him. Her face, as the woman had told him, was blotched and ugly and she held herself taut with suppressed emotion.

'Felicity! I hardly expected to see you. You have changed your mind?'

'No, Allan,' she said. 'I have not changed my mind. But I have thought long over what you said to me and now 'tis *I* have a proposition to put to *you*.'

He waited, puzzled, for her to continue, but her self-control was fragile and she took a moment to master het emotions.

'I have thought it out this way, Allan. I will not part with my little boys and you want them at Heron. Then why not wed me?'

He was completely taken aback by her suggestion and his dismay showed fleetingly before he could hide it.

'I see,' said Felicity. 'Your expression has answered me.' She turned towards the door, intending to pass him, but he put out a restraining arm to block the way.

'Wait. I have said nothing yet,' he protested. 'You are too hasty. I gave you more time to consider my proposition.'

That was true and she hesitated. 'Then take a little longer,' she said coldly. 'Let me put the facts before you as I see them. You wish to bring up Martin's sons and I will not part with them. If you wed me I will bring the boys to Heron. I do not love you but I scarcely know you. I hope I may love you in time. You, for your part, do not love me, and you have caused my lover's death. That might stand between us, although for my part I have already said that I accept it was an accident. You may love me in time. On the financial side—' She shrugged helplessly. 'You will not be gaining a rich wife who will help re-establish the Heron mine. I have almost twenty gold pieces left and you are welcome to that. Also the share of Romney House which Maria intends to settle on the boys. That would be our contribution, small though it may be. I would care for Piers and Lorna when Maria returns to Arnsville – she has told me she is determined to do so. I would be to you all that a wife should be. In fact I should try to make up to you for all the unhappiness of the past few years. Together I believe we could prove, once and for all, that the Gillis curse is meaningless. I would give you sons and daughters and Martin's memory will not stop me from loving you – if you will help me.'

The last five words of the breathless little speech touched

Allan's heart more than all the rest. He was astonished and full of admiration for the girl.

'And will you give me time to consider?' he asked.

'Aye. Five minutes. I will sit here and wait your answer.'

He burst out laughing as, stony-faced, she sat down on the bench beside the beer-stained table, still littered with the remains of last night's carousing.

'Felicity! Forgive me but – oh, this is so unexpected. You have astonished me.'

'You find it humorous,' she said.

'No – that is, in some ways. Did ever a man receive such a proposal! I am not laughing at you but at the two of us. No, maybe at myself. I have been very blind yet thought myself so clever.'

Slowly she allowed herself a glance at his face and at once her own face relaxed a little as she saw the genuine humour in Allan's eyes.

'You have made me laugh!' he told her. 'I think the first time for years. My sweet Felicity, I ought to be angry with you—'

'Angry?'

'Your plan is so much better than my own. And I spent days perfecting mine and you have bettered it in an evening!'

'What do you mean, Allan. I have had no straight answer as yet.'

'And my five minutes? Is it up?' he mocked gently. 'I see it this way. We have both been abandoned in our own ways. Martin and Eloise.' He sighed. 'Yet we both have a lot of love to give. You are a clever girl, Felicity, to put together such a plan. I'm truly dazzled by its brilliant simplicity.'

'But what is your answer, Allan?'

'I accept your offer unconditionally.'

She said 'Oh' and looked down at her fingers, which twisted in her lap. Then she said 'Oh' again in quite a different tone. He moved towards her a step and she stood up.

'Are you going to say "Oh" again?' he asked.

'No,' said Felicity. 'I'm trying to think of something more original. You must give me time.'

'Five minutes?'

She laughed tremulously and put up her hands suddenly to hide her ravaged face. 'My face,' she whispered.

'If I must wed an ugly maid—'

He shrugged and she lowered her hands. 'I have not slept all night,' she said.

'Poor Felicity. I've caused you so much grief. Will you forgive me?'

'I think it has ended well.'

'You think so? Are you still unsure?'

'Is it settled?' she asked him. 'I mean, are we - are you—'

'Am I going to wed you and are you going to bring those two handsome sons to Heron? The answer is "aye" to both questions. I am such a fool, Felicity. I should have offered you that solution.'

' 'Tis of no matter now.'

They looked at each other in disbelief.

'Felicity!' he said. 'We have two yards of filthy floor between us! Why is that do you suppose?'

She looked down, seeing for the first time the dirty straw, scraps of food and splashes of ale.

'Is this really happening?' she whispered, her eyes downcast. 'I can scarce believe it. I was so sure you would say "No". Then I felt that I could tell the twins the truth at some stage and - they would not think so badly of me. And you did not say "no"!'

'Come to me, Felicity.'

He held out his arms and after a moment's hesitation she moved to him and his arms closed round her. He felt her shudder with fresh tears. 'No more tears,' he told her. 'You are ugly enough already - Ah! that's better. Now you are smiling.' He kissed her gently. 'Felicity, let us make a pact. To be happy together. You and me and the boys.'

'And the other children.'

384

'And the others. What d'you say?'

'Aye, let's be happy, Allan. I believe we deserve it.'

They regarded each other solemnly and kissed again. A sound from the door startled them and they found the innkeeper's wife watching suspiciously from the doorway.

'I said no nonsense,' she reminded Allan sourly.

Allan looked at Felicity. 'No nonsense!' he mimicked. 'D'you hear that?'

She smiled shakily and then they both began to laugh and then hugged each other again.

'We are going to be wed,' Allan told her.

'I thought as much,' she said triumphantly. 'Knocking a body up before sun up! 'Tis always the way.'

He didn't bother to disillusion her but asked instead for breakfast. 'And for pity's sake sweep us a clean corner to sit in while we eat it.'

Over breakfast it was decided that Felicity would go back to the cottage to tell Dorothy and Lucas what had happened. She insisted on doing that in her own way, refusing Allan's offer to accompany her. Allan would wait at the inn until she was ready to leave for Heron, refusing to go without her in case she changed her mind while he was gone. He would send a letter home to prepare Maria for their arrival and then he and Felicity and the children would travel back to Devon together. They would wed without further delay.

'And our new life will begin,' said Felicity, her eyes shining with hope.

And Allan, looking into her eyes, felt that it had already done so.

The events of the next few days were confusing. By the time Allan's letter reached Heron, Maria, with Matt and a pack pony, was on her way back to Kent for the sale of Romney House which had been delayed by nearly a week because of the auctioneer's 'indisposition'. He was an elderly man frequently troubled by gout but he was the best in his profession and Maria was not prepared to accept another member of the firm in his place. It therefore came about that while Maria rested and dined at the Blue Boar just outside Salisbury, Allan, Felicity and the twins passed within yards of her. In fact had she sat on the opposite side of the table she would almost certainly have seen them pass the window. She went on towards Kent unaware of the outcome of Allan's visit to Felicity.

The auction attracted a large number of prospective buyers, many from London, one or two from the surrounding area and even two from as far away as Oxford and Aylesbury. The house was full of strangers on their various tours of inspection and their many footsteps echoed on the stairway. The few articles of furniture that Maria was keeping had been stored in the barn prior to despatch. While the auction was in progress Matt would take the relevant items over to Felicity and the rest they would take home. The remainder had been sold already and the rooms were bare. She could not bear to see it so and sat on a stool at the back of the Hall while the room gradually filled up. Benches and a few stools had been provided by the auctioneer, and at the far end a tall lectern had been set up beside a small table on which various documents had been neatly arranged beside a jug and beaker and the small hammer. Maria watched and listened as groups of people drifted in and sat down, intent, comparing their impressions of the property and mostly unaware that Maria was the present owner. She recognized a local man who lived on the outskirts of Rye and he, recognizing her, joined her for a brief chat before the actual proceedings began.

Promptly at two o'clock the auctioneer introduced himself and the auction began. To Maria's surprise and heartfelt relief, it was all over in less than fifteen minutes. The reserve price had been passed with a comfortable margin and she was well pleased with the final price, which was a little more than they had anticipated. The purchaser was from Aylesbury and later he was introduced to Maria and told her how delighted he was to be the new owner.

He was a printer by trade and was planning to move the business further south. The stables would be extended to house the machines, the barn would be demolished and . . .

Maria did not want to hear the details. She wanted to remember the house as it had always been but already it sounded different – empty and cold – and it grew harder to summon up the images of Ruth and Harold. She made her excuses and spoke quickly to the auctioneer about the few matters which remained, then left the house without a backward glance.

From there she rode to Arnsville. Matt would wait for her and she would be able to see Martin's sons before they returned to Devon. Arnsville drew her inexorably and she experienced the strangest lightening of spirits with each passing mile. Once, as a young woman, she had approached it with near dread, but now it seemed to beckon like an old friend. She had not seen it for nearly twelve years, but when she first glimpsed it time stood still. It had not changed at all – but no, that was impossible, she told herself. Always, everywhere, there is imperceptible change. If the buildings were the same then the inhabitants would be altered. She had grown older. They would have aged also. Some would have died. She knew they had a new prioress, Dame Margaret, the wealthy daughter of a family of London merchants. An occasional letter from Katharine had kept her in touch for a few years, but then they had ceased. She reined in her horse and sat looking down at the place which had once been her entire world and one day would be so again. The thought comforted her. Seeing it again crystallized in her the longing for the tranquil lifestyle which she had once found so hard to bear. Now she craved the small quiet cell, the simple life and the companionship of holy women. Astonished and strangely excited, she rode slowly on, savouring the moment, anticipating her arrival with childish eagerness.

A young novice opened the door to her but then Katharine was hurrying towards her, hands outstretched

in a welcome so genuine that tears sprang into Maria's
eyes.

'Katharine! I cannot tell you—'

'Oh how good to see you, Maria! So many years and yet
you look no older.'

They clung together for a moment and the novice was
sent away – to tell the prioress of Maria's arrival and to
alert the kitchen so that refreshment could be sent to the
prioress's quarters.

'Is it true, Maria? You are coming back to us? Tell me
with your own lips or else I dare not believe it.'

' 'Tis true, Katharine. So much has happened – I cannot
tell it all now, 'tis too painful—'

'Then don't! We shall have plenty of time and I so look
forward to hearing everything. Life is as dull as ever!'

'Dull? Oh Katharine, if you knew how I crave a dull
existence! I've changed, Katharine. I have changed so
much.'

'But your husband is dead? The prioress spoke of it. I
was so grieved for you. We prayed for you. And those that
remember you talked of your letter that told us you were
not coming back.'

'That I was going to wed Hugo!'

'Aye. Such a stir, you can imagine! That set the cat
among the pigeons, I can tell you. And now he is dead. My
poor Maria.'

'We won't speak of it,' she said hastily.

At that moment the novice returned to say that the
prioress would receive Maria.

'I'll speak to you again,' she promised Katharine and
followed the girl through the familiar cloisters, past the
chapel where she had made her first penance and from
where she had crept out for a clandestine meeting with
Matt. A smile lit up her face at the memory. She had been
inattentive during the study period which she and Katharine shared: Dame Augusta, who instructed the novices,
reprimanded her not once but twice and finally gave Maria

a penance of an extra hour's prayer on her knees after Compline.

'This way,' said the novice shyly.

Maria smiled at her. 'I know the way like the back of my hand.'

The girl nodded, opened the door and Maria came face to face with the new prioress.

Dame Margaret greeted her quietly and expressed her regret at Maria's recent loss. They sat down and the question of Maria's return – at a time unspecified – was discussed to their joint satisfaction. The financial aspect was then raised and that, too, proved to be in order.

'You will no doubt find many changes,' said the prioress. She was a tall woman with an angular face and cold grey eyes. Her voice betrayed her London origins and her manner was confident to the point of arrogance. Not a woman to tangle with, Maria thought, but with her own maturity the thought gave her no qualms. She was no longer a headstrong young girl, resentful of the limitations of a cloistered existence. She was a tired, lonely woman craving security and a small corner of the world that was hers alone. In Arnsville she would find just that. This austere woman would keep a tight rein on the little group of women and her forbidding presence would deter the troublemakers, maintain the efficient running of the establishment and ensure the even tenor of convent life. Maria could appreciate the need for such a woman and would, she knew, find occasion to be grateful. They drank sweet ale together and Dame Margaret encouraged Maria to talk about her family and the responsibilities which delayed her return to Arnsville. She then spoke briefly of her own connections and of her earlier life in London. Her young husband had died at sea without giving her a child. She had refused to wed again and her parents had settled her at her own request in a convent in Arundel which had been closed like many others by the Dissolution of the monasteries. After two more such setbacks she had moved into Arnsville.

'So you see,' she concluded, 'I, too, have tasted marriage and the ways of the world. But I thank God daily for my decision to take Holy Orders. I have never regretted it. You are making the right decision, my dear.'

'I know I am,' said Maria. 'I shall look forward to my return.'

She little knew, as she spoke, quite how soon that would be.

Katharine was waiting for her when she left the prioress and the two women walked in the flagged courtyard, talking animatedly but in low voices.

'I'm Mistress of the Novices now,' Katharine told her. 'And Dame Agnes has died of a fit, God rest her soul. Dame Augusta left us. She began to quarrel quite dreadfully with the old prioress and the bishop was consulted. On his advice she moved to Ealing, where no doubt she is quarrelling still!'

'Dame Augusta!' said Maria. 'I recall she escorted me when I went to Harold's funeral. She was not quarrelsome then. Strict and so pious – but not quarrelsome.'

' 'Twas her health. She had a troublesome stone and was often laid low with the pain of it. So, I am Mistress of the Novices in her stead. But you, Maria, in those clothes! You look so worldly. How can you bear to give it all up?'

'I cannot speak of it yet, Katharine. My griefs are so recent but I will tell you all in time, if you will be patient. I would come back tomorrow were it not for my two children. I cannot leave them until Allan has wed again. I love them dearly but—' She laughed a little shamefacedly. 'Hugo was the light of my life—'

'As I well recall!'

'Aye. Even the children did not replace him in my affections. My worldly life ended with his death.'

Katharine was silent. Then she said cheerfully, 'How's the devoted Matt? Will he return with you?'

'No. I would not ask it of him, poor Matt. He is happy at Heron, and must end his days there. And, indeed, I don't need him with me the way I did before. Then he was a link with my old life. Now, I do not need such links. But tell me of your own life while I have been gone.'

Katharine threw out her hands despairingly. 'There is nothing to tell,' she said. 'I teach the novices but I have no Maria among them so I am fortunate!' They both laughed. 'I am quite reconciled to my life here and can enjoy the company of most of my sisters – with the exception of Dame Martha. You will not care for her, Maria. She is a thorn in our flesh but we pray for her and are hopeful of a transformation. She fills the dorter with her snores, eats like a pig and smells like a farmyard! But she brought great wealth with her – we have a new orchard full of plum and pear trees and the stables were rebuilt. But there, we tolerate her. We are all God's creatures.'

Katharine's words brought back so clearly the essence of spiritual life. Maria glanced down at the black velvet of her travelling outfit and felt a sudden distaste for the rich fabric and fashionable detail. She thought of the rose-red taffeta and the blue silk and discovered that they had lost their charm. She envied Katharine her sandalled feet, and dark shapeless tunic with its simple cord at the waist. A deep sigh shook her. She would be patient a little longer and then this coveted way of life would be hers again.

Before she left she dined with the prioress in the Guest Room and, at Maria's request, Katharine was invited to join them. Three others shared the meal – one of the young novices and an anxious mother and father who were paying her a first visit. They ate a well-cooked meal of fish soup followed by a brace of baked pheasant – a gift from the visiting parents. Meat was allowed in the Guest Room. The rest of the nuns who dined in the frater were eating mullet and cucumber. Maria joined in the conversation while her thoughts wandered. In this same room she had entertained Ruth Cummins and they had eaten baked heron. And later Hugo had come to see her and they stood together in this very room. Dame Elinor had chosen to wait outside, allowing them a few precious moments alone together. She could see Hugo still in brown and gold, the sleeves of his doublet slashed with red, his brown eyes intense under the dark hair. He had begged her to leave Arnsville and return to Heron. Hannah was ailing and the children needed Maria. *He* needed her! Somehow she had refused, unable to live with him while Hannah was his wife.

After the meal she walked with Katharine a while longer. She saw the old orchard where she had met Matt by moonlight; saw her tiny bare room with its high window where she had worked so hard at her studies; and the long, lofty dorter where they all slept. Aye, she would be patient, she told herself again. Arnsville would wait for her.

From deep under the ground came an excited barking which Nat translated for Lorna's benefit.

'Fox!' he said. 'I reckon we'll have that old devil before long.' He bent forward and, head on one side, listened carefully to the sounds of conflict. Trapped underground, the fox was snarling and snapping at his small attacker. Brin would be braced firm, toes dug well into the sandy floor of the fox's earth, hurling defiance and waiting his chance to pounce. The fox, aware of his desperate position, would fight like one possessed.

'Smell that fox!' cried Nat. 'A real old dog fox!'

Lorna declined the offer, with a toss of her head and an expression of disgust. She was annoyed at Nat Gully. She had walked miles in search of him to regale him with all the exciting events of the past week and she had finally found him near Ladyford digging out a fox – 'the fox that most likely killed all those poor hens,' he told her.

His spade lay beside the enlarged entrance hole and a small mound of newly turned earth lay close by. But the fox had gone deeper still and Brin had gone in to flush him out. Nat's attention was directed to the dog's efforts and Lorna felt, rightly, that her news was not receiving the appreciation it deserved.

'The twins are so bonny,' she exclaimed. 'One with hair

and one without. And one bawls lustily and the other is silent. And Felicity—'

'Hush up! There's summat wrong down there.'

She pursed her lips and stared at him balefully, but he was lying flat out on the grass, his ear to the ground.

'What is wrong?'

' 'Tis hard to say. I heard Brin yelp.'

'The fox! Mayhap 'tis biting him. Oh Brin! Brin!'

'Hush up, I tell you. I can't hear for your noise.' He listened, cursing softly, and then leapt up and began to dig again. He seemed to have forgotten her existence.

'Then I shan't tell you about Felicity and Allan's wedding or which day 'twill be - or that Mama is going away to be a nun and Felicity will care for me - or that a letter is come from Oliver and he is coming home shortly - and Allan is to reopen the mine.' She glanced at his recumbent form then crouched beside him.

'I shan't tell you, I say,' she insisted.

'And hush up, *I* say! 'Tis damned quiet down there. I don't like it at all.' He cupped his hands to his mouth and shouted, 'Brin!'

There was an ominous silence.

'Mayhap they are both dead,' whispered Lorna.

He shouted again and the same silence followed. Nat scrambled into a kneeling position, his face thoughtful, his eyes never leaving the darkness through which either Brin or the fox should appear. Suddenly, without moving, they heard a scuffling and the rear end of the dog came slowly into view. The hind legs were well dug in to the soil and the dog moved backwards with slow jerky movements.

'Damn me if he hasn't got the fox!' cried Nat. 'He's pulling it out. Here, Brin boy! Come, boy!'

Encouraged by the sound of Nat's voice, the terrier redoubled his efforts. As his short tail came within reach, Nat reached down and grasped it with his right hand and pulled hard. The dog emerged *with* the fox, which had fastened its teeth into Brin's snout. Lorna screamed. The fox still hung from the dog's snout as Nat scrambled to his feet, momentarily at a loss how to deal with the situation. Then he shouted to Lorna to hand him the large stone which stood on the folded net to one side of the earth. As she reached for it, Nat snatched at the fox's brush with his left hand and for a second the two animals swung between his two hands like a living rope. Lorna handed him the rock and with one movement he released the dog, allowing it to swing down. Still the fox refused to loosen his hold on the dog and, with an oath, Nat smashed the rock against the fox's skull with a sickening thud. Lorna screamed again, her hands over her face. The fox shuddered, its jaws slackened and the terrier fell to the ground, yelping with pain. Nat struck the fox again. The red-brown body jerked convulsively and was still. He held it up, grinning. 'A big old dog fox,' he said. 'You can open your eyes now. 'Tis all over.'

'And poor Brin!'

'Aye. We must get him home and I'll make him a salve for his poor old nose. Here, boy. Come and show us.'

The terrier crept forward, the small tail wagging.

'You were a brave dog,' Lorna told him, 'but you will soon be well again.' Nat inspected the wound, patted the dog and smiled. 'He'll survive.' Then he plunged his arm down the fox's earth again and drew it out.

'Ah, I thought so,' he said. 'See here, Lorna, I reckon 'tis the fox that killed the Ladyford hens. Once they go for feathers there's no stopping them.' He held out a handful of earth in which a few brown feathers were visible. 'You tell them I've got the culprit and he's well and truly dead and I'll be up in a day or two with the brush for my reward.'

'I will.'

She stood up. While Brin waited, Nat collected up his net and stick and slung the limp body of the fox over his shoulder.

'Now,' he said, 'we'll walk back towards Heron and you shall tell me all that news again. Will you do that?'

Lorna needed no second asking. She gave a little skip, took a deep breath and began all over again.

*

394

Maria knew, before she arrived back at Heron, that Felicity and the twins would be there. She had learned from Lucas of the dramatic change of plans and her anger at the news equalled his dismay. She had made careful plans and now they had all been rendered worthless. Felicity had no right to put forward such a plan, she protested. And Allan had no right to act upon it without consulting her first. Lucas was astonished by her reaction and Dorothy's own hostility towards Maria faded when she saw that the latter's concern was genuine. Nothing would convince Maria that Martin's mistress was the right woman to wed Martin's brother. She could foresee distant problems over the inheritance if Allan adopted the twins. She was sorry for Lucas and told him, quite sincerely, that she believed him to be a far more suitable husband for Felicity. But what, as Dorothy repeatedly asked, could be done about it? Maria assured them of her best endeavours and promised to do anything she could to put matters right on her return. Lucas was still in love with Felicity and would take her back if she would come.

Maria had her doubts but she would try to persuade Felicity and Allan that they were making a mistake.

She rode home in a moody silence and for the first time in his life Matt was heartily glad to see Heron and be rid of her company. She found the household in a delightful uproar which did nothing to soothe her frayed nerves. She had slept badly on the journey home and was in no mood for Minnie's starry eyes or the sight of Ellie cradling the twins, one on each arm.

Without further ado, Maria sent for Allan and her interview with him was short and, on Maria's side, sharp. She demanded that Felicity go back to Lucas and Allan for his part refused to allow it. He remained calm and reasonable and explained that in his view it was a better solution to the problem. He was sorry for Lucas but he pointed out that Felicity had never given Lucas a firm answer – too much had been taken for granted. Now Felicity had made her choice and he was happy to endorse it. He asked her forgiveness for their haste and for not consulting her first. She did not give it and the discussion ended abruptly.

Maria then talked to Felicity who was unhappy to find Maria so hostile to their plans but she, too, remained reasonably calm. Her arguments were the same as Allan's. She believed that what she had suggested was best for the twins.

'And do you pretend to love Allan?' Maria demanded.

'I do not pretend it, no, but I believe I can learn to love him. Did Eloise love him?' Maria, taken aback, hesitated and Felicity went on. 'I believe I shall love him more than Eloise would ever have done. I accept him as he is, with no money and few prospects. Eloise wanted him for what she would gain. I shall be forever in Allan's debt for ensuring my children's future and I shall do my utmost to repay him. He shall have my head, and my heart and my body, I shall make him happy, Maria. Nothing will make me change my mind. I shall wed Allan on the twentieth of November. I should dearly like your approval and your blessing – it would mean a great deal to both of us. But we shall wed with or without it, Maria. Oh do forgive us. Allan is *so* happy. I have never seen him so alive and confident. He feels that at last he has made a good decision; that he has broken the mould of his past disasters and can make a success of the rest of his life. Don't you see, Maria, the change in him?'

Maria had seen it but she made no comment.

'He has lost that haunted look,' Felicity went on. 'He is rid of the Gillises. He is rid of the guilt of Martin's death. Rid of Eloise's ghost. Oh Maria, when you see him with the twins – he loves them, you see. Already he loves them! Be angry with me, if you must, but I beg you not to cast a gloom over *his* new-found joy. We acted hastily. I don't wonder you are angry. You had made generous plans for us. But give us this chance, Maria. If you oppose him, and this fails, I believe he is truly a lost man.'

Maria was touched by the impassioned plea and suddenly her anger left her. She looked at Felicity with a new and grudging respect. Perhaps the girl was right. And perhaps her anger was partly pique at having the matter so neatly taken out of her hands. She tried to be honest with herself. Would she ever have found a suitable girl for Allan? She still blamed herself for hurrying him into a betrothal with Eloise. No, she thought, Eloise had been *their* mistake; hers and Hugo's. Was she likely to make a more successful choice next time? She no longer had Hugo to advise her. It might all be for the best, who could tell? She sighed. She was tired and she did not want to strive any more. Hugo had gone. Allan was the new master of Heron. Felicity was to be his wife. Marriage was not easy. It was fraught with difficulties and disappointments. She could not envy them their future. She pulled herself up abruptly. This will not do, she told herself. Be honest with yourself. You are tired and confused. You are lonely and you long for Arnsville. This is your chance also. Let them have their way and you can leave Heron in younger, maybe wiser, hands. You have lost this fight, Maria. Face the fact and surrender gracefully. By giving them their chance of happiness you do the same for yourself. She sighed again. Felicity waited. Then Maria thought of Hugo and the joy they had given each other. Allan and Felicity believed they had the chance of just such a joy. They were clutching at the chance with both hands. Did she have the right to deny them their chance? She took Felicity's hands and put them to her lips.

'Only love him,' she said, 'and you have my blessing.'

The wedding was a very quiet affair for several reasons. The family was still mourning Martin and Hugo. The relationship with the tinners was still uneasy, although negotiations were going on between management and men to reopen at least one drift. There was no money to spare for a lavish wedding and the presence of Martin's sons was causing plenty of gossip among their neighbours. The family were all invited but Adam Jarman was suffering from a badly infected leg, the result of a dog bite, so he and Abby were unable to attend. Beatrice and her husband accepted with alacrity. Piers came home from school. It went without saying that all at Ladyford would be there.

The only guest to be invited came at Lorna's insistence and that was Nat Gully who stood to one side, self-conscious in his shabby clothes but with a scrubbed and shining face.

The little group gathered at the church porch for the exchange of vows and rings. Felicity wore a simple dress of pale rose taffeta with Maria's pearl head-dress. Allan was in dark blue. Maria still wore black but most of the visitors were soberly dressed with black ribbons on their arms.

Nat Gully watched Lorna standing demurely beside the bride and grinned at the transformation. She looked almost ladylike until, catching his eye, she winked conspiratorially and he knew she was the same tomboy she had ever been. Harum scarum Lorna, he thought. Whom would she marry? And Piers, twelve years old and so solemn. A few more years and he would be a man. The vicar was gabbling through the service as though time was money, his grey head bobbing occasionally to emphasize a word. Allan looked happier than he had ever been and Nat thought him well suited to this calm grey-eyed girl, Felicity, whatever had happened between her and Martin. And Nat knew it all – told him by Lorna in strictest secrecy – a confidence he would honour.

He had no friends or relations so who was he to tell it to, he thought a trifle ruefully. Not that it was a secret. Everywhere he went folk asked him about the truth of the matter and he shook his head and pretended ignorance.

There were no little 'uns at the church, he noticed. The wet nurses from the village had been hired to give an eye to them all under one roof at Heron. Nina's two and Beatrice's youngster and the twins . . . The bridegroom kissed the bride and they moved into the church for the breaking of bread and sipping of wine. Nat thought it all highly entertaining and watched from a safe distance. If he *had* a family it was this one, he mused. And he liked them. Even poor dumb Nina. He thought of her quick darting hands and mobile face and the expressive dark eyes. She didn't need speech, that one. And such a smile. It fair dazzled a man! And Oliver was due back from sea, so Lorna had said. A nice family, the Benets. They had paid him handsomely for the fox and would make use of his services again, no doubt. Ah, now they were passing the holy wine or whatever it might be. And breaking up the bride cake. Soon be done and they could all go back to Heron and enjoy the food. Nat was looking forward to that. He hoped Brin was behaving himself, tied up at the church gate. There was no sound from the little dog. He had been rather subdued since the fox bite and Nat hoped he was properly cured. The salve was a good one, but dogs had been known to die of the bite of a fox - as though the dratted fox liked to have the last word!

Funny things, families, he thought, as he watched the bride and groom kiss and the congratulations begin. Loving each other one minute, hating each other the next. All these smiles and tears and all for what? You're born and you wed and you give birth and you die in your bed if you're lucky. So many mouths to feed and souls to fret over. He was glad he was single. He'd have no wife but he could fend for himself. He'd have no little 'uns but they were no great loss. Love you and leave you, that's what children did. No, this pantomime was not for him.

He grinned. Ah, now they making a move. He slipped out and collected Brin and was away up the hill before the rest of them had quitted the churchyard. He didn't intend to bump his way up to Heron in a creaky old wagon while he'd two good legs could do the journey quicker! He cut across the fields and through the coppice and by the time the rest of the wedding party approached he was ensconced in a corner with Brin beside him. He had a mug of cider in one hand and a chicken leg in the other.

CHAPTER TWENTY

Maggie woke up the next morning with a sore head and sick stomach. She lay in bed a while, tossing and turning in great discomfort and misery until she was finally forced to get up. Outside, the October sky was heavy with cloud and a wind sent the leaves scudding against the house like a whispering voice. She shivered, stretched and scratched. She was stiff and sluggish and depressed. The bowl of cold water was uninviting and she dipped in the edge of the towel and wiped her face briefly, letting the cold cloth rest for a moment against her forehead. It gave her no relief so she wiped her face dry and went quietly downstairs to the kitchen where her clothes lay beside the dying embers of the fire. Snatching up the bellows she blew some life into what remained of the fire, added a handful of wood chips and blew again. The flame grew until the chips glowed and when they caught alight she added a few larger twigs and lastly a log. While the fire increased, she half filled the smallest kettle and hung it over the flames and then poured herself half a mug of wine. A pinch of grated nutmeg and another of cinnamon and a generous spoonful of sugar completed the concoction. When the kettle boiled she would top it up with hot water. It might not cure her headache but it would warm her body and relax her stiff limbs.

Oh Maggie, she told herself, you are nigh on fifty. What can you expect? By the comforting warmth of the fire, she pulled on her clothes and then sat beside it, eyes closed. Some of her misery left her. Forty-nine was not *so* old. There were footsteps and then Melissa joined her. She had dressed upstairs.

'I heard you come downstairs,' she confessed, 'and knew you would make up the fire. You look pale. No, don't rouse yourself. I'll make myself a mug of hot lemon. What are you drinking?' She sniffed the proffered mug and laughed. 'At this hour? You must have the constitution of an ox! But it went well yesterday, didn't it? Felicity looked beautiful.'

'Aye. 'Tis a strange match but it might work. She looked – thoughtful, would you say?'

Melissa nodded, preparing her drink.

'I thought so too. No doubt thinking it should have been Martin, God rest his soul. But poor Maria, in those sombre clothes! I wish she had worn something brighter. The green silk would have looked well. Or even the russet, but black!'

'She is in mourning, remember.'

'But a wedding! I thought it a pity but there – 'tis no concern of mine and now she has no one to advise her. She will mourn Hugo forever. She will want to. That way she will keep his memory fresh in her mind.'

'My heart aches for her.'

'And mine.' She pulled up a stool and sat beside Maggie. 'Is your head bad?'

'My head, aye, and also my belly, my back, my legs and arms, my spleen, my lungs—'

They both laughed.

'And Nina looked bonny,' said Melissa, ever the girl's champion.

'She looked most striking,' Maggie agreed. ' 'Tis her dark eyes and golden skin. The gown became her. And the children were all well behaved. No tears and no tantrums. It went well. Quiet but pleasant enough.'

'Not like Hugo and Maria's wedding,' said Melissa. 'Now that *was* a day to remember.' Her eyes gleamed at the memory. 'Everything was perfect. Fine weather, crowds of well wishers – the town went mad with delight! And the feast after up at Crockern Tor and so many guests! The old hall fairly shook when the dancing began.'

Maggie shook her head. 'Aye, that was the way a Kendal should wed. I think every tinner this side of Dartmoor came, and everyone else who had even the slightest connection with the place.'

Melissa smiled. 'And Minnie was with child again, and Piers and Lorna not even a twinkle in Hugo's eye!'

'Oliver had just left to go to sea. He was so young.'

Melissa nodded. 'I thought I would never see him again. I almost hated Maria.'

'Maria?'

'He was in love with her. She was free then.'

'But Hugo – I mean surely she was betrothed to—'

'Not then. Something happened between them – between Oliver and Maria. I never knew exactly how it happened but Oliver wanted to wed her and she refused.'

'Because of Hugo. I see.'

'No one else knows except Thomas. I have never spoken of it.' She shrugged. 'It all seems a lifetime away now and insignificant but then – Oliver was heartbroken. Soon after Oliver left Maria wed Hugo.'

'He is happy with his Nina,' said Maggie. 'They are a happy family.'

Melissa did not answer, deep in thought. Maggie's head thumped painfully but the nausea had left her. She cast around in her mind for a way to change the subject.

'I wore my green silk,' she said, 'and felt so grand though 'twas a mite too tight and I was bursting at the seams. It never did fit me as it should have done. And we made nigh two hundred pies and Lord knows how many pasties!'

'You were still at the bakery, then. Do you ever miss it?'

'Not a lot. I'm happy wherever I am. Life's too short to let it be otherwise.'

'You should tell Maria that. She is so intense, poor Maria.'

Maggie shook her head. 'Don't pity her,' she said. 'She had the one thing in life she cared for – Hugo. 'Tis more than many of us have had.'

Neither of them spoke of Simon but he was in both their thoughts. There was a loud knock at the door and they exchanged indignant glances. Maggie groaned and put a hand to her head and Melissa went to the door and opened it. A small boy, of ten or eleven years, stood outside.

'Who are you?' she asked. 'Bothering folks before the day's rightly begun. Well, speak up, lad. I'm not going to eat you.'

For all his bold knocking, he was a shy lad and now stood twisting his fingers. 'I'm told to give you a invitation,' he said. 'The new owner of Maudesley says you are to come to visit him at eleven o'clock. He says all of you to come and visit.' He screwed up his face in concentration. 'He says all of you at Ladyford to come and—'

'Aye, I've heard it,' said Melissa. 'And I'm no wiser than I was. Who is this new owner who sends a young lad to rouse us up at this hour of the morning?' She glanced over her shoulder towards Maggie. 'Do you hear this? We're invited to visit at Maudesley—'

'He's a foreigner,' said Maggie. 'They've no manners, any of them - family excepted,' she corrected herself hastily.

The boy said, 'At eleven o'clock.'

'We heard you. Who is this new owner? What is his name and which county does he come from?'

'Ask him where he earns all his money!' cried Maggie and Melissa smiled.

'I don't know anything,' said the boy hurriedly. 'I don't know his name or where he comes from. He just said to give you the message.'

'He speaks English then?'

'Aye.'

'Wait there.'

Melissa closed the door. 'I'd best ask Thomas what we should do. I'd dearly love to see the house now 'tis finished but I mislike his arrogant ways. Tell them to visit at eleven, indeed!'

Thomas, woken from his sleep, was reluctant to accept the invitation but felt it would be discourteous to refuse.

'Mayhap 'tis their way in his country to be so peremptory,' he said. 'We'd best go this once and then the niceties have been observed. If we don't like the fellow we need not go again. On the other hand we may like him and he is our nearest neighbour apart from Heron. Aye, say we will go.'

And he slipped back under the sheets and was almost immediately asleep again.

Melissa relayed the decision to the boy and gave him a large slice of gingerbread.

'Mind you will *all* go?' he insisted. 'Every man jack, he said.'

Melissa stared at him. 'He said that? Then he *does* speak good English. We shall all be there, tell him. And now be off!'

Maudesley was greatly improved. No one could deny that. The windows gleamed with leaded glass and the new roof looked serviceable without looking hard. The decorative brickwork infilling the timber frame extended as far as the new oriel windows on the first floor. Everywhere stone had been replaced with carved wood and intricate mouldings. The party from Ladyford paused to look at it, prepared to be critical, but in all honesty they could not fault it. The effect was of tasteful elegance.

'Well, we cannot sit here all day admiring it,' said Thomas and he urged his horse forward. Melissa rode beside him. Jacob drove the wagon and Maggie, Nina and the children rode with him. Thomas had taken their host at his word. It was 'every man jack' of them! The driveway had been freshly gravelled and the gardens had been cleared. Gone were the piles of timber, bricks and tile. All was neat. Even the autumn leaves had been swept from the grass. At the far end of the garden they caught sight of gardeners, busy with a bonfire. A maid opened the door to them and led the way into the Hall.

It was unfurnished apart from sheepskin rugs on the floor, but three rich wall hangings covered the white walls.

A small table had been set up containing wine, glasses and a plate of biscuits. At the far end of the room a tall man stood at the window, looking out. The maid said, 'I'll tell the master;' and crossed to him. She said, in English, 'They are here, sir.'

He turned and smiled, and for a moment they all stared blankly at the new master of Maudesley – because it was Oliver!

'Oliver?' whispered Melissa in disbelief but Nina, with a gasp, ran forward and threw herself into his arms.

'Oliver?' said Melissa again. She turned to Thomas, still unable to understand what was happening. Thomas, smiling broadly, took her hand gently. 'He said he would come back a rich man! I believe he has done!'

Melissa's eyes widened. 'Oliver – has all this? Has bought – has done – Maudesley belongs to Oliver?'

He nodded.

She turned from Thomas to Maggie who was as dumbstruck as *she* was. 'Oliver owns Maudesley? Oliver is a rich man? I must be dreaming. Maggie, prick me! Thomas! I can't believe it!'

' 'Tis true though,' cried Maggie. 'Oh what a trick to play on us – and it worked so perfectly. Our faces!'

The room echoed with their excited cries, laughter and even a few tears.

'Mama!' cried Oliver. 'Say you are glad to see me.'

'Glad? Dear God, there are no words strong enough.'

He hugged her until she protested that her ribs were in danger and then Thomas, too, received a bear-like hug.

'And you look so grand!' cried Maggie when it was her turn for a hug and a kiss. 'Dear me, I feel I should curtsey. Look at this cloth! 'Tis beautiful. And a jewelled belt!'

'Wait 'til you see the gifts I have brought,' cried Oliver. 'I cannot tell you how I have longed for this moment. Every day has been an agony for me. Ever since we took our prize – and what a prize! A Spanish galleon laden with the spoils of her *own* maraudings! Can you enjoy the sweet irony of that, Papa? They were returning home with *their*

405

ill-gotten gains and *we* take them, lock, stock and barrel! Not without a fight, though. God's nails and that *was* a fight. That was a battle and a half. I have a scar on my leg to prove it and a limp when I'm tired but was it worth it? All this—' He swung round, arms outstretched '—and more! Oh, the Queen has had a small share of it. The dues have all been paid. 'Tis all above board now and no one can take it from me.'

Nina watched him, not understanding much of what he said, for in his excitment he spoke so fast, but she *did* understand that he was home and safe.

Thomas accepted the wine which the maid was pouring somewhat inexpertly. 'And will you stay home now?' he asked.

'Indeed I will. I swore to myself that if I survived that nightmare, rich or poor, I would never go to sea again. And I do not need to.'

'And the scars?' said Melissa.

'Healed long since, Mama. I was very fortunate. Five of our men were killed, seven maimed – but the Spaniards paid dearly for the havoc they wrought us. Don't look that way, Mama. They had killed many to seize what they had taken. Such treasure! Gold and silver, jewels, jade, ivory, satins and silks, even furs. Sixteen of us survived but only three of us had shares in the venture. Oh, the mariners were paid generously. We could afford to be generous.'

'And the other two?' asked Thomas.

'They have gone off again in search for more!' He laughed. 'Good luck to them, I say. After we'd shared the money and all the cargo we sold the galleon to a Dutchman. But now I've done with adventuring. Rest assured I shall not go to sea again. I have such plans. You shall hear them all later.'

Della tugged at Nina's skirt, anxious to see the rest of the house.

'Aye, go and explore, my pretty little dove,' said Oliver. 'This is your home now. Your new home.' He swung her into the air, spun her round and hugged her. 'You and

Jason and Mama and me – we will all live here in Maudesley. I chose it so that you will be able to see Grandmama, Grandpapa and Maggie whenever you wish. Ladyford is so near.'

Della pointed to Jacob, who grinned self-consciously.

'Aye, and Jacob. We mustn't forget him. Now run along.'

They watched her run off, full of curiosity and Oliver raised his glass. 'A toast to Maudesley, our new home.'

They all raised their glasses, which were of a delicate green, and drank.

'Italian,' said Oliver, seeing Thomas' interest. 'Oh, there are so many beautiful things. They are stored upstairs waiting to be unpacked when the house is furnished. I thought Nina and I should choose the various items together. There is a wood carver in Plymouth who is making us chests and a bed. They will be here shortly. There is no one to touch him for craftsmanship. And there are more wall hangings – one for you and Papa, one for Maria—'

He broke off and his face darkened. 'I heard about Hugo and Martin. 'Tis a bad business.'

'And the wedding? Have you heard that also?' cried Thomas, trying not to let the sad business spoil Oliver's moment of triumph.

'Aye, last night when I arrived. I so longed to come home earlier but dared not leave the ship until the shares were fairly apportioned and mine secure. I have learned to trust no one.'

'But how did you know?' cried Maggie. 'That Maudesley was for sale? And why did the workmen say you were a foreigner?'

'I let them believe it. I wanted to surprise you so I pretended to be acting for the real purchaser. The Tuckers knew, of course, but they, too, were sworn to secrecy. In fact my early negotiations took place while we were anchored off Portugal, so 'twas easy enough to maintain the deception. As for Maudesley, 'twas *not* for sale and I had the devil of a job to persuade them to part with it. But, what is money for if not to buy your heart's desire?'

The maid refilled the glasses at a sign from Oliver.

'Oh,' he said, 'this young lady is our first maid. She's the daughter of the tile-maker who provided our new roof. Engaging the rest of the servants will be Nina's responsibility, though she will need your help Mama.'

Melissa nodded. 'And the boy who came to the house with the message?'

'Son of the timber merchant in Ashburton. He has helped tidy the garden and I may keep him on to help in the stables. He is older than he looks. But now let me show off my house. I am inordinately proud of it. You must bear with me, but I have risked my life for it and now I long to share it with my dearest Nina. She waited so patiently for me to return and she loved me when I had nothing!' He kissed her fondly and led the way upstairs. As they went from room to room he carried Jason on his right arm and kept his left arm round Nina's waist. Maggie felt a lump in her throat as she watched them together. He told them of the rest of his plans – to go into partnership in the Heron mine, if Allan would agree. He had enough money to bring over a new consultant if Bucher still refused to return. They no longer needed finance from London. With the capital Oliver had available there should be no question that the mine would thrive again.

Melissa and Thomas walked hand in hand marvelling, as Oliver described his plans for the future. Maggie followed with Jacob. Della ran from room to room and up the stairs and down again, her footsteps echoing throughout the house.

The garden, too. Great plans had been made for that. Exotic trees and shrubs had been ordered and would all arrive in the course of time. As they stood outside a little later, preparing to remount and ride back to Ladyford, Melissa looked at Thomas. Her cheeks were flushed with excitement and her eyes shone.

'Thomas!' she whispered. 'It does seem that the bad

times are over. Dare I hope? I am so afeared that I shall wake up and find it all a dream.'

' 'Tis no dream,' said Thomas. 'I believe the pendulum for Heron, for the Kendals, indeed for *all* of us, is swinging the other way at last.'

Christmas came and went, taking the old year with it. Snow fell at the end of January and was washed away by the fierce February rains. March heralded the traditional winds but there was no more snow. Heron huddled bleakly in the lee of the moor and waited impatiently for April and the first real signs of spring. It came at last and straggly yellow catkins appeared in the hedgerow and the pale sunshine drew forth green shoots from the ground and coaxed open the buds on the trees.

In the big bed at Heron, Felicity opened her eyes and at once blinked herself into true wakefulness. The mattress, of goose feathers, was delightfully warm and the heavy blue bed drapes were pulled back to allow the warmth from the fire to reach them. Raising herself on one arm she glanced in the direction of the hearth and saw that a few embers still glowed dully. There might be time to save it. The small silver table clock showed ten past five so the rest of the household would not stir for another hour. She looked down at Allan, sleeping beside her. He slept so soundly as usual. It amused her each morning to see the difficulty with which he struggled out of his dreams and into reality. Moving gently, she lowered herself to the floor and tiptoed to the fire. A smile played at the corners of her mouth as she began to scrape the embers together. Then she blew softly to promote a flame and when that happened she arranged small logs over it and sat back on her heels to watch it flare. The smile returned and she stood up and crossed to the chest which stood at the end of the bed. She lifted the lid from its depths, took a flagon of madeira wine and two of the green wine glasses which Oliver had given them. Closing the lid, she set the flagon of wine and the glasses on top of the chest and returned to the fire. Another log went on and she sat beside it for a while, eyes closed, enjoying the warmth. When finally it blazed to her satisfaction, she found her hairbrush and began to brush her long hair until it floated round her shoulders, tangle-free, framing her face which was still rosy from the fire. Her grey eyes sparkled with mischief as she dabbed lavender oil between her breasts and behind her ears. Then, her preparations complete, she slipped between the sheets once more and began the slow, but pleasant, task of wakening her sleeping partner.

Allan lay with his back to her, his knees curled up, his face hidden below the bedcovers which were pulled well up around his head. Carefully she fitted her own body round his, and slid one arm down over his body to his thigh and let it rest there, unmoving. Softly she nuzzled her face into the back of his neck below the tousled blond hair. She kissed his neck and his left shoulder, edging down the covers to reveal the fine sprinkling of gold hairs which covered his shoulders and thickened over his arms. The skin of his back was pale and freckled and his shoulder blades showed like two budding wings. She kissed the one she could reach and then, as he still slept, she smiled and nestled against him for a moment, her cheek against his back, her arm thrown over his long, lean body so oblivious to hers. They had been married exactly five months and only now were they beginning to feel at ease in their new situation. The household had accepted their union and Felicity was given as much respect as any previous mistress of Heron. Piers and Lorna, now growing rapidly, treated her with affection and Melissa visited occasionally. Allan and Felicity had twice been invited to dine at Maudesley and Beatrice had written to them, promising a visit when the weather improved. Poor Martin had been their only problem. His charming face had haunted Felicity's dreams and she had several times woken to find that she was calling his name aloud. Fortunately Allan slept too soundly to have heard but Felicity had been shaken and distressed.

Many times she had surprised Allan staring at the twins with an expression of deep remorse but she had made no comment. Frequently, however, she brought Martin's name into the conversation, determined that his death should be regarded as any other and not locked away in Allan's mind, to become a forbidden subject.

Her relationship with Allan had slowly deepened and already there were moments of joy, the occasional spark of passion or a shared tenderness. Felicity was beginning to believe that their marriage would prove a happy one. Gradually she had seen the terrible darkness fade from Allan's eyes and knew that he too felt the first stirrings of hope.

It was time to wake him up, she decided, and slid her hand down over his body, smoothing the firm buttocks, reaching gently between his legs. Slowly, softly, she anticipated the growing excitement that would finally rouse his body from its dreaming state. He grunted softly, and stirred, rolling onto his back, so that she had to move out of his way. She ran her hand over his firm abdomen up and up to his chest, brushing the nipples lightly with her fingertips. He gasped and suddenly his eyes were wide open and he was staring at her in astonishment.

' 'Tis no dream, then!' he whispered delightedly.

'No dream, sweet Allan.'

She leaned over and kissed his mouth and he pulled her down on top of him, trapping her, ignoring her protests.

'I thought I dreamed,' he said. 'I was reluctant to waken and then . . . So my wife is a baggage!'

He laughed as she tried to wriggle free. A log shifted and he noticed for the first time that the fire blazed.

'So you have mended the fire, too!' he teased. 'This is a fine start to the day. Why do you try to pull free of my arms? You cannot wake me with such promises and then fight shy of me.'

'I don't fight shy,' she protested, 'but my strategy is not yet complete. Look there – at the foot of the bed.'

He struggled to a sitting position and laughed aloud.

411

'Wine, too! And before cockcrow! My little Felicity! What has gotten into that pretty head of yours? I thought you a sober maid.'

'Then you misjudged me, husband. Come, 'tis for you to pour. A toast to us on our anniversary. Five months wed to the day and no regrets.'

He knelt on the bed, still rumpled from sleep, looking like an excited child.

'And after the toast?' he asked.

She nodded, smiling, and for a moment they clung together. Then he released her and moved to the foot of the bed to pour the wine. He handed her both glasses to hold while he pulled the drapes, hiding them from view if one of the children or a servant should surprise them at their love-making. When they were thus secure, Allan raised his glass.

'What shall we drink to?' he asked. 'This is your notion.'

Felicity raised her glass to touch his.

'To you, to me and to the twins,' she said, 'and to Martin who brought us together.'

For a second or two they looked steadily into each other's eyes.

Then Allan nodded, approvingly.

'I'll drink to that,' he said.

Devon, July 1581

Felicity waited at the bend in the road, a hand shading her eyes from the evening sun through which Allan would ride at any moment. Or so she hoped. She had waited impatiently there for what seemed an eternity but was in fact less than half an hour. She held a letter from Maria in her hand and she had only read it through once. Then it had seemed a good idea to waylay Allan on his way back from the mine and share it with him. Now she could wait no longer and sat down on a grassy mound to read it for a second time. After the usual greetings Maria spoke of Arnsville with affection:

' 'Tis as though I never have been away. The first year was difficult for me as I wrote you and each letter from Lorna tugged at my heart. But, suddenly, I feel as though I have come home. You will not understand it, I scarce do myself, but 'tis true. I am content at last. My days are full of work and prayer. My sewing is so admired that I have replaced the old chambress whose eyesight is failing. Katharine is a good friend and Dame Veronica makes us both laugh. She is so outspoken and will not take us seriously. I am now mercifully removed from Dame Martha and her snores. She is at one end of the room and I am at the other and can sleep soundly at nights. I also work in the garden twice a week and enjoy the fresh air and exercise and my appetite is quite returned.'

Felicity scanned the page, looking for the paragraph about Rochester.

'A letter from Abby arrived last week. Her eldest son is to wed on August the seventh and I have applied for permission to attend. Will I see you all there? I pray so. If I must take a chaperone with me I shall ask for Katharine and hope the prioress is agreeable. Abby speaks also of Eloise. She is now wed and has a child. Poor Adam suffers still from his leg which is now badly ulcerated and, she says, will likely never heal . . .'

She thought of Eloise for a moment then pushed the image from her. Standing up, she shaded her eyes again. There was still no sign of Allan so she began to walk on in the direction from which he would come.

Maria was obviously delighted by the progress being made at the Heron mine. Allan would be pleased, she thought – and deservedly so. The mine was flourishing again. With Oliver's money and Allan's experience, they made a good partnership. But then Allan and Oliver had always been firm friends, more like brothers, she thought, even as boys, from what Minnie told her. It was reasonable that they would work well together. And Bucher had come

over to England again! Only for six months and only at
great expense and with stringent safeguards for his protec-
tion – but he had come. And he had proved his worth. The
new machinery was built and installed and the new shaft
was progressing more rapidly than they had ever believed
possible. They had also reopened an old adit, to be
reworked with the improved techniques made possible by
Bucher. They owed him a great deal.

The road climbed steeply and at the top she caught the
full force of the breeze which ruffled her hair under its slim
head-dress and whipped at the hem of her skirt. Make
haste, my love, she thought. I have so much to tell you.
And even if she had nothing else to say, she could tell him
that she loved him. Minnie teased her – a woman does not
fall in love with her own husband! But Felicity had done
so.

She sat down again and opened the letter once more,
turning her back on the breeze so that it did not tear the
page from her fingers.

'. . . what news of Beatrice? I trust the sickness does not
still trouble her. Another child after so long. Mayhap 'twill
be another girl . . .'

Maria did not ask the question that must be uppermost
in her mind, thought Felicity. When would she, Felicity,
give Allan a child? It was to Maria's credit that she did not
ask. Felicity smiled. Soon she would write to Maria and
tell her what she longed to hear. That their first child
would be born in six months' time, at the end of January.
Even Allan did not know yet! Felicity had waited for the
right moment.

'I long to see the twins,' Maria continued. 'When they
are a little older mayhap you will bring them to visit me –
or I will come to Heron on some pretext. To arrange Piers'
betrothal, mayhap. Lucas . . .'

Hastily she folded the letter. She did not want to
remember that Lucas was still unwed. Poor Lucas – but
surely he would wed in time. Deliberately she thought of
Allan, of their nights together, of their tender loving

moments during which their child had been conceived. Felicity had discovered a deep love for Allan and gradually he, too, had felt the stirrings of real love where before there had been only respect and affection. Now even their bodies were in harmony and the final seal was set on Allan's happiness. But perhaps not the *final* seal. That would come with her news of the coming child. Faintly the echo of hoof-beats reached her and she stood up, folded the letter and walked towards the sound. As horse and rider rounded the hill, she saw Allan outlined against the sun and waved her hand.

'Allan!'

He raised his hand in greeting and she knew instinctively that he smiled. She stood for a moment watching him as he drew nearer. Suddenly she glanced around. There was no one else in sight. She put her cupped hands to her mouth and shouted.

'Allan Kendal! I love you, Allan Kendal!'

She heard his amused laughter. 'And I have news for you, Allan Kendal!' she whispered as, smiling, she gathered up her skirts, and ran towards him.